Irv Kupcinet

March - '63

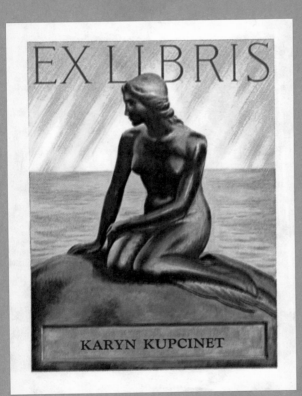

EX LIBRIS

KARYN KUPCINET

Passages marked by KK

NOT ALL OF YOUR LAUGHTER,
NOT ALL OF YOUR TEARS

Books by Steve Allen

NOT ALL OF YOUR LAUGHTER, NOT ALL OF YOUR TEARS

Steve Allen

PUBLISHED BY
BERNARD GEIS ASSOCIATES
DISTRIBUTED BY RANDOM HOUSE

This Book Is Dedicated
To Whom It May Concern

But if in your fear you would seek only love's peace and love's pleasure,

Then it is better for you that you cover your nakedness and pass out of love's threshing-floor,

Into the seasonless world where you shall laugh, but not all of your laughter, and weep, but not all of your tears.

—KAHLIL GIBRAN
from *The Prophet*

NOT ALL OF YOUR LAUGHTER, NOT ALL OF YOUR TEARS

CHAPTER
ONE

Walking through the sand was awkward, but it seemed to Daniel Scanlon the only way that he could avoid coming into contact with people—the few who sauntered along the highway, or those who parked their cars by the roadside and sat looking at the ocean, munching sandwiches, or talking, or fondling each other. They were immersed in living; he wanted to escape from it and the ocean tempted him.

The damp sand near the water's edge was firmer underfoot. All afternoon dark clouds and scattered wisps of fog had contended with the sun for control of the waterfront, and now they had won. The sea was gray as death, cold and quietly ominous, rolling and bunching its muscles, curling the lips of contemptuous waves, mumbling and hissing. Dan passed a spot where, not many weeks before, he had romped and swum with the children. The sea, then, had been friendly but now it was a stranger and it frightened him, seeming, as it lifted its dark bulk, to be a potential agent of God's vengeance.

Because of the hour and the chill in the air the water was empty of people as far as he could see, except for two surfboarders, floating dejectedly in the distance, their glistening boards rising and falling slowly. He stopped walking and massaged the small of his back, inhaling deeply. A stronger wave than the rest suddenly attacked his shoes, with a sibilant swoosh. He swore, hopping clumsily backwards to drier ground. Then he laughed, for only a moment before he had been considering walking slowly out into the water, wondering if it was a quick means of self-destruction, and now the instinct of self-preservation or—even more absurd—the simple, practical dislike of getting one's feet wet had sent him scrambling back to safety. At this his already extreme self-contempt was increased by the knowledge that he did not have the courage to kill himself. The mingled smells of wet sand, iodine, seaweed and salted mist were sucked down into his lungs as he stood breathing heavily, staring down at his slightly soggy shoes.

He considered, for an idle moment, the question of whether he should, the sea having attacked him, hate it. He decided that to do so would be as reasonable as to love it. There seemed to be in his life, and possibly in the whole universe, no formal method of loving or hating. One could learn, scientifically, to play the piano or to construct a bridge, but there was no instruction in emotion. Everyone, therefore, was passionate rather ineptly.

At this moment of his life, as he stood staring at the Pacific Ocean in the year 1952, he was beginning to discover, painfully, that he was a prisoner of the past: both his own and that of his species. The knowledge inclined him toward pessimism. It had not yet occurred to him that it is always possible to escape from a prison.

Before driving down to the beach he had stopped at a bar in Santa Monica and had two drinks. The alcohol still muddled his mind and yet, in another way, cleared it. Thoughts floated freely to the surface and, because of his solitude, because of the privacy afforded by the steady soft roar of the sea, he was not ashamed to speak aloud at those moments when it occurred to him to do so.

Oh, Mother. Where are you?

She could not be found, ever, because she was not real. His real mother was alive, and indeed living less than two miles

4

from the spot where he stood, but she was not the one he was seeking, although in the form in which she had existed some thirty years before she was *part* of the image. But it was another—an ideal figure of perfection and beauty and soft, feminine warmth formed in the animal mind of an infant permitted to conceive an attachment but not to consciously develop it—to whom he cried out. There was difficulty in distinguishing among what was, and what was not, and what was represented by something else.

He would often sit with his head in his hands and think of how he had met her, and wonder what his life would have been like if he had not. Looking back he had the impression that he had not been paying close attention when she had dropped into his life. You rarely seemed to know, while things were happening, whether or not they were important. The sense of importance came later. Perhaps every minute of your existence you stood at a crossroads, in a fog, able perchance to see only one path open; and then later, sometimes many years later, you could look back and know that there had been another road, another direction you might have taken. You could stand on a high hill, looking back and to one side, and could consider what it might have been like on the other road. But the strange thing was that in the very moment of your looking back you might be standing at a new and unrecognized crossroads.

You could bump into strangers on elevators or be introduced to them at cocktail parties. You could say "How do you do?" and never know that at some future moment you might love one of these people, or kill one of them, or help one of them to wash his car.

Dan Scanlon had always been mildly amused by the fact that he could not remember how he had met any of his friends.

"The only person I know that I met at a particular time and place," he would say, "is my mother. The others just drifted into my life when I wasn't looking."

Although he was not technically equipped to compose legitimate music, he had always hoped that somehow he might someday be able to attempt the background score for a dramatic

5

motion picture. Tiomkin or Steiner, he realized, could make it absurdly easy for an audience to correctly evaluate the significance of characters, actions and events in a motion picture, for they could make a violin passage say, "This man has just met the only girl in the world," or "These lovers are parting, knowing they will never meet again." It was unfortunate, he thought, that there was not some mysterious cosmic orchestra that underscored the daily, seemingly humdrum activities in which people were engaged. If, in the moment he had met Elaine, he had heard a sudden wild chord, a sad minor passage that openly foretold doom, he might have stepped back and terminated the scene.

But warning there was none, and so he had smiled and said, "Nice to meet you."

He had been sitting, with some radio people, at a table in the bar of Brittingham's restaurant, next to the CBS studios on Sunset Boulevard. It was pleasant in the dimly lit room. The cooling system warded off the heat of the afternoon sun; the conversation was soft and lighthearted. He was waiting for Manny Wolpin, the publisher, who was in Studio B seeing Bob Crosby, and he was talking about golf with some of the people who worked on the Eve Arden program.

He had stepped to the bar to get cigarettes for one of the girls and when he sat down again there was a strange woman at the table. Someone was making introductions. He didn't catch the new woman's name.

"Nice to meet you," he said, smiling, and somewhere there was muffled laughter among the gods, a vicious sniggling and poking and pointing, a cruel anticipation. But for him there was no warning of any kind.

His reaction to her was immediate, normal and moderate but animal and in no way unlike the reaction of the average man to the average attractive woman. During the next several minutes he regarded her from time to time when he was certain she was not looking in his direction and he was respectfully impressed by her eyes, which were almost too large, and blue.

There had been nothing extraordinary about the meeting, he remembered. The incident was commonplace, merely another instance of the first-sight attraction that customarily dis-

6

sipated itself within twenty minutes because of an unattractive feature suddenly perceived or a disillusioning word allowed to fall from a mouth. The single man sees in every strange and intriguing woman a possible conquest, even a possible love; the married man reacts in the first moment according to the detached compulsion of his animal self and five seconds later, when the fog of morality, habit and loyalty has snuffed out the almost imperceptibly flickering fire of interest, according to what he knows is expected of him. Dan had met scores of beautiful women during his nine years of marriage.

They had not interested him, in the main. One or two had occupied his thoughts for perhaps twenty-four hours. With two or three others he had carried on brief, largely platonic relationships, taking them to casual dinners, going for unplanned drives, talking, then veering away from them as unconcernedly as he had drifted toward them.

This time he had no reason to suppose things would be in any regard different. He held a match to the new girl's cigarette, spoke to her briefly, somewhat stiffly, learned that she worked for a talent agency on the Strip, and that she was "going with" an arranger who worked at the network. The conversation was casual, underplayed, and the expressed ideas held scant interest. Wolpin came into the bar after a while and said, "Why don't we all have dinner together?"

The group had dwindled somewhat and when they went outside and walked around the block to the parking lot only Dan, Manny, Manny's secretary and the new woman were left.

"Let's go to the Villa Nova," Manny said. "I'm in the mood for some Italian food."

They got into Dan's car and he drove out Sunset Boulevard. The windows were open and he drove fast so that the wind would blow into the car. A colorful late-afternoon sky was beginning to piece itself together over the ocean.

They all joked and made small talk, discussed the latest pictures, toyed with the idea of going to other restaurants.

The new girl sat in the front seat next to Dan but he paid no inappropriate amount of attention to her. The wind felt good on his face and he made them all laugh heartily, telling them the latest Joe Frisco story. He even mentioned his family.

7

"Helen told me that one the other day."

"How is she?" Manny asked.

"Fine," he said. "She's bowling tonight."

"How are the kids?"

"Great."

At dinner, which they ate sitting at a round table in the back room, Dan talked business and laughed a great deal.

"I almost got the assignment to write *Are You With It,*" he said, "but at the last minute they found out I was without it."

They had a few drinks and at one point Manny and his secretary wandered off to another table to talk to new arrivals, and in the next minute Dan felt hot in the face and shy because he had lifted his head and looked into the girl's eyes for a split second too long.

She seemed amused. After a moment the tenseness passed and they retreated to small talk. Dan's stomach felt strangely leaden again a few minutes later, and he frowned and shook his head, staring at the tablecloth.

"What's the matter?" the girl said.

"I don't know," he said soberly. "I feel funny."

"I do, too, a little."

"Who did you say you worked for?"

"The Darby office. Frank Darby." She mentioned the name of several entertainers represented by the firm.

"You married?" His tone was casual, his face expressionless.

"I was."

"Oh, I'm sorry."

"It's all right. Over and done with."

"I see."

"You're married, aren't you?"

"Yes," he said, somehow glad to be reminded of it. He told her boastfully about the children, their ages, what wonderful youngsters they were, what they looked like. While he was speaking he could smell her perfume. He became slightly morose and stopped drinking.

"Excuse me," she said, getting up. As she walked back to the rest room he watched her ankles, her hips. She was tall and graceful. Looking at her made his stomach knot up again.

He felt relieved and strangely grateful when she came back to the table.

There was a small piano, a half-size instrument, wedged into a narrow area near a stairway and after a while he strolled over to it and sat down and began playing. She stood next to him, leaning her elbows on the piano top, singing snatches of the melodies she could recall.

"Play some of *your* things," she said.

"All right," he said. He ran over a few bars of each of his hits.

"I didn't know you'd written so *many*," she said. " 'Now We Know' is one of my favorites."

"I just wrote the music," he said. "Hank Lazarus did the lyric."

Manny had come over to the piano and pushed himself in behind the girl. She was forced to stand closer to Dan and once, when she stooped down to pick up a bobby-pin she had dropped, her hair brushed against his face.

"I guess I'd better call it a day," he said, standing up.

"What's the matter, Danny boy?" Manny asked. "Cashing in?"

"Yes," Dan said. He felt tired and disturbed and suddenly wanted to go home and watch television, sitting on the familiar large sofa in the den, with the children piled around him. The new girl lived closest to the Villa Nova so he drove her home first, then took Manny to the Player's Club. The secretary had disappeared.

When he got home the children were in bed. He kissed Helen automatically, standing beside her in the kitchen as she took hot, dry dishes out of the automatic washer.

"I thought you were bowling," he said.

"Rose couldn't make it, and we were going in her car, so we called it off."

"That's too bad," he said. He hung his suit-coat up, walked into the den and sat watching *Kukla, Fran and Ollie* for a few minutes. Helen came in and curled up beside him.

"Anything happen?" she said.

"Wolpin didn't go for the tune, but he took me to dinner."

"That's too bad," she said. "Where'd you go?"

"The Villa Nova," he said, with a trace of irritation. "Why?"

"Why what?"

"Why did you ask me where we went?"

"No reason," she said. "Don't bite my head off. I simply happened to ask you where you had dinner. Is there anything wrong in that?"

"Oh, God, never mind," he said quietly. "I'm sorry. I'm not feeling well."

"What's the matter?"

"I don't know. Nothing, really. I guess I'm just tired."

"That's too bad, hon," she said, looking at him closely. He put his arm around her and patted her shoulder.

"Patrick cut himself this afternoon," she said.

"Good Lord. How?"

"He fell off the swing or something. I didn't quite get the story straight. Banged his head on one of the cross-bars, I think."

"Is he all right?"

"Oh, sure. Had a bump for a while, but I put ice on it."

He walked into the bedroom that Patrick shared with his baby sister and listened to the two of them breathing. The baby thrashed around in her crib and Dan held his breath, hoping he had not awakened her. When the thrashing stopped he sat down on Patrick's bed. For several minutes he looked at him lying in the semi-darkness and then kissed him on the head and tip-toed out of the room.

"Michael okay?" he asked when he walked back into the den.

"Yes. He and Mrs. Walsh fell asleep about an hour ago."

The house had three bedrooms and a den, but because there were three children one of them had to sleep on a small bed in the housekeeper's room.

After a few minutes Dan stretched out full length on the sofa and fell sound asleep. Helen left the house and walked across the street to visit. When he woke up the den was cold and he felt stiff. Helen was in bed reading.

10

He undressed, brushed his teeth, and climbed in beside her, opening a book. Later, lying in the darkness, his thoughts went back to Brittingham's bar, to the Villa Nova, to the large eyes, and the full breasts, and the perfume. He rolled and gritted his teeth.

"Can't you sleep?"

Her voice frightened him and for a moment he half imagined that she had known what he was thinking.

"Oh, sure," he said. "I'm all right. I guess falling alseep in the den like that sort of took the edge off my tiredness."

"Good night, honey," she said, turning and kissing him lightly, drily, on the lips.

In the morning when he awakened, he was alone in the bed. Helen had been up early, getting Michael off to school, sending Patrick out to play, tending to Barbara, the baby. Dan lay vegetatively, looking out the window, scratching his head and yawning.

The sky was gray and sombre. He rolled over and tried to wrap the shreds of sleep about himself but without success. His mouth felt sour and his face stiff. In the kitchen Helen set orange juice and a cup of coffee before him. He read the paper, with another part of his mind listening to the radio on the drainboard, then put the glass and cup in the sink and went to shave, shower and dress.

He walked around the back yard for a time, examining gopher holes and considering whether or not he should get a spray for the weeds that were beginning to choke the grass. In the next yard he saw the woman who had just moved into the neighborhood. Middle-aged, small, unsmiling, she moved energetically about the yard, snipping leaves and branches, cutting flowers. He knew it would be a matter of little time before she began to talk to Helen over the concrete block fence, and only a while after that that she would begin to say things like "My, your husband certainly has nice hours, hasn't he?"

When they found out he was a song-writer, some of them took it to mean simply that he was out of work. To most people it didn't seem proper for a grown man to be at home in the afternoon, mowing the lawn, or sitting in the house playing the piano.

He wandered morosely about the yard, out beyond the white-fenced lawn, out among the high weeds that surrounded the eight dying peach trees. When they had moved into the neighborhood, two years ago, the real-estate man had said, "Don't know how much more life there is in these peach trees but if you water them they might last another year or two."

At first he had watered the trees a great deal, perhaps too much. The dry San Fernando Valley soil blotted up the water, and the sun, thwarted at not finding desert on the spot as in times past, viciously baked the trees. Now, after two years, they were withered dry, almost lifeless.

It was while he was standing in the pungent high weeds near the trees that he thought of the girl. At first he simply considered her, without emotion, recalling her as part of the previous day, giving her no more importance than his conference with Wolpin, the dinner at the Villa Nova, the ride home.

Then he discovered that he could not, at least at that moment, stop thinking of her. The scent of orange blossoms floated across the warm valley, drifted to him on the light breeze, rustled the small dry leaves of the peach trees, and reminded him of her perfume.

Never in nine years of married life had he been affected by a woman precisely in this way. It troubled him and he determined to put the thing out of his mind, literally throwing his shoulders back in a gesture of affirmative renunciation. He kept overly busy the rest of the afternoon, shopped at a supermarket, called a man about having the cesspool drained, and tidied up some books that had fallen out of a crate in the garage.

It helped.

He did not think of her again that day, and the next few days she crossed his mind only fleetingly and at widely separated intervals.

Friday he walked into Brittingham's and saw her sitting alone at a table.

12

"Well, hello," she said.

"Hello, there," he said, forgetting her name for the moment. "Having lunch?" he heard himself say, as if listening to the voice of another.

"Yes," she said. "Care to sit down?"

"Well . . ." He could think of no reason to say no. "Do you eat here often?" he said, sitting opposite her.

"No," she said. "I'm meeting a girl friend of mine who works at CBS. She's a little late."

"Oh," he said, looking at her blankly. He felt slightly angry and did not know why.

"Seen Manny?"

"No, I haven't, as a matter of fact," he said. "Have you?"

"No," she said. There was a brief uncomfortable pause. It seemed difficult to get the conversation off the ground.

Sitting in the harsh afternoon sunlight that slanted through the plate-glass window, she looked a year or two older than he had thought. Perhaps thirty-two. He examined the slight lines at the corners of her eyes, looking for imperfections, in a slightly desperate way hoping to find them, suddenly realizing, albeit dimly, that he *had* to find them, and promptly.

"You know a girl named Bobbe Hotchkiss?" she asked.

"Why, yes," he said. "I believe I do. Why?"

"No reason, really. I just met her the other night and she said she knew you."

"Is that right?"

"Yes."

The conversation still was leaden. So she had been discussing him. Well, now. He looked at the large blue eyes, the downcast mascaraed lashes, the soft, short brown hair. She was wearing a dark blue dress with a white collar, which made her look more business-like, more like a secretary than she had the other evening. He thought, as he regarded her sitting there toying with the orange-colored melon on her plate, that she was the most beautiful woman he had ever seen. The thought exploded silently in his mind and slowly filtered downward through his body in an almost physical sense, inducing in him a strange melting sensation such as he could recall having experienced from having drunk hot cocoa in the snow of

December or a cold glass of beer on an empty stomach in the heat of August.

"Say," he said, listening to the tension in his voice, hearing it float to him as if from afar, "I wonder if I might have your phone number. I might want to give you a call sometime." He laughed, trying to be casual, and his heart pounded.

"Well," she said. "That's . . . that's funny."

"I didn't mean any offense," he said. "I just thought some time maybe we might have a drink together."

"Surely," she said. "It would be quite all right."

"Of course," he said, his palms moist. He frowned and wondered what he was doing. Had he asked a girl for her telephone number? Something was wrong. The sun lay warm on the tablecloth and on his back. He wiped his brow and felt frightened, as if he were about to be accused, as if a hand were about to fall on his shoulder. On the surface he was non-chalant. Silently, in the uneasy privacy of his mind he said her name. Elaine. Elaine.

"I think I have a pencil here somewhere," he said, chuckling offhandedly. "Now, what was that number?"

She told him and he wrote it down on the back of an envelope and put the envelope in his inside jacket pocket.

She regarded him with a steady, level glance and took a cigarette from a pack in her purse. His hand trembled slightly as he lighted it.

"You're a strange one," she said.

"Why do you say that?"

"I don't know," she said. "I just have a feeling that there's something odd going on. Something I don't quite understand. Did you ever have a feeling like that?"

"No," he said. "But I have it at this moment."

Something had happened that, in a mysterious way, melted the ice that had blocked the flow of conversation, the exchange of ideas between them. They talked now feverishly, without interruption for over an hour, discussing many things trivial and grave. He learned that she had been divorced three years, that she was from Milwaukee, that she had married her husband four weeks after she'd been introduced to him and then regretted it, that she was learning to speak French in her spare time, that she was not satisfied with her job and felt that she had been cut out to do more important things, that she was an amateur artist, dabbling in oils, that she liked to water-ski at Lake Arrowhead, that she had gone for a time with a man who was a Christian Scientist and thought there was a great deal to be said for the religion, that she was glad that skirts were getting a little shorter, that she lived with her mother, that she had worked for a while as a secretary for a producer at MGM, that reading Thomas Wolfe could sometimes make her cry, that she could recite dozens of Emily Dickinson's poems, that her father was dead and that he had been, of all things, a bartender, that she loved to drink cold milk, that she was about seven pounds overweight, that she used to bargain with God when she was a child, that she had never wanted to be a model or an actress although goodness knows she had had plenty of offers, and that she did not now care whether or not her friend showed up because she was having such a perfectly marvelous time talking to him except that she thought she was boring him.

From time to time, as she spoke, his mind wandered, so that he once or twice lost track of what she was saying, distracted by her face, by the movement of her red, creamy lips, the rise and fall of her eyelids and lashes. At one point he studied her face carefully, touring it with his eyes, from the delicately rounded chin up to the full fire-truck red lips, the square white teeth, the moist pink tongue, the handsome nose, the wide, expressive eyes, in the blue depths of which it seemed that something else lay watching *him* from a separate distance, something that dwelt behind the surface of her, something that called a silent message, a message having nothing to do with what she was actually saying. He had a sudden impulse, the utter absurdity of which he fully appreciated, to reach out and pat her head, as one might pat a kitten or a puppy.

CHAPTER
TWO

So that was the way it had started, in something akin to innocence, certainly in naivete.

When he got home that afternoon he noticed an astounding thing. *The house and all the objects in it appeared to be of a different, new size and the colors in the rugs and wallpaper were changed slightly.*

Even the children looked like strange lovable gnomes to him as he saw them playing in the back yard, stretching an old army blanket over a rope, making a tent.

When he walked into the kitchen and looked at Helen he felt as if he had been far away from her for a very long time. She, too, had changed in what seemed the intervening years.

She was ironing shirts in the back vestibule. A blue oxford button-down was on the ironing-board and several others, already done, had been put on hangers against the wall.

"I wonder why it is," he said, "that so many wives leave ironing on display until the man of the house gets home."

"I don't know," she said, accepting the kiss on the cheek, brushing a wisp of blond hair away from her unmascaraed eyes, "maybe we're just showing off. Maybe we just want a little credit."

16

"They look fine," he said. "But why didn't you let Mrs. Walsh do them?"

"Oh," she said, "she never seems to do the collars right. There's coffee made."

"Thanks." He poured himself a cup from the chrome coffee-maker on the tile sideboard and sat down at the yellow formica table.

"What happened today?"

"What?" He swallowed and felt a curious wary blankness.

"Any news?"

"No. Nothing much. I went down to CBS to see some of the guys. Had lunch at Brittingham's." The coffee lay bitter on his tongue. He felt light-headed.

"Why don't you take off your coat?"

He rose and removed his jacket, placing it over the back of his chair. Turning halfway around, he took his wallet and the envelope with Elaine's phone number on it out of the inside pocket.

He placed the wallet on the table and slid the envelope under it.

"You want me to go to the store for anything?" he said.

"I don't think so. We still have the chops left over and I can whip up a salad."

"Well," he said, inhaling deeply, "I just thought maybe I'd go down to the drugstore and if there's anything you want . . ."

"What do you need at the drugstore?"

The question brought him face to face with the realization that he was manufacturing a lie.

"Razor blades."

"There's a new pack in the back bathroom."

A telephone call. He could have driven down to the drug-store and made a telephone call, in the end booth, speaking softly and close to the mouthpiece. He could have said, "Hello," and "Guess who?" and "I was just thinking of you," and "I'd like to see you tomorrow," and "Oh, my God, where do we go from here?"

But there was a new package of razor blades in the back bathroom. It was just as well, he tried to tell himself, but his

17

clenched knuckles were white and he was privately angry.

He stayed angry, mainly at himself, for the next three days, although Helen did not seem to notice it.

Sunday morning he got up at eleven fifteen and took Michael and Patrick to twelve o'clock mass.

It was always the same on Sundays. Helen in a housecoat, fixing breakfast, dressing the boys in clean suits, combing their hair, putting the baby out in the back yard to play in her play pen and then walking to the door to watch Dan drive off to church with Mike and Pat.

They rarely discussed religion any more, although there had been mildly bitter arguments in the early days of their relationship. Helen's parents had not wanted her to marry a Catholic and Dan's mother had not wanted him to marry at all, least of all a Protestant, until he was older. Once, about six months before she and Dan got married, they had broken up after a wrangle about religion.

"Don't get me wrong," he had said, sullenly. "I'm not trying to convert you. It doesn't matter to me whether you're a Catholic or not. I wish you were, but you're not, and I love you."

"Oh," she said, her tone verging on the tearful, "you say it doesn't make any difference, but it does. I can tell. Besides, it makes a difference to me. Mama says she knows of one couple, friends of hers, and the woman is Catholic and the man isn't, and she says they fight all the time about it."

"So what if they do?" Dan snapped. "They're not us. Are you going to let your mother make up your mind about our getting married or are you going to make up your own mind?"

The argument had increased in volume and tempo and finally she had given him back his ring, the pitifully cheap ring he had purchased at the little jewelry store in downtown Phoenix. He had remained bitter for two days and then mooned around town for three more, trying not to call her, trying to get along without her. But at last he knew that he could not and he called her on the telephone and they had had a happy, tear-streaked reconciliation.

Other than that, they had never had a real argument about religion. There were differences based on faith between them,

18

and important differences, but they chose to keep them bottled up. He never discussed the matter with anyone at all, with the exception of his mother, and only then against his better judgment.

At first she had been disturbed at the news that Helen was a non-Catholic. It didn't really matter what she *was,* it was simply a matter of what she *wasn't.*

Helen's people had been opposed to the match, too, although not as volubly as Dan's mother. The strange thing was that when at last everyone knew the marriage was inevitable it was his mother who did the most to help them, who loaned them money, who arranged for a small wedding-party at the Paso Robles Inn, in the little town near Camp Roberts.

She had had the wisdom to succumb to the inevitable, and when Dan had been drafted and sent to the sprawling Infantry Replacement Training Center in the mountains of central California, when he had written to Helen and implored her to come to him and marry him before he was shipped overseas, it was his mother who had made the trip with the girl and helped her to set up a little place for Dan in Paso Robles.

They had been married in one of the post chapels, right across from the machine gun range where Dan had that morning been occupied in learning to load and fire a 50-calibre weapon, and then three weeks later the thin, bald, irritable officer at the camp hospital had decided that Dan's asthma was too severe a handicap for an infantryman and a recommendation had been made that he be given an honorable medical discharge.

Because he had never actually been called upon to face true danger, and because the thirteen week stay at Camp Roberts had been an exciting, stimulating experience, and because he had married a girl he had loved for over a year— because of all these things he was always thereafter able to look back on his army days as rather pleasant.

He could always recall the thrill he had felt the hot June day, waiting at the front gate of the camp, seeing Helen running toward him in a white, summery dress. He had never had any difficulty remembering the excited, frantic pace of the few days just before the ceremony in the chapel, the nights of

19

holding hands, walking around the camp, drinking milkshakes at the PX, playing the jukeboxes, sitting under the moonlight on the side of the tawny, lion-haunch hills that ringed the post. He could always clearly remember lying at night with Helen on the grassy hills, looking down into the camp at the miles and miles of twinkling lights in the humming barracks, lying dreamily with his head in her lap, her fingers running through his hair.

They had stayed at a cheap hotel the first honeymoon night, but it had seemed like a pleasant enough place at the time. There had been fumbling attempts at lovemaking before they were married, in cars, on front porches; but now, lying shyly under a sheet in a dingy room on the third floor of the little hotel, they had been swamped by the giddy, thoughtless abandon that only the very young in love can know, and they had not been even too saddened by the unsatisfactory, partly embarrassing nature of their physical experience that first night.

Helen had cried and been frightened and Dan, in his eagerness, had been unable to satisfy her. She was afraid of becoming pregnant and in the instant, although they did not realize it at the time, lost as they were in the golden haze of their first privacy and matedness, there was born a spectre that was to haunt them all the years of their married life.

Sitting next to the boys in church now, Dan tried to pray but could not seem to clear his mind. Michael was sitting solemnly, his serious brown eyes looking straight ahead; but blue-eyed, carefree Patrick was standing on the seat next to Dan, smiling at the people behind them, flirting self-consciously.

In the habituated tranquility that prevailed in the church, Dan thought of Elaine and considered that he had the strength to forget about her. He bowed his head slightly, closed his eyes and tried to participate actively in the sacrifice of the mass, tried to pray; but praying to forget a particular face was an extremely delicate operation, for when one closed one's eyes to concentrate one saw the very face one was trying to forget.

He opened his eyes and stared at the large crucifix on the altar, a focal point for his concentration in moments of stress.

20

At such times he would often think sadly of the days of his youthful innocence. He would see himself walking back up the aisle from the communion rail, hands pressed flat together, head bowed, or kneeling alone in a silent chapel, making an afternoon visit, staring transfixed at the flame of a candle, imagining that the candlelight was his soul and that its flickerings represented little weakenings in his determination to be good.

"If the candle flame holds still till I count to ten," he would say to himself, "that means I will be a good boy all day today." Then he would stare fiercely, unblinking, at the candle, his lips moving, counting, his heart aching with the pure lust for virtue (or was it approval?) until he had either reached ten or the gust of a breeze had whipped at the flame and made it flutter.

He glanced sideways now at Michael, the one of the three children who looked most like him, and felt a brief wave of sadness that the child was destined to grow up and be obliged to come to grips with whatever wayward and antagonistic forces would beset him.

At that moment, Patrick dropped a red glass marble. The clatter as it bounced on the wooden seat caused a wave of turned heads and disapproving looks. Angrily Dan stared back at the bolder of those who had turned, and in that significant instant he experienced a feeling of surrender to evil, a fit of despair at man's inability ever to accumulate more than a few seconds of uninterrupted goodness. You knelt piously in church—and the young woman in front of you had on a tight silk dress. You woke up in the morning and promised yourself or God to practice selfless charity—and before you had gotten into your slippers you were silently cursing at your wife for having failed to close the window against the biting cold.

You had rules that were rules until they inconvenienced you and then you broke them. You affirmed that it was wrong to lie, and then you said, "Sorry, Charlie, we can't make it Tuesday night, because we already have a dinner date," when the truth of the matter was that Charlie and his wife were dull and boring and you didn't want to spend an evening with them. You drove back from church on Sunday with a feeling

21

of smug self-satisfaction and warmth in your heart, until another driver tried to cut in and force you over a little and then you stuck your head out the window and shouted, "Watch out, you stupid bastard!"

Driving the car into the garage, Dan was still angry. He opened the door for the boys and then followed them out into the back yard and stood looking at the pale flowers that grew along the fence. He felt a strange gnawing in his stomach that was not hunger, and he knew damn well then that before the day was over he was going to get to a telephone and call Elaine. He wanted to hear the speech-sounds come out of the red mouth.

Later in the afternoon his chance came. Helen did some laundry. When she went out into the yard to hang the clothes on the line he hurried into the bedroom and dialed Elaine's number. There was no answer.

CHAPTER

THREE

H<small>E</small> controlled himself for the next three days, his unspoken misery mounting. On Thursday evening he met his partner, Hank Lazarus, at the Brown Derby and together they went to station KNX to be interviewed by Al Stevens, the late night disc jockey and comedian. When they arrived at the CBS Building, a fuzz-cheeked usher showed them to the control room of Studio B. "You can wait right in here," he said. "Mr. Stevens has already started his warmup."

They entered the small, overly air-conditioned cubicle with the slanted plate glass front that overlooked the stage, seated themselves on aluminum and black leatherette chairs, received a curt over-the-shoulder smile from an engineer and looked out at Alan Stevens' back and beyond him at the upturned faces of the studio audience.

"I'd like to take a little survey," Stevens was saying. "Now, let's see. Would those of you who have never been here before please raise your hands?"

About ninety per cent of the people lifted their hands, some innocently, others smirking wisely, suspecting the joke that, knowing Stevens, they felt sure would follow.

"That's fine," he said, seemingly very earnest. "Now may I

see the hands of those who are here tonight for the *first time?*"

Most of those who had raised their hands did so again and then slowly the audience started to build a moderate roar of laughter as the realization of the trick Stevens had played on them began to dawn.

"Funny bit," Hank said.

"Yeah," said the engineer, touching a dial. "I've been listening to that same joke every night for the last two years. For some reason every time I see those hands go up the second time I break up."

"We'll be on the air in just a few minutes," Stevens said, pushing a lock of hair off his forehead, "and since this is supposed to be a comedy show I—uh—I suppose I'd better show you some comedy. I mean I suppose you'd better agree to laugh it up. In fact, as an added inducement we have some very nice prizes to give away. For example, the lady who laughs the loudest tonight is going to receive a beautiful five-pound box of wet sand."

"He does the warmup just the same every night?" Hank asked.

"Yeah," the engineer said. "The ad-libbing starts when we go on the air."

"And we have some other wonderful prizes too," Stevens said. "Seriously, we're going to find out tonight who the oldest lady in the audience is. And we have a marvelous present for her."

The elderly women in the audience giggled in anticipation, while those who had attended the program before smiled knowingly.

"When we find the oldest lady," Stevens said with a convincing display of sincerity, "we're going to give her . . . the oldest *man.*"

A hair-thin black indicator-needle on the control board jumped all the way to the right side of a small dial as a shout of laughter blasted into the studio microphones.

"Don't laugh," Stevens continued. "The first time we tried this . . . I distinctly remember . . . was one night about ten years ago. We had a very nice lady in our audience. She was 87 years old, as I recall. We introduced her that evening to a man from Chicago who was 96 and shortly thereafter, believe it or not, they were married. It was a very lovely story. And that wasn't the end of it either. I read in the paper recently where that woman has just given birth to a beautiful 47-year-old baby boy!"

"What time do we go on?" Dan said.

"First he does a few minutes by himself," Hank explained. "Then he does a commercial or two, then he'll either bring us right out or else he'll go into the studio audience and do some interviews."

"That's my favorite part of the show," the engineer said. "Man, we don't know *what's* gonna happen out there. I have to keep my hand on this pot, too, because they come up with some pretty wild lines when he jumps down there with the hand-mike."

"Well," Stevens was saying, looking carefully at his wrist. "It's about time to go on the air and I really don't know what I'm looking at here because my watch is in hock."

Hank laughed and said, "This guy's pretty off-beat."

"He does things like that all the time," the engineer said. "Like the other night I put a cigarette into my mouth and Al holds up this lighter and begins clicking it, trying to give me a light and then all of a sudden I notice that it's not a lighter at all, just a house key that he's flicking with his fingernail. He's a nut."

The large clock on the control-room wall buzzed briefly, its minute-hand wiggled and snapped smartly into the straight-up notch of twelve and Stevens said, "Ladies and gentlemen, we have a late news report, a late news report from the CBS newsroom. The Kaiser's troops have just marched into Belgium!"

After the crowd had stopped chuckling, he said with a solemn face, "Listen, what's so funny? If that isn't the latest news report *you* ever heard I'll put in with ya. And I wonder where the heck *that* expression originated. I'll put *what* in *where?*"

"This all done without script?" Dan said.

"One hundred per cent," the engineer said. "He just says whatever comes into his head."

"When does he go on the air?" Hank said, looking at the wall clock with a puzzled frown.

"We're already on," the engineer said.

"That's pretty weird," Hank said. "No announcer tonight?"

"Yeah, McGraw's here, but Al usually opens the show cold."

At that moment a tall plump man with a jovial expression walked on-stage carrying a handful of papers and seated himself silently at a table upon which rested a microphone.

"Tom McGraw just sauntered in," Stevens said. "Tom, I hope I don't have to speak to you again about *sauntering*. I'll thank you to have the decency to *walk* like the rest of us, or else stride manfully, stalk determinedly or even slouch dejectedly, but no sauntering."

McGraw guffawed heartily. "All right, Al," he said. "To tell you the truth I don't think I was sauntering. Inasmuch as I was about five minutes late getting down here from upstairs I actually intended to *sneak* in."

"Then I'll thank you to wear your sneakers," Stevens said, adding, "There must be *something* I can thank you for."

"I can't imagine what it would be."

"Then," said Stevens, "I'll thank you to keep a civil tongue in your head—which is a scene from the picture *Where Else?* But I don't mind, Tom. If you've *got* a civil tongue you can keep it in a cigar box for all of me."

Seating himself suddenly at a concert piano, the lank comic played an arpeggio and sang "All of me—why not take all of me?"

"Jeez," Dan said. "This guy is the original Mr. Free Association."

"Yeah," Hank said. "He'll make more money out of stream-of-consciousness than Joyce ever did."

"Well," Stevens continued, "we've got some pretty interesting items in the old mail bag tonight. And why are the mail bags that radio people refer to invariably described as *old*? Same question goes for the old clocks on the wall. Someday I want to turn on my radio and hear a guy say, 'Well, folks, I see by the new clock on the wall that it's time to go.' But anyway, as I was saying when I was so rudely interrupted by my

26

subconscious, we have a lot of interesting items in the mail bag tonight."

"Get many letters this week?" McGraw said.

"No," Stevens said. "No letters. Just interesting items. For example, I find in the old mail bag tonight two paper clips, four skrumbles of lint, and a—"

"Four *whats* of lint?" McGraw said, giggling.

"Tom," Stevens said, "I've got to hand it to you. (And don't drop it.) But your noticing the word skrumble—that shows you're paying attention. To tell the truth it's just a word I made up on the spot (and when you're on the spot you've got to do *something*)."

Hank lit a cigarette. "Half this guy's remarks," he said, "are made up of parenthetical clauses. He's closer to Proust than to Milton Berle."

Dan made a mental note to find out who the hell Proust was and resumed listening.

"Anyway," Stevens was saying, "what would *you* call pieces of lint? The question, of course, is rhetorical and was submitted by an oracle named Rhett who will receive as a prize a handsome Bakelite twenty-one jewel garter belt personally autographed by Roy Rogers *and* Trigger. Or, if this is not satisfactory, an unreasonable facsimile. Does that answer your question, Tom McGraw?"

"Look," McGraw said, "why don't you let me go through the formality of starting the show and then I'll get out of your way."

"You're not *in* my way, Tom," Stevens said. "But as for introducing the program, you can write your own ticket (if you remember to use carbon paper)."

McGraw made a formal announcement that it was time once again to present from Columbia Square that square from Columbia, Alan Stevens. The engineer piped in a recording of Stevens' theme "Laughing Boy" and when McGraw said, "And now here he is, your friend and mine, Alan Stevens," the audience burst into applause for Stevens for the second time.

"Hello there, friends and neighbors," Stevens said, "and how seldom neighbors *are,* now that I think of it. Well, let's get right to the mail. A lady in Pasadena, Eileen Hackle or Hockle, I guess it is, wants to know if I really have to wear glasses or, as she so cleverly puts it, 'Do you really have to wear glasses?' Well, no, Eileen, only when I see. To tell you the truth I'm very nearsighted. In fact, so far as I know I'm the only man in town who has to wear contact lenses to see his glasses.

"Now let's see. We have a card here from a man in—in—uh —in—cahoots. No, I mean in San Diego. (By the way, what are cahoots and how do you get in them? From the top, maybe? Or perhaps there's a little sliding panel in the *side* of the cahoot. A sliding cahoot-panel, or as they would say in the army: Panel, cahoot, sliding, M-one.) But where was I? (And if it was nice there why did I move out?) Oh, yes. The man from San Diego. (Say, that sounds like a movie-title, doesn't it? Republic Pictures presents John Wayne in *The Man from San Diego!* Coming!!! To your neighborhood meat market soon. You'll *thrill* as the usher punches you right in the mouth, *gasp* as the lobby drinking fountain squirts up your nose!"

Stevens was speaking more loudly now, abandoning his stock radio Truman Bradleyish suavity, getting wild, banging out mock movie-theme chords at the piano. The crowd was beginning to whoop it up with him, giggling and shouting encouragement.

"Christ," Hank said, laughing, "this is like a revival in a nut-house."

"Yes," Stevens was exclaiming, "you'll see two thousand wild automobiles stampeding across an Arizona drive-in! You'll see five thousand hot-dogs eaten alive by panicky suburbanities! You'll see ten thousand ants crawling all over a dropped Eskimo Pie! Don't fail to miss this monumental tribute to the brave men who pilot our elevators at the Broadway Department Store. See *The Man from San Diego,* starring John Wayne, Mabel Wayne, Bernie Wayne, Frances Wayne, *pouring* wain, soaking wet, and sick in bed! You'll be glad you did. Remember, it's the best friend your car ever had!"

At this, Stevens hit a sustained trumpet-blast of a chord

signifying that his free-swinging impressionistic tirade was concluded and the audience erupted into applause.

"We're supposed to follow *that?*" Dan said.

But later when the interview started it went well.

"How did you gentlemen meet?" Stevens asked.

"That's a rather embarrassing story," Dan said. "Hank had been writing with another fellow, who shall be nameless,—"

"And talentless?" Stevens said.

"By no means," Dan said. "But the other fellow went off to Europe to study music or something. I read about it in the trades and wrote a letter to Hank telling him that if he was in the market for a new collaborator I was his man."

"Do such stratagems really work?" Stevens said.

"This one did," Hank said. "Dan sent me a recording of a bunch of his melodies. It lay around the house for several weeks and then one day, just for want of something better to do, I decided to listen to it. The songs were great. I called him up and we went right to work. It was that simple."

"Let's see, now," Stevens said. "I understand that, unlike most songwriting teams, you both write words and music. Is that right?"

"Yes, it is," Hank said. "On most of our tunes Dan writes the music and I do the words, but each of us also functions as an editor for the other and each of us contributes valuable suggestions to the other."

"How'd you break into the game?" Stevens said.

"Oh, accidentally," Hank responded. "The usual way. You know, started out to do something else. I was going to the University of Pittsburgh, studying law. Somewhere along the line I goofed and began to write words and music. The usual bit. School shows, numbers of kids around town, occasional parodies and what-have-you for acts that were playing Pittsburgh. Johnny Crane's band played a one-nighter in our neighborhood once. I caught him with his guard down and showed him some novelty material. He liked it. One of the numbers, 'Watch Your Step,' was a big record. On the strength of that one I went to New York and began making the rounds."

"When did you begin writing for pictures?"

"Let's see," Hank said. "That would be about 1939. I had

written the score of a Broadway revue. The show only lasted about two weeks but everybody seemed to like the music so I got a call to do some things for Class B musicals at Columbia. The rest, as the saying goes, is history."

"Now how about you, Dan?" Stevens said.

"My story is considerably less interesting," Dan said. "I was going to school in Arizona, majoring in journalism. I never did bother to finish college. Marriage seemed like a more attractive proposition, and when you're married you have to win the old bread. So I quit school, took a job in a clothing store, and began trying to write during my free time."

"Write?"

"Yes. Short stories, poetry, songs, a novel—anything. As a youngster I had taken a few piano lessons and I had the knack of playing by ear. Nobody seemed the least bit interested in my poetry and stories so I began to concentrate on the songs. I saved up a little money, moved over here to the coast about six years ago, got a job in the newsroom at one of your rival radio stations down the street rewriting stuff off the teletype for eighty bucks a week. Eventually I met Hank. That's all there was to it."

Stevens played recordings of several of their songs, discussed the pictures for which they had created scores, solicited their opinions on various trends in the music business, and eventually—complimenting them lavishly—concluded the interview. As Dan walked off the stage and past the control room the engineer called to him from within the booth.

"Call for you," he said, nodding toward the telephone. When Dan heard the voice at the other end he was almost overcome with a sudden dizzying mixture of nervousness, guilt, and sexual excitement.

"Where are you?" he said.

"Over at a friend's," Elaine said, sounding gay and relaxed. "We just happened to catch your interview and I thought I'd call and tell you how much I enjoyed it."

"Can I see you?"

"Well," she said, "I don't know. I don't think so. I mean, I'm with these people. You're not alone, are you?"

"No, Hank is still here, but that's no problem."

There was a pause.

"I'm sorry," Elaine said. "I really don't think I can get away from where I am. Sorry to turn this into a hang-up, Dan, but I just thought I'd say hello."

"I'm glad you did," he said, stiff with a strange, tense weariness. "Thanks for calling." The engineer looked up, puzzled, as he slammed down the phone and hurried out of the booth.

"Who was that?" Hank said, as they headed toward the parking lot.

"Wrong number," Dan said.

CHAPTER
FOUR

LONG the ocean, in the coastal towns, the first wispy trace of autumn was in the air in the early mornings, and sometimes at night it slipped in and out of the warm fogs that drifted up from the sombre sea, over the hills, laced themselves through the oil derricks, stretched out in droplets on the hoods and windshields of parked cars.

In the valley, however, autumn had not as yet made its appearance. The afternoon sun burned painfully into the Van Nuys soil, dried the Encino orange groves, sapped the strength from the walnut trees in Reseda. The children still played in the yard in their swimming trunks on the hotter days, splashing in and out of the green plastic wading pool that Dan had brought home.

One day he sat in the small plastic circle himself, in his shorts, laughing and gasping as the boys climbed over him, splashing water up onto his face and his chest. Through the semi-transparent bottom of the pool he could see the pattern of the crushed grass, matted down and twisted by the weight of the water in which he sat.

At last he rose and the children screamed, "Daddy, Daddy, don't go in the house! Play with us some more." But he laughed and wrestled with them, glad that the water on his face made it impossible for them to see that he was beginning to cry, and went into the house and took a shower and got dressed and got into the car and drove into Hollywood slowly, regretfully, with his hands gripping the steering wheel hard.

His mouth was a straight line and he felt drained of emotion. He felt neither guilt nor elation, only a sense of inescapable futility. He had fought a battle within himself for days, and lost it. There had been no moment during those days, really, when he had seemed to be winning the fight, but at least he had tried to keep himself fired up for that long a time. Then at last, sitting sloshing in the wading pool, surrounded by his own children, with the sun hot on his naked back, he had given up.

He drove down Vine Street and turned right on Sunset Boulevard. Two blocks from the Darby office he parked, went into a drugstore and telephoned Elaine.

The voice of an older woman came through the receiver.

"Is Elaine there?" he said.

"Why, no, but she'll be back soon. Who shall I say called?"

"Mr. Scanlon." It was hot in the booth. He ran his finger around his collar and bit his lower lip. "Did you say she'd be right back?"

"Why, yes. I think so."

There was a flat silence.

"Well," he said, "I'll call back. Could she be at the office, do you think?"

"No, I don't think she'd go back there this afternoon. I'll tell her you called."

"All right. Thank you."

He sat at the cool marble soda fountain counter and drank a Coca Cola, looking at his wrist watch every few minutes. He looked, too, at his reflection in the mirror behind the counter and had the distinct feeling that he was looking at someone other than himself. At five-thirty-six he stepped into the booth again. When he heard her voice say "Yes?" he exhaled deeply, although not altogether with relief.

"Hi," he said. "This is Dan."

"Who?"

"Dan Scanlon." He felt a tremor of fear.

33

"Oh, yes. I'm sorry. How are you?"

"I'm fine. Listen, I was wondering if I could see you tonight."

"Oh." There was a pause. Then, "I'm terribly sorry, Dan, but I've got a date tonight. Maybe some—"

"That's too bad. I'm very anxious to see you." He felt irritated at the ineptitude with which he was handling the conversation. He was like a sixteen-year-old boy, unsure of himself, awkward, unable to keep the breathy note of anxiety out of his voice.

"Well," she said.

"Look, maybe you could have a drink with me right now, before dinner?"

"Well," she said, "I really don't know. I couldn't spend much time with you because I—" There was another pause. "Well, I guess it would be all right for just a few minutes. How soon could you come over?"

"I can be there in five minutes."

Outside he jerked the car away from the curb furiously and spun it out into the car-swarm. Weaving dangerously in and out of traffic, he turned left off Sunset and wound through the shopping section of Beverly Hills. As he pulled up to her building he saw her standing on the steps.

"What took you so long?" she said jokingly.

"Stiff headwind," he said smiling as she climbed into the car. They got back on Sunset Boulevard and headed west, toward the ocean.

"Where are we going?" she asked, taking out a cigarette.

"Why," he said, "nowhere in particular. I just wanted to see you."

She smiled noncommittally. "That's nice."

Silence lay like a rock on the seat between them.

"I've been thinking about you."

"Have you?" she said.

"Yes."

"I've been thinking about you, too." At the words his heart leaped and he looked at her fiercely. Unable to think of any words that could appropriately express his emotion, he drove silently for several minutes, steering with one hand, the other arm thrown up on the back of the seat. She sat turned toward him, her back against the door.

"That's a pretty dress," he said, lamely, wanting to shout, to cry out he knew not what.

"Thank you."

The dress was pale lavender, cotton, tight around the waist, cut low in front, complemented by deep purple cotton shoes with very high heels. Her legs were crossed and he felt something like a sickness in his stomach as he looked at her ankles.

"Pretty sunset," he said, squinting ahead.

"Yes," she answered. "It's hard driving into it."

"Do you have to hurry right back?" There was a plaintive note in his voice, for which he detested himself.

"Well, not right this minute if that's what you mean. Why?"

"Hell," he said. "I don't know why. I don't even know what I'm doing here. I just had to see you, that's all. I hope I don't sound like an idiot."

She leaned over and patted his arm.

"No, dear," she said quietly. "You don't at all."

After that it was a little easier, talking. They drove to a small bar in Bel Air and each of them had two drinks at a table against the wall, near a fireplace. After the second drink he said, feeling foolish at the trite sound of the words, "You look very beautiful by firelight."

"Who doesn't?" she said. They laughed. Her long, slim fingers were knotted together, holding up her chin as she regarded him levelly. He could look at her now without feeling shy.

"I was afraid to look you in the eye the first day I met you," he said.

"Why in the world were you afraid?"

"I don't know. I just felt that if you saw me looking right at you, you'd discover something about me."

"Discover what?"

"That's the funny part of it. I haven't the slightest idea. All I know is that I could only look at you when you weren't looking at me. And another thing: you look *familiar* to me."

In the next instant he had reached out and taken her hand. She did not withdraw it.

35

"It's getting late," she said.

"Please," he said, a bit louder than he had intended.

She smiled forgivingly.

"All right," she said.

"You have pretty hands," he said. "And this is a lovely bracelet." He fingered the gold chain with the tiny charms attached to it.

"Maybe charm bracelets are old hat," she said, "but I like them."

"Where did you get this?" he asked, touching a small golden Eiffel Tower.

"In Paris," she said. "Frank and several of us from the office were there this spring with Jackie Barton."

Barton was Darby's most important client, one of the nation's top comedians.

"You were there all spring?" Dan said clumsily, retreating before some sudden phantasm of rejection.

"Yes, Jackie wanted to do a few of his shows from there so we all went over. It was wonderful."

A black-winged fear fluttered shadowlike in the remotest part of Dan's mind.

"I suppose all the girls from the office went over?" he said, looking away.

"Why, no," she said. "I'm Frank's number-one girl so I was the only one of us who made the trip. Although I could have used a little help."

"Oh," he said. "I'll bet you had a lot of fun, the only girl with all those men."

She did not seem to grasp his implication immediately.

"Most of the time it was work, work, work," she said, "but I did see quite a bit of Paris. I'll never be happy till I go back."

Dan suddenly was assailed by an icy numbness in his chest that he had not known for many years. It was the feeling he had always had on Sunday nights at boarding school when his mother, or his aunt, or his grandmother would kiss him good-bye and get into a taxi at the school gate and say, "Good-bye, Danny. I'll see you soon, sweetheart."

It was the feeling that had come over him at those long-gone times when he would stand on the gravel driveway looking through the school gate at the disappearing cab, looking at the strange cars speeding past, ever past, on the exciting highway outside. It was the feeling he would have in his stomach all through dinner, all through the lifeless cold plate and hot tea Sunday night dinners that the nuns would fix for the children who had spent the day in town soaking up chocolate sodas and banana splits.

It was the feeling that would lay heavily on his chest after all the children had gone to bed and he would lie in the heavy darkness of the dormitory, listening to the creakings of the old, gray building and the water dripping in the deserted soap-smelling showers, and hearing too the tragic distant ghostly wail of the trains that hurried past in the night toward or away from Chicago.

He would rise and lean on one elbow and look out the third floor window, peering out into the darkness like a small monkey in a pet shop window in the middle of the night, looking at the lights that sparkled in the distant town, and sniffing deeply to suck into his lungs the lovely, rich far-away smell of the train smoke.

There had been so many times when he had been happy on trains. Usually being on a train had meant he was going to see his mother or that he was going some place with his mother. Going some place where he was wanted and loved, by someone. He delighted in lying in the Pullman berth at night, sleeping and then waking up when the train jostled in some lonely little water-stop town. He loved to look out the windows and see the steam licking up the sides of his Pullman car and see the dark, coated forms walking by in the night with lanterns, calling to each other in strange and mysterious tongues. He loved to walk up and down on trains, on the Pennsylvania line that had the green and red checkerboard linoleum floors and on the other railroad lines that had taken him out West where the cowboys and the sun-washed palm trees were, sometime long ago in the almost forgotten past.

He loved trains very much and had wanted perhaps when he grew up to drive a train and to lean out of the window of his locomotive and wave good-naturedly to little boys in the exact way that kindly engineers had waved to him when he had stood in the streets of Chicago looking up the long, steep cindered hills that wound through the city and supported the neat rows of gleaming rails.

The lonely Sunday-night feeling of being abandoned hit him now, unaccountably, although there was a reason that he could not have perceived.

"What's the matter?" Elaine was saying. She had to say it twice. He was looking into the fire and felt very afraid.

"I'm sorry," he said, without knowing what he was sorry for.

"Why," she said, laughing, "if I didn't know you better I would have thought you were going to burst into tears there for a minute. Such a face!"

He turned toward her eagerly and searched her face, staring in a frightened and supremely attentive way into her eyes.

"I felt cold all of a sudden," he said. "Let's go."

During the trip back to her apartment they talked but little and he apologized twice for detaining her. She was sitting close beside him on the way back but they did not touch each other.

"I'd like to see you again," he said, frowning at her when the time had come to say good-bye.

"All right, Dan," she said. "Call me any time."

He could not sleep that night and after Helen's breathing had become regular and heavy he got up and prowled about the house. He had eaten a gluttonous dinner, but now he felt ravenously hungry again and he walked into the kitchen and made hot Ovaltine and buttered four pieces of raisin-bread toast. The food gave him new energy and then he could not get to sleep at all. At dawn he was sitting in the den reading a book.

When Helen walked in he turned white with shock.

"What's the matter?" she said.

"Nothing," he whispered, in the traditional tone in which people speak at dawn. "You scared me."

"Haven't you been asleep at all?" She stood in the doorway

38

between the bedroom and the den looking pale and haggard in the cold blue light of early morning. Her feet were bare and her nightgown hung unattractively and straight from her naked, bony shoulders. She looked displeased.

"Go back to bed," he said. "Don't worry about me."

"All right," she said. He listened as she padded down the hall, winced as she sat in the bathroom urinating, the door open. Then he heard her flush the toilet and yawn and go back to bed. Distantly the baby whimpered and thrashed in her crib.

He closed his book and sat looking out into the bleak morning. The grass was wet and birds twittered weakly, cheerlessly, in the dying peach trees. Somewhere in the house there was a thin, electric whine, almost inaudible. He felt tired now and knew that there were circles under his eyes. He shivered and pulled his bare feet up onto the seat of the chair on which he sat.

He talked to himself a bit, swore at himself, silently moving his mouth so that he could hear the spittle parting as the lips separated and moved against each other in the silence of the den. He tried to pray and then laughed aloud at himself for making the effort.

He thought of Elaine in Paris and pictured her laughing in bars, walking beneath the god-damned chestnut trees, arm-in-arm with some man. A murderous hatred for the man, whoever he was, even if he did not exist, welled up in Dan's heart and left him trembling with jealousy and despair.

He thought of the children and of Helen and of his mother and of the grease stains on the floor of the garage and of a song he was working on and wondered what Elaine's body might look like naked. And then he pounded his fist against his forehead and stood up quickly and walked back and forth over the chocolate-brown *bouclé* carpeting in the den and said, "Oh, God, oh, God, oh, God," and dug his fingernails savagely into his folded arms.

Later in the morning Dan took one of Helen's Dexedrine tablets that the doctor had prescribed to help her reduce. After lunch he fell asleep, lying clothed on one of the children's beds, and then after Michael and Patrick came home from

39

school he took them over to see his mother because he had been promising to do so for many days and he now snatched at any excuse to get away from the house.

His mother lived in a dingy, depressing room in Santa Monica. When she heard the boys clattering up the stairs, shouting "Grandma! Grandma Agnes," she opened the hall door at the head of the back stairs and clasped her hands under her chin and smiled and said, "Oh, dear. Well, look who's coming to visit Grandma. My goodness! Look at these two little old things that love their Grandma so much they're just running up these old stairs. Give Grandma a big kiss. That's it. Oh, my! They're getting so heavy!"

Dan curtly kissed her on the cheek and sat quietly by in a large rocking chair while she played with the boys and gave them pencils and a writing tablet and opened bottles of Seven-Up for them and gave them each a dark red rubber ball that she had got for them at the dime store.

At last she sighed and sat back and looked at Dan. "You look tired," she said. She always said he looked tired whether he did or not, but this time he knew she was right.

"Did a little late work last night," he said, picking up a newspaper.

"You ought to take it easy," she said. "You're always pushing yourself too hard."

"I'm all right," he said, annoyed.

"My God," she said. "Take it easy, Dan. You don't see the lazy Whartons working themselves very hard."

He made a soft clicking sound with his tongue against his teeth, indicating displeasure. It was going to start again, the interminable railing against Helen's family, the unbelievably mistaken deduction, the twisted logic with which his mother could assemble facts until she had them lined up in such a way as to make it sound almost plausible that the Whartons were always at Helen's elbow, urging her to get every penny she could out of him, to work him to the grave, to neglect him, to hurt him in any way possible.

"You don't see her lazy slob of a brother working all hours of the night," she was saying.

He always promised himself that he would not answer her,

that he would just let her spew out the ridiculous venom until her system was cleansed of it. Sometimes it would work that way. Sometimes she would rail at the whole world for perhaps forty-five minutes or an hour while he sat reading a paper, hardly listening, and then at last when all the loneliness and bitter regret and unhappiness that was stored up within her had been exhausted and cast forth she would unexpectedly turn completely about and exhibit a genuine warm affection for Helen and a completely honest if puzzling respect for the contributions the Whartons had made to the welfare of his marriage.

But this time, because of his irritable state, and because of his mingled feelings of guilt and affection toward Helen, he could not control his tongue.

"I don't care anything about Helen's brother," he snapped. "He means absolutely nothing to me. Nothing whatsoever! I don't care if he's lazy or ambitious, do you understand? What in the name of God has he to do with me?"

"Oh, my God," she mumbled waspishly, while she was thinking of an answer. "Do you remember the time in Phoenix when you were deathly ill and I came over and found you sick as a dog on the couch in the front room, not even in bed, mind you, but just stretched out on the couch like a damned charity patient and I said to Helen, I said, 'Where are you going? Why aren't you staying home to take care of Danny?' And she said, 'Oh, he'll be all right. I have to go downtown to meet my brother Willy.' And I said, 'Well, my God,' I said, 'Whatever you have to do with Willy, couldn't it wait till your own husband is up and around?' and she said, 'But he's not sick.' And I said, 'Not sick,' I said, 'My God,' I said, 'Look at him,' I said, 'Why anybody can see he's *plenty* sick,' I said. But did she stay with you? No, not her. She had to go running off downtown to shop or something with that no-good brother."

"Does that make Willy no good," Dan shouted, "just because his sister went downtown to meet him?"

"Oh, sure," his mother said, raising her voice. "You *never* think *I'm* right, do you? You never have. Well, the time will come. You mark my words. The time will come when you'll look back and realize I wasn't a complete simpleton. Why, I remember when you and Helen were so anxious to get married that you didn't even know I was on earth and I . . ."

And so the voice would inundate him with story after story, accusation after bitter accusation. Eventually he would either get his emotions under firm enough control to resist answering her or else, if the children were not present, he would finally blow up and shout at her and tell her that he thought she was losing her mind and that he was sick and tired of listening to her foolishness and that he didn't care if he never saw her again. After such battles he would stay away from her for two or three weeks at a time, but eventually the hard core of bitterness in his heart would soften and melt away and then he would feel sorry for her and finally something like love for her would manifest itself within him and he would go back and visit her again and sit there in the dingy room reading the paper, sometimes hardly listening while she talked to him in an endless rambling monologue.

This time he cut her short after a few minutes by pointing to the children, who were playing with paper airplanes, but probably listening, and then after a while her mood magically changed and she was all warmth and good nature.

"How is Helen *feeling?*" she asked.

"Fine," Dan said.

"You shouldn't let her do all that ironing, Dan," she said. "Why don't you get her one of those big ironers? I saw one on television the other day and they're wonderful."

"I'll get one one of these days," he said.

"Yes, you really ought to. Helen's got enough to do taking care of three children without having to iron all your shirts. And you know how particular you are about things like that."

In her pleasant moods his mother was lively, animated, socially uncouth but completely charming. In the past, before he had learned that it was utterly useless to hope that she could sustain a happy mood for longer than a few days at a time, before he learned that she was flatly unable to control the black fits of depression and resentment that would sweep over her, they had experimented a few times with her living in the house with them all. But it had not worked out, of course. There had been frightening battles and one time Dan had become so incensed that he had wanted to strike her, and in his rage he had shouted and kicked a coffee table to pieces. He and Helen had gone visiting in the afternoon leaving his mother to take care of the children. She had stood smiling on the front lawn, waving to them and saying, "Have a good time. Take your time. Don't hurry back. Don't worry about a thing."

And then when they had returned late in the day she had been sitting in the kitchen, drunk. The corners of her mouth were turned down and when Dan stepped into the back washroom and found water all over the floor and wet clothes hanging out of the washing machine, and he said, "What the hell happened here?" she flew at him and drunkenly shouted, "What the hell kind of god-damned washing machine have you got that the clothes get all tangled up when you try to wring them? And what's the idea of staying out so late? Didn't you know I had a lot of work to do here?"

He shouted, "Shut up! You're drunk!" And she shouted back, "Don't talk to me like that, you ungrateful whelp! You never talk to the Whartons like that so you're not going to hand *me* any of that crap!"

He stood in front of her, his chest heaving, his fists clenched. "Shut up! Shut up!"

"No, sir! No, siree! How dare you talk to your mother like that! No, sir. The Whartons don't have to take all your abuse and your nasty temper so there's no reason in God's world why I should take any of it!"

"What have the Whartons got to do with *this?*" He pointed at the water on the floor and the slopped clothing.

"Oh, nothing," she cried, self-righteously, taking a new tack, "and you can bet your last dollar they never would either. Do you think any of *them* would come over here and take care of your children and do your washing? No, siree! Not them. They've got their own little lives to live over there in Phoenix and I don't notice them running over here to offer to help anybody at all."

Helen rushed out from the children's room, livid.

"My mother and father have done the washing here plenty of times," she shouted.

"Stay out of this, honey," Dan said. "Don't pay any attention to her!"

"That's it," his mother screamed. "Take sides against me! Well, I've had about enough of this!" She staggered past them and got her hat and coat and said, brokenly, "You tell those babies good-bye for me, you ungrateful sons-of-bitches!" And then she lurched out to the front porch and walked across the lawn, still pulling her coat about her, fumbling for one sleeve. Helen looked at her leaving and groaned and said, "This will give the neighbors plenty to talk about."

"Don't come back!" Dan shouted through the open front door, his rage so maniacal that he slammed the door and screamed, *God damn it!* and kicked the coffee table that lay in his path. It crashed across the room, collapsing, and he ran and picked up one of the pieces of it and broke it over his knee.

Most of the big vicious scenes had taken place when Michael and Patrick were very young, before Barbara was born. There had been many of them but now there would be no more, for they all knew now that it was impossible for his mother to live in the same house with his family, or for that matter with any family.

When he was not angry with her he would feel genuinely and deeply sorry for her, for she was plainly the victim of a delusion of persecution, and life had kicked her about so often and so cruelly that now she had difficulty in placing her trust in anyone in a very lasting way. Though she was fiercely Catholic, she had long seemed to Dan to be singularly un-Christian, for her deepest emotions, so far as one could determine from what appeared on the surface, were negative rather than positive. She had never been especially free or gifted at demonstrating love, but she was masterful and creative at manifesting hatred. Dan had never heard her express a word of affection for God, Christ, or Church, but he had heard a million words of invective about the Jews, the Protestants, the Communists, the liberals, the Roosevelts, or those among her kin or associates who had harmed or displeased her in any way.

44

Dan himself had little interest in political matters, and had always had to force himself to get out and vote in presidential elections. He had never felt any interest in state or local elections. What little knowledge he had of political, economic or social matters had been mainly acquired, oddly enough, not during the process of his formal education, but from reading Father Coughlin's *Social Justice,* copies of which he recalled having seen on the dining room table during several of the years of his boyhood in Chicago. In later years, the simple matter of widening the circle of his social environment, reading, and maturing had convinced him that the political climate in which he had grown up was to some extent anti-Semitic, and in a very true and simple sense un- (if not exactly anti-) American. He was convinced that his mother, and the many like her that he knew, did not really approve of freedom of speech and of the press, except for themselves, that they did not really approve of the freedom to worship any God or no God, but only fiercely insisted that their own religious activities be unrestricted, that they did not truly believe in the American ideal of equality except in a selfishly oriented fashion, and that not only were she and her kind poor excuses for American citizens but they were even sadder excuses for Catholics. For he believed that God was more important than Caesar, and that therefore Church came before State, although each was obliged to treat the other with tolerance and fairness.

He had tried to educate his mother and other relatives to the point where they could understand that Christianity was not meant to be a combative faith and finally, realizing that he could not accomplish this by personal persuasion, had given them subscriptions to the *Commonweal* and *America,* Catholic magazines noted for the dignity, liberality, and rationality of their editorial policies. This experiment too, alas, proved to be a failure. His mother still preferred to read those Catholic publications that devoted much of their space to the militant call to arms against American Communists. This, so long as it was conducted reasonably and legally, seemed in essence a worth-while journalistic endeavor, but he observed over the course of the years that abuses were frequent and that what started out as a campaign against communism deteriorated in time into a campaign against New Dealism, liberalism, organized labor, desegregation, and other ill-chosen targets.

He thought of these things this day and knew, sadly, that it was too late for his mother to change. As he watched her talking to the boys he felt that he was the parent and she was the wayward child.

He was glad that when he left she was in a good mood. "Don't forget," she said, "if there's anything I can do for Helen at all, just tell her to let me know. After all," she said, "Helen and me have a lot of laughs sometimes."

"All right," he said, helping the boys downstairs. Whenever he would leave he would stand looking back up at her and feel a sad love when he saw her standing alone, in her poor out-of-style Chicago South Side clothes, waving good-bye.

He wondered, as he drove back toward the Valley, through the Sepulveda Pass, if there were any men in the world who could confide in their mothers. He wanted to talk to somebody about Elaine; he wanted advice of some kind. But the very last person in the whole world he would have thought of going to for help with his problem was his mother. He wondered if this was unusual or if any man might have said the same thing.

From his observations of his friends, he had finally concluded that it was a rare adult who did not disapprove of his parents to some extent. He had never known his father, for Dan had been only eighteen months old when the man's appendix ruptured while he was on a train going somewhere to play a vaudeville date.

His mother had carried on and had become a moderately well-known singer. Even today, Dan would meet older people here and there who would say, "You mean to tell me you're Agnes Scanlon's son? Why, your mother was really something!"

"You're late," Helen said when he walked in with the boys.

"I'm sorry," he said. "Traffic was heavy."

"How was your mother?"

"Oh, fine. She said to give you her love."

46

CHAPTER

FIVE

T HE next day Dan left the house late in the morning, telling Helen he had a luncheon appointment. Mechanically he sped into the Sunset Strip neighborhood, parked the car and walked to a telephone booth. He dialed the Darby office.

"Elaine?"

"Yes. Who is this? Dan?"

"Yes. I just happened to be in the neighborhood. Thought you might join me for lunch."

"Why, all right."

Somehow when she walked out of the office and got into the car she leaned against him, sitting up off the seat a little to straighten her skirt, and in that instant he put his right hand on the back of her head and kissed her on the mouth.

"I'm sorry," he said. "I didn't know I was going to do that."

"Why does a man say he's sorry the first time he kisses a new girl?"

"I don't know. I guess I said it because I really am sorry."

"Well," she said, looking straight ahead, "where will we eat?"

"Are you angry?" he asked, as they pulled away from the curb.

"No."

"You *look* angry."

"I'm frowning, but I'm not angry. I'm just puzzled."

"About what?"

"Oh, skip it." She turned suddenly and looked at him and he thought he saw something hard in her eyes.

"Dan," she said, "I'm not in the market for just a flirtation."

"What do you mean?"

"I'm not too sure what I do mean. I mean I hope you know what you're doing."

"That's too bad," he said, "because I don't. I haven't known what I was doing from the first moment I met you. I keep saying to myself 'What is this? What's happening to me?' "

"You told me you were married."

"That's right," he said. "I am."

"Well?"

"Well, what?"

"What's the score? Are you happily married?"

"I don't know. I always thought I was. If somebody had asked me that question a couple of weeks ago I would have said 'Sure! You bet I'm happily married.' But now I don't know. All I know is that I have some terrible need that I never was aware of before, a need that it seems only you can satisfy. But the whole thing is hazy in my mind. I can't seem to grasp any of the realities."

"Maybe we'd better just call it a day then while it's still easy."

"That's what we should do," he said. "I *know* that, but it's too late for it to be easy."

"I'm sorry," she said.

"Oh, that's all right," he said. "It's not your fault. It's funny, but the thing is I just can't seem to stop thinking of you. Isn't that ridiculous?"

"I guess so," she said. "But it happens to the best of us."

He had intended to take her to a good restaurant but now he pulled into a drive-in so that they could talk in complete privacy. They ordered cheeseburgers and coffee.

"I don't know how to handle a thing like this," Dan said,

48

"if I may be frank. This is the first time I ever—" He fumbled for words.

"Really? The first?"

"I swear it."

"It's strange. I should feel sad or guilty about that but it makes me feel good. That's awful of me, isn't it?"

"No," he said. "I guess you just mean you're glad I'm coming to you sort of fresh."

"Yes, but that's a horrible, decadent thing to think. I shouldn't be thinking of you at all. I should be sending you home."

"*Have* you been thinking of me?"

"Yes."

She took his hand and held it in her lap and looked at it sadly.

"How many children have you?" she said.

"Three. Two boys and a girl."

"Do they look like you?"

"Yes," he said, smiling, taking out his wallet. "Here's a picture of them."

"Ah," she said, shaking her head. "They're beautiful."

"Thank you," he said. "They're wonderful kids."

"Baby," she said, patting his hand, "go on back. Right now."

"All right," he answered simply.

"You're wonderful, but just—go on back."

"All right."

Driving back to her office his eyes became moist and he swallowed hard and turned his face away so that she would not notice. When he pulled up in front of the pale green stucco building she hopped out, then leaned down and looked in the window.

"Good-bye, Dan," she said, smiling. "Don't worry about anything, honey. It will all work out all right."

He sat silently watching her move away, watching her hips as she walked into the building.

That night he had a nightmare. Helen woke him up.

"What's the matter, honey?"

"What?" he said.

"You were moaning. Were you having a nightmare?"

"Yes," he said. "I guess I was."

She patted him affectionately and rolled over, pushing her back up to him. He lay quietly for a moment and then a wave of sensuality engulfed him and he turned toward her and ran his hand along her leg, from the knee up to her hips.

She purred contentedly and tried to slip back into sleep.

He put his mouth against the back of her neck and moved his body close against her. And then in the next few minutes they were making love.

"You're wild," she said, moaning in his ear.

He was more excited than he had been with her for months, and freer, more abandoned than he had been for longer than he could remember. They became noisy and she whispered, "Ssshh—the children." But soon they forgot all restraint. When at last the fever had left them Dan lay back exhausted and thought that perhaps he would be able after all to forget the new woman that had come into his life. It did not occur to him till almost a week later that he had been able to make such violent love to his wife only because the new woman had built up a deep, high-dammed and dangerous lake of desire within him.

In another week he was being driven to the point of desperation again by the desire to see Elaine and he now found himself completely helpless in the face of the compulsion. One night he left the Brown Derby about eleven o'clock to go home and then suddenly walked back inside and called Elaine's number. Her mother answered.

"I expect her home any minute," she said. "She's been up at Arrowhead over the weekend, you know, with her friend Kay, and they should have been back before now."

He drove out to her neighborhood, parked his car in front of her apartment and sat there waiting. After about twenty minutes a car pulled up across the street and Elaine got out. There were laughing good-byes and an exchange of shouted jokes. Then the car sped away. As Elaine was coming across the street she saw him sitting in his automobile.

50

Without a word she walked around the car and got in the door on the far side.

"Who were you with?" he asked, curtly.

"Kay and some friends of ours," she said. "How long have you been here?"

"I just drove up a few minutes ago. Your mother told me you'd be right home. What did you do at Arrowhead? Did you stay there overnight?"

"Of course," she said. "What is this, the third degree?"

"I'm sorry," he said. "Do you want to hear something funny? I'm jealous."

"That's not funny, Dan." She looked at him. "What's the matter, baby? I thought you were going to stay away."

"I thought I could do it," he said. "But here I am."

She shook her head slowly from side to side and pulled her knees up under her. He watched her from his corner of the front seat and felt that she was at a great strange distance, looking at him down a long, dark and forbidding hallway.

Suddenly she said, "Well, what the hell," and lunged toward him and put her mouth on his. He sighed and pulled her down into his arms, turning her over so that the side of her face was pressed against his chest and her mouth was turned up toward him. His hand circled her waist tentatively and marveled at its slimness.

He paused for breath and then kissed her again. When her mouth opened he trembled and started to run his hands over her body. She wriggled free and sat up, straightening her hair.

"Hold the phone," she gasped.

"I'm sorry."

"That's right," she said. "You're the original Mr. Sorry. I forgot."

He sat looking straight ahead, far down the dark street, wondering what was going on at just that moment in his home.

"Listen," he said, "I've got to know. Are you in love with anyone else?"

"No," she said. "What gave you that idea?"

"I didn't have the idea, exactly. I just wanted to know. I thought perhaps you were up at Arrowhead with a man."

"I told you I was there with Kay Rosner," she said. "She and I go up there all the time."

"There were men in that car just now."

"That's right. We met them up there."

"Do the two of you go up there just hoping to meet men?"

"No," she said. "Or, I don't know. Maybe we do. Is that supposed to be a crime?"

He said quietly, "Ah, this is strange. Here I am torn apart with jealousy and I'm being cruel and insulting and all I really want to do is hold you in my arms and say—"

He paused, startled.

"What's the matter?"

"I don't know," he said.

"What is it you wish you were saying?"

"I love you."

"Honey, you *can't* sit there and say that. Don't you see?"

"Now, please," he said. "Don't ask me to deal in logic. Don't bring up a thing like common sense at a time like this. I *know* none of this makes any sense. I've said it before—I don't even know what I'm doing here. I don't know what's happening to me. I don't even know for sure that I love you, if you see what I mean. All I know is that I want to say to you that I love you."

"You must be very desperate for love."

He shrugged.

"Dan," she said, moving up close to him, looking at him closely, so that her eyes were less than five inches from his own, "I feel something like that myself. I don't understand it exactly, but I think you're wonderful. You're gentle. You're funny. But . . . it's not that simple. Can't you see that?"

"It's no use preaching to me," he said, grim-lipped. "I know everything you're going to say. Do you think I haven't thought this thing out from all angles? I've been almost out of my mind these last few weeks. I can't understand myself. I love Helen, or I thought I did. I love my children. I wish everything was the way it was a few weeks ago. But it's not. And one thing I know for sure. I want you. I've got to have you."

They clung together then in the car and kissed and wept and talked for almost two hours until at last they reached a sort of

52

emotional doldrums. And while in that deceptively calm state they made a mistake that sinful lovers have made down through all time. They supposed that because at that given moment they felt no especially strong physical desire for each other they would be able to say good-bye and mean it and make it stick. And so, accordingly, they went through the formality of another tearful farewell.

Dan drove home that night fearfully wiping her lipstick off his face. He was depressed and believed he really had seen her for the last time.

He stopped at a Richfield station and while the car was being filled up with gas walked into the rest room and inspected his face in the mirror. The area around his mouth looked pink. He put soap and water on his mouth and rubbed it hard with a paper towel. At last his face looked clean. Because his handkerchief was stained he threw it in the wastebasket under the sink, walked out and got back in the car and drove home.

The next night a music publisher he knew called him and invited him to the opening of Les Brown's orchestra at the Palladium.

"It won't hurt you to be there," the publisher said. "Les has got *What's Yours Is Mine* in the books and if you talk to him he'll probably give it a few air-shots."

Dan asked Helen if she wanted to go to the opening but she said she had a cold and was going to bed early. At the Palladium he moved among the tables, saying hello to the big and small fry of the music business. At last he thought of Elaine and began drinking.

He sat disconsolately at the publisher's table, fingering a glass of Scotch and ice-cubes and watching the dancers. The teen-agers fascinated him in that they seemed determined not to alter the lizard-like immobility of their faces no matter how they exerted themselves physically. He watched one little girl wearing saddle-shoes and a lavender Angora sweater. She danced well, her hips moving from side to side rhythmically under her tight gray tweed skirt, but she did not look at her partner nor did she allow the expression of the slightest emotion to appear on her face. After a few moments he noticed that she was chewing gum, but the slow movement of her jaws was the only indication that her face was not a frozen mask.

He was quite drunk when he got home and he fell asleep on the couch in the den with his clothes on.

The next day, while Helen was at the grocery store and Mrs. Walsh was hanging up clothes, he furtively slipped into the front bedroom and dialed Elaine's number.

"This is Dan," he said, looking out the window at the children in the back yard. "I can't talk now. I've got to see you."

"All right," she said, weakly. "When?"

"I'll be there sometime within two hours."

He made an excuse to absent himself and then showered and changed clothes and drove like a madman through the mountains. He picked her up and they drove to the ocean and he pulled the car up a dirt road. They got out and walked up a hill until finally, turning, they could look down on the ocean-front and see a beautiful misty panorama, stretching from the Palos Verdes Hills to the far peninsulas above Malibu. They lay in the wind-swept grass and weeds high above the ocean while gulls floated on hot updrafts about them and they clung together, her face wet with tears which he kissed away, and knew that at last they had lost the battle forever and irrevocably. They unashamedly made plans to be together, alone. It was a Saturday. He was not able to get back to her until Monday.

CHAPTER

SIX

THEY drove out Sunset Boulevard to the ocean highway. The sky was overcast and the ocean was a flat, gray pol-
ished slate rimmed with white chalk at the edges. As they came
to the beach road they felt a curious combination of guilt and
elation.

He drove with his left hand on the steering wheel and his
right resting lightly on her knee. From time to time she would
lift his hand to her mouth and press her warm lips to it.

"Where is the place?" he asked.

"Not far from here," she said.

"Did you have any trouble?"

"No. The lady was very nice. I left a deposit and told her
we'd be back this evening."

"Who are we?"

"What?"

"Who are we . . . on the register?"

"Oh," she said. "I gave them my ex-husband's name. We're
the Sterlings."

He felt a momentary flicker of displeasure but his elation
at her nearness wiped the feeling out.

"I love you," he said.

"I love you."

She turned to him and kissed him three times on the side of his face. The warmth of her mouth excited him but he became aware in the instant of an overpowering sense of unreality that cast a shadow over the scene, somewhat weakened his sensitivity to physical stimulus, and confused his emotional reactions.

"I wish the sun were shining," he said.

"It *is* dark, isn't it? Oh," twisting in the seat next to him, "that's the place up ahead. The Las Palmas, redundantly enough."

The *Las Palmas* was a two-story motel that faced the ocean, its green neon sign looming dully through the fog that was beginning to drift in off the gray, rolling water. Parking the car in the small asphalt lot behind the building, he saw a deserted swimming pool behind a hedge.

"Too bad it's too cold to swim," he said, trying to be casual.

His palms were moist as he gripped the handle of his empty suitcase and he had an uneasy feeling that at any moment unknown forces might manifest themselves to prevent the completion of the experience they were about to undergo.

"Yes," she said, her heels clicking on the pavement before him as they walked to the unattended side door of the building. He began to speak more loudly than his emotions dictated and he forced himself to laugh unconcernedly so that if anyone were observing them no suspicion could be excited by any action or word that might be construed as furtive. It did not occur to him, in his innocence, that the proprietors could not have cared less.

When they were in the room he sat down on the edge of the bed, took out a handkerchief and wiped his palms. Then he rose and came up behind her as she was hanging her coat in the closet and took her in his arms and buried his face in her soft brown hair. After a long time she stepped away from him playfully and closed one of the venetian blinds to block out the depressing gray light of the sombre afternoon. When she turned on a lamp on the table he saw the bucket with the champagne bottle inside of it.

56

He smiled at her and she looked down shyly.

"You're wonderful," he said. "Champagne."

"I'm sure it sounds corny," she said, "but I wanted this to be something special. I wouldn't really have cared if we were in a cave, but as far as was in my power—well, I wanted to dress things up."

"I love you," he said, feeling a great tenderness that for the moment had nothing of the physical in it. She must have realized, he thought, that he had been depressed by the moral sordidness of their relationship and, though he too would not have cared if he made love to her in a cave, he was suddenly so overcome with appreciation of her gesture that his eyes filled and he had to hold her tightly to him to prevent her noticing that he was on the point of tears.

While she was showering, he undressed and stretched out on the bed, feeling sensitive and exposed and frightened. When the water was turned off he shouted to her, "I'm lonesome." She appeared wrapped in a blue bath-towel and opened her suitcase.

"Here," she said, handing him two books.

"What's this?"

"I brought along two of my volumes of Emily Dickinson. After we open the champagne we can lie here and read."

"You," he said, "are either an abandoned pagan or the most sensitive, civilized woman who ever lived. In either case, I love you."

They sat side by side on the bed and drank two glasses of champagne each, out of plain kitchen glasses, clinking the glasses and proposing toasts and laughing quietly, sometimes pointlessly. Then they placed the glasses on the floor and flung themselves back onto the bed and kissed for a long time and then, luxuriating in the knowledge that there was no hurry, tore themselves away from each other, pulled a sheet up over their bodies and opened one of the Dickinson books.

"I love her," Elaine said of the poet, and in the quivering emotionalism of the moment she began to weep over a particular passage. Dan finally was unable to concentrate on the words in the book. They began to swim before him, or he would read half a page and then realize that the words had not reached his brain. His body began to tremble and he kissed the back of her neck as she lay on her stomach reading. There was no definite moment when they stopped reading and began making love. Later he could not remember a transition at all. One moment they were reading, relaxed, joking, guilty, uneasy, eager, tender, pathetic, thoughtful, detached, and playful. At another moment, sometime shortly after, there were none of these things. They were not in essential control of themselves at all but were crushed in the grip of primeval energies that rendered them automatons. There was the sound of her breathing in his ears and the sound of cars whispering by in the fog outside and the sound of the Pacific ocean waves breaking on the deserted beach. There were the smells of soap, of perfume, of hair, of warm flesh. Finally they began to speak to each other, to entreat, to plead. Their pleas turned to demands, their demands to undeniable summonses to realms of existence that he had never before explored. They spoke a tongue previously unknown to him and he reveled in the sudden freedom, the unexpected vigor with which he found himself able to convey his lightning-like conceptions and reactions to her.

Her body, alternately yielding and compulsive, became at once to him marvelously strange and yet mysteriously reassuring and familiar. So it came to pass that, when there was no turning back, no possibility of pausing to prolong the experience, no choice but to rush headlong and in complete and literal madness into the last wild and frenzied moments of the act, in that instant he heard her moan "Oh, Jim!" And, miraculously, the words did not sink like a cold knife into his heart. But later, when they had rested, eyes closed, recovering their dignity, a sullen resentment forced itself to the top of his mind and he said, "I guess you didn't notice, but you called me by another man's name."

She regarded him with something like amusement.

"I what?"

"You called me Jim."

She spoke calmly. "No, I didn't, sweetheart."

"It's all right, hon," he said. "I have no justifiable complaint. You weren't born yesterday. If you knew . . ."

"But wait a minute, baby. I didn't call you Jim, or Tom or

Dick or Harry. I love you. I wasn't thinking of anyone but you."

"But I heard you."

"You must have heard me wrong. I don't even *know* a Jim."

"That's ridiculous. Everybody knows dozens of Jims." There was an edge to his voice.

"All right, so I know some men named Jim, but I've never made love to any of them. That's what I meant, baby. I've never been in love with anyone named Jim."

"It's all right, sweetheart. You don't have to lie to keep me from being hurt."

"Dan," she said, sitting up in the bed, pulling the sheet over her, "I *didn't* lie to you. Maybe I said something else, maybe I said '*gimme*' or '*in*' or '*damn*' or *something* and you thought I said Jim. I swear it. I swear it as God is my judge. I didn't call you by any other name."

After that he could say nothing more to her. He believed her. He thought he had been mistaken. But later, many times, when plunged into moods of depression or jealousy, he would reach into his subconscious and take out the ugly, spiteful memory of "Oh, Jim" and consider it at length and allow himself to build up a great and awful rage against her. Never, in all the long, long time of their relationship, had he been able completely and with finality to dismiss the matter. It was added to his secret hoard of monstrous and evil fears, and eventually he grew to feel hatred toward himself for his inability to believe in her integrity unreservedly and at all times. If someone had said, "Well, come now, when all is said and done, do you believe her or don't you?" he would have answered in the affirmative and with genuine sincerity and conviction. But he never knew at what moment the memory would pounce out at him from whatever dark and mysterious shadowed place in which it lurked to scream and sink its claws into his mind.

The next few weeks were nerve-wracking, exciting and depressing. He took to drinking rather more than usual and twice made excuses to skip attending mass. For the first time in his life he felt that prayer was a fruitless exercise.

It was entirely possible, he supposed, that faith could move mountains. The only trouble was it never had. It did a great many things, perhaps, in its battle against whatever force it was designed to combat. But in the end the force always seemed to win and the bullets *did* tear into the lungs and the forest fires *did* make the green leaves hiss and blacken and the war department *did* send the telegrams and the cancers *did* kill millions and the rain *did* fall on the car before you had driven a block away from the wash-rack on Sunset Boulevard.

Sitting in the heavy blue-velvet chair in The Celebrity's house, he furtively, privately lowered his lids until they were almost closed. Under the lashes he could still see his lap and his two hands in it, holding the drink. By looking slightly to the left he could see the ankles and feet of a woman, partly obscured by the edge of a coffee-table, the nyloned toes protruding through openings in the toes of the snakeskin shoes. The feet were small and the ankles were dainty and as he looked at them in an unnoticed and sidelong manner they excited him to an almost perceptible manifestation of physical interest. He did not know whose feet they were and he decided to sit looking at them until he could remember. The right ankle, under the stocking, was circled by a thin, faint band of gold chain. For a moment he shifted his eyes to the rounded-edged cubes of ice jiggling in his glass and thought in a sodden, unemotional way of suicide, and then he looked back at the right ankle, at the honey-colored stocking, at the snakeskin and the high heel.

It could be The Celebrity's wife. Or the girl who had come with Hank. Or the movie starlet who had had the fight on the front lawn with her boy friend. They were the only three with trim ankles and now, as the unfilterable virus of the perfume spread itself in an invisible smoke about him, he realized that it must be one of them, for the gold band and the spike heel and the *Jicky* bespoke a woman who wanted to be desired in an immediate and practical way. That meant it could not have been Helen, his wife. That meant it could not have been any of the other four or five women in the room.

60

Where are you, baby? Where is your big mouth and where are your square little white teeth and your warm pink tongue? It's one-thirty-eight in the morning, flower-face, and I wonder where you are right now, you old pinky-pants. Where are you and where is the ocean and where are the sea gulls right now, the ones that flew by the day we climbed to the top of the hill and looked at the white lace ruffle that ran from the northward jutting north of Santa Monica to the misted-in Palos Verdes Hills? It's noisy here, kid, but it's not getting me down. I can still sit over here in the corner and do the osmosis bit with the ossification-juice and look at this lady's ankles over here and wish they were yours, old strawberry-mouth. Good-bye, friend. It's been nice. It's been so very nice, in fact, that I just possibly may not be able to do without it, how do you like them apples? I don't like myself, Elly. Maybe that's the worst part: the conflict, the guilt, the two-falls-out-of-three with the conscience.

But that's all pretty tricky, that sort of thinking, and when you get hold of an idea it melts in your hand. Ideas are ice. The iceman cometh. The come-man iceth. The income taxeth. The—"

"You falling asleep?"

He started up in panic, wide-eyed, mentally buttoning himself. It was Helen.

"What?"

"You looked like you were falling asleep. You want to go home?"

"Oh, it doesn't make much difference. I'm ready if you are."

He stood, weak from the adrenaline that had pumped into his heart. It was ridiculous, the feeling that she might have some knowledge of his thoughts. But her face, looming unexpectedly, had frightened him. He drained the glass in his hand, walked steadily to The Celebrity.

"Baby!" cried The Celebrity. "Not going?"

"Got to, old man," Dan said. "The dawn comes up like thunder."

"But we were just going to ask you to play."

"Some other time."

"How do you like this guy?" The Celebrity said to the snakeskin shoes, who had just walked across the room. "Drinks my booze all night and then folds his tent."

"Aw," said the ankle-band, "why *don't* you stick around? I'd love to hear you play."

It was the starlet. She had red hair and a green dress. Looking over her shoulder he saw Helen coming out of the bedroom, one arm in a sleeve of her coat. Her hair was blond and she was pretty. Prettier, really, inside and out, than the starlet. He thought for a moment that something was wrong with a man when he could be more attracted to a scatter-brained stranger with thin ankles and a tight, green dress than he was to a better, prettier woman whose only drawback was that she happened to be his wife. While muttering his farewell apologies, he tried not to look at the redhead's breasts, then winced at his weakness. He felt guilty and then, walking across the lawn to the car, he giggled. Helen wanted to know what he was laughing at and he had to say, "Why, nothing, really," because he could not tell her that it was funny about his feeling guilt because in the instant he had experienced it he had felt a sense of obligation both to Helen, his wife, and to Elaine, the woman he loved. Helen-Elaine, Elaine-Helen. A two-headed mother-figure, or figure of some god-damned sort, an idol frowning down at him in disapproval.

They drove out of the mists of Beverly Hills and beetled through the mountains to the desert air of the valley.

Two weeks later Hank Lazarus and Dan were dismissed, with appropriate regrets, by Paramount. Dan alternately laughed and swore at himself for considering it the retribution of God.

CHAPTER
SEVEN

O NE AFTERNOON he was alone in town, killing time until Elaine got off work. He put the car in the parking lot on Vine Street, across from the Broadway-Hollywood department store, and walked into the Derby to see if anyone he knew was at the bar. The bamboo-paneled room seemed deserted, so he walked out again and crossed the street.

A crowd of tourists were lined up in front of the radio studio opposite the Derby. As he passed among them some of them accosted him furtively, whispering, "Any tickets? Ya got any tickets?"

He told them he did not and walked to the Whelan's drugstore on the corner, where he bought a pack of cigarettes and a new ball-point pen.

Half way down the block he stopped before the window of Sy Devore's haberdashery and surveyed a display of expensive sport shirts. The shirts, he thought, must have looked strange to the people from Iowa and Minnesota who frequented the neighborhood, looking for movie stars and pleading for broadcast tickets.

The navy shantungs, the glowing prints and the pearl-buttoned jerseys must have seemed foreign, affected, perhaps even effeminate to the rough-hewn men from North Dakota and Kansas and Tennessee, strolling with their sturdy, gawking wives. One could see them daily, wandering about the tiny area that was the heart of Hollywood, peering hopefully into the faces of any passersby who wore dark glasses. Often, Dan thought, they must be staring at each other, mistaking each other for movie stars. He did not entirely disdain their naivete, their eagerness to rub shoulders with the gods. He had been in Hollywood for nine years and had never entirely lost the fairyland feel of the town. It was phony and tinsel. It was all the things that people said about it when they were being critical and obvious, but still it was a magnet and a magic place.

A hardened Hollywood agent, a song-plugger, an assistant director, an actor, a writer, any of them would act bored about the town, but nevertheless they could all feel that plain, simple Des Moines, Iowa, small lift in their throats when Cary Grant sat down at the next table at Chasen's, or when somebody pointed out Marion Davies' old beach mansion, or when they circled over Los Angeles on the Mercury flight early in the morning, with the city lying green and misty beside the ocean, sprawling across the checkered valley beneath them.

It was in several respects a miserable town, but it just happened to be one of the most beautiful places to live in the whole world, Dan thought, as he moved away from the shop window. He walked into Coffee Dan's restaurant and stood by the door for a moment, looking at profiles, the backs of heads, looking for anyone he knew. He didn't mind bumming around town in the afternoons, killing time between appointments, but he didn't like to be alone too long.

Coffee Dan's was like a good many restaurants in Hollywood. Too much money spent on decor, not enough on a chef. But it didn't matter. Perhaps the decor was more important than the food after all. No one, to Dan's knowledge, had ever gone there only to eat. It was a hangout, a spot to meet the boys, to mark time waiting to see publishers, to meet a girl, to have a cup of coffee and read the papers.

"Danny boy!"

It was a song-plugger connected with the Harms office. Dan could not remember his name.

"Want to sit down?"

"Yeah," Dan said. "Thanks." He slid into the semicircular green leather booth. "How've you been?"

"Same," said the song-plugger. "You?"

"Fine," Dan said, feeling slightly embarrassed at not being able to recall the name that lurked and bobbed in his subconscious, coming close enough to the foreground to make his tongue move experimentally in his closed mouth. Stan. Sid. Steve?

"Understand you're not with Paramount any more," Stan, or Sid, or Steve said.

"No," Dan answered, caught off guard. "I wasn't . . . that is, Hank and I weren't under any long-term contract or anything. We were, you know, just working on a few things. When Carson finished making *Girls, Ahoy,* we checked out."

"As if you had to worry," Sy, or Sam, or Sol said, looking at his watch. Dan noticed he was wearing giant cuff links made of gold and turquoise.

"Like 'em?" Sonny, or Sid, or Sam said. "Present from Perry."

"Como?"

"Yeah. He's a real sweetheart." The pluggers all liked Perry. Dan recalled a line Hank had thrown at a party once. Somebody was talking about Perry, saying that he was a real sweetheart, saying that he was one of those rare guys everybody liked.

"You're wrong," Hank had said. "I understand he didn't get along very well with Will Rogers."

"I'm meeting him across the street in a few minutes," Harry said. It was Harry after all, Dan realized, and not Sid, or Steve, or Sam, or Sol.

"NBC?" Dan said.

"Yeah," Harry said. "They break in about ten minutes."

A tall, blond man with glasses sat down next to Dan.

"Hiya, Gene," Harry said. "Dan, you know Gene Haskell."

"Yes," Dan said, "we've met." Haskell was a disc-jockey,

one of the most successful. He had always seemed to Dan outwardly scholarly and a bit dull, somehow inappropriately collegiate. In person his speaking voice was pleasant if undistinguished but on the air he had the habit of speaking with his lips no more than half an inch from the microphone, which made his voice resound with a breathy, baritone intimacy and accounted for his popularity with the thousands of women who lay awake late in the Los Angeles night, listening to bedside radios.

"List' to me, chickadee," he was in the habit of saying to his listeners. "It's neighbor Gene, on the scene, tapping lightly at the window again, asking to be let in to show my wares." Disc-jockeys were forever talking like a cross between Bing Crosby and a rhyming dictionary, Dan thought. Some of them had the sense to talk like human beings but the public seemed to make no distinction between those who spoke radioese and those who spoke American so it evidently didn't matter.

A girl in the next booth eyed Dan frankly, with an expression of mingled boredom and interest, then looked away, exhaling cigarette smoke. A secretary in one of the publishers' offices, maybe a girl from NBC, or perhaps just a visitor to town, looking for excitement; she could be any of these. But no, probably not a visitor. The black hair was too sleek, the green neckerchief too artfully knotted, the black jersey blouse too tight over the breasts, the eyes too devoid of expression. There were rarely wives in Coffee Dan's, it seemed, only passersby. Girls you knew just slightly. Receptionists from Capitol Records upstairs, girl friends of radio-network ushers, dancers from the night clubs. They would come in by twos usually, and there would be much table-hopping, idle banter, pointless, half-hearted flirting, a little laughter. Sometimes it seemed that the faces in the restaurant never changed. Perhaps they were only the faces of dummies that the management shifted from table to table to keep a fresh look to the place. It was always the same faintly familiar girls, the slick well-groomed Hollywood girls with the inexpensive dresses, the same seedy, hungry-looking not-quite-successful songwriters, the same flashily dressed pluggers, the same harried, tired-eyed, curt waitresses, the same impersonal bus boys, scurrying around like agitated wraiths, leaning into conversations, never noticed.

"I have to cut," Harry announced, throwing a dollar on the table. "This will cover my wheat cakes."

"Good to see you," Dan said.

"See ya," Gene Haskell said. The waitress came to the table and they both ordered coffee.

"What are you working on, Dan?" Haskell asked. It was a stock Vine Street question. It means "What songs have you written lately? What numbers are you hoping will make the grade? What recordings have you been able to secure?"

"Oh, nothing much right now," Dan said. "I'm just taking it kind of easy."

"Nice to be able to afford to," Haskell said, and for a moment Dan wondered if there could have been the faint suggestion of the unkind about the comment. It had begun very simply; the word had gotten around town that he was no longer with Paramount and at once the small talk had started. Dan hadn't had a real hit in two years, but what the hell, he told himself, a lot of other guys were doing worse. He was worrying needlessly about what people thought. Maybe they hadn't even noticed. He wasn't asking anybody for money. He wasn't mooching around, running up bills.

People had their own problems. Why should they be conscious of his? The dark-haired girl was eyeing him again, and it interrupted his train of thought. She looked familiar. If you looked around long enough everybody began to look familiar. Maybe there were only about thirteen thousand kinds of faces and eventually you got to a point where every new face was like one out of your memory-file. He looked at her again and her mouth reminded him of Elaine's. He felt a flicker of guilt and turned back to Haskell, who was stolidly drinking coffee, his eyes half-closed.

Through the giant plate glass window at the front of the restaurant Dan could see the sleek, gaudy lines of the pistachio-green NBC building across the street and, beyond it to the right, palm trees standing on Sunset Boulevard, tall and thin, looking like solidified explosions of Fourth of July fireworks.

Two soldiers sauntered past the window, carrying small

leather zippered objects in their right hands. Dan had never understood exactly what it was that off-duty soldiers in Los Angeles always seemed to be carrying. He only knew that it was something small, and made of leather, and zippered. Probably a case containing toilet articles.

He could clearly recall the exaggerated importance such things could assume to a mind inhibited and numbed by the monotony of service life, and had assumed for him when he was in the Army. A clean shirt or a new comb were very much more important to a soldier than to a civilian. Being a soldier was in some respects like being a child again. Little things counted once more. He mentally discarded the phrase "little things," his song-writer's mind disdaining the cliché, considering a replacement, then wondering if perhaps it would be better to keep the line in.

"It's the little things that count," he said.

"What?" Haskell said.

"I was just thinking of a song title," Dan said. "It's the little things that count. Probably been done a million times."

"Probably," Haskell said. "Say, what happened with the score of *Girls, Ahoy?*"

"Nothing very big," Dan said. "The numbers didn't get much exploitation."

"Didn't Freddy Martin record 'Don't Say It's Love'?"

"Yes, he did. It sold fairly well."

"Really?" said Haskell. Dan saw that his eyebrows were lifted.

"Well, nothing sensational, but . . . you know . . . good enough." The record had enjoyed less than a modest sale. Dan felt annoyance begin to well up inside of him. He wanted to stop talking to Haskell, to leave Coffee Dan's. None of the really big writers ever hung around the place. It was more a hangout for the second-raters, the up-and-coming talents. He would have preferred lunching at Lakeside, sitting around playing poker with the club bunch. But Helen had insisted that he cancel his membership, to save money. He had argued with her deceitfully, letting her win a debate he had intended to lose from the first. Was it so she would feel guilty at depriving him of the club's pleasures? He was not sure. But at Lakeside there would have been no song-pluggers, no disc-jockies trying to stare through your eyes into your mind, or through your jacket into your checkbook. Maybe it would have been better to bluff it through at the club, to gamble on making the right contact, and to hell with the expense.

After a while, bored, he forced a cordial word of good-bye, paid the check and left. You never let a disc-jockey pick up a check. Haskell was a funny geezer, he thought, as he strolled up Vine Street. There was no real Gene Haskell, or if there was the world would probably never know him. There was only a front, a smooth, glib façade. Dan himself realized that he was to a degree socially inhibited but he hoped that he was not *all* front, as Haskell appeared to be.

A wry smile crossed his lips as it occurred to him that Haskell might have made the same evaluation of him. He knew that he tended, perhaps to an extreme degree, to adapt his personality to the people with whom he came into extended contact, out of a desire to put them (or himself) at ease by seeming to be like them. Dull men, consequently, would have reported, he was sure, that *he* was dull. Humorless people must have felt that he lacked humor, witty people seemed to think that he was amusing, and bright people, unless he flattered himself unduly, probably found him bright. Too, he had met a few reflective neurotics who had professed to see in his character dark, subterranean streams that ran swift and treacherous.

He walked up to the corner of Hollywood and Vine, that esthetically pointless intersection so disappointing to the tourists who had been educated to expect more by the jokes of a generation of radio comedians. Seating himself on a bench, feeling comfortable and relaxed in the sun, he idly watched the passersby, recalling that watching people had always been a practice of which he was fond. In Chicago, he remembered, he had sometimes skipped school, traveled downtown, seated himself on the steps of the public library or at some other heavily traveled spot and watched the passing faces for hours at a time. Hank had told him that the custom was more common in other parts of the world than in America. In Italy, for example, he had said, the people love to watch one another as they stroll through the streets. There was only one rule to the game, wherever it was played, as far as Dan could tell: it was not proper for two people to watch each other simultaneously. Otherwise the eyes would exchange emotion, unnecessary, undesired emotion: annoyance, disdain, interest, sexual curiosity, embarrassment—whatever.

People preferred to look upon one another, it seemed, rather as they were in the habit of observing animals at the zoo. One would as soon consider making needless random human contact with a stranger as one would think of becoming emotionally involved with an ostrich or panther seen behind bars.

When, later in the afternoon, he met Elaine he found her depressed. They sat in his car, in a small park in Beverly Hills, with the windows open, inhaling the scent of warm grass.

"For two days," Elaine said, "I've been fooling myself. I've been thinking that I had the strength to give you up. I've been concentrating on your children, thinking that would do it. When you look into a case like this from the outside you have no sympathy for the woman playing my role. I'm the *other* woman, the home-wrecker. And that's right. I think that way myself. So I gave you up." She laughed, bitterly.

"I know," he said, taking her hand.

"First," she continued, "I cried, as I haven't cried since I was an infant, hiding in the bathroom so my mother wouldn't ask questions. Then after I was all cried out a strange calm came over me, a strange sort of—I don't know what the right word is—unaliveness. It was as though the world was a big bowl of clear Jello through which I moved somehow. People's voices came to me from a distance, and any simple movement required extra effort. I stood by and watched myself do things. If I smoked a cigarette I actually watched my hand reach down, lift the cigarette from the ashtray. I picked up a book of Picasso prints, a book I had looked at many times before, and yet it looked strange to me. The pictures looked sombre and depressing. I suppose I sound idiotic."

"No," he said, his eyes narrowing compassionately as he looked at her, his head shaking slowly from side to side as if to say no-no-no-no.

"Anyway," she continued, "while I was in that state I thought to myself 'Well, I guess I can stand *this,* for a few days, or weeks, or years, or however the hell long it takes to get over a thing like this.' I didn't know that the calm state was just a lull between storms. The lull I can take. When the storms start, I guess I'm a sissy. I just lie there and keep repeating your name as if there was some sort of magic to it. Oh, baby!" she said, her eyes beginning to brim. "What do we do now?"

He kissed her then, hard, not caring about the people in passing cars, not caring about anything except her.

When he got home, the first thing Helen said to him was, "Your mouth looks red." He went cold with fear.

"What?" he said, rubbing his lips with his fingers and putting on a falsely puzzled frown. He had wiped his lips with a handkerchief in the car but, still in a daze of mixed desire and depression, had forgotten to look at his face in the rear-view mirror.

Helen stood in the kitchen, drying a dish, regarding him with a peculiar expression.

"Oh," he suddenly said, smiling, manufacturing a lie, "it's that damned demonstrative Terri Jackson. I went down to CBS to give her a new piece of material and—you know Terri —as soon as she got off the air she ran over and gave me a big kiss."

"Her show's at one o'clock," Helen said. "You been walking around like that all afternoon?"

"Guess so," he said, his skin crawling, literally beginning to itch, perspire, under his T-shirt.

At that moment something happened to Dan Scanlon that made him rear back with deep horror, inwardly, while he forced the muscles that controlled his face to remain motionless, to communicate no emotion.

"Guess I'll wash up," he said, fighting to keep his voice low. Without waiting for her response he turned and hurried into the back bathroom. Locking the door he took off his jacket, started cold water running in the sink, and glared into the mirror with shocked revulsion. Not twenty seconds before he had looked at his wife, his own dear blonde, gray-eyed wife, the mother of his children, and thought to himself in some vague, diseased, fleeting way that he *wished she would die or be killed or*—or what? He did not know. He rejected the thought now, vomiting it up out of his mind with a violent shudder. But the important thing was: *the thought had occurred to him.* No amount of virtuous denial could erase that simple fact. A lifetime of repentance, of righteous self-contempt, could not suffice now to make him forget that he had, albeit in one lightning flash of time, wished his wife's death!

Good God, what was he? What sort of monster? He had never actually evaluated himself morally, but had he taken occasion to do so he would have given himself fairly high marks. He rarely drank to excess, rarely smoked, did not philander, was easy-going, charitable, well-liked, suffered from a minimum of social prejudices.

Now he knew, for the first time in his life, that he was, morally, an animal. A tame one, certainly enough, but an animal. For it was animals that killed one another, in the jungles and forests of the world, when crazed by sexual desire. But no. He was *lower* than the beasts, for it was only the males who attacked and sometimes killed one another, fighting over a particular female. He was lower, more evil than that. He *had* a female, and he had wished her dead that he might take another.

He looked at himself in the mirror, his face contorted in horror, and said, whispering, "You son of a bitch!" And now his horror increased as he discovered that something about the fear and passion of the moment had actually stimulated his physical desire so that he stood there trembling, his body tensed and tight, wanting Elaine, wanting her at that moment, furiously, wildly, and at the same time loathing himself, regarding himself warily, with strange caution, as if at any moment he might be attacked by the wild-eyed image he saw glaring back at him in the mirror. In the next moment he considered directing his desire toward Helen but, in the circumstances, that seemed criminal.

"I cannot get a divorce," he said to himself in the mirror. "You Catholic son of a bitch," he whispered. "You can *not* get a divorce!"

When the sink was full of cold water he lowered his face

into it, deep, up to the ears. Then again and again he scooped up double handfuls of water and bathed his burning features. After a few minutes his fever seemed to abate and his self-control flowed back in, as if a power-current had been turned on. He combed his hair, hung his tie over a doorknob, and walked out into the yard to play with the children.

When they saw him coming they squealed with delight. He picked them up one by one and kissed them fiercely, to their consternation and the amusement of two neighborhood children who stood watching.

CHAPTER

EIGHT

ONE NIGHT, when he arrived home late after having seen Elaine, Helen happened to be watering the front lawn. As he opened the door of the car and stepped out something fell to the ground. It was one of Elaine's handkerchiefs, perfumed, and covered with stains of lipstick. Helen, since she had come over to greet him, was close enough to pick it up. For a moment she stared at it and then she said, in a strange voice, "What's this?"

"Beats me," he said. "How's everything on the home front?"

"Don't lie to me," she said. "Where did this handkerchief come from?"

"I don't know," he said.

"You don't know," she said, contemptuously. "A woman's god-damned handkerchief is in your car, full of lipstick, and you don't know how it got there."

"Let's see," he said, trying to mask his panic. "Maybe I gave somebody a lift today. By golly, I did. I dropped Hank and his date off at La Rue."

"Were they necking in the car, in the front seat?"

"Of course not. Look," he said, "I've heard about enough of this nonsense. Either you trust me or you don't. Now let's drop it."

There was nothing more she could say. She did not believe him but there was nothing more she could do or say. From that moment, however, she never trusted him again, although she tried to tell herself that she must, that if she did not then the future yawned before them long and dark and hopeless.

Once a month Dan took his mother to dinner at a restaurant. He counted the evening successful if they could get through it without an angry word. This night she lit a cigarette as she got out of the car. It always displeased him to see her, an old woman, smoke on the street, but he could not recall whether or not he had ever told her so. There was some sort of residual shame left over from the sensitive days of his childhood, a feeling that had something to do with the fact that neither his mother nor any of her sisters and brothers had any taste in clothes or furniture or paintings or wallpaper or anything, really, when he stopped to think of it. Their coats always hung open, their hats were always somehow slightly askew, their attire always seemed somehow poor-looking and sad, regardless of what it had cost.

As they walked into the restaurant, she stepped to the curb to discard her cigarette. Then, walking behind him, she said softly, as they entered the café, "Aren't you wearing your pants a little too short?"

Later, at the table she said, "It's Friday. I hope they have some decent fish." While he was inspecting the menu she looked at him and said, "You look tired."

"I had ten hours sleep last night," he said. "I feel fine."

"Oh, sure," she said, sarcastically. "I'm wrong again."

He did not respond.

"This place used to do a good business," she said, "but it's been running downhill terribly." When the waiter came to take their order she said to Dan in a loud voice, "You don't mind if I have a bottle of beer, do you?"

"Of course not," he said, although he did. While they were waiting for the beer she said, "I had roast beef here the other night and it was so tough I could hardly eat it. And I don't know what's the matter with the tomatoes out here. They don't seem to have any flavor."

Her employment of the phrase "out here" fascinated him. She was always complaining about the "eggs out here," or the "coffee out here," or the "rain out here," or the "people out here." Her sense of bitter alienation, although almost certainly unconscious, was unmistakable.

When they were having coffee she said, "Oh, I heard that new song of yours. It's very nice."

"Thank you," he said.

"I don't like the way what's-his-name sings it," she said, "it sounds so draggy. Have you ever tried to write any *peppy* numbers like Johnny Mercer or that Cole—what's-his-name—Porter?"

"No," he said, "they have their own styles."

"Well," she said, "I think people like peppy numbers, not all that damned draggy stuff."

She droned on, for another hour. He answered her politely and laughed, genuinely, when she said amusing things. And he was grateful, in an almost childish sense, when she said something gentle and compassionate. But most of her conversation was critical, of people, of food, of prices, of government, of service, of the weather, of Helen, of him. Sometimes as she rambled on he would disconnect his mind for a moment and look at her tired, sad old blue eyes and think, "What happened to you? What went wrong, way back somewhere long ago? At what point did you start to turn from a giggling three-year-old child into a bitter, sarcastic, suspicious woman? Who did it to you? *What* did it to you? You couldn't have decided, yourself, to just become a perpetually angry human being, so something must have done it to you, and early. Even, perhaps, before you were born." He was not gifted enough to develop the theory further.

Dan made the decision to leave town in a sudden and natural way, the way an animal decides to flee a forest fire or run to a water hole or skitter at the shadow of a cloud passing over the full moon.

It came about in a simple way. A wire arrived from Dave Halliburton in New York. It said, "Will you call me Friday about writing score for *Not This Time?*" On Friday, at Hank's apartment, they put the call through.

"Hello?" Hank said, speaking loudly.

Even decades after Alexander Graham Bell people still didn't trust long-distance lines. Across town it was just "Hello," but across country it was always the incredulous, high-pitched "*Hello?*"

Halliburton was on the line. "Hello, Hank?" he said.

"Dave?" Hank asked.

"Yeah," Halliburton said. "How are ya?"

"Fine, you old son of a bitch! How's yourself?" Hank was talking loudly, and laughing. There was that, too, about long-distance. You not only talked loudly even when the connection was perfect, but you laughed more than was necessary. You called friends old sons of bitches, and old bastards, smiling the while. Perhaps it was the awareness that the call cost money and lulls in the conversation were nickel-wasting traps to be avoided even at the cost of a great deal of falsely hearty profanity, and hemming and hawing. Customarily you perspired more when making a long distance call, or you drummed your fingers on the table more, or made more doodles on the scratch-pad on your desk.

Halliburton explained that he had had to hold up production of his new show because of his dissatisfaction with the songs written by Larry Vine. Dan remembered having read in Earl Wilson's column that Halliburton and Vine had had an argument about the show and gone their separate ways. Dan got on the line and was surprised to hear himself say, "Look, Dave, if you're moving fast maybe we'd better come back there and get close to the thing."

"I wish you would," Halliburton said. "It would be much better, really."

"All right," Dan said. "I'll let you know when I'm leaving. We might even have some things to show you when we get there."

When the call had been completed Hank said, "I didn't figure on going right back but I guess it'll be all right. How soon do you plan on leaving?"

"I don't know," Dan said. "For some reason or other I'd like to get at it right away."

That night he lay in bed wide-awake, listening to Helen toss and turn, trying to get up enough courage to tell her he was going to New York. About half past three he slipped out of bed, padded barefoot into the kitchen, and poured himself a cold bottle of beer. He was startled when Helen walked in and stood before him, grimly silent.

"What's the matter?" she said.

"Nothing," he said. "Go back to sleep."

"Something's wrong," she said. "Something's been wrong for a long time. We haven't made love in weeks and you've been prowling around the house like a caged tiger. What is it?"

"I have to go to New York."

"Why?" She looked frightened.

"It's a great break, actually," he said, hoping to calm her. "You know Dave Halliburton, the big producer? Well, he wants Hank and me to do the score for his next show. I'll have to go back there for a while."

"How soon?"

"I was figuring on leaving the next day or so."

"Do you have your tickets and reservations and everything?"

"I was figuring on driving back," he said.

To himself he said, during the pause that followed, "My God. I might as well be planning a bank robbery or a murder."

"Driving?" Helen said, frowning in disbelief. "Why drive all that distance?"

"I don't know," he said. "It might be good for me. I've felt a little—I don't know, sort of like I've needed a vacation lately. The open road for a few days might do me some good."

"You're lying."

The skin on his stomach began to itch. "What the hell," he said, "would I be lying about?"

"Who is Elaine Sterling?" Helen said.

Instead of fright he suddenly experienced an emotional numbness, a sense of cold withdrawal.

"Who?" he said, avoiding her eyes, toying with the beer glass.

78

"Elaine Sterling," she said, flatly. "When I sent your brown jacket to the cleaners a couple of weeks ago I found a piece of paper with her name and telephone number on it. Who is she?"

"Let's see," he said, still numb. "I know that name all right, but for the life of me I can't seem to remember just who it is."

"You're a god-damned liar," she said, reaching into the pocket of her housecoat and taking out a small laundered handkerchief. At the sight he almost jumped. It was the handkerchief that had fallen out of the car that night. She had picked it up at the time and now it had been washed and pressed. She opened it and he saw, for the first time, the initials E.S. stitched in one corner with pale green thread.

He sat silently and then, after a moment, he reached for the glass of beer, his heart pounding. After taking a long drink he stood up and faced her.

"All right," he said. "You are right. I *am* a god-damned liar. I am a god-damned liar and a cheat and an adulterer and a son-of-a-bitch of the worst sort. No matter what you think of me it can't compare with what I think of myself."

Her lips began to tremble and she seemed no longer angry. "Oh, Dan," she whimpered, "have you been—have you been untrue to me?" Something about the simplicity and old-fashionedness of the phrase moved him more than anything she could have said.

He looked at her with his heart overflowing with tenderness and a love very much like that which he felt for their children. Biting his lip he reached out and took her in his arms.

"I've wanted to kill myself," he said, struggling to keep his voice level, speaking softly so as not to awaken the children or be overheard by the housekeeper. He looked down at her faded housecoat, at her tired, wet, sad eyes, her hair hanging unkempt over her brow.

"I never wanted to hurt *you*," he said. Then he could no longer, in his torment of guilt, bear to touch her. It would have been like receiving communion with mortal sin on his soul. He felt unworthy in a simple physical sense, as if he were covered with some sort of horrible slime.

"How did it happen?" she said. Then she stepped back and

raised her voice, saying, "No. No, god damn it. Don't tell me. I don't want to think of you in parked cars, or worse, with that bitch, whoever she is. I'll kill her, god damn it!"

"Don't," he said. "Please don't talk like that. What good will that do? I've told you I'm sorry."

"Aghh," she gasped. "I feel like I'm going to throw up."

He shook his head from side to side helplessly.

"And now," she said, "after telling me this, now you're running out. Going to New York."

"I've got to go back there because of my work," he said. "I won't be gone long. I promise."

"Promise," she said. "You bastard, what good are your promises? You promised something when we got married in your god-damned church and now look!"

The word *church* startled him and stirred up the murky waters at the bottom of his mind. A fearful shape began to emerge from the depths, lifting its hideous bulk up to the surface. In a moment he recognized it as the thought that he wanted her to scream at him that she hated him and wanted a *divorce*.

It would be a solution, he thought. A terrible one. A painful one. An insane one. But a solution of sorts. In the next moment she lunged at him and tried to slap his face. He warded off the blow and grabbed her wrists.

"Let me go," she said, raising her voice.

"Please," he said. "Keep your voice down. Remember the children."

"Oh, that's beautiful, that is," she said. "Remember the children. Did *you* remember the children when you were with that *whore?* Did you? Answer me, *did* you?"

He hung his head.

"What does that slut say about the children?" she said. "Or does she even know about them? Does she even know you're married?"

"Shut up," he said, in an almost apologetic tone.

"Tell me about her," she cried, her eyes blazing. "How *is* she? What has she got?"

"Don't talk like that," he said, anger rising within him.

"Oh, great," she said. "What are you going to do now, *de-*

fend the whore? That's just great. How about me? Who's going to defend me? Who's going to care about me?"

At that she broke down, seating herself and flinging her head down upon the yellow formica table, sobbing hysterically.

Patting her shoulder, saying, "Ssshh, that's it, dear. Ssshh. Come to bed," he finally got her into the bedroom. They fought and cried for another hour. It was dawn before they fell into a sour, troubled sleep.

When he awakened the house was empty. A note on the kitchen table said, "I've taken the kids to visit some friends. We will be back this evening."

When they came home he played with the children. But after they had been put to bed he discovered that Helen would not speak to him. After a while he walked out, slamming the front door.

He stayed out all night, sleeping at Hank's place. When he returned the next day at lunch time he found Helen sweeping the patio.

"Well," she said coldly. "Look who's here. Where did you spend the night?"

"With Hank," he said. "I suppose you don't believe me."

"What's the difference?" she said.

"Yeah," he said, tiredly. "What's the difference?" He stood watching her, not knowing what to do next.

"Look," he said. "I still have to go to New York."

She did not answer.

That night at dinner sullen resentment lay like a large ugly toad on the dining room table. The children were eating grilled cheese sandwiches in the den, watching a cowboy program and gravely spilling bits of potato chip on the floor.

"You're not eating," Dan said, watching Helen toy with a piece of meat loaf.

"I'm not hungry." Her hand lay listlessly on the lace tablecloth, holding a fork. Her eyes were red-rimmed.

"Dave Halliburton called again this afternoon from New York."

"Oh."

"He wants me to come back there right away. You see, he's got this new show in mind."

She looked up at him suddenly, anger at the corners of her mouth.

"You're really going?"

"I suppose I'll have to."

"Why?"

"What do you mean 'why'? He wants me to write some numbers for him. I can do a better job of it back there."

She allowed the fork to slip through her numb fingers and sat staring down at her plate. He felt his stomach knot up and knew there was going to be a storm.

"That's fine," she said. "Just go off to New York. Just like that."

"What difference does it make to you whether I stay? What the hell is so desirable about the state of affairs here?"

"What am I supposed to do while you're gone?"

"What do you mean? I've been away before. You never acted like this!"

"You never acted like this before either," she said. "Does anyone else know you're going?"

The image of Elaine leaped like a phantom between them but neither would say her name.

"No, I've just made up my mind for sure this afternoon." He wanted to get back to talking about the mechanics of the trip and about the work he had to do. He was afraid Elaine's name would come into the conversation.

"When will you come back?"

"Oh, it's hard to say. Probably before too long."

"What about the children?"

"What do you mean?"

"Oh, for God's sake stop asking me what I mean. I mean will I tell them you'll be gone for a long time or just for a few days?"

He looked sorrowfully at her plate. Grease had begun to congeal on the meat loaf and the bright green peas looked cold and wrinkled and pathetic. He felt an unexplainable tenderness for a moment and wanted to ask her to eat and not to worry and not to cry or be sad or be hurt but it was all impossible and he knew he could do nothing but sit there and watch her writhe on the rack of his inability to love her as she wanted to be loved. His skin fairly crawled with guilt at the poleaxed-steer expression on her face as she mirrored pride and love and despair.

"I don't know just how long Dave will want me to stay back there," he said, trying to sound relaxed and comforting. "Perhaps your mother could come over from Phoenix for a while."

"Don't worry about me," she said, her voice breaking. "You just go running off where you want. It's a little late to start being solicitous."

They paused momentarily as Mrs. Walsh entered the room and circumspectly poured coffee. When she had walked back into the kitchen Helen said softly, "Must you drive back? Why don't you fly?"

"I don't know," he said, but already his mind was conjuring pictures of a motor trip with Elaine. He could see the two of them, sitting side-by-side in the Buick, speeding down a magazine-ad sort of highway, smiling. Now at the table he considered briefly whether he might be losing his mind.

The gloom of the present shortly overwhelmed Dan and Helen completely and they had a brittle, snapping, whispered argument after which Helen left the table and ran into the front bathroom and locked the door. He walked after her and stood in the hall and for a moment was frightened by the possibility that she might try to drink something in the medicine cabinet and kill herself. But after he had stood outside the bathroom door for a few seconds listening to her crying and blowing her nose he walked numbly into the back bedroom and began putting things into a suitcase. When he had two bags packed he carried them furtively out to the front porch and then came back into the house and walked into the den.

The boys were sitting flung in relaxed positions on the sofa, wearing brightly colored pajamas, staring transfixed at the television screen. Barbara crawled on the floor. He walked over and sat down between Michael and Patrick, pulling the baby onto his lap.

"Hi, Fatso," he said, kissing the back of the moist neck, just over the pink collar.

"Hi, da," Barbara said. "Don't you tickle me."

He looked at Michael's serious, handsome face in profile and felt a small knot come into his throat. He would have to work hard to underplay the scene.

"What's up, Mike-o?" he said.

"I don't know," Mike said without turning.

"Did you eat all your sandwich?"

"Uh-huh."

"Did you drink all your Ovaltine?"

"Uh-huh. Pakowww!" He fired a forefinger at the screen.

"Daddy," Patrick said, trying to slide onto his lap, pushing the baby, "where's Mama?"

"She's in the kitchen, I think. And she's kind of tired, too. You boys be good boys for her tonight, will you? And every night."

"Sure. Where are you going?"

They always seemed to know when he planned to walk out of the house, whether he was going to the corner for a magazine or to the end of the world. A parent sitting down with a child to attempt a controlled good-bye must communicate some sort of reserve and false joviality that a child's sensitive emotional mechanism can detect. Michael turned now and regarded him briefly.

"You going out?"

"Yep," he said. "I'm going out. Pretty far this time, too. Have to go all the way to New York."

"Where's New York?"

The baby said, "Where's New Rok?"

"Oh, it's not *really* so far away," he said, with a slight smile of reassurance. "Just across the country is all it really is. Just across the United States."

"Is it a million billion miles?" Patrick asked.

"No, not quite. It's only three thousand."

"Three *thousand?*" Patrick said, wide-eyed. "That sounds like more than a million billion to me."

They all roared. Patrick could always make the family laugh. He seemed to have an unconscious sense of the comic, a mysterious talent for the ridiculous, possibly, Dan thought, inherited from his paternal grandmother.

One time Patrick had been playing on his bed, jumping up and down with Michael, and had hurt his mouth slightly so that a small amount of blood flowed from an almost invisible cut on his tongue.

"What happened?" Dan had said, touching his lips with a cold washcloth.

"I bit my throat," Patrick had said, and for weeks they had repeated the line to neighbors and friends and ever after they could make each other smile by saying, when someone had sustained a small injury, "What happened? You bite your throat?"

"When are you going?" Michael said, still facing the television screen.

"Well, to tell you the truth," Dan said, "I think I may have to leave right about now. But don't you kids worry about a thing, because I'll write to you and I'll see you before very long and . . . I love you very much."

They looked at him with some faint trace of embarrassment and he smiled with a fair imitation of conviction and mussed up their hair and wrestled with them and tickled them and made them laugh and then said, "You kids sit right here and go on watching television and I'll be seeing you. Okay?"

"Okay, Daddy," they all said and he grinned again and told them they were the best children in the whole world and then he strolled stiffly out of the den without looking back and walked around through the front room and down the hall and put on a coat. Helen was in the kitchen. When she saw him walk in with his topcoat on she frowned and looked startled.

"Are you . . . You're . . ."

"It won't be any easier tomorrow," he said. "And I just had a nice talk with the children. They're all right."

"Oh, sure," she said. "They're all right. You won't have to be here with them, to answer their questions."

"What the hell would it mean if I took my coat off right now and stayed?" he snapped. "What good would it do?"

"Well, then go. Go right now. Go ahead."

"Why do you act like that?" he said. It was a meaningless question for he knew that he was the transgressor, not she.

She had a right to act any way she wanted, for he had given her provocation. He even felt a certain measure or relief that he was leaving her in anger. It was easier that way. He expected her fury and it was easier to take than innocent incomprehension, an air of mute, helpless dejection. So that when at last she swore at him and told him to get out he seized upon the excuse and hurried out into the foggy night, throwing his suitcases angrily into the back seat of the car and roaring off down the street with the transmission in low. He was close to tears at leaving the children, and he was so full to overflowing with guilt and remorse that his face twitched and he shook his head violently back and forth to blot out the picture of Helen's pathetic expression. He could not understand himself at all. The emotions that drove him to push his car swiftly through the night and point it toward the mountain passes that led to Beverly Hills were a swirling, confused mass in his mind. For at least a minute he considered committing suicide, wondered if just driving off over one of the high mountain curves ahead would surely kill him.

At the corner of Ventura and Sepulveda he parked the car and rushed into an outdoor phone booth.

"Hello?" It was her mother's voice.

"Hello," he said quietly. "Is Elaine in, please?"

"Who's calling?"

"Mr. Scanlon."

"Just a moment." He could hear the clatter of the phone being put down on a table, then the sound of heels on a wooden floor.

"Dan?"

"Hello, baby?"

"Where are you?"

"I'm in a phone booth on Ventura. I . . . I just left the house."

"What do you mean?"

"I mean I just left it for good, for a while that is. I don't know what I'm saying. What I mean is I'm going to New York. I talked to Dave Halliburton again this afternoon and he wants me to come right back there and do some work on the show he's putting together."

"That's wonderful."

"I want you to come with me." He had not truly known that he was going to say it, although part of his mind had hoarded the idea for a long time, keeping it secret from the other parts.

"Oh, Dan."

"I can't help it, baby. I know it's not a bright idea, but I've been going out of my mind. I have the car right now. I can leave this minute and drive back. Will you come with me?"

"Yes."

He felt weak and heard himself chuckle, hollowly.

"I don't know what I would have done if you hadn't said that."

"When did you say you wanted to leave?"

"Well, right now. Or tomorrow. What about you? Can you just up and leave like this? What about your mother?"

"It's no matter," she said. "I can tell her I'm going to stay with Kay or something. I've got my two weeks coming at the office. I'll pack right now. How soon can you be here?"

"I love you," he said. "I can be there in fifteen minutes."

"I love you, but that's too soon. Why don't you go have a cup of coffee some place and be downstairs in an hour."

"Will that give you enough time?"

"Yes. I'll just pack two or three bags and send for more things later. Dan . . ." There was a pause.

"What?"

"Oh, I don't know. Are you sure you love me?"

"Yes, darling. I know this doesn't make any sense, but I do love you. Does this thing make you feel . . . funny?"

"Yes," she said. "I feel excited, but it's as if I were robbing a bank."

"I know. I feel that way too. It's terrible."

"All right, sweetheart. You be downstairs in an hour and just honk. I'll come down."

"All right. Good-bye."

He walked back to the car and sat behind the wheel with his heart pounding and his mouth dry. He felt frightened and confused. Because the gas tank was almost empty he pulled into the station on the corner and had it filled. While the attendant was wiping off the windshield he asked, almost furtively, for a road map.

Driving slowly through the pass that led from the valley to the coastal areas he tried not to think of Helen and the children. He listened to a newscast on the car radio, stopped at a drugstore and bought a toothbrush and razor blades and then drove to a drive-in restaurant on Wilshire Boulevard in Beverly Hills and had a steaming mug of coffee and a piece of apple pie. Twenty minutes before the hour was up he pulled around the corner near Elaine's house and stopped the car in front of her building. Sitting there listening to the radio he glanced nervously at his watch and looked out the window from time to time up at the balcony of her apartment on the second floor. Once again when he was looking out he saw her carrying suitcases into the vestibule of the building. He leaped out and ran up the steps to her.

"I didn't know you were here," she said. "I was just getting the bags down here so I'd be ready when you showed up."

He kissed her awkwardly on the forehead and put the bags in the back seat with his own. Then they drove off toward downtown Los Angeles to pick up the main highway going east.

They drove for a long time without speaking, hypnotized by the overpowering oddity of the experience they were undergoing, fearful that at any moment a restraining hand would be laid upon them, fearful that a flat tire, a policeman, an earthquake, a flood, a war, a motor breakdown, or the end of the world would shoulder its way into their experience and put a stop to their strange illicit adventure. At one point Dan said to himself, "I am a criminal. I am an adulterer. I am destroying myself."

Later the two of them smiled nervously and squeezed each other's hands.

It was a long time before they began to relax and breathe deeply.

CHAPTER

NINE

THEY drove as far as Palm Springs and spent the night at a motel.

In the morning they took a dip in the motel's blue, jewell-like swimming pool, breakfasted to the point of gluttony, and pulled out of town at ten o'clock, driving fast.

Driving across the desert they talked for a while about subjects in which neither of them was particularly interested. At last they fell silent. Once when they stopped for gas Elaine took over the wheel. Dan sat sideways on the front seat, facing her, and as he looked at her profile he thought to himself, "Good-bye. Good-bye there, pretty-face. I don't know where we're going, but I know that when we get there we won't be able to stay long."

Phoenix brought back the fear strongly. "This is where I went to high school," he said. And in the suburb of Tempe, "This is where I went to college for a few months."

"You met Helen here?"

"Yes."

"Let's not stop."

"I had fun here, though," he said. "I was majoring in journalism. Thought I was going to be a great writer in those days. Didn't know I'd end up writing tin-pan alley slop."

"You don't write slop."

"Not exclusively," he said. "I write some things I'm proud of, but sometimes I write slop. People don't want to buy much class. You can't dictate to them. You've got to write what they're buying."

"But what about the show?"

"Oh, that's different. For a show you can write as good as you want or as good as you're able. But even there as often as not the really well-thought-out numbers are buried with the show. It's the light stuff that sometimes gets into the hit class."

"You haven't told me yet. Are you doing this one alone?"

"No," he said. "I'm still working with Hank Lazarus."

"He does the music, doesn't he? Or no, it's you."

"We're a funny team. We both write words and we both write music. I like it that way."

"Oh, that's right," she said. "I remember that interview. Listen, it'll take you a few days to get set up. Where will you be staying?"

"I don't know. The Warwick. The Barbizon-Plaza."

"I won't move in with you, of course."

"I guess it would be awkward. I'll be seeing so many people."

"Sweetie . . ."

"What?"

"Why don't we just turn around and go back?"

"You want to?"

There was a long pause.

"No."

"I don't either."

"But I just had the oddest feeling. I just thought to myself 'What in the name of God am I doing driving across Arizona in a car with a man who has a wife and three children?' "

"Would it make you feel any better to get off in Albuquerque or some place and take a train?"

"That's not it," she said.

"Look," he said. "This isn't exactly running away to a desert island the way Gauguin did. I *have* to go to New York on business, after all. I have work to do there. It's not as if I were going there forever."

"How long *will* you stay?"

"I don't know," he said. "Lord, I've been saying 'I don't know' ever since I met you. I'm getting to hate the sound of the words."

"Do you think we'll ever get married?"

"I don't know."

They spent the night in a small town in New Mexico, huddled together under a grayish sheet and a thin bedspread. There was no heat in the room and in the morning the water was too cold for a shower.

When at last they were driving through Texas Dan told her about the time he ran away from home, when he was sixteen.

"Why did you do it?"

"It's hard to say," he said. "I just hated my existence. I couldn't get along with my mother, I lived in a miserable rooming house, I wasn't doing very well in school, I was in love with a girl who couldn't see me for dust, and I had sexual problems."

"Like what?"

"Nothing unusual," he laughed. "The same problems every growing boy faces. There just wasn't anything about my life that I liked so I decided to run away to South America."

"You didn't make it?"

"No."

"Is this a pattern of yours, running away?"

"I don't think so," he said, "although come to think of it when I was very little I used to get lost pretty often. One time they found me on a viaduct or something, walking along a railroad track. I told them I was going to walk all the way to New York to see my mama."

"And then at sixteen you were running away from her."

"That's the usual set-up, I guess," he sighed.

He remembered the other flight clearly.

On the bicycle, thinking he was going to school, but then, dazedly, past the school grounds, out Stony Island Avenue, through South Chicago, through Gary. The exultation of realizing that in the first hour he was out of Illinois. In another state. In Indiana. The Hoosier State. The Hoosier Hotshots. Hoosier little whozis? Who do you love?

And other songs, played on jukeboxes, at roadside hamburger stands, when he would turn his cycle in across gravelled parking lots, wearily. "Marie," by Tommy Dorsey and his orchestra, with Jack Leonard singing. And "Who?" by Tommy Dorsey. And later as he progressed South, nameless and similar hillbilly records, seemingly one with the glaring neon signs, *Hi-way Eats, Jack's Place, Thompson's Shack, Pop's Diner,* and *Bessie's Fried Chicken* (*Trucks Stop Here*).

The blaring jukeboxes and the red and green neon signs. His legs had given out two hundred miles out of Chicago, "Hey, mister, can I leave this bike here in your garage for a couple of days?"

"I guess so."

"Right over here be all right?"

"Yeah, I guess so."

It had been a good bike. White and blue. New Departure brakes. Balloon tires. Fast. It had been fun coasting down long hills, easing along with the wind at his back. But for every downhill there was an uphill. For every tail-wind there was a head-wind. And so he had left it at the garage in the small town in Indiana. Coming back in a few days. Pick it up again. But he had never gone back.

Often later he thought of the bike. Of riding girls on the bar in front of the seat. Of showing off on the streets near his home. Turning corners without touching the handle bars. Look, ma; no hands, as the saying goes.

He had hitchhiked before. To school. Downtown. Now on the highway, it was different. The cars slipped past, cutting the air, tires whining on the oil-stained concrete. At first it didn't matter much that they weren't stopping. It didn't matter much about each individual car. There was always the next one. It was three days before he became accustomed to the bitter desperation that is the hiker's. But his first ride had been a lucky one. A truck was stopped at a fork in the road, pulled off in the dirt, guarded by red flags and lanterns before and aft along the highway. The driver was changing a tire, and he had stopped to help, hoping. It was almost dark and he offered to hold a flashlight. Then the eternal question:

"Say, you goin' down this way?" The truck was *headed* this way.

"Yeah. As far as Louisville." The breath held. A strike. A bonanza. A full house. A jackpot. But . . .

"Mind if I ride along?"

"No. I guess it'll be all right. How far you going?"

"Oh, Texas." It was the first time he had thought of going to Texas. Up until that moment the answer would have been, "Oh, I'm going back to Chicago." But the logical answer in turn would have been, "Headed in the wrong direction, ain't you?" so he had to say:

"Oh, Texas."

The man's name was Jim French. For hours at a time they had ridden in silence, the fierce hum of the engine vibrating the cab, the windows, the steering wheel, the leather seat, his brain, the world. Then:

"Bastard won't turn off his brights!" Or:

"Kinda gettin' in the mood for a cuppa coffee." Or:

"Looks like the son of a bitch is using oil again." Or:

"Texas, huh?"

"What?" Sleepily.

"You say you're goin' on down to Texas?"

"Oh. Oh, yeah. Got nothing else to do." Another monotonous hour of the kidney-numbing vibration, the grinding motor-hum. Then:

"Say, you can give me a hand when we get to Louisville."

"How's that?"

"Just help me unload what's in back."

"Sure thing." In the dim light from the dashboard their faces loomed before them on the windshield, ghostlike, seemingly in space.

They stopped at a trucker's diner. Hamburgers. Bright red cherry pie. Coffee.

"This is on me," French said.

"No, thanks. I have money."

"Naw, it's okay. I'll get this one."

"All right."

The ill-kept toilet out back. Ten thousand evil-smelling ill-kept toilets strung along highways. Writing on the walls. A. C. Kenney, 1934. Mabel Kirshner, Adams 4691. Bulls with short horns, please stand close. Dutch Flam, U.S. Navy, November 14, 1936. The waitress here has big tits. Chicago, or die trying. Crude pencilled drawings, child-like in technique, degenerate in substance. Names carved in wood. More signs of the Depression, of poverty. Dirty roll-towels. Empty paper-towel racks. Dried-up soap dispensers. Bars of Lava. Moist containers of Dutch Cleanser. Rusty hot water faucets dripping ice-water. Cracked stained toilet-seats. Cigarette butts in urinals, dissolving. Splashed floors, with broken concrete. Cracked, blackened mirrors. Doors and walls with many coats of thick paints, chipped, peeling, many colors visible. Oh, beautiful for spacious skies.

Strangers lurching in, bumping past. Belching, or vomiting, or laughing, throwing cigarettes in the urinal. The short hiss as the glowing red ash touched the water. He had always been appalled by dirty toilets, the infinite number of them out back of roadside diners, lonely gas stations.

In the morning he awoke stiff, cold, and aching, conscious at first only that the brain-numbing growl still enveloped him, that he was being vibrated, jostled. They were in Louisville and the city looked fresh and city-waking-upish in the morning sun. Backing the truck up against the platform at a warehouse of some kind. Jim French disappearing, saying:

"Just stack the boxes up on this platform here. I'll be back in a few minutes."

The boxes were heavy. Much heavier than he had expected. Each cardboard crate was full of tin cans. He could not remember now what had been in the cans. Syrup or pineapple or something. He dragged and pushed four boxes to the platform, then, weak and exhausted, slunk off to explore Louisville. The South. The Deep South. Hush ma mouth. Is it true what they say about Dixie? Magnolias. Mint juleps. Yo' all.

Louisville, or what he saw of it, was a disappointment. He wandered through a colored neighborhood. Stiff ragged clothing hanging in back yards in the morning mist. Smoke coming from shacks that seemed never to have been painted.

Sullen brown faces turned toward him as he ambled past. Black eyes regarded him dully. Rusting piles of scrap metal in grassless back yards. Chickens cackling tiredly, hopping among broken glass and waste paper.

His money lasted till he reached Houston. It took seven days, and in that time he had spent exactly seven dollars. In Evansville, Indiana he stood in front of the New Era hotel. The clerk demanded payment in advance. No baggage. The colored porter showing him to a dingy second-floor room. Then, as the door was opened:

"Shall I send the girl up now?"

"What?"

"You want the girl here now?" The sudden hotness in the face when he realized what the man was talking about. No expression though. Act big.

"No. I guess not. I'm pretty tired."

"Yas, suh." The closed door. Washing socks and underwear in the sink with the tiny bar of hotel soap. Thinking of the girl. Wondering what it would have been like. Waking up in the morning, not knowing where he was. Familiar feeling. Sometimes he could lie awake for as long as fifteen seconds and not know where he was. Twelve hour sleep this time. No shave. No razor blade.

One day spent in Hot Springs. Burning his mouth at a public fountain. Hot spring water. Why make the fountain look like a drinking font when the water was hot?

One night in Texarkana. Sleeping on the cement steps of a motor court, waiting for the salesman who had given him a lift that far. The prowl car sliding unheard to the curb. The flashlight suddenly in his face.

"You all right, boy?" The soft, not unkind Southern voice.

"Oh, sure."

"Better move around. You can't sleep there all night."

"Okay." They had been nice about it. He would be glad to move around. Flies with honey.

Sleeping out in the open was becoming commonplace. It

was warm for late September. In Houston, sleeping on a ledge in an alley, waking up covered with a white, powdery frost. Crystallized fog. Using his hat and folded arm for a pillow. Not bad. Not bad at all. Necessity is the mother of invention. Necessity is the mother of vinegar. You catch more flies with honey.

And there had been honey. The experience was not all vinegar. The man in Houston who had overheard him say in the restaurant, at the cashier's desk:

"I guess I'll have to wash dishes for you, mister. I don't have any money."

The man, without a word, throwing a dollar on the marble surface, looking at the proprietor, nodding. Gone before he could be thanked.

He had tried the trick again, a week later, in Del Rio, Texas. On the border. The Bluebird Café. Two hot roast beef sandwiches with mashed potatoes and gravy. Then:

"I don't have any money." Stupefaction on the waiter's face. Then suspicion.

"You don't what?"

"I don't have any money. You want any dishes washed?"

"Hey, Harry. Come here. Guy eats and then says he ain't got any money."

"That right?"

"Yep." The proprietor stepped casually to a telephone and called the police. Seated by the door, young Dan could have stepped out into the street, hurried off. Strangely, he had no desire to escape.

"Why didn't you tell me first you didn't have any money?"

"I don't know. I was just hungry."

"You should have asked me for something to eat, then. That's a hell of a note. No money." Presently, a friendly Texan walked in, khaki-clad, visor-capped.

"This the man?"

"Yep."

"What's the trouble, son?"

"No trouble. I was just hungry, so I had two roast beef sandwiches, then told the guy I didn't have any money."

"That's no way to do."

"I guess not."

At the jail they fingerprinted him, questioned him politely, showed him into a cell. It was clean. There was a hard bunk in the corner. After the alley ledge it was luxury. In the morning an inspection of his cell. A barred window with a not unpleasant view. A toilet in the corner with no wooden seat. No privacy. Only open bars separated the cells.

A heavy-set elderly man unlocked the door and walked in with a steaming bucket of oatmeal, ladled some out into a large, flat dishpan, gave him a giant, bent tablespoon. Another man came in with flat, weak coffee. The oatmeal was good, even without milk. There was a little sugar in it.

Later in the day, standing at the window, his fingers touched a razor blade on the ledge. It was cut along one edge, shaped like a key! Playfully he inserted the flimsy key in the lock. He had no desire to escape. The tumbler started to turn and then the blade snapped. He could not get it out of the lock. Then, for the first time in the jail, he was afraid. If the lock was jammed they would think he had done it deliberately. Later, when they unlocked it to take him out for a little exercise it operated smoothly. Sigh of relief.

"Weren't you afraid?" Elaine asked.

"Believe it or not," he said, "most of the time I wasn't. I think there's something essential in the way of emotional equipment that you must lack when you're a teen-ager. Why, I would no more hop a freight train today or sleep all night in a field than—well, what I mean is I'd be terrified today to do some of the things I did then. But when you're sixteen you're too stupid to feel the correct amount of fear. At least I was."

"I guess you're so impressed with the new experiences that life throws at you that you don't have time to be afraid."

"You think you know so much then, too," he said. "That's a big part of it. You're so impressed with the new body that you've just gotten that you think you can use it to run the world."

They pressed on, driving fast. It was not until he was

traveling through East Texas that Dan remembered he had forgotten to tell Hank that he was leaving. Well, time enough to call him when they got to New York. Time enough, he knew, to solve all his problems, or at least to conclude them somehow, for better or for worse.

CHAPTER

TEN

SPEEDING NORTH through Arkansas, Dan became slightly feverish and decided to let Elaine drive again. When they stopped for gas at a country crossroads he climbed into the back seat, stretched out as best he could and later, when they were on the road again, fell into a troubled sleep. The faces of the children loomed before him and at one point, as something seemed about to strike him, he cried out, waking himself.

"What's the matter, baby?" he heard Elaine saying. "Nightmare?"

"Yes, I guess so," he said, sitting up and rubbing his eyes. The back of her slim neck looked so beautiful to him that he leaned forward and kissed it. She reached back with her right hand and patted his cheek.

"I want you," he said.

"So I gather," she said, looking straight ahead. "Look, while you were asleep I worked a few things out in my mind. I have a girl friend I can stay with. She lives on 55th Street. When we get to the next big town I'll send her a wire and tell her I'm coming. I know she'll be thrilled as long as I agree to pay half the rent. She's always starving."

"Fine," he said. "I guess I'll put up at the Barbizon-Plaza. That's only three blocks away."

"Three blocks is too far," she said, smiling at him in the rear-view mirror. "I want you three inches away."

He kissed the back of her neck again and laughed.

"What's funny?"

"The word *Barbizon*," he said. "It sounds like double-talk. Put the frenistan in the barbizon."

"That's right."

"I have a collection of words like that in my head," he said. "They're all real, but they sound like nonsense if you stop to think about it."

"For example?"

"*Storm-drain*," he said, "and *crevice*, and *retina*, and *tantamount*."

She giggled. "How about *plethora?*" she said.

"Perfect," he chuckled. "It goes right at the head of my list. Listen, you know what's fun? Try to make up sentences containing several of the words. If you say them fast it sounds as if you're talking complete nonsense."

"Try me," she said.

"All right," he said. "There's a *crevice* in the *storm-drain* running from the *Croydon* to the *Waldorf*."

"I love you," she said, "but I want you to know that that's *tantamount* to a *plethora* of *Tarletons* at the *Bryn Mawr*."

"Stop the car," Dan said. "I want to get in the front seat with you." When she pulled over to the side of the highway, startling a small herd of cows in a meadow, he said, "I'll drive for a while."

Before starting the car again he took her in his arms. The warmth of her mouth excited him to such an extent that he began to run his hands over her body.

"Wait a minute," she said, smiling. "We're out here in broad daylight."

"Okay," he said, turning the ignition key.

A few minutes later they passed over the body of a small, recently killed animal, the blood of which was splattered along the asphalt, streaked with tiremarks. Elaine averted her eyes.

"Did that bother you?" he said.

"I'm not too brave about blood," she said.

"The sight of something *dead* doesn't bother me," he said, "but I can't stand to see things, or people, suffering."

"That's strange," she replied. "Death is worse than suffering, since death can't be stopped or reversed and suffering can. But most of us find it easier to look at death."

"For some reason," he said, "I've always had a hatred of violence. I saw too many bullies as a kid."

"Did you grow up in a tough neighborhood?"

"Oh, moderately," he said. "I guess there are worse neighborhoods. It's a funny bit, these days men like to brag about how tough the neighborhood was that they grew up in. I guess it's a kind of sneaky way to brag about your own toughness. Ours was tough, all right. That is, there were kids around who seemed to like to fight, but now that I think back to my early background, what disturbs me is some sort of distortion of values."

"What do you mean?"

"Well, take just two types of sin. Sexual sin and sins of violence. Now where I come from a man feels very deep guilt if he masturbates or touches a girl. But he feels practically no guilt at all about beating up another human being or throwing a brick through a Jew's window. In the first case what is involved is *loving,* although it may be twisted or misapplied. But it's loving, and my people were guilty and scared about it. In the second case what is involved is cruelty and violence. As for that, well, it was just kids letting off steam, just a laughable prank. I say now that there's some sort of terrible distortion of values in a situation like that, though I'm not enough of a scholar to get the thing all straight in my mind."

"Are you sorry you grew up in Chicago?" she said.

"No," he said. "Growing up in Chicago wasn't really a handicap. As a matter of fact being raised in a tough neighborhood may even be a good thing for a kid. It kicks him around a little and he gets the idea early that it's not going to be an easy road. Besides, Chicago has never avoided facing the question of juvenile delinquency. Years ago it realized it had the obligation to get its children off the streets. And it fulfilled that obligation. It took its young people off the streets and put them into nice warm saloons."

"I wish I'd known you then," she said, smiling reflectively. "We would have gone to school together and gone dancing and held hands and gone to the movies."

"You wouldn't have looked at me then," he said. "I'm pretty astonished that you love me *now,* but in those days you wouldn't have given me a tumble. I was a tall, skinny kid with a prominent Adam's apple, shy as hell, and always mooning around."

"I would have loved you," she said.

"No," he said. "Beautiful girls like you always went with the captain of the football team or something. The girls who seemed genuinely fond of me usually had thick ankles or wore heavy glasses and no make-up. A lover-boy I was not."

"I'll bet you were smart in school."

"You're wrong," he said. "Oh, I did all right in the subjects that I liked, but in general I was something of a goof. In my junior year I got in the habit of ditching school and spending the day in the park or wandering around the Museum of Science and Industry or sitting on the beach, staring out at the waves of Lake Michigan."

He told her a bit more about his school days and then after a while the conversation dwindled off as they hurtled along the highway, traveling north and east. His mind wandered back to Chicago, to the old days.

That night they stayed at a dismal, second-rate hotel. After they had gotten into bed Dan noticed a Gideon Bible on the small bedside table, picked it up and opened it.

"Read me the Song of Solomon," Elaine said.

"What's that?" Dan said.

"You're kidding."

"About what?"

"About not knowing what the Song of Solomon is."

"No," he said, defensively. "When I'm kidding I get laughs. I'm sorry. I just don't know a great deal about the Bible. I

102

mean I *know* quite a bit about it, but I've never really read much of it, except the New Testament."

"Well," she said, taking the book from him and riffling the pages, "you just do this till you see where it says the Song of Solomon in black print at the top of the page. Here. Here it is."

"Thank you," he said, as she handed the Bible back to him. Looking at the ceiling he said, "My God, this is weird."

"What is?"

"I feel as if I have a lot of nerve. Here I am running away, running across the country with a woman I'm not married to, fearful that at any minute God will strike me with a lightning bolt, and yet I'm sitting here in this big warm bed with you, reading the Bible. Well, this whole thing is so unreal that I don't know what I'm doing anyway."

"Whatever will be, will be. Read to me." And she huddled under the covers next to him, her head resting on his bare shoulder.

"The song of songs, which is Solomon's," he read slowly. *"Let him kiss me with the kisses of his mouth: for thy love is better than wine."* He stopped, frowning. "I thought that Solomon wrote this," he said, "but the speaker is a woman."

"Christopher Morley wrote *Kitty Foyle,*" Elaine said.

"Did he get an answer?" Dan said.

"No," Elaine said, laughing. "She was out of town at the time."

Dan ran his finger down the page. *"I have compared thee, O my love, to a company of horses in Pharaoh's chariots,"* he read. *"Thy cheeks are comely with rows of jewels, thy neck with chains of gold. We will make thee borders of gold filled with studs of silver. While the king sitteth at his table, my spikenard sendeth forth the smell thereof. A bundle of myrrh is my well-beloved unto me; he shall lie all night betwixt my breasts."*

Lifting her head, Elaine kissed him on the mouth.

"I cannot see that this has anything whatever to do with religion," Dan said, "but it's very beautiful poetry."

"Read more," Elaine said.

"I am the rose of Sharon, and the lily of the valleys. As the lily among thorns, so is my love among the daughters. As the apple tree among the trees of the wood, so is my beloved among the sons. I sat down under his shadow with great delight, and his fruit was sweet to my taste. He brought me to the banqueting house, and his banner over me was love. Stay me with flagons, comfort me with apples, for I am sick of love. His left hand is under my head, and his right hand doth embrace me."

At that Dan carefully placed the book, the pages opened, on the bed beside them. He put his left hand under Elaine's head and with his right arm embraced her.

"I love you," she said, looking up at him with half-closed eyes. "I love the sound of your voice, saying those words. Or any words."

"I charge you, O ye daughters of Jerusalem," Dan read softly, *"by the roes, and by the hinds of the fields, that ye stir not up, nor awake my love, till he please. The voice of my beloved! Behold, he cometh leaping upon the mountains, skipping upon the hills. My beloved is like a roe or a young hart. Behold, he standeth behind our wall, he looked forth at the windows, showing himself through the lattice. My beloved spake and said unto me 'Rise up, my love, my fair one, and come away. For, lo, the winter is past, the rain is over and gone; the flowers appear on the earth; the time of the singing of birds is come, and the voice of the turtle is heard in our land.' "*

He stopped, kissed her once on each eye, lightly, and resumed reading.

"O, my dove, that art in the clefts of the rock, in the secret places of the stairs, let me see thy countenance, let me hear thy voice; for sweet is thy voice, and thy countenance is comely. Take us the foxes, the little foxes, that spoil the vines: for our vines have tender grapes. My beloved is mine and I am his; he feedeth among the lillies."

With one open hand he felt, tenderly, the warmth of her stomach as he continued.

"How beautiful are thy feet with shoes, O prince's daughter! The joints of thy thighs are like jewels, the work of the hands

of a cunning workman. Thy navel is like a round goblet, which wanteth not liquor; thy belly is like a heap of wheat set about with lillies. Thy two breasts are like two young roes that are twins."

Sighing, she turned toward him.

"How fair and how pleasant art thou, my love, for delights! This thy stature is like to a palm tree, and thy breasts to clusters of grapes. I said, I will go up to the palm tree, I will take hold of the boughs thereof; now also thy breasts shall be as clusters of the vine, and the smell of thy nose like apples. And the roof of thy mouth like the best wine for my beloved, that goeth down sweetly, causing the lips of those that are asleep to speak. I am my beloved's and his desire is toward me."

Reaching back across the bed Dan turned off the light.

"This is strange," he said, whispering, caressing her face, "so strange. This, we are told, is the word of God. And reading these words has moved me to powerful desire for you. I love you. I love you as the man loved who wrote this poem. I love your warm breasts and your neck and your mouth in just that same way. Where, I wonder, is the good and the evil in all of this?"

"Kiss me," she said, "hold me close. I am happy and afraid and I want you to hold me."

CHAPTER

ELEVEN

WHEN THEY arrived in New York he drove her directly to the apartment of her friend on 55th Street, carried her bags upstairs and kissed her good-bye before she rang the doorbell.

"It might be awkward," he said, "if you have to explain who I am right off the bat. I'll go up to the Barbizon now and get a room. It's only eight-fifteen. I think I'll have some breakfast and then take a nap. Call me later in the day."

That evening they had dinner together at a small Italian restaurant. Later, as they strolled about the midtown area, he stopped in at a Western Union office and sent a telegram to Helen saying, "Am safely in New York. Have started work on Halliburton's show. Will let you know what is going on. Love to the children. Dan."

As they turned the corner of 56th Street and Seventh Avenue a short man suddenly bounded up to Dan, his tanned face beaming.

"Danny-boy," he shouted. "How are ya?"

"Oh, hello, Al," Dan said, startled. "Good to see you. Oh, Miss Sterling, this is Al Schwartz. He publishes some of my music."

"How do you do?" Elaine said.

"Pleasure," Al said. "When'd ya get in town?"

"Why, uh," Dan said, "a little—a couple of days ago. I'm here to do some work on a show."

"Great," Al said. "Listen, give us a call if you're gonna be around, okay?"

"Sure," Dan said. "You bet."

"I gotta run," the man said. "Me and Pete are going over to the Copa to see Dean and Jerry. Listen, you guys wanna come with us?"

"Well, thanks, Al," Dan said, "but—uh—we've got other plans."

"No problem," the man said. "Nice to meet you, miss. See you later, Dan. Give us a call now, you hear?"

"Sure thing," Dan said as the man hurried away, whistling for a taxi.

"Miss Sterling," Elaine said, thoughtfully.

"Oh, God," Dan said. "Now comes that problem. Running into people. At least he didn't ask me how Helen was."

"He would have if he hadn't been in a hurry. Dan, you're going to run into a lot of people who are going to ask you how Helen and the kids are. And you're going to ask yourself how they are."

"I know," he said. "That thought was in my mind every minute of the way across the country."

"Look," she said, "how would it be if I borrowed plane fare from you right now and went back in the morning?"

"Please," he said. "Don't leave me. That is, unless you want to."

"I don't," she said. "I love you, Dan. I love you more than I ever dreamed it was possible to love anyone."

They were under a street lamp at that moment. He stopped walking and looked intently, furiously, into her face, into her eyes.

"It's ridiculous," he said. "My heart is so full of emotion it's ready to burst and all I can think of to say is: I love you."

Within a week he decided that he was spending too much money at the Barbizon. A friend happened to be moving out of a one-room-and-kitchenette apartment on 55th between Park and Madison so Dan took it, to cut expenses. Then, too, the move solved the problem of Elaine's visiting him. He had gotten the idea, at the hotel, that the bellboys and floor managers had regarded him suspiciously every time the two of them had walked through the lobby together.

By this time Hank Lazarus had joined him in New York. One day Hank called him and made an appointment to get cracking. "We'll have a bite of lunch," he said, "and then go over to see Halliburton." They met at the corner of 54th and Madison.

"Where do you want to eat?" Dan said.

"Doesn't much matter to me," Hank said.

Dan looked down the street. Near the corner there was a sign: *Hamburger Heaven*.

"How about over there?" Hank said.

"All right," Dan said, "but I don't like the name. I think somebody in this town ought to open up a little place where they burn all the meat. Call it Hamburger Hell."

After lunch they went directly to Halliburton's apartment to talk about the show. Dave Halliburton was fifty-one years old. He had gone to Princeton, Dan thought, recalling an ancient *New Yorker* profile, although it might have been Harvard. He had white hair slicked down neatly and parted near the middle. Although he was a middle-aged man he dressed youthfully and somehow it was all right. He liked to wear contrasting slacks and sports jackets, Brooks Brothers button-down shirts, and bow-ties. He was sophisticated and very New York, Dan thought, reflecting that he felt a trifle ill-at-ease, slightly inadequate in the presence of such men. Halliburton unquestionably had "class," a word that Dan had always hated, possibly because he had always suspected that he himself did not have it. He felt that he was socially above taxi drivers and gamblers and mailmen but a man like Halliburton could make him feel relatively inferior. Sitting in the spacious living room of Halliburton's apartment in the East Sixties, Dan was suddenly conscious that his shoes needed shining, and that there was a very small spot on his slacks, just above the left knee.

"I think we'll have fun," Halliburton was saying. "Have you read the book?"

"The book?" Dan said.

"I mean the original story, *Where Were We?*"

"No," Dan said. "You read it, Hank?"

"Just the reviews."

"All right," Halliburton said, turning to his secretary. "Sugar-plum, see that the boys each get a copy this afternoon, will you?"

Sugar-plum made a note.

"It's a simple idea, really," Halliburton said. "It's been touched upon by several writers but not, up to now, strictly for laughs. Basically the story is in two parts. First, atom bombs blow everything all to hell. Second, our characters get together and start from scratch."

"Doesn't sound very funny," Hank said.

"You're right," Halliburton said, "but read the book. It *is* funny. Satirical. Bitter. But funny. There's a lot of business that's hysterical. The guy, Billy, finds a stack of thousand dollar bills but, of course, with life reduced to its essentials, the money has no value, no meaning."

"I can see where you might get a laugh or two out of a set-up like that. Guy lighting a cigarette with a big bill or something," Hank said.

"Leave the laughs to us," Halliburton said. "From you boys we just want the best damned songs you've ever written, that's all."

Dan knew that the laughs, in Halliburton's hands, would be forthcoming. He had a long list of successful musical comedies to his credit. He was alternately a producer or a director as suited his whim and he rarely missed. If it was a Halliburton show it was almost certain to be a hit. The silver-haired man with the long boyish legs and the blue eyes had had a dozen hits, three wives, and one nervous breakdown. He had an apartment in town, a home in Connecticut, and his name was frequently in the columns. He lunched at Sardi's, at Twenty-One, and at the Stork. He was only slightly effeminate, without being homosexual, slightly less anti-Semitic, although his second wife had been Jewish, and his speech was only slightly affected, Ivy League. Dan decided he liked him.

"Understand you've got Patty Arlen," Hank said.

Patty was an energetic singer with red hair and big eyes who had given up swimming against the tide in Hollywood and suddenly made good on Broadway.

"Patty's no Merman," Dave said, "but she'll be great for this thing. She looks good, sings good, and dances fair. Don't worry about her."

"Al got the book ready?" Hank said.

"More or less. It needs a lot of work but you can look it over. See how the scenes break down, you know."

The book for the show was being written by Al Lewis, ex-radio gag-writer who had hit the jackpot with his first effort three years earlier and decided to stay with the theatre.

"Al's a little weak on character," David said, "but I'll fix up that part of it." He stood up. "I've got a late lunch," he said. "Hope you'll forgive me."

"Oh, sure," they said, rising.

Later they spent half an hour jotting down ideas over a steak at a restaurant on 54th Street.

"What do you think?" Hank said.

"I've got some melodies and things at my place," Dan said. "Why don't we get together tomorrow morning and run over some stuff?"

"Fine. I have a few loose things, too."

"We'll have to arrange to get at a piano, of course."

It always seemed to start that way, with old music, snatches of old lyrics that had never been published. Later, the pressure of a deadline or the ambition to excel would squeeze fresh inspiration out of them. There was time enough.

Dan liked working with Hank. He himself was richest in melodic ideas, Hank was richest in lyrics. Each served as astute advisor for the other.

They read the story in the form of the original satirical novel, then went over Al Lewis' version.

"What do you think?" Hank said.

"Beats me," Dan answered. "At this stage they either look

110

good or bad depending on your digestion. Who knows how to tell a hit from—"

"All right," Hank said. "No speeches." He poured a drink. "I have an idea," he said, "for the spot in the first act where Billy runs into Patty, or whatever they call her in the book."

"Miss Miller."

"Yeah. It's where they meet, ya know, on the outskirts of the town. I have a title—'We Haven't Been Properly Introduced.' "

Dan looked at the ceiling, repeating the title.

"Sounds okay," he said.

"I think it can be cute," Hank said. "You see the bit. As far as they know they're the only people in the world and it's funny if they don't speak because they haven't been introduced. Billy should lead into the number because he's the square, you see? He's the society boy. Miss Miller, the waitress, she's ready, but Billy is still the gentleman, even standing there in his dirty T-shirt or whatever the hell he's wearing."

In a week they had finished the number and Hank had started working on another lyric to a melody of Dan's.

"It's beautiful," he said, running it over at the piano in Al Schwartz's office, reading a lead sheet. "This how it goes?"

"Yes," Dan said, listening, smiling.

"Beautiful."

"Wait," Dan said, "don't play that chord right there, the E flat minor. Makes it sound too much like the change in 'You Go To My Head.' "

"Yeah, you're right."

"Here," Dan said, walking to the piano, leaning over Hank's shoulders to hit the chord. "Don't get up."

Hank laughed.

"What's funny?"

"That don't-get-up bit. Ever notice at a party where there are seventy thousand piano players they all keep screaming 'don't get up' to each other and at the same time they're climbing all over the poor guy at the piano?"

Dan hit the chord change again.

"You got it now?"

111

"Yes."

It felt good to be at work but after a few days they began to realize that things were going slowly. Since Dan felt that it was his fault he was first to mention it.

"Forget it," Hank said. "So you've got problems on your mind. That's okay. We'll get it."

There was a pause, as Dan listlessly fingered chords at the piano.

"How's Elaine?" Hank said.

"Fine."

"Look," Hank said, "I'm not prying, you know that."

"Certainly," Dan said.

"I'm neutral in this thing. I like you. I like Helen. But I also like Elaine. She's quite a hunk of woman."

"I didn't realize you knew her that well."

"Oh, yeah. Didn't I ever tell you? I've known her for a long time. Through Barton. In fact I took her out once, just once, about two years ago, I think it was."

"Who was she going with at the time?" Dan had no clear idea as to why he had asked the question.

"I don't know," Hank said. "Nobody special that I ever knew of. I mean, you know, she was just one of a million girls around town."

Dan looked up with a slight frown.

"I didn't mean that the way it sounded," Hank said. "You know what I mean. She was just working for Barton, and any guy who happened to be around—Oh, the hell with it. Let's get back to work."

Dan stood up. "I guess I can't come up with anything right now," he said. "Let's forget it for today."

That night, as he and Elaine were riding in a cab toward Luchow's restaurant, Dan said, "How long have you known Hank?"

"Gosh," Elaine said. "Let me see. I guess I met him a couple of years ago. I hadn't seen him for a long time, though, until I met you."

"Who were you going with at the time?"

"Why, sweetie? Why do you want to know?"

"No special reason."

112

"Well, you must have had a reason to ask the question."

"Why don't you just answer it, then," he said, "and stop trying to psychoanalyze me?"

"I'm not trying to psychoanalyze you," she said. "That's a ridiculous thing to say."

"Oh, hell," he said. "What are we fighting about?"

"Nothing," she said.

They rode on in silence. He was still concerned that she had not answered his question. For the next several days he was in a depressed state.

One midnight he lay in the darkness, wide-eyed, wondering if she had fallen asleep. Angled strips of light from the street lamps came in through the venetian blind and made a dimly discernible pattern on the ceiling. For a while he counted the light bars in the pattern, first from one side, then the other.

"One, two, buckle my shoe," he said to himself. "Three, four, shut the door, in the morning we'll hunt for wi-uld boar. Five, six, pick up sticks, I see you're up to your same old tricks. Seven, eight, lay them straight. I'll meet you in the alley at half past eight."

Elaine breathed noisily, rolling toward him, and put her hand on his chest.

"You asleep?" she asked.

"What?" he said, although he had heard her.

"You alseep?"

"No, why?"

"I just wondered. I can't sleep either."

"It's the noise," he said. "There's no silence in the city. Listen."

"To what?"

"Everything. If you try you can even hear the refrigerator."

"Are you sure?" she said, after a moment.

"Well, something is humming," he said. "Just listen. There's some kind of a small, electric whirring, like something hidden deep in the walls, humming to itself."

They lay still for a few moments.

"You're right," she said. "I never noticed it before."

"There's no silence in the city at night," he said. "Listen to the clock ticking, and the floor creaking. Listen to the cars going by outside. Listen to your blood pounding in your head. Listen to the mockingbird."

She laughed and patted his stomach.

"You losing weight?" she asked.

"No," he said. "It's just this haircut."

"What?"

"I got a haircut today. Haircuts always make you look like you're losing weight."

"Why?"

"I don't know. I guess your head looks smaller."

"Have you weighed yourself lately?"

"No."

"Your stomach feels like you're losing weight."

"That tickles," he said, turning toward her. He put his hand on her stomach, playfully, then felt for her mouth in the darkness and kissed her vigorously as a flicker of desire shook him.

"That was good," she said, when their mouths separated.

"Yes, baby," he said, whispering, pulling her to him. He touched her hips lightly, and she made a soft, sleepy animal sound, slipping her arms under his shoulders.

"Ah, you're beautiful," he said, throwing back the blanket. It fell about their knees and she kicked it away impatiently, her body suddenly abandoned and eager.

For a long time they embraced, clinging together almost fearfully while a storm of passion raged, shaking the world with its violent gusts and unexpected tremors, blinding them with its remorseless force and fury, frightening them with its overpowering strength, maddening them with its compulsion. When the hurricane reached its insensate climax they shrieked wildly, like buffeted animals, then slowly relaxed as the winds stopped howling in the corners of their minds. Whimpering slightly, utterly exhausted, holding each other, they helped each other to higher ground.

"That was good," she said.

"I love you," he said. "I'm sleepy."

"Don't go to sleep just yet," she said. "I want to talk."

"About what?"

"Not about anything, exactly. I just want to talk."

114

"Cabbages and kings," he said idly, slowly, his eyes closed. "Corn beef and cabbage. Maggie and Jiggs. Abercrombie and Fitch. Wheeler and Woolsey. Finan haddie. I have to go to the toilet."

"Well, go."

"I'm too tired."

"You're a lazy bum," she said, kissing him, as she stood up beside the bed.

"You're sure pretty," he said, observing her through half-closed eyes. She stepped toward the window and stood looking through the venetian blind out into the night, faint bars of light falling upon her breasts, stomach and legs.

"You're a zebra," he said.

"All right," she said, yawning. "It's pretty out. Maybe we can go for a ride tomorrow."

"I should do some work."

"Have you seen Hank?"

"No."

"Are you going to call him?"

"To hell with him. Let him call me."

"What if he says the same thing?"

"Then to hell with him."

"Fine thing."

"You may have a song title there," he said.

"What?" she said.

"Fine thing. It's not a bad title." he said. "You said you loved me—no. You promised you would love me. Hold no one above me. Now you're stepping out. Fine thing. You said you wouldn't leave me. Something about deceive me. Something about untrue. Fine thing."

"Why don't you work on a few things by yourself, if you're not happy working with Hank?" she asked.

"I didn't say I was unhappy working with Hank," he said. "I suppose I could write a few lyrics of my own again, although since 'Take My Heart' I haven't come up with much."

"That thing you were playing at the party the other night didn't sound bad."

"It didn't sound good." He sat up and put his bare feet on the floor, moving them past the edge of the rug. The wood felt

115

cold and comforting against the soles of his feet. "I don't know," he said. "This slop they're writing today. It's a crazy market. Sometimes I don't know which way to turn."

She came up behind him, kneeling on the bed, and kissed his back.

"You hungry?" she said.

"You?" he asked.

"A little."

"What do you feel like?"

"I don't know. How does milk toast sound?"

"I think it goes plop-squish," he said.

The next day, feeling slightly more cheerful, he telephoned Hank and made an appointment to meet him at Al Schwartz's office in the Brill Building on Broadway. Some writers he knew were standing on the sidewalk outside the building but he put his head down so that his hat covered his face and walked in without speaking to them.

He walked into the elevator and stood stiffly, trying to hold himself apart from the people pressed in around him. His eyes were only four or five inches away from the neck of the man in front of him. The neck was reddened and creased, and the hair too long, curling in random wisps over the collar. He looked at the ceiling and coughed apologetically as the elevator stopped suddenly, causing him to sway against the woman at his side.

"Three out," the operator said. There was pressure from the rear of the car and the man with the red neck stepped out into the hall. Dan followed him and they stood aside to let a short, stocky woman out.

You always felt smug and condescending when you stepped out of an elevator to make an exit easier for another passenger, Dan thought. When you stepped back into the car it was difficult to suppress a very slight but nonetheless undeniable feeling of pride in the graciousness of your gesture.

When he reached Schwartz's office Hank was already there. They went to the small room with the piano and got right to work.

CHAPTER
TWELVE

DAN and Hank had gone to the Inkwell before. It was a smallish café on Third Avenue that served as a hangout for the newspaper crowd, but at its mention this time Dan drew back in what almost seemed like genuine alarm.

"The Inkwell?" he said thickly. "You won't catch me eating in a joint with a name like that. Inkwell! Pooey!"

"What's the matter with the Inkwell?" Hank asked. He was beginning to get a little irked at Dan's drunken good spirits.

"They probably sauté their meatballs in Parker's Quink, that's what's the matter," Dan said, contorting his face and turning his head slowly from side to side. "Besides, I don't like 'hangouts,' if you know what I mean."

"What *do* you mean?" Hank said.

"I mean I don't like to go to a place just because it's a place that particular groups of people go to."

"You're drunk," Hank said.

"Up yours," Dan said. "I'm not drunk. I just don't like to be going to a place to eat just because it's a place where newspaper people go."

"Look, Dan," Hank said, "I'm going there to eat. I don't give much of a damn who else eats there, but now that you make such a point of it the place isn't exactly a joint. It was good enough for Hemingway."

"I didn't say it was a joint," Dan mumbled. "So let's eat there and to hell with it. And to hell with Hemingway." He was singing softly as they got into a cab. "Across the River and into the Trees . . . to grandmother's house we go."

"Where to, Mac?" the driver said, without turning around.

"Driver, go to the corner of 34th and Caterpillar and step on it," Dan said, chuckling. "That's a joke I heard on the radio once, driver."

"Shut up," Hank said. "Go to Third Avenue and turn left. I'll tell you when to stop."

At the restaurant they ordered drinks, then for a few minutes examined the menu in a silence of indecision.

"I'm not very hungry," Dan said. "Maybe a sandwich . . ."

"Do you like tongue?" Hank said.

Dan made a face. "No," he said. "When I taste something, I don't like to have it taste me back."

"You're still drunk," Hank said. A waiter appeared from nowhere and stood beside the table, head cocked slightly to one side in the familiar birdlike attitude customarily struck by people waiting deferentially for orders.

"I'll have the ground sirloin," Dan said, "on the lunch." The waiter wrote silently, then cocked his head in Hank's direction.

"The same," Hank said. "Coffee *now,* please." When the man was gone Dan said, "You can't get a bad cup of coffee in New York. I wonder why."

"You're probably not trying hard enough," Hank said. "But it's the water. Wonderful water here. They ought to bottle it. Anybody who couldn't make a good cup of coffee with this water ought to give up." Carried away he reached for the glass of water before him and drained it.

"This is a great town," Dan said. "I feel sort of at home here."

"Yeah," Hank said, "but who can say anything new about New York? It's all been said already. Too many guys have taken a crack at it. Even what I'm saying right now must have been said before."

118

Dan fell silent and sat listening to the hum and clink and soft babble of the restaurant, then he said suddenly, "Look, Hank, I'm really not drunk. I'm just pleasantly high, which I guess is obvious, but I know what I'm talking about. And I want to apologize for not having come up with the stuff lately, you know?"

"Forget it," Hank said. "You know that when it comes to writing you can't force it. Either it's there or it's not."

"Yeah."

"Besides, I presume that the song-writing hang-up is incidental and minor. I guess the main problem is Elaine, isn't it?"

"Yes."

Hank sat twiddling the ice cubes in his Scotch and soda with a small, blue plastic stick, while Dan told him the complete story, filling in details he had not before revealed. From time to time he would say, "Uh-huh," or very quietly "Wow," or "Rough," or "That's too bad." At last he said, "Look, I'm not sure what role I should be playing here. I mean, am I just the sympathetic friend, just an open ear, just a sounding board? Or do you want advice, do you want my opinion?"

"Certainly I do," Dan said.

"I don't think so," Hank said.

"What?"

"You heard me. When a guy's in a spot like yours I think all he wants is somebody to tell his troubles to. That's why bartenders are so popular. I don't think you really want any advice."

"I don't know," Dan said. "Maybe you're right. Maybe the reason I'm not too keen on soliciting advice is that the advice I think I'm going to get is just the order to straighten myself out, to go back to Helen, to get Elaine out of my system, and that, as I've learned, is all wasted breath. It's like telling an alcoholic 'You really ought to stop drinking, pal.' "

Hank caught a waiter's eye and raised two fingers.

"This is a hell of an imposition, I know," Dan said. "And that's another terrible part of the deal. Not only am I hung up myself but I have, over to one side, the knowledge that I've become something of a drag to my friends. I'm afraid that I'm carrying my problem around like a large rock on my shoulders.

It keeps getting into conversations whether I want it to or not."

"I just got through saying I wasn't going to hand out any advice," Hank said, "but I feel a few ideas coming out. Why the hell don't you just get a divorce from Helen and get it over with? You know—pull the tooth and stop the ache."

"If I could bring myself to do that I'd be in a better spot, I suppose. But I can't seem to make any decision and then make it stick."

"Is it a religious hang-up? Is that it?" Hank said.

"Oh, to a great extent, sure."

"Too bad," Hank said. "That makes it difficult for me to speak."

"What do you mean?"

"Well, I have some ideas but they might not sit too well with you because you're a Catholic."

"No, go ahead. Shoot. We're friends."

"That's probably what they said to Servetus before he shot off his mouth," Hank said, smiling.

"So?" Dan said, not bothering to admit that he didn't know who Servetus was.

"Well," Hank said, "I think half of your problem is real, and simple and rough. I don't underestimate it a bit. But I think half of it is, well, imaginary. I think that half is brought into existence simply because you're an Irish Catholic. Now, does my saying this bug you?"

"No," Dan said. "Say whatever you want."

"Well, to begin with," Hank said, "I don't think you would have gotten into this spot if you weren't Catholic."

"How the hell do you figure that?"

"Here's what I mean. To me it's obvious that you're married to a woman for whom you're completely unsuited. She's a nice gal, but not for you. From what I've observed of my fellow man this sort of thing is much more apt to happen to a Catholic, at least in this country, in this society, than it is to, say, a Jew. Or a Protestant. Or a nothing. The reason is that you people make such a god-damned big bugaboo of sex that when it finally looms in your life you're very apt to get thrown by it. Other people can play it down, can laugh it off, can muddle through it. But you people often get hung up. If you

120

get the breaks and make a good marriage, and I'm sure a lot of you do, all well and good. But as often as not a young Catholic kid like you gets hot pants and, wham, he marries the first girl he sleeps with."

In spite of his determination to listen open-mindedly Dan began to feel in his stomach a certain unpleasant traditional reaction, a certain resentment and withdrawal. Hank did not seem to notice it.

"It's my guess that's what happened to you. As I say, it's far less likely to happen to a Jewish boy. Jews are, I don't know exactly how to put it, more sophisticated about sex, at least relatively. Don't misunderstand me. Jewish kids, girls particularly, are very serious about sex and virginity and marriage. What the hell, who *isn't?* What I mean is that the religious Jews don't take it all lightly, but on the other hand they don't *avoid* the subject. They don't let it loom as a great big threatening monster. So as a rule they make pretty good marriages. That doesn't mean there aren't plenty of neurotics among us and plenty who get a bum shake or marry too early to the wrong person, but in general—well, you know what I mean. Now, a divorce to a Jew, to a religious Jew, let's say, is a great tragedy. But if it has to be, it has to be. It's a terrible, terrible thing but it happens and you do the best you can to rebuild your life. For a guy in your position, though, it seems to me the divorce will probably come to pass anyway in the long run but it may wreck the entire rest of your life because you'll *never* stop feeling guilt, you'll never stop feeling like a worthless sinner. And you realize that, I'm sure. It's partly that thought that makes you draw back from the break, that frightens you. Am I right?"

"Yes," Dan said, looking at the tablecloth.

"Let me ask this," Hank said. "Could you get a divorce and remain a Catholic?"

"Technically," Dan said, "it could happen. In practice I don't think it ever works out. Oh, if you're seventy-five years old I don't suppose it makes any difference to you whether you're married or not as long as you've got three squares a day and somebody to talk to. But when you're a young Catholic and you're divorced what the hell are you supposed to do? Live the life of an ascetic? Lotsaluck. So it all adds up to the fact that if you do get a divorce you're pretty much blowing your life anyway, because either you still feel a Catholic intellectually and emotionally but you can't live a Catholic life while cut loose from your moorings or else—or else—"

"Or else what?" Hank said.

"I don't know," Dan said. "I forget how I was going to end the sentence."

"That's interesting," Hank said.

"What's so interesting about it?"

"Well, it seemed to me you were going to consider the possibility of leaving the Church but suddenly your mind just blotted out the idea."

Dan frowned. "I guess you're right," he said. "That prospect does frighten me. It would kill my people."

"Your people, your people," Hank said. "Frig 'em! Consider this problem in terms of the *principals* involved. You, Helen, the children, Elaine. That's all. To hell with your people. You've got enough trouble without muddling up the issue with what your relatives think."

"But you don't understand," Dan said. "To the Irish—"

"Ah," Hank laughed, sardonically, "the Irish. I'm no expert on the subject, mind you, but it seems to me you Irish would be more concerned in a difficulty like this with what your mothers and uncles and society would think than with what God would think."

"God?" Dan said, blankly.

"Yes."

"I thought you weren't a religious Jew," Dan said.

"I'm not," Hank said. "I'm sort of a free-lance Unitarian operating individually. But not an atheist. My idea of God isn't what yours is but I figure something had to make the universe. It's that simple. But what is it with you Irish? You don't even seem to get the laughs or beauty out of your religion that the French and Italians and Mexicans do. I don't say the Spaniards because they're a special case and a gloomy one, I think. But other American Catholics seem to have an idea of the width and breadth of their religion. You Irish seem to have a very narrow concept of it. It's a funny thing; I grew up in San Francisco so I didn't have the problem of living with Boston Irish or Chicago Irish or New York Irish and getting my head kicked in like a lot of Jews I know. To me the Irish always seemed a likeable, fun-loving people, dripping with charm. There's no mystery about where I got the idea, of course. All I knew about the Irish I gathered from the standard theatrical sources. The Irish to me were all like Pat O'Brien or Jimmy Cagney or Spencer Tracy or Barry Fitzgerald. They seemed gay and poetic and jovial. They seemed almost Jewish, if you dig what I mean. When I went East it came as a shock to me to learn that the big-city middle- or lower-class Irish were nothing at all as Hollywood and legend had pictured them. You still want me to level with you?"

"Certainly," Dan said, feeling a mixture of fascination and resentment, but determined to mask the resentment part.

"Well," Hank continued, "I now understand, I think, why the American Irish are what they are. I've learned about the nineteenth century misery they went through; the terrible poverty in the old country, the famines, the hatred of the English and the Protestants. I know all about the harsh treatment the English gave them. And I know about the shocking welcome they got here in the land of the free and the brave. The crummy slums they were forced into, like the Puerto Ricans today; the uppity airs of the earlier immigrants, the 'No Irish Need Apply' signs in windows and in want-ads. Believe me, it takes a Jew to feel sympathy with a set of circumstances of that sort. We've had it. And we're still having it. The Irish aren't the only people who were ever oppressed. But they seem reluctant to let go of the old hatreds. They seem so brain-washed in intolerance directed against themselves that they've sopped up that intolerance and now are determined to give the world more than they got, more than good measure."

"I can't argue with you there," Dan said, "except to point out what you already know, that we're dealing in generalizations. But you're right on that last point. It has taken me

123

years to get over my early indoctrination as an *against er*. We Irish were against the Jews, against the Protestants, against just about everybody, I guess, often including ourselves."

"Right," Hank said. "And where the hell is the charity and Christianity in that? Where is the brotherly love? What happened to turn-the-other-cheek? Oh, I know there are some saintly priests and nuns, but they're the exceptions, right?"

"Right," Dan said.

"But we're digressing," Hank said. "All I wanted to establish is that you, being Irish, may not even understand your own religion completely. I've been to Italy. I've lived in Rome and I can tell you for a fact that those Catholics who are in your Holy City have a far more relaxed and compassionate sort of faith than you American Irish Catholics. Now does any of this help you with your problem?"

"I don't know," Dan said, "but I appreciate your taking the time to talk it out with me."

"Well," Hank said, "it just bugs me that people never appreciate their own resources. Americans today don't appreciate what Americanism really means. Most Jews I know don't understand their heritage. And from observation of my Catholic friends I would guess that not one of you in a thousand has any real feeling for what your Church is. For all I know there may be something in your religion that could give you the strength to pull yourself out of a difficulty like this, although I doubt it because I think you've stumbled into a trap from which religion can't be the thing that will free you. But the point is that to most of you people your religion seems to be a matter of church attendance, hating the Communists, lighting candles, praying for the impossible, and reading some second-rate diocesan newspaper. Let me ask you this: have you ever read Aquinas?"

"No," Dan said.

"Augustine? Meister Eckhardt? St. John of the Cross? The Papal Encyclicals?"

"No, I haven't," Dan said, "but how the hell do you know about all these things?"

"Courses in comparative religion and philosophy at college," Hank said, "plus the influence of my old man who used to read everything in the world. We had a great library in our home. I've looked into the Church. It wasn't for me but at least I have a pretty good idea of its dimensions. You don't. And you're not the exception. What do you think of the Inquisition?"

"I don't know," Dan said, automatically resenting the question. "I guess I'm sort of ashamed of it by proxy."

"All right," Hank said, "but you should also know that the position of the Inquisitors is far from completely indefensible. You probably aren't aware that in the fourteenth century the rivalry between the Franciscans and the Dominicans was so rough that it makes the rivalry betwen the Republicans and the Democrats today in this country look like child's play. Religion, in that day, was to the common man what politics is today. In our time we don't seem to find it strange that men are imprisoned or even put to death for political heresy, so in that time it wasn't strange that men were punished for theological heresy. But forgive me; I didn't mean to turn this into a lecture. I just wanted to make the point that you shouldn't regard your religion just as a terrible big black figure of authority, something that points the finger at you because of the mess you've gotten yourself into. In one sense the Church is just people. About four hundred million people, practically none of whom gives a good god-damn *what* you do."

CHAPTER

THIRTEEN

THE FIRST five weeks in New York seemed to go quickly, and then it was Christmastime and Dan flew home to visit with the children. Helen was stiff and prim but not cold. When, however, after two days she realized he was going back to New York she became alternately morose and sarcastic.

"Well," she said, standing in the driveway as he put his bags back into the car, "I hope we didn't keep you from your work."

"I don't want to argue," Dan said. "I'm sorry I have to stay on in New York but I do, that's all. You can't write a Broadway musical from three thousand miles away."

"Oh, that's all right," she said. "Don't worry about me, I'm only your wife."

On the plane going East he felt drained of emotion, unable to feel excitement even at the prospect of being reunited with Elaine.

Once back in town he threw himself into his work. A first draft of the book of the show had been completed and Dan and Hank read it avidly, noting the places where songs were called for, making additional suggestions of their own as to positions for musical numbers.

"Al has done a hell of a job, I think," Hank said, seated at the small piano that Dan had rented.

"I agree. The ending of the first act needs to be punched up, but in general the thing looks good. What do you think of writing a new lyric to 'A Good Time Was Had by All' for the opening number?"

"The song that was cut from the Carson picture?"

"Yes."

"Okay by me. It's good and peppy. Got any ideas?"

"Yes," Dan said. "In the scene here where Al has Tommy coming back up out of Carlsbad Caverns to find that civilization seems to have been misplaced, the script calls for a song with the dummy title 'Where Did Everybody Go?' I think that hits it a little too much right on the head. How about something like 'As I Was Saying'?"

"When I was so rudely interrupted?"

"Right," Dan said, playing the familiar melody they had written three years earlier but which had never been published and recorded. "The title will have to go right at the top."

"Yeah," Hank said. For a minute he bit his lip and stared at the carpet. Then, rising, he tentatively sang, "As I was saying, when I was so rudely interrupted . . . As I was saying, just the other day . . . You have to take the bitter with the sweet . . . er—something about—you have to learn to land on your feet."

"We can change the melody at the end of the first four bars," Dan said, "to make it fit."

In half an hour the song was finished, at which point they decided they didn't like it after all, discarded it, and made a fresh start.

"You know what?" Dan said. "Maybe 'Where Did Everybody Go?' isn't such a bad title after all."

"Let's try it," Hank said. "How about something to the effect that Tommy is forgetful, absent-minded. Always mislaying things."

"I get you," Dan said. "So now he's misplaced the whole human race."

"That's it."

"Memory," Dan said speaking very slowly, toying with words. "Forget. Elephant. Elephants never forget. I consider it wholly irrelevant . . . to observe that an Indian elephant . . . has a memory vastly superior . . . to mine. Can you rhyme elephant and irrelevant?"

"They're close enough," Hank said.

In a week they had four songs completed. Halliburton liked three of them. Dan could scarcely wait to tell Elaine the good news.

"That's wonderful, honey," she said, setting a dinner of creamed salmon and peas in front of him.

"He was very complimentary," Dan said. "And I could tell he meant it."

"Oh, I *hope* the show's a hit for you," Elaine said. "If it is you won't have to worry about money at all, will you?"

"No," he said. "But I have no serious worries now. There's enough to take care of Helen and the kids back home, you and me here, and my mother, too. The only thing is we'll just have to be a little careful, that's all."

"I don't want you to think I'm prying into your financial affairs," she said.

"No problem, angel. Thanks chiefly to ASCAP I can count on about forty thousand a year. God, it's funny. When I was a kid if anybody had told me I'd have to pull in my belt a little on forty thousand dollars a year I would have told him he was crazy. But I guess that's the American way; no matter how much money you make you always seem to spend just a few more dollars than you're taking in."

"It does seem that you ought to be able to manage nicely on that amount."

"Sure," he said. "Don't worry. We'll make out. It's just that the house payments run a little high and then maintaining two separate set-ups is going to, you know, add up. But to hell with it. Frankly I've never cared much about money. As long as there's enough around to get by on I don't get neurotic about not having a lot in the bank. And as far as you and I are concerned I wouldn't care if we lived in a shack."

128

"I wouldn't either," she said, squeezing his hand across the table.

Later that night they were lying in bed when the people upstairs began to fight. The people upstairs were always fighting. The man would get drunk and shout at the woman and she would shout back and they would swear and threaten each other and now and then there would be a thud or a slight crash as if somebody had been shoved or a drinking glass had been thrown. Dan and Elaine would sit listening, their eyes on the ceiling, looking at each other and giggling, or gasping with mock horror. No matter how violent the argument it always seemed somehow comic to them.

This particular night the debate started in a low key and Dan pressed his ear against the wall to hear better, but soon the voices were raised and, though they were muffled, words began to come through distinctly.

"And another thing," the man said drunkenly, "tell that lousy brother of yours to stay outta here!"

"Never mind my brother," the woman shouted. "Just you worry about your own half-ass relatives! Your mother comes in here once more makin' cracks about the wallpaper and everything and I'm gonna tell her which end is up!"

The man was evidently livid at the introduction of his mother's name into the argument. He let out a bellow of rage and at that Dan walked to the door and boldly opened it to hear better.

"Do you think we ought to call the police?" Elaine whispered, wide-eyed.

"No, they're all right," Dan said. "Listen!"

"My mother?" the man screamed and then he said a line that Dan and Elaine repeated to each other for months. It could always make them laugh.

"My mother?" he said. "Listen! I hope *your* mother is half as decent as *my* mother will *ever* be!"

The line always reminded Dan of something a bus driver had said to him one morning at the Greyhound station in Los Angeles. It was years before when he had first gone to Los Angeles. Helen was coming in on an early bus and he had gone to the station to meet her, but she had not been on the bus when it came in nor was she on the one that arrived half an hour later. He walked over to the driver of the second bus.

"Pardon me," he said, "but if a person wasn't on one of these two buses would she be on one of the others arriving this morning?"

"Well," the driver said, "that's hard to say. Tell me . . . where do you want to see somebody from?"

In time he came to half-suspect that his love affair with the city of New York was partly a palliative, something to make him stop thinking of himself and his predicament.

They did the town feverishly, rushing from spot to spot, while Dan did more than his usual amount of drinking. They kissed openly in taxis and held hands under tables and most of the time were very gay and happy.

On rainy days, if the mood would come upon them, they would haunt the museums and art galleries. Sometimes a walk down 57th Street would satisfy them, and they would pause before the gilt-framed canvases in the windows of the exclusive dealers.

One time Elaine referred to one of the shops as an "exclusive salon" and Dan picked the phrase up and worried it back and forth. "I wonder why this town is full of exclusive salons, and exclusive restaurants, and exclusive hotels, and exclusive shops," he said. "The word really doesn't mean much any more. Just whom do these places exclude?"

Elaine said, "One-legged Eskimos without enough money," and they both laughed and concentrated again on the high-priced paintings in the windows.

At other times nothing but the Museum of Modern Art or the Metropolitan itself would do. They would gorge their esthetic appetite, hurrying from canvas to canvas, absorbing in one afternoon the artistic output of a thousand years. Once, when a guide's back was turned, at the Metropolitan, Dan furtively fingered the brittle brush-clumps of oil applied by Van Gogh to one of his late-period canvases. It gave him a curious thrill to feel the actual paint, the selfsame colors that had once lain moist and shiny on the canvas, oozing slightly in the warmth of a long-gone afternoon in the south of France.

At the Museum of Modern Art they were fascinated by a giant work of Tchelitchev's, a wild, churning cauldron of reds and greens that at first inspection seemed to depict a violently twisted tree. As they stared at it the limbs of the tree and the spaces between the limbs, the crotches and forks of the branches, became the ghostly outlines of gnomish children and strange foetus-like sprites. They stood hypnotized before the painting for a full half hour, every few seconds deciphering a part of the puzzle. It reminded Dan of the old "How-many-faces-can-you-find-in-this-picture?" advertisements that used to run in pulp magazines years ago, but he was deeply impressed and admitted it. The title of the work, "Hide-and-Seek," they found somehow tawdry and obvious, but Elaine guessed that perhaps the original title had been Russian and something had happened to it in translation.

The colors were unlike anything they had seen before. Just bright greens and glowing reds, but there was something unique about them. The green was glaring, mint-jello, jungle-glen, emeralds in the sun, merging into darker, bile-like shades. The red was fire-truck, blood on snow, maraschino, danger-sign, and in patches it swirled and faded off into lighter shades like flesh bleeding slowly in still water.

Dan sat down on a bench and began making notes on the back of an envelope.

"What are you writing?" Elaine asked.

"Just a little something," Dan said. "Got a sort of Edgar Allan Poe type idea from this Technicolor nightmare here. It's about a deranged artist who, living in sepulchral solitude, paints strange, sullen canvases using no paints, no palette . . ."

"No paints?" Elaine said.

"That's right," Dan said, scribbling again. "Instead he has a freshly killed cadaver stretched out on a marble-topped table. The blood, humours, and juices of the corpse serve as paints and colors."

"Blood for red and that sort of thing?" Elaine suggested.

131

"Yes," he frowned, "although blood turns brown after it dries. Anyway, it's an idea I may be able to use sometime."

"I seem to recall from Biology One that the gall bladder has oodles of green in it."

"Sure. Using fat-tissue and lymph for mixing solvent, I imagine . . ." His words trailed off as he wrote, then putting the envelope back in an inside pocket, he rose, took her arm, and they left the museum.

Outside, the city looked as bleak as a garbage dump on a rainy day. The days were getting shorter now, and feeling the need of a gloom-chaser they stopped in for a drink at a small restaurant on 54th Street.

When they came out darkness had fallen. Here and there up through the asphalt streets steam flowed from the subway vents under the surface and swirled briefly, billowing like frothy white tulle against the black velvet of the macadam.

One unusually warmish Sunday in March they went to the East River to paint. Dan parked the car on 116th Street and they piled canvas, Bristol board, paints, sweaters, and a paper bag containing sandwiches and a carton of milk into each other's arms, then hurried across the East River Drive when the endless line of traffic faltered momentarily. An iron-spike fence bordering the drive blocked their path and they had to take turns climbing over, transferring their paraphernalia from one to the other until at last, breathless and laughing, they were over the fence, across the strip of grass, and on the sidewalk that led to the 114th Street promontory.

From time to time while they painted, their backs aching, shadows would fall across their canvases and, looking up, they would see that people had stopped to appraise their work. At first Dan resented the presence of the gawkers, but after a few minutes he became used to it and once or twice even shifted his painting so a passing critic could get a better look.

"I guess there are three times when it's okay for strangers to stop and act like old friends," Dan said. "When they see you with a puppy, a baby, or a painting."

That week Walter Winchell printed an item to the effect that Mrs. Dan Scanlon no longer liked Mr. Dan Scanlon's words and music. After that Dan did not try to hide Elaine. They appeared openly in public. They visited many people in the city although their absorption in each other tended to prohibit any extensive enlargement of their circle of friendships.

One day Dan took Elaine along to Halliburton's apartment. She seemed to find the older man charming.

"Aha," he said, "you must be the reason friend Daniel is taking so long to come up with a score." They all laughed but the remark made Dan uncomfortable.

Twice during the afternoon he noticed that Halliburton was staring at Elaine and when they had left his apartment Dan mentioned it.

"Sweetheart," Elaine said, "don't be silly. Naturally I was *pleasant*. What did you want me to be, *rude?*"

"Of course not," Dan said, "but did you have to sit so close to him on the sofa?"

"Angel," Elaine said, "I didn't sit close to *him*. He sat close to me. I was seated there first."

"Oh, hell," Dan said. "You know what I mean."

"No, to tell the truth, I don't. What *do* you mean?"

"Aw, let's not turn this into the Lincoln-Douglas debates," Dan said sullenly. "I just didn't like the attention he was paying you, that's all."

"Well, then bite *his* head off, not mine."

Suddenly Elaine stopped in her tracks as they approached Fifth Avenue. "Look," she said, "what do I have to do to prove my love for you? I've given up my job, I've come all the way back here. My friends are finding out that I'm living with you. I know what some people are saying, even the most sophisticated of them. But I'm not complaining. I'm here with you because I love you. If you don't believe that I do then what am I trying to prove? Where are we headed?"

Dan walked on, grim-lipped.

"What is it?" Elaine said. "Is this nastiness on your part just because of your guilt feelings? Are you trying to take it out on me?"

"I'm not trying to do anything," Dan said, wearily. "And now, if you don't mind, I'll just drop you off at Polly's."

Later that night, repentant, he telephoned, but Polly answered.

"Elaine's not here," Polly said. "She's having dinner with an old friend of hers from Philadelphia."

The next day Dan discovered that the gentleman was seventy-four years old, but the experience unnerved him.

Another evening Elaine walked into the apartment while he was on the phone talking to Helen and the children, telling them that he didn't expect to be in New York too much longer. They had a quick, bitter argument, after which Elaine swore at him and walked out. When, in a few minutes, his anger had subsided he was filled with a deep longing and a sense of hopelessness. Something of the desperation he felt at that moment led him to concoct a plan. The only way he might ever be able to break away from her, he thought, was to become interested in some new woman, to deliberately, callously, form an attachment, even if it was only sexual, that would serve as a pain-killer. He called up a couple of women he knew and took one of them to dinner. Three or four days passed in confusion, guilt, and loneliness.

This time, after a while, his longing for Elaine assumed the form of jealousy. Coming out of his building he met an old friend he hadn't seen in over fifteen years. They had gone to high school together.

"Well, Dan, you old son of a gun."

"Sid Franklin! Well, I'll be darned. Old Sid."

"How you doin', you old bastard?"

"Oh, just fine. How's yourself?"

"Great. I'm just in town for two days. What are you doing now?"

They continued with all the clichés and just when they were getting down to the "Let's-get-together's" and "Listen-let-me-hear-from-you-once-in-a-while's" Sid said, "Say, I'm going to a sort of party this evening. If you're not doing anything why don't you come along? You may know some of the people."

Dan said it would be all right. He met Sid after dinner and went with him to the party. He didn't know any of the people and was the only unattached man in the room. He had two drinks, became morose and on a sudden irresistible impulse walked up to the hostess.

"Pardon me," he said, "but I was wondering if I might use your telephone for a minute. It's just a local call."

"Why, certainly," the woman said. "It's in there on the table, right by the little girls' room."

He walked in and sat down on the bed by the little girls' room. There were no little girls in it but almost immediately thereafter a big girl entered and threw up in the sink. While she was running the water and moaning softly he dialed the familiar number. The line was busy. He sat on the bed for a few minutes looking around the room and then dialed again.

Still busy.

Who the hell was she talking to? He went into the living room and talked to Sid for a few minutes, looking at his watch and trying to get interested in the party-talk. None of the people, it appeared, was in show business. Sid was in the infant's wear line and one of the women seemed to be a writer of some sort. It was hard to tell about the others. He looked at his watch, stalked back into the bedroom and began poking a vicious forefinger into the number holes. This time the phone began ringing at the other end of the line and he breathed deeply in relief. It rang twice, three times, four times.

Let it ring. She might be in the tub, or in the kitchen fixing a snack for Polly and herself, or asleep. He hung up and gritted his teeth and dialed again on the small chance that his finger might have made a mistake the first time. The phone began ringing again and he waited, perched tensely on the edge of the bed, his tongue licking his lips. After a long wait he put the phone back on the cradle softly, then tiptoed into the vestibule, picked up his trench coat and slipped out of the front door without saying good-bye to anyone. His mouth was a straight venomous line and there were tears of anger in his eyes. Where was she? It was only a little after ten o'clock. Out on a date with some operator probably. Or maybe, please, with Polly. Or maybe just out for the late papers and a cup of coffee at the drugstore.

By the time he found himself out in the street he could concentrate only on the idea that she was with some other man. The pictures that flashed before his mind's eye made him feel ill. He was at 79th and Park when he started walking and some time later he found himself sitting on the stone steps of the Plaza fountain, at 59th and Fifth Avenue, with his head in his hands.

He could scarcely remember having walked all that distance except that his feet were tired and his back ached. He sat there speaking in whispers, first to himself and then to her, asking her where she was and why she had gone out with someone else. He could take another girl out, laugh with her, kiss her goodnight, perhaps even sleep with her and think nothing of it, never bothering to see the girl again and never wanting to. But the thought of Elaine's even having a drink with another man could leave him weak and panting and frightened. He sat on the steps blowing his nose noisily until his eyes were dry and his back was thoroughly cold and tired, then he walked back to his room, stopping in a drugstore on the way for papers, toothpaste and razor blades. By the time he opened the door of his room he had fallen apart inside again. He stumbled into the room and dropped his package and newspapers on the floor, sobbing.

Like a snarling jackal he pounced on the phone and dialed her number. It wouldn't do any good, god-damn it! She'd still be out with that son-of-a-bitch, whoever he was. She still wouldn't be home and he would just have to sit up all night, calling her every few minutes until he found her in.

She wouldn't be home for—

"Hello?"

At the sound of her voice he drew in his breath and made a great effort to sound normal.

"Elaine?"

"Yes. Dan?"

"Yes, baby. It's me. I—were you out?"

"Yes, sweetie. Polly and I saw a movie and I—"

He had been wrong. God love her, she hadn't been with another man at all. His nose started to run.

"Baby, what's the matter?" she said.

"Nothing," he said. "I'm all right. I just—I'm just going crazy, that's all."

"Oh, sweetheart," she said, slowly. He could see her shaking her head from side to side. Then he broke down.

"Baby," she said. "What's the matter, honey? Don't cry, darling. Dan, listen to me. Where are you?"

"I'm here in my room," he said, fighting to control himself, losing the fight. "I want you. I want you. I can't help it. I just want you, that's all, and I can't help it. I want you." With some small separate part of his mind he knew he sounded like an idiot.

"Darling," she said, "listen. Are you all right for a minute?"

"What?"

"Never mind. Just sit right there, sweetheart. Don't move. I'll be there in five minutes."

"Will you, baby? Will you really? I love you so much . . . I—"

"Never mind, honey. Just sit right there. I'll be with you in just a few minutes."

The phone clicked in his ear and he put it back on the glass-topped desk. He sat right there in the chair, occasionally blowing his nose, till he heard a soft scuffle in the carpeted hall and a click as the door-handle turned. She was wearing a fur coat over a green silk print dress and her hair was disarrayed from the wind. She flew at him and flung herself on the floor, kneeling in front of him, smelling of perfume, her face feeling wonderfully cold against his warm brow.

"Darling, what's the matter?" she said, as if talking to a child.

"I'm sorry," he said. "I just couldn't do it. I tried. For days I tried. I just didn't have the strength, I guess."

She saw the newspapers and the package on the floor.

"What happened?"

"I don't know," he said. "When I walked in I fell apart. I guess I dropped everything."

"Oh, you poor angel," she said, patting his hand, kissing it. "What are we going to do?"

"I don't know," he said, frowning. "It seems that I just can't make it without you. Do you love me?"

She put her arms around him and kissed his forehead.

"If you know anything in the whole world for certain," she said, "you know I love you. I'll always love you. Sweetheart, we'll— Oh, I don't know. It's not up to me. We'll do whatever you want. If you want me to go, I'll go, but if you want me with you I'll stay with you and love you and fight for you and take care of you and cook for you and make a home for you and try to make you laugh when you're sad."

For no clear reason he laughed. They smiled at each other and he pulled her up onto his lap, patting her shoulder as if she were an infant. They never knew such tenderness and love as in these moments of reconciliation. Their hearts would swell and almost burst with emotion and they would sit smiling and staring at each other's faces as if they had never seen each other before or as if each moment might be the last not merely for themselves but for the whole precious universe. For a long time there would be a kind of simple, burning tenderness without passion that would bathe them in a warm haze that blotted out all the rest of the world and then, at a word or a movement, desire would suddenly leap into flame and consume them.

It hit them now, hard, and her nails dug lovingly into the back of his neck as he breathed into her ear. Without a word he stood and locked the door and they began hanging up their clothing, pausing to kiss and cling together. When she had removed her shoes and stockings but not yet her dress, they sat down on the bed for a moment and somehow never got up. She had stopped at her apartment long enough to put a dash of perfume between her breasts and he was inflamed now at the scent and at the warmth of her.

After a long time they lay back on the bed, their hands touching, fingers interlocked.

"My goodness," she said, smiling, mocking him, "the least you could have done was wait till I got my dress off."

"It's good silk," he said. "I don't think it'll wrinkle." He turned over and lay on his stomach looking down at her. "Darling, let's make a go of it this time. I'll try real hard, really I will."

"All right, angel," she said. "Remember, I love you. You're

all I want. I'll do anything to make you happy. I know you'll feel blue now and then . . . about the children . . . and your mother . . . and maybe you'll think that God doesn't love you, but I'll try to convince you that He does."

"Oh, it isn't that."

"Well, whatever it is, baby, I'll try to make it all right for you. I just love you so much. Do you get tired of hearing me say that?"

And so they lay together asking each other the timeless questions that lovers have asked throughout eternity, making the same evergreen jokes, swearing to the obvious vows, being very happy and very confident that the tomorrows would be better than the yesterdays.

After a while they left and went to Joe King's Rathskeller on Third Avenue for a late snack. It was an ancient, beery, German, musty, friendly place where college kids hung out on weekend nights and carved initials in the woodwork and the tables were covered with checkered tablecloths and the waiters were elderly and bored but competent. They walked downstairs to the bar and got into a conversation with a tall, burly good-looking Irishman who turned out to be Joe King. King was an expansive Irishman, one of the husky, placid, likeable sort who often end up as big-city politicians or heads of Catholic high schools or police officials. He was the Spencer Tracy–Pat O'Brien type of Irishman and it was easy for him to make Elaine and Dan feel at home. They each drank two glasses of dark beer and then walked upstairs to the street-level dining room and had dinner.

Placing a forkful of *Sauerbraten* in his mouth, Dan lifted his eyes and looked at a moose head jutting out of the wall near the ceiling. It was the largest he had ever seen and the drinking he had done before dinner made him see it in a fresh and twisted way.

Surely, he thought, there could be no more fantastic creature on Mars than a moose. Here was an animal who didn't stop growing on top as one might expect but whose skeleton kept right on growing through the top of his head, reaching up into the meatless air.

"What are you looking at?" Elaine said.

"Just a moose," Dan said. "Who was it that said every time he saw a moose head sticking out of a wall he couldn't help visualizing the rest of the beast attached right behind the head, buried in about eight feet of plaster and concrete?"

"I don't know," Elaine said, "but whoever he was I like him."

"Me, too," Dan said, signaling the waiter.

"Yes, sir?"

"I'd like some brown bread and butter, please," Dan said.

"I'm sorry, sir," the waiter said, apologetically. "We're all out of brown bread."

"Then bring me some white bread and Shinola."

The waiter frowned, puzzled. He disappeared and returned with a basket of rolls.

"I have an idea for you," Elaine said a few minutes later, buttering a roll. "Why don't you check the list of best-selling books as a source of good song titles?"

"That is a good idea," Dan said. "A lot of big hits have been named after novels. There was 'Stars Fell on Alabama' . . ."

"And 'I Cover the Waterfront.' "

"That's right. And 'Gone with the Wind.' "

"And 'Farewell to Arms.' "

"Right again," Dan said. "And let us not forget 'Tom Swift and His Flying Machine.' Nor must we overlook 'The Rover Boys at Vassar.' "

"Go ahead," Elaine said. "Be funny. But I still say you could keep a close check on what books are coming out, what the important novelists are writing, and get some really useful title ideas."

"Baby," Dan asked, "are you worried?"

"About what?"

"About my being able to write any more?"

The mood was changing again. Out of laughter so often would come the sudden, swooping numbness, the insidious pall. Elaine forced herself to smile.

"Don't be silly," she said. "You can write as well as you ever could."

"I wish I'd said that."

"Joke if you want to, but don't ever get the idea that I don't have confidence in you."

"Oh, I know you're for me, sweetie, but . . . I don't know. Maybe I need to be pushed, I need to have you tell me to get to work, but sometimes the pushing seems to be shoving. You can't write songs mechanically, although some guys do. A song just sort of comes to you while you're brushing your teeth."

"But isn't there such a thing as waiting too long for inspiration?"

"Only if you're waiting at a corner where it doesn't stop." He put down his fork and gripped his napkin nervously. "It's the same, really, whether you're talking about writing songs or designing skyscrapers. Relatively few of the world's worthwhile ideas have been arrived at as a result of painstaking study. The phenomenon of an idea's creation, it seems to me, is more often a sudden, mysterious thing. It almost seems as if all ideas hang waiting to be discovered in a dim—" he fumbled for the word, "in a dim psychical forest and man, stumbling headlong through the dusk, feels them suddenly brush against his face. The ideas, at least as I see it, seem to have a pre-existence and they await only accidental discovery."

"If there's a God who knows all things, including the future, there must be something in what you say, but . . ."

The discussion became too metaphysical to hold onto and it slipped from their fingers and was gone.

"The *Sauerbraten* was good," Dan said, wiping his mouth.

"You didn't eat your vegetables."

"So I didn't," he said, his mind thumbing through its files of unanswered questions, coming up with the pertinent one.

"I wonder," he said, "why man has to make such a fuss about getting a balanced diet, eating certain amounts of this and certain amounts of that when most animals eat simply meat or grass and seem to get along just fine."

"Maybe it's because animals can't read advertisements. They're not suckers for salesmen like people are."

"Clever, but not valid. We actually need the various vitamins and things. Without them our teeth fall out or our eyes get weak or our bones turn rubbery. But how come Lassie doesn't need orange juice?"

CHAPTER
FOURTEEN

DURING the next few weeks Hank and Dan spent a great deal of time together but Dan could not seem to make any productive contribution to the score. He contented himself with comments and criticisms on the lyrics and melodies that Hank suggested. One morning Hank said, "Look, Dan, here's a number I've finished myself. If you like you can work it over and make whatever changes seem good to you. But for right now I'm going to turn this in to Halliburton and tell him that the two of us wrote it."

"Why the hell are you going to do that?" Dan said.

"He's getting impatient, that's why. We should have finished at least the first draft of the score long before now. We can't put him off much longer."

"Ah, hell," Dan said, "we're weeks away from rehearsal. What's the big rush?"

Hank was silent.

"All right," Dan said. "I'm sorry. You're right. I don't know what's the matter with me. I just can't seem to get going."

"I understand," Hank said. "You've got other problems on your mind."

"Yeah."

"I don't want to butt into your affairs, but how are things going? Are you going to get a divorce?"

"I don't know," Dan said. "I doubt it."

In May he decided to make another trip home. When he told Elaine of his decision she said, "Certainly, baby. You ought to be out to see the children more often anyway. The trip will do you good."

"I've missed the kids very much," he said.

"Of course you have, sweetheart," she said. "It will do you a world of good to see them. I'll be here waiting for you. And if you decide not to come back to me, well, I won't approve, but I'll understand."

He kissed her.

"God, but I sound noble," she said. "I don't feel it at all. But I do mean what I'm saying."

In the cab on the way to the airport Dan felt wrung out, excited at the prospect of seeing the children, already embarrassed at the thought of seeing Helen and his mother. What would he say to them after all this time? He decided not to mention to Helen the trouble he was having with the show, with Halliburton. If suddenly Halliburton should call the deal off Dan would be left with no excuse for staying in New York and he found the prospect alarming.

His mother, of course, would by now have gotten the general story from Helen, albeit in biased form. But no, whatever she had said against him, she was right. She was entitled to a full measure of hatred, sarcasm, contempt. He had it coming.

An odd thing about this trip home was that it seemed more real than the first one, at Christmas. Then Dan's mind had been more confused, more withdrawn. He had moved and spoken as in a dream. Now he was conscious of the sensations of travel, the expectation of emotional exchanges. He felt more securely positioned in space and time.

He boarded the plane tiredly and sat with his chin in his hand looking out the window. On the ground two men in dirty white overalls were pushing a luggage-cart. He watched them as they came up close to the plane and disappeared into the foreground beneath his line of vision. The stewardesses walked back and forth up the aisle, speaking softly, hanging up overcoats, joking with passengers.

After a few minutes one of the plane's motors coughed and spat a puff of blue smoke. He watched a propeller TURN . . . TURN . . . TURN . . . turn . . . turn . . . turn-turn-turn-turn-turrnnnnn—and blur into disappearance as the pilot warmed the motors and the plane surged gently against its brakes.

A pale green light ordered that seat belts be fastened and the passengers complied, feeling faint twinges of tension in their stomachs, as well as the delicate mixture of elation and fear that seems to center in the solar plexus when one is about to take off in an airplane or leap from a diving board or ride on a roller coaster. The motors were roaring angrily now and the plane bucked slightly, anxious to be released. With a graceful movement it suddenly began to roll, turning slowly in a wide arc, and then laboriously it waddled out and away from the airport buildings and onto the wide straight open spaces of the field.

Dan's thoughts turned calmly and without panic to the possibility that there might be an accident during the take-off, but at such times he was never able to grant the idea more than temporary asylum. His thoughts turned, too, to God in a rather detached and indefinite way. He could rarely put into words what he felt at such times although now and then he would cheerfully mutter "God help us" as he sat pressed lightly against the back of the seat by the force of the craft's take-off, and when the wheels lifted and he felt the quick lack of contact with the ground and the pressure of his body down against the seat that indicated the plane was lifting itself rapidly, he would feel a quick flicker of gratitude that all had gone well. His emotion could not have been accurately labeled fear. It was a mild tension, a concentrated concern that always seemed to be in him when he flew.

The plane drifted up lazily through clouds, circled the sprawling smoky city and headed west.

He read leatherette-bound copies of *Time, Life,* and *Reader's Digest,* dozed, went to the toilet, took out a note-pad and jotted down a few ideas. Finally he fell into a heavy sleep.

"Sir, would you mind—"

A voice awakened him and he closed his dry mouth.

"We'll be landing soon. Is your seat belt fastened?"

The hostess loomed close over him, smiling. He nodded and said, "Oh," and closed the buckle of his seat belt with sleep-numbed fingers. They were landing at Chicago.

He got off the plane and had a cup of coffee in the airport lunch room. He was not certain but the faces of the employees seemed to look a little different from the New York faces. There were more blondes and there seemed something more Slavic in the faces.

He stopped at the cigar counter, bought postcards showing Soldier's Field, Michigan Boulevard, and The Wrigley Building for the children, picked up a pocket comb and a copy of the *Chicago Times*, walked around outside to stretch his legs and then got back on the plane.

It was too dark now to see the green and tawny quilt-patterned landscape of the Middle West as it rolled by far below. Now and then lights would glow dully in the bottomless darkness or a river would reflect for an instant a three-quarter moon that hung off to the right, but otherwise there was nothing to see when he looked through the window but the ghostly, gloomy reflection of his own face in the double glass.

Occasionally one of the pilots would address the passengers by means of a scratchy public address system but because of the insistent growling of the motors it was difficult to catch the message.

He sat with a cool, small pillow behind his head, his eyes closed, thinking of Elaine behind him in New York and Helen awaiting him in Los Angeles. He felt a longing without knowing what it was he desired and the pleasure of the trip was to a degree lessened by the fear that when he looked again into Helen's face he would see the same old expression of innocence and pain that had haunted him for so long.

He slept again for a short time and then was awakened by the smell of food. The dinner was good. Swiss steak with lima beans, a small green salad, a shortcake-like dessert made with blueberries and a too-sweet whipped cream, and a cup of coffee. He asked for more coffee, chatted briefly with the man seated on his left, who turned out to be a lawyer from Boston, read for a while and then dozed again.

He awakened hours later, feeling stiff and uncomfortably warm.

"I guess we're coming in," the man from Boston said.

"I guess so," Dan said, looking out the window. A million lights twinkled on the invisible ground thousands of feet under the plane, lights that lined up in partly orderly fashion, as if they were diamonds that had been neatly placed on black velvet by a meticulous jeweler who had then jostled the table slightly with his elbow. Here and there wisps of cloud and fog put a filmy layer of gauze over the diamonds and now, as the plane neared the more thickly populated parts of the Los Angeles area, colored neon jewels appeared.

The plane lurched suddenly and wheeled sharply to the left as the pilot began to line up with the field. Dan could look to his left and down across the aisle now and see the city-floor climbing crazily up the windows on the left side of the plane as the giant craft slipped down, turning through the night. Like a gull lowering its claws, feeling for sand to land on, the plane discharged its landing gear and lowered its wing-flaps, and though its speed was actually decreasing it seemed that they were traveling faster and faster as the four-motored giant hurried down and down, close to roof tops and oil towers and telephone wires and winking neon signs. In a moment the ship was traveling parallel to the ground at a height of about ten feet and then with a quick screech of rubber on concrete and an almost imperceptible thud the earth pressed up firmly against the wheels and the passengers relaxed their stomach muscles and began looking out the windows, trying to get their bearings, trying to see if familiar faces and forms were outlined against the airport buildings. When the plane stopped rolling Dan stood up, smiled a good-bye to the man from Boston and the stewardesses and put on his trench coat. He stepped out into the cool California night air and sniffed at it hungrily. It felt familiar and exciting to his nose. There was a peculiar smell of moist earth and growing things and the sea that he could always sense whenever he arrived suddenly, by

146

air, in California, although after a few minutes he could not notice it. It reminded him of the time years before in Chicago when he had spent an entire day at the stockyards. He had always before felt slightly ill driving past the yards, especially on hot summer days when the dusty red streetcar would loiter past the blocks of cattle pens and slaughter houses and the musty stench of death and urine, fecal matter and chemicals would assail queazy stomachs, but this particular day he had been astounded to learn that after half an hour inside the yards he could not notice the odor and that, by contrast, when at the end of the day he left the neighborhood, the relatively fresh air of the areas beyond the yards seemed for a moment foreign to his olfactory nerves. So it was that now as he walked into the waiting room at the Los Angeles airport he began to get used to the smell of the air, and after a few minutes it seemed normal and unnoticeable to him.

He had wired ahead that there was no point in her driving to pick him up. Within twenty minutes he had rented a car and was ready to head for the valley.

When he pulled into the driveway the house looked small and foreign to him. He felt that he had been away from it for many years, that he was a tired Ulysses returning from his travels. Helen opened the front door the moment his headlights arced across the front picture window and strolled out to meet him.

"Hi," he said, embarrassed, as he stepped out of the car.

"Hi," she said. "It's a little past the kids' bedtime but I kept them up. They've been so excited all day."

"That's good," he said. "I can't wait to see them."

Carrying one of his bags he stepped briskly across the lawn, put his right hand on Helen's shoulder, and kissed her quickly on the forehead. She smiled wanly.

"You're looking well," she said.

"Thanks," he said. "So are you. You've taken off some weight, haven't you?"

"A pound or two," she said. "I'm wearing my hair a little different, a little higher on top. I guess that's what makes me look thinner."

"Well," he said, feeling slightly giddy, "you look just fine."

The moment he walked into the house and saw the children he decided, privately, that he would have to stay there, right in the house, come hell or high water, come any manner of suffering, any degree of torture over not having Elaine. The children squealed and came at him like halfbacks, smothering him with kisses and embraces and laughter. He noticed first that Barbara was now walking with complete assurance and that she looked much taller than when he had last seen her.

Helen fixed a pot of coffee and served it in the den, where the five of them sat, regarding each other with mingled love and embarrassment.

"Can you stay home now, Daddy?" Patrick said.

"Well, Patto," Dan heard himself saying, "I'll be here for the next couple of days anyway, and maybe even much longer than that."

"What does that mean?" Helen asked, not unpleasantly.

"I'm sort of ad-libbing it," he said. "I mean I may have to go back to do some more work. But I'm not sure. It might work out that I could—uh—you know, handle things from this end, by mail or something. We'll see."

He asked the children about school and kissed them every few minutes. When it was time for them to go to bed he held Barbara in his arms for a long while before putting her into her crib and then he sat beside Michael and Patrick for almost an hour, telling them the story of Goldilocks and the Three Bears, purposely getting the details confused to make them laugh. They howled and giggled and pleaded for a retelling, and another, and another.

Later, Dan walked into the kitchen. Helen was putting dishes into the automatic dishwasher. He picked up a cardboard box full of wastepaper.

"I'll burn this stuff," he said, turning on the light over the back door. Outside he sat before the incinerator on an upended wooden crate, poking at the burning papers from time to time with a blackened switch. The moon was behind clouds and the darkness pressed in around the incinerator, retreating fitfully when a vagrant gust gave the flames sudden strength.

After a while he squatted before the incinerator and scraped a few embers out onto the dark earth. They glowed orange and crawled in the blackness when the breeze touched them. He spat into the incinerator, closed its door, stepped on the ashes he had scattered on the ground and went back into the house.

Helen was putting bottles of beer into the refrigerator.

"You know," he said, "if you stand up in front of an incinerator on a very dark night and scrape a few ashes out onto the ground and squint your eyes a little you can get the impression that you're high up in an airplane looking down at the lights of a city."

"I guess so," said Helen. She seemed tired. "You want a beer?" she said.

"No, thanks," he said. "It's certainly nice out. I'll miss it when I go back."

"The weather?"

"Yes. But not only the weather. I wish I could stay."

"Why don't you?"

"Oh, I've got to check into the possibility of doing a new show, you know, as well as the project with Halliburton, which we've been having some trouble with. I think I may connect with something this time, and I've got to get back to stay close to it, to nail it down."

"Is that all there is to it?" Helen said.

"What do you mean?"

"I mean is that all you have to tell me?"

"What else can I tell you? We both know what the situation is."

"I don't, really," she said.

"I mean we know what the general problem is. So why talk about it? I could say that I'm sorry I've hurt you and all that, but doesn't that go without saying? I've wanted to kill myself because of what I've done. I don't defend myself at all. But what's the sense of saying all this? Can't we just concentrate on the fact that I—well, that I came home for a little visit and let it go at that?"

"Oh, I guess if that's the way you want it," Helen said.

"I don't *want* it like this at all," he said, with an edge to his voice. "Oh, God, please don't let's fight. I don't want to say anything unkind. It seems that that's about all I'm good for any more is to make people suffer. It's not a very nice spot to be in."

"I don't want to nag you, Dan," Helen said. "I'm just trying to find out, for the children's sake, what's in the cards for us."

"I don't know," he said. "I guess I still need more time to make up my mind."

"You've had almost six months," she said.

"Right. And I need more. If there was anything I could say right now I'd say it. I just don't know what's going to happen. Sometimes I think one thing and then the next day I think something else."

"Well," she said, "if you have to go back to New York when will you be out again? What shall I tell the children?"

"Oh, Christ," he said, very softly. "I don't know. How's the Chevrolet holding up?"

"Fine," she said.

"Maybe beer's not a bad idea after all," Dan decided.

He opened two bottles of cold Schlitz and they sat in the kitchen drinking, sunk in depression.

The next day they kept the children home from school and he played with them the entire day, rolling with them on the lawn in the back yard, throwing a football with them in the street, picking them up and kissing them, taking them to a drive-in restaurant for malted milks, joking with them, making them laugh. Again at one point during the day he made what he believed was the firm decision to remain with them. But later, when he began to face the problem of how he could break the news to Elaine, he realized that he could not do it, that he did not want to do it, that he wanted her more than anything else in the world.

Two days later he was back in New York, wondering what was going to happen next. As the weeks passed he lost weight and became more irritable.

It sometimes seemed that the three most painless times were when he was waking up, when he was falling asleep and when the second drink had begun to affect him. There were things understandable then that not only were not clear to him at other times but that did not even exist for him at other times.

To be sure, some of them were not very important things. One morning, in winter, with the window open he could hear a shovel scraping in the street and men's voices quietly joking. For a time he listened to the sounds while asleep and they were wound up in his dreams. Then for a few minutes he lay half awake, listening. He heard one man laugh loudly and say, "I thought you said you knew how to drive that thing." It was not a very cruel thing to say, but lying there half-awake he felt what cruelty there was to it and he half-smiled in sympathy with the anonymous victim to whom the subtle, joking insult was directed. There was cruelty all day long, unrecognized. "Say, you're putting on a little weight, aren't you?" "I distinctly *told* you I wanted three carbons, not two." "Don't get me wrong, there's nothing *wrong* with your wearing low-heeled shoes to my mother's party." Moving fast through the stream you could scarcely feel it. But lying still, half-awake, feeling, it was there, brushing against your face.

The matter of degree puzzled him. He could grasp the extremes easily enough. War and peace. Good and evil. Up and down. Hot and cold. Heaven and hell. Mutt and Jeff. Punch and Judy. Fine and dandy. No, even the extremes were a problem. How carefully could you back up from peace before you found yourself at war? How slowly could you move, measuring with delicate instruments, moving away from the complete good, through the relative good, and the less good, before you found you were surrounded by evil? It was like the old question: Can you step anyway but south when you're standing on the North Pole?

Another idea he had when half-asleep: Could you make a chart of the spectrum, relating the colors to virtues and vices? Of course you could, but it would be worthless. Or of course you could not. Unless perhaps you wanted to try it anyway. He used to have the feeling that great truths were just barely eluding him when he was falling asleep. If only he had the energy to wake up fully and make some notes, he used to think. And then in the next minute the elusive truths were part of his dreams, and such commotion there was then!

CHAPTER

FIFTEEN

H<small>E</small> was sitting alone on the studio couch in his stocking feet one day when a knock came at the door, and at once he felt helpless and trapped. There was really nothing wrong, he realized. It wasn't his mother, or the law, or God. It was probably just a delivery boy or Western Union but there was something about being forced to go to the door in your stocking feet that made you feel inferior to whatever fully shod creature might be waiting to face you. Dignity was a fragile thing, he reflected, that it could be imparted by a pair of shoes or a clean shirt or a wisp of hair patted into place.

He recalled a story he had heard during the war, about a group of Russians captured by the Germans, or had it been the other way around? Anyway, the captives had been forced by their captors to strip, and standing naked in a field in the broad daylight they had presented such a pathetic spectacle, they had been so completely lacking in human dignity that the officer whose duty it was to command a firing squad to shoot them down had been unable to give the order. So the nude unfortunates had been ordered to reclothe themselves and only then, when they had drawn about themselves a rightful measure of pride and military hauteur, had they been cut down.

It was Hank.

"I've been calling you for two days," he said.

"Oh, I'm sorry," Dan said. "I haven't been answering the phone. I thought it was Elaine. We've had another little scuffle." *Little scuffle.* The words echoed in his mind as Hank entered the room and seated himself. Always the attempt to minimize problems and dangers, even to himself. Especially to himself.

"Look," Hank said, "I've got some work I can do back on the Coast so I thought we ought to kick things around for a minute. The deal with Halliburton may go down the drain, as you know. If it does, well, personally I haven't any reason to hang around town. Unless you've got something definite you want to work on, or a few tunes you want to finish up, I'll be going back."

"Okay," Dan said. "I guess you're right."

"Fine," Hank said. "So much for music. Now, what about the other scene? Why don't you get your god-damned divorce and marry Elaine and get it over with? You can't hurt Helen any more than you have. You obviously don't want to go back to her. So why not cut her loose and let her start rebuilding her life?"

"I can't answer that," Dan said. "It sounds like good enough advice, but I don't seem capable of acting on it. It would kill my mother, for one thing."

"Balls!" Hank exclaimed. "With all due respect to your mother I still propose a toast to Philip Wylie. But anyway, don't you think your mother wants you to be happy? And you're certainly not happy now."

"I don't know whether my problem is my mother or religion or what-the-hell," Dan said.

Hank poured himself a drink.

"This business of morals gets so complicated," Dan said. "Maybe it would have been better if man had quit while he was ahead: after conceiving the Golden Rule."

"Not at all," Hank said. "The Golden Rule is a very inadequate guide to conduct. It's only practical for men who are already good."

"I don't follow you."

"There are whole classes of people for whom the idea of do-unto-others-as-you-would-have-others-do-unto-you is obviously impractical, at least in relation to the good of society. Take masochists, for example. Or, if you think that's too limited a group, how about nymphomaniacs or prostitutes or alcoholics? Oddly enough those groups *do* apply the Rule, in a twisted sense, but I'm sure the result is not one that moralists would approve of."

"I guess you're right in regard to these exceptions," Dan said, "but it's still a wise idea for the rest of us who—"

"Not necessarily," Hank said. "I seem to be limiting myself to the area of sex but then who doesn't? But what I'm getting at is this—forget the exceptions, the psychopathic cases. Consider the normal people. Take me, for example, if I may flatter myself. When I go to a party and meet, say, Lana Turner, do you know what I want to do unto her and what I want her to do unto me?"

Dan laughed and said, "But you don't do it. You behave yourself."

"Of course," Hank said, "and for reasons that have nothing to do with the Golden Rule. But the simple wanting is there. There may be men who say they *don't* want an attractive woman but unless they're ill, old, momentarily jaded or sexually abnormal they delude themselves. What actually happens is that they smother their desire so fast that in many cases they're honestly not aware of its existence. It has nothing to do with evil, really, nothing to do with morals. It's no more evil, in its essential simplicity—the desire, I mean, not the act—than is the desire of a thirsty man for a glass of water he sees on a table. Now he may decide for good and sufficient reasons not to drink that particular glass of water. He may find out that it was poured out for somebody else. Or he may learn that the water is poisoned. Or he might have been ordered by his doctor to cut down on his liquid intake. Or he might belong to some nutty religion that tells him drinking water is sinful, you have to get your liquid from fruit juice or something. But his reaction is the simple pure one of an animal that God created. So when you apply this idea of essential desires to the areas of sex and social contact, when you also consider the infinity of psychological quirks to which man is susceptible, you begin to see that the Golden Rule is not the all-encompassing guide that it at first seems."

"Then the Church is right after all in insisting on the Ten Commandments," Dan said.

"A friend of mine wrote a play once," Hank said, "that has one great line in it. He said he would have a lot more use for the Ten Commandments if they had been called the Ten Suggestions."

"But people pay them little enough heed as it is," Dan said. "If they were only suggestions they'd have even less effect on us than they do now."

"I can't agree with you," Hank said. "A commandment is a form of pressure. Pressure builds up resistance—and there are no exceptions to that, my friend. Resistance, given enough time to become powerful, needs only a certain type of stimulus to trigger it off. The Orientals have a better understanding of this sort of thing than we do. Their commandments usually *are* in the form of suggestions, words to the wise. But we dictate, we dogmatize. Fortunately today we don't threaten thunder and lightning and hell-fire as we did in ages past but the general idea has rarely been specifically repudiated. And here again you Christians are worse offenders than the Jews. Luckily enough, though, despite man's intellectual insistence on treating the Commandments as just that, as strict rules of conduct, in practice, since he's really run by his emotions whether he knows it or not, he has a certain inner wisdom that *does* regard the Commandments as only suggestions."

"I'm afraid I can't agree with you," Dan said.

"Skipping over for the moment the possible psychological significance of your use of the word *afraid*," Hank said, "I'll just say that of course you can't agree with me. Someday you might, but I don't think it can happen now. But let me explain what I meant. Take any Commandment at random. Honor thy Father and thy Mother. Good advice. Very good advice. But I know a guy whose mother was a whore and whose father sold heroin. I know another man whose old man was a notorious gangster and rum-runner. I know another fella whose mother was an alcoholic and whose father was a part-time homosexual. I know another—"

"All right," Dan said, "I concede the point."

"Okay," Hank said. "Obviously there are millions of people in the world who couldn't possibly honor their mothers and fathers. The only intelligent thing for them to do is get as far from their parents as possible, and as early in life as possible. Help them, surely. Don't let them go hungry. Try to get them straightened out, get them to a doctor, or a psychiatrist, or to church or whatever. Love them, if possible. But *honor* them? *Honor* whores, murderers, sexual psychopaths, raving neurotics? Of course not. And I'm happy to say that in practice nobody ever does, the Commandment of God to the contrary notwithstanding. Or take another example. Thou Shalt Not Kill. Very fine advice. Except that Western man, Christian man if you will, has been killing his fellows for two thousand years just as fast as he could. We engage in religious wars, wars of all sorts, and the ministers of God solemnly assure all participants that they are on God's side. And we refuse to do away with the barbarous institution of the death penalty, although I'm beginning to believe that there are signs of its being on the way out. But the point is overly obvious. We preach Thou Shalt Not Kill, but in practice we kill whenever and wherever it seems convenient for us to do so. So the Commandments *are* only suggestions, after all."

"You're a lot brighter than I am," Dan said. "I wish you had my problem and I had a piece of watermelon."

"I *couldn't* have your problem," Hank said. "Don't you see? I couldn't even be in your predicament. Our backgrounds aren't the same. Oh, I can get hung up. What the hell, I did. I was married. She was a nice girl who turned out to be a nut. When she became more nutty than nice we split. It was that simple. Not easy, you understand, in fact very rough for a while. But simple. I knew what had to be done. One of these days I'll find somebody who makes sense to me and I'll try it again. But your problem I couldn't have."

"I wonder," Dan said. "You said our backgrounds were different. I wonder if certain backgrounds have certain types of traps, problems, built into them. Not everybody will fall into the traps, maybe, but they're there."

"I think you're right."

"What is it like being Jewish?" Dan said. It was the kind of question that is rarely asked in this world, not because there are only a few people who could ask it, or only a few who could answer it, but because it is the kind of question that has to hurdle one of the higher invisible barriers of reserve.

"It's largely just having a feeling that you're different," Hank said, "although that's an oversimplification. When you're the only Jew at a Gentile country club it reminds you a little of the feeling you get when you go to the beach for the first time and come out of the bath house white as a fish's belly and see the beach strewn with tanned bodies, bodies that belong, bodies that seem to be at home. Probably nobody is looking at you but it doesn't make any difference because you think they are, and if you think they are, they might as well be."

"I see," Dan said.

"No, I don't think you'll ever exactly *see,*" Hank said. "If being a Jew simply meant being different it wouldn't be so bad because, what the hell, we're all different. But the worst thing of all is that other people think you are inferior to them. In a certain sense my Jewishness exists to a large extent in the minds of others."

"That's another reason why anti-Semitism is such a mystery. People usually hate what they fear and I don't think you can fear something unless you feel somehow inferior to it."

"I don't know," Hank said. "It's a mystery to us, too. We don't feel we're better than you or worse. We think we're just as good."

"Obviously you are," Dan said, "or else better. I do think you're smarter. I've met very few stupid Jews. Maybe none. It must be a very unfortunate thing to be hated for the wrong reason, or for no reason at all." He put two more ice cubes into his glass and added a dash of Vat 69. He sat back, looking at the ceiling, then laughed.

"What's funny?" Hank said.

"I was just thinking," Dan said, "I know what it feels like

to be Jewish. Once or twice, maybe more, I've gone through what you must go through almost every day of your life."

"How could you?"

"It's hard to explain," Dan said, "but several times I've been in groups of people when some stupid bastard dropped a clumsy remark about the Jews. I've felt a tense, awkward emotion take hold of the room because the thought had suddenly passed through the minds of some of the people present that *I* might be Jewish."

"You?"

"Yes. You know, I have dark hair, dark eyes, sort of a prominent nose. If I said I *was* Jewish nobody would argue with me. Anyway, it's hard to explain, but I would catch somebody maybe looking at me out of the corner of his eye, or nervously putting out a cigarette or something and for a few seconds I actually would feel that there was a legitimate reason for the chill that filled the room, because I *was* a Jew. It's hard to explain."

"I get you," Hank said. "It's something a little like what used to happen to me in school. Some kid would shoot a spitball or break a window and the teacher would whirl on the class and begin bawling us all out, trying to put her finger on the kid that caused the trouble. I can still remember the feeling of guilt that used to well up in me. I'd get frightened and my heart would pound. I'd feel guilty as hell."

"Maybe it's like reading an article about cancer in *Reader's Digest* and then sitting around looking at the moles on your arm. Whatever it is in your mind that makes you believe these strange things about yourself is the same thing that the hypnotist reaches when he induces you to believe that you're a cucumber or Lily St. Cyr."

"God," Dan said, leaping to his feet and striding to the window. "The first really fresh and startling thought I've ever had in all my life has just occurred to me and it is this—that in all my life I've never had a really fresh and startling thought. Every man, I guess, comes eventually to the disturbing realization that, where women are concerned, imagination sets you up for some kind of an eventual letdown, no matter how great the woman that you're involved with might be. I guess another way of saying this is the old barracks-philosophy, 'There is no sense running after a streetcar once you've caught it.' But can it be that this is true not only of women but of everything in life?"

"Well," Hank said, "not to coin a phrase, it's all in the way you look at it. This feeling that you mention, it's not just you, it's everybody who makes the mistake of looking only ahead and up, wanting only what those have who seem better situated. You've got to remember to take a 360-degree view at all times, to look back at those who are poorer than you, who drive older cars, who have poorer health. Or do I sound like Norman Vincent Peale?"

"I feel guilty," Dan said, "about being dissatisfied with what my life was. After all, what the hell right have I to expect things to be any better than they are? So all right; so everybody in my neighborhood out there tries to live the way people do in *Good Housekeeping* magazine; so we're all sort of like bees in a giant hive, mowing our lawns and going to our supermarkets and bowling alleys and drive-in movies. Who the hell am I to say this isn't really the great American dream?"

"Danny," Hank said, "you're asking some pretty subversive questions. You start knocking power-mowers and TV sets and you're shaking the foundations. The fact is we're all hung up with *things,* with stuff. We're so busy surrounding ourselves with all the props and scenery that we lose interest in the plot and the drama. In fact, the only time the actual drama really comes into the lives of most of us is when, usually against what we call our better judgment, passion explodes in our lives and takes over. In other words when somebody marries, when somebody dies, when somebody falls in love, or gets drunk and gets into a fight. This is the real thing and it usually scares the hell out of us. We feel much more secure when we're just saving money or trading in savings stamps or buying a new car. And then, too, a lot of people retreat further from what is really important by leaning on religion."

"Don't you think religion has a reality of its own?" Dan asked.

"Sure," Hank said, "but I've told you before—there isn't one churchgoer out of a thousand who ever perceives that reality or who really understands what the founders of his religion had in mind. Personally, organized religion seems to me to be a big charade, a sort of pleasant game that men agree to play with each other, but I'll be the first to admit that I might be wrong about this, and that there might be something to it after all. But I will *not* admit I am wrong about your average churchgoer. He's not looking for enlightenment; he's looking for security. He doesn't go to church because it makes him feel *bad;* he does it because it makes him feel so damned self-contented when he comes walking out of a church into the sunshine on Sunday morning with his family, looking like somebody on the cover of the *Saturday Evening Post*. It seems to me that people go to church largely to have their prejudices confirmed. And the same thing goes for books. This is really a shame, too, because reading could do it; I mean, reading could melt the ice in most people's brains, but the thing that prevents it is that people have a way of smelling, at a range of 200 yards, that a certain book might disturb their beliefs, so they just automatically stay away from it. What they really want to read is books that tell them how right they are.

"You see," Hank continued, "almost all of us, the smart people as well as the jerks, make one basic mistake—we think that everything is going to work out all right if we can somehow get with the right philosophy, the right church, the right party, the right movement. I say there is no such thing. You show me what you call the right group and I'll point out a million people inside of it who are all hung up. The fact is that if you go at it the right way you can be reasonably happy in *any* camp. Unless the breaks go against you. There is no philosophy that's ever been invented, or will be, that can make it possible for a man to take in his stride earthquakes or getting struck by lightning or having a depression wipe out his savings or having a Mongoloid idiot for a son or something of that sort."

"Where I come from," Dan said, "people think that bad breaks are punishments sent by God."

"Man," Hank said, "I'm always astounded by the fact that people think that just because *they* are lousy then *God* has got

160

to be lousy. If only bad people got bad breaks, why then there would be some sort of a cause-and-effect relationship that would suggest, if not prove, that there might be something in this punishment-from-God idea. But anybody with even a half-open mind can see the bad breaks are distributed very democratically and that for the most part breaks in life are just as unplotted as breaks in a crap game. Does the good guy always win in a crap game? Of course not. Does the bad guy lose when he plays poker? Certainly not. I'll tell you a funny thing about me. I seem antireligious but I'm really not. What I mean is that I dig the bare bones of the idea of religion. Being sure there was a God up there looking out for me would bring me a certain degree of comfort. But every time I stop thinking of religion with a capital R, in other words, every time I look at some particular *thing* about religion, it always seems a hundred per cent fertilizer."

"Well, to hell with it," Dan said. "You want to go get something to eat?"

"Sure," Hank said.

Dan picked up a paper and began looking at restaurant and club ads, hoping to find some new and interesting place.

"Look at this," he said after a moment, pointing at a sentence in the paper. "The Bal Tabarin, 225 West 46th, is eager to divert you with a Can-Can." He folded the newspaper, sank back in his chair and assumed an attitude of resignation and disgust. "As far as I'm concerned," he said, "the Can-Can is the biggest nothing in entertainment history. Oh, I suppose if you were in Paris and the girls didn't have any pants on and you had about four drinks under your belt you might enjoy watching the Can-Can, but if any one of those three conditions were lacking it would be a complete waste of time."

"That's what I like about you," Hank said, laughing. "You don't know how to live, you can't keep your affairs in order and you plan to contribute nothing to posterity, but when it comes to a really meaningless issue, you think as clearly as anybody I know."

It was taking Dan a long while to get used to the language of the New York streets, to the beat of the city's music, to the colors and shapes and lights of the metropolis. He had grown up in Chicago so he did not see the big city through the gawking eyes of a farmer, but he had lived so long in the West that, though he could take the city in his stride, he was still acutely sensitive to its noises and outbursts and electric cracklings.

On his ear, which was used to picking out the rhythms and tones of all sounds, whether they were hog-grunt, railroad-clicking, mimeograph-rattling or coyote-howling, the speech patterns of the city fell with a confusing freshness. One day he got in a cab and said to the driver, "Eighty-fifth and Park." The driver sped through Times Square in the wrong direction and for two blocks Dan let him go, thinking there must have been some problem about making a left turn.

Finally, "Say, aren't you making kind of a wide swing?"

"What's that, Mac?"

"Aren't you going the wrong way? I want Eighty-fifth."

"Oh," the driver said, laughing, *"Eighty*-fit. I thought you said *Tayty*-fit."

Unlike the weary, preoccupied New Yorkers who daily clambered in and out of cabs without noticing the drivers or devoting any of their attention to the details of the trips they took, Dan was fascinated by the hackies and he was able to maintain his fascination for several months.

One day he got into a cab driven by an elderly, polite, warm-natured colored man who told him the complete history of a small town in Iowa.

"I used to chauffeur for old Mr. Morris," the man said. "That was even before he built the flour mill on the river. That's where he made most of his early money, you know, with that mill. His son Edward now, he owns half the town."

By the time Dan got out of that particular cab he had the feeling he had just finished reading a novel by Sinclair Lewis, so intimate had been his narrator's expository technique.

Another time he got into a taxi driven by a man who appeared to be subject to a strange sort of fit. The man twitched his head from side to side and pretended, at each twitch, to be looking out the windows at the traffic behind him. He was evidently unable to control the jerks and convulsions that

162

seized his body and at first Dan was apprehensive that during one of the spasms the man would lose control of the vehicle. His affliction did not appear to affect his driving in any way, however, so after a few minutes Dan settled back and watched with calm, unblinking fascination. Finally he felt welled up with sympathy and when he got out he gave the driver such a large tip that he felt a little sheepish about it and turned around and walked away fast.

Another time, getting out of a cab with Elaine, Dan fumbled in his overcoat pocket for change for a tip and finding only twelve cents, a dime and two pennies, handed this amount to the driver. The driver said, "Thanks," and then after they had left the cab he evidently noticed the two pennies and became incensed.

"Here, buddy," he shouted, venomously, and threw the two pennies out into the street at Dan's feet as he drove away.

For a moment Dan stood looking after him, puzzled, and then he became furious and shook his fist at the driver and would have welcomed a fight.

He almost got into a fight with another hackie. At Grand Central late one afternoon he jumped into a cab, settled back, opened a newspaper and flicked the overhead light button. The light did not go on.

"Your light work?" he asked the driver.

"I guess not," the man said.

Dan stepped out of the cab. "Sorry," he said. "There's something I want to read." He walked back to the next cab in line and climbed in. The inside light went on and he opened his paper.

"Fifty-ninth and Sixth," he said.

Suddenly the door was jerked open.

"You owe me for the flag," the driver of the first cab said, peering in at Dan.

"What?" The phrase was incomprehensible.

"You owe me twenty cents for the flag."

"I don't get you, Mac. I didn't go any place in your cab."

"Listen, god-dammit, I dropped the flag on the meter when you got in. You think I'm supposed to pay the company myself?"

"I don't know about that, Charlie, but I know I didn't go any place in your cab so *I* don't owe you a thing. It's not my fault your light wasn't working!"

The man's face reddened and he made a threatening gesture.

"You lousy tightwad," he said. "You son of a bitch! You got the money. Why don't you give it to me?"

Horns were beginning to honk now and a policeman, far down the line, began walking toward them. Dan felt tight and nervous and shaken and wanted to get out of the cab and either hit the driver or make him listen to reason.

"Listen," he said. "I'll tell you what I'll do. I'll pay two dollars or whatever the hell it costs to have your god-damned light repaired but I wouldn't give you that particular twenty cents under any circumstances."

"You cheap son of a bitch," the driver shouted. "I hope the money does you a lot of good."

"You listen to me," Dan shouted, pointing at him. "You listen to me—"

The policeman loomed behind the driver.

"All right," he said, in an almost blasé tone, "let's break this up. Traffic has to get through here."

The driver whirled and ran back to his cab, shaking his fist in Dan's direction. He raced his motor and drove away. Dan was left on an emotional cliff.

"Crazy bastard," he said to his driver.

"Yeah," the driver said, embarrassed. "He had no right to shoot his mouth off like that. His equipment is supposed to be in working order at all times. He could of got a citation from the cop."

"It wasn't the twenty cents," Dan said.

"Yeah," the driver said.

Dan was angry and his stomach was knotted up the rest of the evening because neither party had gotten any satisfaction out of the argument at all. They were both right and they were both wrong.

He had many adventures in the city and they were mostly without significance and always without plot or reason, but they impressed him. Later, at odd times, he would talk about them to people, saying, "I remember a funny thing happened to me one night," or "I just happened to think of something." A face would say, "What?" and he would begin to talk, squinting slightly as if trying to recognize details in a fog, looking away at a wall or a ceiling or the floor or his hands.

One night he was on the subway. It was almost four in the morning and there were only three or four people on the train. He was seated on one of the long benches facing the aisle when, at a midtown stop, a dark-haired young man with a dirty leather jacket stepped into the train and sat down on the seat almost directly across the aisle. The man was wearing a khaki shirt, opened at the collar, and his shoes were wing-tipped and pointed but scuffed and out of shape. His face was brown and Latin and he had a thin, scraggly mustache. He looked drunk and cold as he sat huddled in the front corner of the car, shivering and spitting on the floor.

At first Dan took no special notice of the fact that the man was spitting but then once he happened to be looking at the man as he spat and he was surprised at the vehemence with which he directed an almost invisible bit of saliva to the floor. The man looked as if he were spitting out a deadly and bitter poison. He would shudder and twist his face into an ugly expression of horror, shutting his eyes and jerking his face quickly from side to side as he worked his jaws to summon up a supply of saliva.

After each expectoration he exhaled vigorously, mumbling, "Son of a bitch!" or "Oh!" or "God!" as he wiped his lips with the back of his hand. He would sit quietly for a few seconds, head nodding, eyes half closed and then begin again, trying to rid himself of something that had lain foreign and terrible in his mouth.

He did not cough nor did he clear his throat. There was no congestion in his lungs, no bronchial inflammation that caused him to hack and spit. He spat because he wanted to get rid of something and for long minutes Dan sat staring at him, trying to decipher the mystery that he represented. Once the man glanced in his direction and Dan looked quickly but casually away, in the manner of people who have been caught staring impolitely. But the man's eyes were glazed and though he looked for a moment into Dan's face there seemed to be no glint of contact and in another instant he screwed his face up, grimacing horribly, and bent over and emptied his mouth.

Then it was time for Dan to get off at 87th Street and he stood up and walked off the train and never saw the man again and never found out what was wrong with him. The incident was without meaning but sometimes, when he would see someone spit, he would think of the man and wonder what manner of experience he might have had before he got on the subway that night.

CHAPTER

SIXTEEN

Dan made two more trips to the Coast to see Helen and the children. By now, he was surprised to discover, they had become used to the idea of his absence. He could not tell if he imagined it or there was actually the merest trace of coolness in Michael's attitude. Eventually he decided that there was, accepted it as inevitable, and internalized the painful knowledge, using it to stir up the other, older ingredients of his torment.

There began to form, in the back of his mind, the idea that there might be some value—what, he was not sure—in having Helen and the children visit with him briefly in the East. This gave him the excuse to move out of the room on 55th Street, the expense be damned, and take a five-room apartment on upper Park Avenue. Elaine, who had not inquired into the motivation of his decision, was overjoyed. She began to decorate the place, selecting inexpensive paintings and prints, crocheting doilies and pot-holders, putting up drapes and curtains. The apartment had two large bathrooms, with deep tubs and heavy, old-fashioned showers. They splashed gaily in the showers together, rubbing soapsuds on each other's bodies, singing harmony, laughing, kissing and embracing.

But as the days wore on they began to have more frequent arguments over trivial matters and each began to display more jealousy of the other. One night they gave a dull little party where the guests stood around and criticized everything they had seen or heard in the way of entertainment during the previous week. Dan sat listening to one knot of people for ten minutes and in that time did not hear any of them say a complimentary word about anything or anybody. First they cut a new musical to pieces, then they made scathing remarks about several television shows; next they delivered themselves of nasty opinions about an aging motion-picture actress who had married a younger man, and finally they discussed several new plays, arriving at the aggregate conclusion that they approved of none of them.

Dan decided that such parties should be called Criticism Parties and that engraved invitations should be sent out saying, "Come to a party at our house prepared to be as nasty as you please. If you have anything insulting to say about a new play, book, or motion picture, by all means save it for the night of June 19, 9 PM till 2 AM."

He got into several conversations but became annoyed because their threads were constantly snapped off without rhyme or reason. Nobody, it seemed, was interested in following anything through.

They were talking about a man named Milton.

"He has beautiful eyes," said a Mrs. Gardner to a group gathered around her. "So large and brown."

"I used to have large eyes when I was a child," said Dan, who had started to drink, "but they seemed to get smaller as I grew older."

"Personally I'd rather have green eyes," said Mrs. Gardner, "but in a man I like them brown."

"Maybe it's not that my eyes got smaller," Dan said. "Maybe they just didn't grow any after I was about eight years old and my head kept on growing so that in the end it seemed that my eyes were not as large as they once had been. That must be it. And another thing—there doesn't seem to be much relationship between the size of an animal and the size of its eyes. By that I mean a man's eyes aren't any larger than a dog's. And a horse, or even an elephant, doesn't have very large eyes in relation to its over-all bulk."

"Yes," said Mrs. Gardner, "that was the first thing I noticed about him was his eyes. I think it was at Shirley Greenberg's place—that was when she was Shirley Totter, of course, before she married Eddie Greenberg. She had a cute little place, just off Ventura Boulevard."

"Where *is* Shirley?" someone asked.

"God knows," said Mrs. Gardner. "Last I heard she was in Chicago with an agency or something, but you know Shirley. No, I don't think it was Chicago now that I think of it. It was Cleveland or someplace like that."

"Is she still with Eddie?"

"Lord, no. That was over and done with ages ago. I could have told you that the day they got married. Good God, he was a million years old to begin with, and then you know Shirley and how she had to have money and everything. They just weren't right for each other."

"It's awful," someone said.

"Well, you know how those things are," Mrs. Gardner said. "But I always liked Eddie myself. I mean, he was a million years old and a lot of people thought he acted, you know, sort of snooty, but I always liked him. Better than I liked his brother, anyway."

"Which brother was that?" someone asked.

"Charles," Mrs. Gardner said. "Oh, I know. You're thinking of Saul. No, Saul was an angel. It was Charlie who was no good. At least to my mind he wasn't. But Saul . . . there was a dear if there ever was one. It was Saul who originally made all the money the family had, you know. Certainly they had nothing until Saul made good and then of course they did all right; at least after Eddie got in at Paramount *he* did all right. By the way, I hear they're not *doing* much out there right now."

"That's right," somebody said. "The lot looks like White Sands Proving Grounds."

"Well, my God," Mrs. Gardner said, "I told them two years ago, I said, listen, I said, when television hits it's really going to hit, but a lot of those monkeys out there won't listen to anybody, you know. It's the same way all over town. But you know something?"

"What?"

"I'd like to be out there right now, soaking up some of that sunshine. Oh, I mean New York is wonderful. It's the greatest city in the whole world, but what the hell, there are still times, like right now, when . . . I don't know . . . I'd just as soon chuck it all and go back out there and take the house in Encino again and just *live*. There's nothing like it."

"Give *me* New York," someone said.

"Don't get me wrong," said Mrs. Gardner, "I'm here because I love it, but once in a while I just sort of get homesick for the Coast, that's all. That crazy ocean and those open convertibles and all that. But don't get me wrong, there's nothing chauvinistic in my attitude. I think that sort of thinking is ridiculous. That's for idiots who applaud at radio programs when somebody says Brooklyn or Texas. That's not the way I feel about it at all. You can say anything you want against California, it's all right with me. I'm just saying that once in a while I get sort of itchy to be back out there, that's all."

"But the winters are getting so mild *here*," someone said.

"Aren't they, though?" Mrs. Gardner said. "I was reading something just the other day about some professor or somebody who says that this part of the world is getting a little warmer each year. He had it all worked out with charts or something. But I think he said in another two hundred years it'll be as warm here as it is in Miami, or something like that. May I have some more soda in my drink?"

"Sure," someone said.

"There's some soda on the table," Mrs. Gardner said. "It's White Rock. I had some other kind the other day but it seemed sort of flat. Of course this is more expensive, but I think it's worth it. That delicatessen of mine is awful, though. You have to keep your eye on 'em all the time or it's two cents here and eight cents there and before you know it they've cheated you out of two or three dollars. It all adds up, you know."

"You have to watch them," someone said.

"Oh, yes. And I do, too, let me tell you. Nobody puts anything over on me. Why I was in a little dress shop the other day, and this girl said, 'You'd better move your purse.' This is the dress I was picking up, incidentally—"

"It's stunning," someone said.

"Do you think so?" Mrs. Gardner asked. "It's nothing especially fancy but it *is* nice, I think. And it's got that new thing with the shoulders, you know, with the sort of cape effect. I thought it was cute when I saw it in the window. Incidentally, did anyone get a load of what Faye Emerson was wearing the other night on that panel show?"

"No," someone said.

"Well," said Mrs. Gardner, "I thought I'd die. Here she is with a sweater of some sort on, very tight, and some kind of fur all up around the neck."

"Oh," someone said, "I love those new sweaters and fur things."

"No," said Mrs. Gardner, "I know what you're talking about. This was different. You're talking about those Angoras and things with just the very small fur trims at the cuffs and on the collar. They had a picture of one of them in the *Times* this morning, as a matter of fact. No, I think it was the *Trib*. I always get them mixed up anyway. You know, it's funny, but you live in one town for so many years and you get used to the names of the newspapers and then you move to some other town and it takes you ten years to get used to the papers again. I'm forever asking a newsboy for the *Herald-American* or something here in New York."

The talk went on like that for a long time and finally it occurred to Dan that he had heard enough. He walked over to Elaine and said, "What ever happened to talking about *something?*"

Some people were sitting down at the party and others were standing up. The two groups rarely conversed with each other for it was awkward for the standees to stoop to talk to those who were seated, and because of the great volume of talk-noise in the room it was necessary to get your face quite close to the face of the person you were addressing. As a result the party was stratified: there was the stand-up stratum, the sit-down stratum, and the nonconformist, uninhibited plop-on-the-floor stratum. Now and then, of course, an individual would move from one to the other.

Dan looked over once and saw that a man with black, straight hair and a suntan was leaning close to Elaine, holding one of her hands. He felt a flicker of jealousy, looked away and forced himself to forget the incident, but his subconscious slyly filed the matter away for future reference.

Finally the people drifted away into the night, leaving a desolate scene of lipstick-stained glasses, cigarette butts, empty bottles and disarranged furniture. When the party had been running full swing it was not night, nor was it day. It was just party-ness and electric lighting and cigarette smoke and talk and music. It was no time at all. But when the people had gone, when all the good-byes and promises to call had been said, then the night, which had been lurking outside in the courtway and on top of the building, crept in suddenly through the open windows and overcame the room.

They undressed feeling tired and slightly antagonistic toward each other. Dan lay in bed and thought, "The only trouble with an affair like this is that it is disastrous if it becomes commonplace. It must remain glamorous and exciting and perfect because if it becomes very much less than that then conscience has a field day. An ordinary love affair has its own little problems and they are difficult enough but a love affair that has been established at the cost of defiance of society and conscience has all these problems multiplied by two, for one goes into the affair partly against one's will; part of one is always trying to slip out unnoticed, to go back, to sacrifice *want* for *ought*."

In the morning he was tired and irritable. His bed looked as if a herd of buffalo had run through it, and at the breakfast table he felt overly sensitive. He sat morosely beside her in the kitchen, listening to the peculiar tiny ripping sound made by the flesh of a grapefruit being pulled away from the skin as the point of a spoon knifed down into the fruit along the pulpy inner wall of the rind.

He stood up and put two pieces of whole-wheat bread into the toaster and wondered what was wrong with him that he

172

could simply stand making toast and feeling angry. It had been like that sometimes with Helen, too. He could remember subtle, unconscious cruelties he had inflicted upon her without ever having admitted to himself that they existed and of course without ever understanding the reasons for his behavior.

He had resented it, for example, if she became ill. Not consciously exactly, and he certainly would have denied entertaining the feeling, but still there had been something in his attitude, something in the set of his mouth that became more important than all the little exterior kindnesses, all the dainties brought for dessert, all the fruit juices served in bed, all the back massages and the bedside chats.

There was something in him at those times that Helen could detect. She would say, "What's wrong?" and he would say, "Nothing," or "What do you mean, what's wrong?" and the old small argument would start. It was always a difficult and exhausting and frustrating argument because neither of them ever knew exactly what it was that they were arguing about.

There was always the split in his thinking, the best and the worst of him at war. Most of him would be genuinely solicitous and loving when she was ill, but there was always one small part that thought her illnesses were psychological and that thus, illogically enough, they were not real, that she was just playing sick to get a little rest, to avoid having to take care of the children, to get attention. He might have made some progress with the problem if he had admitted to himself that it existed, but in the old days he had simply closed off the part of his mind that generated this particular antagonism, had walled it up and denied that it contained anything at all.

Now, with Elaine, he finally was beginning to face this specific reality, although the result was only that he liked himself less and his energies immediately spiraled off into pointless self-criticism and guilt-feelings.

He and Elaine had an argument now while he was putting butter and jam on the toast and at last he stood up and said in a loud voice, "Here's the toast. *You* can butter it and jam it—and you know where," and they laughed in spite of themselves and it helped a bit so that the argument dissolved and they continued eating breakfast. His mind seemed unable to

173

resist the twisting of phrases, the playing with words for comic effect, no matter how serious his thoughts might be at a given moment. Part of him seemed almost a joke-machine although he did not realize that the phenomenon was one of his defense mechanisms against the thrusts of reality.

"Dan," Elaine said, washing the dishes, "are you really happy with me?"

"Sure," he said, "although sometimes I'm a little sorry that for me happiness has to be a positive thing."

"What do you mean?"

"I mean that to a great many people happiness is a negative quality. It involves not so much the presence of pleasure as the absence of pain. These people are content with little. They've learned that happiness can consist not in having the stomach full of food but in not having the stomach empty. To them the presence of a loved one is never so vital a sensation as the suffering brought about by the loved one's loss."

"I think you're better off. People who feel like that are probably more concerned with the mechanics of simply staying alive than you are. They sound closer to the earth."

He pulled her down onto his lap and kissed the side of her neck.

"I feel pretty good," he said. "Have my number-one boy bring me my rifle."

"Yes, *bwana*," she said.

"I think I'll go out today and hunt Stromberg."

"You want the rest of the coffee?" she asked.

"No," he said, pushing the saucer and cup half an inch away. "Hey, did you just notice what I did? People do that all the time."

"Do what?"

"To indicate that they're through eating something they push their plate about two-thirds of an inch away from them. Silly, isn't it?"

"You know, when it comes to making unimportant but fascinating observations you're the world's champion."

"Why not?" he said, making a face. "I'm an unimportant but fascinating man. And there's something else that just occurred to me," he continued, looking at a small pile of toast crusts on the table. "When you're eating there comes inevitably a precise moment of magic when the material on your plate ceases to be *food* and becomes *garbage*."

"I can take a hint," she said, struggling up off his lap as he patted her hips. Deftly she swept the refuse from their meal into a paper bag and put it in the can outside the back door.

"And now, lady," he said, "if you'll pardon me, I've got to get to work."

He had rented a small piano for the new apartment and now he noodled reflectively at it for about half an hour and jotted down a few ideas. But nothing worthwhile would come.

"What would you like to do?" he said to Elaine, when she walked in from the kitchen.

"Go for a ride on a ferryboat," she said.

"I love you," he said. "Let's do it."

They drove down to the foot of Manhattan Island, took a ferry across the river, standing out in the sunlight all the way over and back, then drove to midtown and put the car into a garage.

Walking about at random they saw a group of people milling in front of the Roosevelt Hotel. It was a small, ragged crowd and the people on its edges faltered indecisively, some standing on tiptoe to focus their attention on the nucleus of the cell as it glided along the sidewalk, others walking away slowly, a little regretfully, the way people walk away from a body in the street.

For a moment Dan thought someone had fainted or that there had been a fist fight or an accident, but then along one side the crowd opened up like clouds before the wind and he caught a glimpse of a photographer waving his arms and trying to pose two people who were ready to jump into a waiting limousine.

"It's Vogeler," Elaine said, and automatically they stepped up closer. The photographer was saying, "No, the other arm!" and Robert Vogeler, the man who had just been released after seventeen months imprisonment in a Hungarian Communist jail, tiredly lifted his left hand and waved it at the camera. Clinging to his right arm was a wide-eyed, brilliantly blonde woman. Dan recognized her from the newsreels as his wife.

175

She looked girlishly happy, all white teeth and yellow hair, laughing and digging her red fingernails into the dark blue of her husband's sleeve. To her right stood a slightly taller blonde woman, obviously her sister, who was beautiful in the same chorus-girl sort of way. A gust of hot, dusty New York air swept over the group and the sister laughed too, pushing her long hair out of her face. A flash bulb washed the scene ghost-white for a split second and Dan stepped back, touching Elaine's arm, faintly feeling an odd sort of guilt. A man and his wife were trying to get into an automobile, and people were standing around staring at them. There were no great moral issues involved in the act, but it was really very much like staring impertinently through a window, Dan thought, so he stepped away from the crowd.

You were always stumbling into crowds in the city, and yet they formed inconsistently. Sometimes a man would slump to the pavement and lie for perhaps a quarter of an hour before a Samaritan came along. People would pause momentarily, or not at all, reacting as they might be expected to do if the body on the sidewalk had been a dog's rather than a man's.

Then you could turn a corner and find fifty or sixty people pressed up close against the plate glass window of a restaurant, watching a white-frocked short-order magician whip scrambled eggs into a high, spiraled mound.

CHAPTER

SEVENTEEN

"IT ISN'T quite what I expected," Elaine said, when they explored Greenwich Village one evening.

"What is, these days?" he said. "But it's not the fault of the Village. It's probably always looked like this. You just build up a phony picture in your mind. You're expecting a movie set."

"I'm thirsty," she said.

"Me, too. Let's go in here and have a beer."

They walked into a brightly lighted saloon and sat on high stools at the bar. The seats of the stools were saddles. Behind the bar buggy-whips, stirrups and old riding prints littered the walls.

A piano was playing in a back room, accompanying several male voices which sang drunkenly "My Wild Irish Rose."

"Two beers," Dan said. The bartender set them up without speaking, placed an ash tray on the bar and walked away. At the far end of the bar a television set glowed grayly. The fights were on.

"Carter is absorbing a lot of punishment in there," said the announcer.

On the screen a tough-looking heavy-set Italian was punching wildly at a tall Negro. The Italian shouldered the Negro into the ropes and swung an overhand right, causing the Negro's knees to buckle slightly.

"Rocky caught him again," shouted the announcer. "Listen to that crowd!"

"Who's fighting?" Elaine asked.

"Who isn't, these days?" Dan said.

"Half a minute to go in round eight," said the announcer. "Rocky is throwing plenty of leather in there. Carter hasn't been knocked down in his last six fights but he's definitely in trouble in there right now."

The Negro grimaced as a punch bobbed his head back, then ducked and moved in close, throwing his arms around his opponent's shoulders.

"Carter is hanging on," observed the announcer. "Rocky tagged him good with that right, but he's game. Carter is as game as they come. No, sir. They don't come any gamer than this gladiator from Detroit. He's got plenty of heart."

The crowd screamed again as Carter, suddenly rising out of a crouch, shuffled forward, feinted with his left, and sent his right fist squarely into the white man's face. The Italian sagged, retreated, and pawed at the air, blinking.

"Brother, what action!" shouted the announcer. "Billy Carter just turned the tables on Lazzeri! Rocky got a little overconfident, a little careless in there, and this Carter is always dangerous."

The bell sounded and three girls' voices came melodiously out of the set.

"Friends are coming, things are humming, what, oh, what to do?" they sang. "Get some Riker's, Riker's Pilsner, good old Riker's brew!"

On the screen another announcer smiled casually.

"Unexpected guests dropping in?" he said. "Better make sure the ice-box is well stocked with Riker's! Not just *any* beer, mind you, but Riker's, the brew of perfection."

So saying he poured beer into a graceful cone-shaped glass, took a tentative sip and smiled directly into the camera, winking knowingly.

"Ahhhh," he said. "I'd know it anywhere. And you'll know

178

you're doing the right thing when you serve Riker's. Ask for it tomorrow, in the new no-deposit bottle."

Dan blew his nose and when he looked back at the screen the Italian was crowding the Negro into a corner, clinching, hooking right-hand punches to the side of the Negro's head.

"Manny Berg did a good job with that eye," the announcer was saying, "but Rocky has opened it up again and the claret is beginning to flow. Doctor Nardiello looked Carter over between rounds, but he's not going to stop the fight."

"I'm glad they don't have color television yet," Elaine said. "I wouldn't like to see the blood."

"It's still flowing," Dan said.

"I know, but as long as I can't *see* it . . ."

The crowd shrieked and the announcer said, "No! The referee says that was no knockdown. It was a slip. No knockdown. Carter just slipped."

The Italian bulled the Negro into the ropes, punching determinedly at his stomach.

"Carter has absorbed plenty of punishment in there tonight," the announcer said, "but he's a hard man to stop."

Dan drained his glass and wiped moisture from his lips with the back of his hand as Carter, moving awkwardly backwards, caught a pile-driving right-hand punch between the eyes and sat down hard on the floor of the ring.

"Carter's down," the announcer shouted. "It was no slip that time. Lazzeri has been waved to a neutral corner! He's trying to get up. Billy's trying to get up! The count is four . . . five . . . He's going to make it! Rocky tagged him that time, but he's going to stay with it. The referee is wiping the rosin off his gloves now and here comes Rocky!"

"Get him," the bartender shouted, punching the air in the direction of the television set. "Get him!"

The Italian leaped forward, blocked a wavering right, and hit the Negro high on the side of the head.

"Come on, hit the son-of-a-bitch," a man seated near Dan shouted. "Hit him!"

"Rocky is pouring it on now," said the announcer. "He's trying for the knockout. He needs it to win and he's giving it everything in there. Oooooh! Almost! It's a good thing for Carter *that* one missed!"

The crowd groaned and whistled as Lazzeri missed again, then roared savagely as he looped his left hand solidly into Carter's right ear. The Negro's neck contorted and for a moment his head was cocked as if he were trying to hear a distant voice. Without bending his knees more than slightly he toppled back, tree-like, and crashed to the canvas. For a moment he lay on his side, legs quivering, one glove lifted to his face, as if to shade his eyes. Then, rolling over on his back he lay motionless.

"That's it," the announcer was saying. "One minute and thirty-odd seconds of the ninth round and it's all over! This was the Rocky Lazzeri of old in there tonight, and he just would not be denied!"

"I told you," the bartender said, to the whole room. "I told you. I knew he was ready!"

"Well, sir, Riker's hopes you had your share of thrills tonight, ladies and gentlemen, and believe you me, that's the way it was from the first round in there tonight. Billy Carter fought a game fight, and was, I think, ahead on points going into the eighth, but Rocky Lazzeri came back strong and laid the big one on him in the ninth and that did it!"

The Negro was being helped to his feet. He looked down at the canvas and shook his head, as if saying no to a small child. His seconds led him to his corner and sat him on his stool, where he stared at the floor and shook his head again from side to side. The Italian leaped around the ring, ran to the Negro, patted him affectionately on the head, and waved at the television cameras.

Dan put fifty cents on the bar and they walked out. Going across the cobblestone street he took Elaine's arm. It was bare and almost imperceptibly moist where he gripped it just above the elbow.

"Your arm feels wonderful," he said. "I think there are few things as pleasant as holding a woman's warm, bare arm on a hot summer night."

"Thank you," she said. "What'll we do now?"

"Let's just walk," he said. Turning the corner they strolled along a quiet, darkened street where a building was in the process of being torn down. Red oil lanterns glowed here and there along the edges of the ruins. A drunk stopped some fifty feet in front of them, stepped uncertainly to a pile of lumber and began urinating. Dan took Elaine's arm and they stepped out into the street, walking parallel to the curb.

"I'm taking a good old-fashioned pee," said the drunk, quietly to himself. A taxi drove past and Dan could hear someone in the back seat singing.

"This is a little more like the Village," he said. "You want to go home?"

"No," she said. "I'm fine."

The night was truly warm. It was shirt-sleeve weather; sitting-on-the-front-steps weather, and the sweet stillness of the air gave it a buoyant quality on which summer-night sounds were borne lightly. When they would pass a bar the neon lights would contract the pupils of their eyes slightly, the cool smell of beer would fill their noses and remind them of old saloons dimly connected with their respective childhoods, and the gabble and laughter and jukebox noise would float out to them clearly, heavy as smoke on the warm, quiet air.

They came to a darkened church and, turning a corner, passed the parochial school that nestled beneath its spire. Elaine stopped to read a small sign Scotch taped to the door of the school. Printed in crayon, it said, "Tin soldiers and Flowers come to Sister Felicita's room. Please call for the children *after* the program, not before. The Chorus Girls in room 7 on the second floor, Sister Aloysius' classroom."

Elaine clapped her hands. "It's delicious," she said. "Tin soldiers! And flowers! Can't you just see them? Standing in line, giggling, being shushed. Marching into the hall with mothers and fathers and aunts and grandmothers looking at them."

"And *chorus* girls," Dan said. "Who gave you your start as a chorus girl, my dear, Florenz Ziegfeld? No, Sister Aloysius!"

They laughed some more and walked on, exploring the Village. Dan stopped at a small open-fronted fruit and vegetable store and bought a pound of cherries which they ate as they walked along.

"I wonder why lb. is the abbreviation for pound," he said, spitting out a cherry stone.

"I don't know," Elaine said. "I think it has something to do with the Latin, but I don't know."

"Cherry is a pretty word," Dan said. "Loveliest of trees, the cherry now is hung with bloom along the bough."

"I've always loved that," Elaine said.

There was a silence. He could hear the summer sounds, the sibilant radio in a passing prowl car, the roar of a distant elevated train, faint music from a point of undetermined origin.

"Be a pretty word in a song title," Dan said.

"There *was* a song called 'Cherry,' " Elaine pointed out.

"I know," Dan said, feeling a faint flicker of annoyance. "I know that very well. I was just thinking of using the word in combination." It always annoyed him to be told something he already knew. They had discussed the matter once and Dan has guessed the annoyance might have originally been that of a precocious child anxious to exhibit superiority. He was afraid now that Elaine had noticed the edge in his voice and for a moment he was silent, penitent.

"There was another number," he said after a while, "something about 'It Looks Like Rain.' That's it! 'It Looks Like Rain in Cherry Blossom Lane.' "

Elaine did not answer.

"It's a pretty word," Dan said. "Let's see. Something like 'Cherry Blossom Kisses' . . . or 'Cherry Blossom Time' . . . or 'Under the Cherry Tree.' "

"Sounds good," Elaine said.

Dan suddenly swore and his mood changed.

"It sounds lousy," he said. "All I've got is an idea, a mood, and I can't seem to put it into words."

"It doesn't matter," Elaine replied, helpfully. "Can't you let Hank turn out your lyrics for a while?"

"Of course I can," Dan said, "but I don't want to. I've got to do some thinking of my own."

"Don't get yourself all disturbed, honey. It'll be all right," Elaine said. "Everything will be fine."

"Oh, sure," Dan said, too abruptly. "Everything will be just dandy."

He was angry, and then, as if over to one side, he was angry with himself for being angry. Sometimes anger would burn in him like a long, twisting worm, feeding on itself. More and more, lately, he had been aware that his emotional balance was disturbed, that often he would feel a double emotion, or two emotions simultaneously.

Laughing, he could suddenly feel cold and alone, or feeling creative, he could be overcome by an inability to create. Even his physical relationship with Elaine was becoming emotionally more complicated. There were times when excessive passion consumed itself unexpectedly and he would be surprised, the way a drunk is surprised when he tips a supposedly half-full bottle into a glass and finds it empty. Then they would pass through long days in a sort of sister-brother relationship. Unaccountably, in the middle of one of these periods he would sometimes experience not desire but a desire for desire. Sometimes, making love to her, he would become aware that haunting, nameless spectres had slipped into his mind, distracting him, making him falter, disturbing his concentration, like so many mosquitoes. Or again, fighting with her, hating her, swearing at her, he would be shaken with passion, with unannounced gusts of emotion that blew upon him from an unguarded direction, either making him despise himself for the abjection of his dependence upon her, or overcoming him completely and forcing him to run to her, unashamedly.

A car full of noisy young bucks sped by now in the night, trailing blue gasoline exhaust and loud obscenities.

"Hey, baby," shouted a voice from the car, "want to go for a ride?"

Dan's ugly mental condition boiled up in a momentary explosion of murderous rage.

"Sons of bitches!" He shouted after the car, shaking his fist, "Punky bastards!"

"Honey," Elaine said, "what's the matter?"

"Ah, shut up," Dan said. "What do you mean what's the matter? I suppose you enjoy that kind of talk!"

Elaine pursed her lips in annoyance. The conversation stopped and hung, broken off in mid-air. Dan could think of nothing to say. Unaccountably there came to his mind something he had read once, an opinion expressed by a psychologist that most thinking was done with words, however jerkily and incompletely, and thinking of it now Dan disagreed. He felt anger and resentment and despondency, but he could think of no words, or seemed not to be able to.

"It's funny," he said after a while. "I was just thinking that I can't think of any words and that's what started this whole damned thing, not being able to think of any words."

Elaine pressed his hand.

"It's all right," she said. "It will be all right."

"But you've got to admit it's funny," he said. "I've always been pretty handy with words. In school I ran the gamut of stock situations for a young man with 'literary' talent. High school paper, essay contests and all that. Placed a few poems. Wrote half a novel. Began writing songs. And yet when I try hardest to select the right words in conversation they elude me. Like the times we've said good-bye. I can just stand there and think and feel, but I can't really talk. And lately, when I'm trying hard, trying very hard to get some work done again on a song or two, I can't seem to think of the right words. It's funny."

"I see what you mean," Elaine said, "but try not to worry about it. Maybe if you just relax the words will come."

He resumed eating cherries from the small paper bag, and said nothing more about songs.

They stopped in at a clean-looking bar for a drink, but the lighting was too subdued for their tastes, and sitting next to them at the bar were two women with short hair and slacks.

"You could have knocked me over with a feather," one of them was saying. "Coming around at four in the morning and then getting sore because I wouldn't let her in!"

"Don't tell me about that one," said the other woman. "I've had enough of her to do me for a long, long time. Just a troublemaker."

"That's it exactly," said the first woman. "A troublemaker. And I'm glad you see it my way. I thought you were pretty fond of her."

"Me?" said the other. "Don't make me laugh. Would I be here now if I gave a damn about *her?*"

184

Turning to regard them, Dan saw that the women were holding hands.

"This must be a lez joint," Elaine said.

Later, on the street, Dan said, "I guess they're happier here."

"How do you mean?"

"In New York, in the Village. They're not freaks here like they are in Sioux City and Portland and Tucson."

"I should imagine they're unhappier here," Elaine said, "because here they can give in to themselves. In Sioux City they might never even know . . . I mean they might just turn out to be respectable old maids, or gym teachers, or nurses or something."

"Perhaps you're right," Dan said. "Here it's easy for them to follow their inclinations. If they're susceptible to a feeling of guilt they must be very unhappy here."

"Perhaps they feel no guilt," Elaine said. "Abnormal isn't *synonymous* with sinful, after all."

"I suppose not," Dan said, "although it's very difficult to even tell what the word normal means."

"It's difficult to tell what any word means," Elaine said.

Dan leaned over and kissed her on the side of the neck. "Do you know you're a very bright girl?" he said.

"Oh, well," Elaine said, "I guess there's no use trying to settle the problems of the world right here on Fourth Street."

"I think that was Fourth back there," Dan said. "The streets here are all twisted up. Never saw such a neighborhood. Twisted every which way."

It was fitting, Dan thought, that in such a neighborhood the streets should be twisted. Many of the people were twisted, their lives were twisted. It was too bad there wasn't some way of straightening it all out. Perhaps if the small Scotch-taped sign could say, "Little flowers and tin soldiers and lesbians and drunks taking old-fashioned pees will please gather in Sister Felicita's room for instructions on . . ."

A police car slipped quietly by, interrupting Dan's train of thought. By the time it had disappeared his mind had moved on to other things. A chill had crept into the midnight air. From far away, out in the harbor, came the hollow, throaty

185

scream of a boat picking its way through the darkness. Dan hailed a cab and they went home.

During the ride uptown Elaine said, "I wonder if the deviates who live in the Village feel that they're wrong. Or do they construct some sort of defense for themselves?"

"Sure," Dan said. "They must. That's one of the troubles with the world. Everybody's right."

"Come again?"

"In the world of reality we don't have enough people dressed in black, going around in sneaky movie mustaches and sneers. Everybody is a good guy. Luther was a good guy. Torquemada was a good guy. Napoleon was a good guy. What the hell are wars but disagreements between one group of good people, the Germans, say, against another group of good people, the English, or the French? Every *schmuck* who ever lived, no matter what sort of trouble he caused, could usually make out a good case for himself. What is that thing that Shakespeare said? Something to the effect that in religion there's no damned error so plain that some pious soul can't find a Biblical quotation to support it. Not quoting directly, but that's the gist of it."

While they were eating a late snack Elaine said, "But you still *do* feel that you've done something terribly wrong."

"Certainly," he said. "People have been hurt. I have no defense."

186

CHAPTER

EIGHTEEN

The FOLLOWING morning Hank called. "Dan," he said, "we can't put Halliburton off any longer. I talked to him last night. He as much as came right out and said that we'd better have lots of material to show him by Monday morning."

"Or else?"

"That's about the size of it."

"So let's get to work."

"Thatta boy. I'll be over in twenty minutes. Okay?"

Dan looked across the room at Elaine's sleeping form, at the pouting child's mouth, open in sleep, the full breasts partly covered by her folded arms. Suddenly he regarded Hank, and more importantly Halliburton, as intruders.

"What time is it?" he asked Hank.

"About one-thirty. Did I get you up?"

"Well, I—we were out pretty late last night. Give me an hour or so to have breakfast and shave."

"All right," Hank said wearily. "I'll see you at three, how's that?"

"Fine."

When he had hung up, Elaine rolled over, yawned, and said, "Who was that?"

"Hank."

"What did he want?"

"He's coming over to do some work."

"You want me to make brunch for the two of you?"

"No, honey." He rose and moved to her bed. "Can I bring you orange juice?"

"Yum-yum," she said appreciatively, her eyes still closed. While they drank the sudsy juice, into which Dan had dropped ice cubes, he said, "I don't feel like working."

"What *do* you feel like doing?"

"Making love to you."

"Who's stopping you?"

He pulled back the covers and kissed her right knee.

"Wait a minute," she said, smiling. She leaped from the bed, ran to the bathroom, brushed her teeth and in two minutes raced back into the room, executing a comic leap onto the bed.

"I was reading something in the paper this morning," Dan said. "One of those quizzes that are supposed to help you pick the right mate."

"Did you pass?"

"I didn't actually take the test, or fill in the blanks, or whatever. But what I got wondering about was this. The guy who made out the test was trying to tell people that they just can't go around marrying *any*body—they've got to be careful they don't marry somebody who's too mixed up. So all right. So a guy fills in the blanks and finds out that he shouldn't marry Miss So-and-So. Good. But the question that keeps worrying me is: just who is poor Miss So-and-So supposed to marry? Who are the *millions* of poor Mr. and Miss So-and-So's supposed to marry?"

"You're supposed to marry me," Elaine said, opening her arms to him and smiling sleepily. He was in the instant seized by such a powerful desire for her that just embracing her, just making love to her, would not have been enough. Not knowing what it was he wanted to do to express the full strength of his love he suddenly picked her up bodily from the bed and carried her about the room.

"Put me down," she said, laughing. "I'm heavy."

188

"You're a baby," he said, depositing her on top of the large bureau.

"Ouch," she said. "This glass is *cold!*"

They took so long making love that when Hank rang the doorbell at three o'clock Dan was still in his robe and slippers, unshaven.

"I'll be right with you," he said as he waved Hank into the living room. "Have a drink."

It was close to four by the time they actually got down to work. Dan felt in the mood to compose but the only melodies that would come out were love songs. After he had played the third one Hank said, "That's beautiful, too, man, but it's not what we're trying to find."

"What *are* we trying to find?"

"You know, something *up*. Something to go with the 'People Will Talk' lyric. I was thinking of something with a Latin beat. Maybe a beguine."

"Sometimes I think Halliburton has handed us a lemon," Dan said, feeling resentful at Hank's lack of interest in his three ballad melodies.

"What do you mean?"

"Well, what the hell's so funny about atom bombs and the end of civilization?"

"In reality, nothing at all. But that's just the point of humor, isn't it? Aren't most jokes about bad news?"

"What do you mean?"

"Well, aren't most jokes about how fat people are, or how stingy or how broke or how cross-eyed or how stupid or how hard-up or how drunk or something? The whole point of this show, as I see it, is to use the weapon of humor to show people how idiotic it is for them to think that nuclear war could ever be a reasonable, sensible solution for the world's problems. In comedy you can make people swallow a pill that might otherwise be too bitter for them."

"I don't know about that, but I know we never had all this trouble when we were writing for pictures. Hell, I can write as good as I ever did so it must be something about this god-damned play we're stuck with here."

"There *is* another possibility," Hank said.

"What's that crack supposed to mean?"

"Nothing," Hank said. "Forget it."

But Dan could not forget it. By six o'clock they had completed one song, most of which was created by Hank. This only added fuel to the fires of Dan's resentment.

"Look, Dan," Hank said, "it's Friday night. By Monday we've got to come up with the goods. But you don't seem to feel like working right now. You want to get together tomorrow morning?"

"Not particularly."

"Then what do you want to do?"

"Tell Halliburton what he can do with his god-damn Commie play."

"What the hell are you talking about?" Hank said. "What are you now, a big political expert? You and I are a couple of song writers. We were hired to do a job. Do we do it or not? That's the only question we ought to be talking about."

"Would you mind keeping your voice down?" Dan said. "I don't want Elaine to hear you." He walked nervously to the portable bar and poured himself a drink. Swallowing the bourbon fast so that it stung his tongue and throat, he turned and found himself pointlessly aware of the lines in Hank's face, at the serious, concerned, hurt expression in his eyes. To his dismay he discovered that he felt like laughing. Then he heard himself chuckle.

"What's so funny?" Hank said.

"I don't know," Dan said. "Bad habit of mine. Sometimes, in an emotional moment, I just feel like laughing. I don't know why."

"Dan," Hank said, "I hope you won't take offense at this but have you thought of analysis?"

"Of what?"

"Seeing a psychiatrist."

"What the hell are you talking about?"

"Oh, never mind," Hank said. "I told you not to get sore. It was just a friendly suggestion, that's all."

"What the hell's supposed to be so friendly about suggesting that I'm nuts?"

"I didn't say that, man."

"The hell you didn't!"

At that moment Elaine walked into the room.

"What's the trouble?" she said.

"Nothing," Dan said, embarrassed.

"Hello, Elaine," Hank said. "How've you been, dear?" She moved toward him for the usual peck on the cheek. For some reason it had always annoyed Dan to see Hank kiss her even in so impersonal and sexless a manner.

"What were you boys arguing about?" Despite her blank expression Dan had the feeling that she had heard every word.

"Oh," Hank said casually, "I—uh—I was just saying to Dan that I—uh—"

"He was just saying that I need medical help," Dan said, seating himself at the piano and staring at the keys.

"Well," Elaine said, "whatever he said I'm sure he meant to be helpful."

So she was taking sides against him. "God-damn it," Dan said. "Why doesn't everybody just try to run his own life and let it go at that." The alcohol was beginning to go to his head.

"Well," Hank said, moving to the door, picking up his hat, "I've got to be running along. I'll see you two later."

Dan did not answer or turn around. When Hank was gone, Elaine said, "Now, what was the idea of that outburst?"

"Outburst!" Dan said indignantly. "Where the hell was the outburst? I didn't say a damn word."

"But, honey, Hank only—"

"Oh, Hank only my ass. I'm sorry. Pardon my language. I just don't like his insults, that's all."

"But he's your friend. He wants to help you. And I like him for it."

"Sure you do. I noticed how you never miss a chance to have him kiss you."

"Dan!"

"Ah, shut up."

"But, honey—"

"Never mind. I know you like Hank. So all right. He's a big man. He's had a better education than I have. He dresses better than I do. He knows how to order wine and—"

191

"Dan, what are you talking about?"

"I just wish the Jew son-of-a-bitch would leave me alone."

"Dan!"

"Well, I just wish he'd leave me alone."

"But what about the show?"

"Screw the show."

At that moment Dan rose and left the apartment. Out on the street he walked for several blocks until the knot in his stomach had dissolved. Then he felt ashamed. Thank God he hadn't called Hank a Jew son-of-a-bitch to his face. So he was a true Scanlon after all. The realization of the significance of his outburst, however, only lessened his self esteem, so that for an hour or so he could not even bring himself to go back to the apartment and face Elaine. That was the day that it first occurred to Dan Scanlon that there might be something *wrong* with him, something essential that had really nothing to do with the predicament in which he found himself.

During the next two days, penitent though he was, he could not bring himself to pick up the phone and call Hank. On Monday he received a wire. "Sorry to have had to tell Halliburton that we were checking off the lot," it said. "Am going back to the Coast. Best regards. Hank."

That evening, Elaine stood before the bathroom mirror, drying herself with a large green towel.

"This is awful," she said, and through the partly opened door he could see that she was pinching her stomach, "I've simply got to go on a diet."

"I like you the way you are," Dan said.

"But really," she said. "This is too much. This is the limit. Tomorrow, I swear, tomorrow I start."

"All right," Dan said, reading the paper, listening with only one ear.

"It's funny," Elaine said. "It's funny how easy it is to say you'll go on a diet just after you've eaten a big meal."

How true, Dan thought, and how undependable were resolutions born of satiety. The alcoholic, bloated and shaking, his tissues aching from the absorption of liquor, could summon up a quavery sort of righteousness and solemnly promise himself that he would never touch another drop. The gambler, depressed by losses, could rise above his fever, resolve to handle his money more wisely. Dan allowed the paper to fall to the floor beside the bed, and looked at Elaine combing her hair.

How deceptively easy it was for him to shake himself and decide that he must leave her when, sated with happiness, physically satisfied, settled into a calm, domestic groove, he would unexpectedly exhaust his capacity for appreciating her. He would clutch eagerly at the ecstasy their relationship held out to him, take it, hold it, drown himself in it and then eventually find that, for a short while, he was unable to respond to it emotionally. That, he now had come to realize, was the dangerous time, for it was then, when he discovered that he could do without her for twelve hours, that he would imagine he might be able to do without her forever. It was almost always out of such times, such moods, that their arguments and separations sprang. For it was the same with her. She could appreciate him just so much at one time, laugh just so much at his whimsicality, thrill just so much to the feel of his hands on her body, be delighted just so much by his conversation, and then would come an emotional lull and, after the lull, a storm.

They would unexpectedly find themselves apart, often without quite realizing how or why. For the first day it was almost always all right. She would visit Polly and toy with the idea of calling other men. He would laugh and joke and talk to himself about the children, about Helen. The pleasant daydreams would sustain him for perhaps another day or two. During this period he was apt to telephone the West Coast, or write an overly sentimental letter, and then, along about the third day the periods of thinking about Elaine would lengthen. Sleeping would become more difficult; he would lurk near the telephone, wanting to call her. Sometimes, on the third or fourth day of a separation, he would try dating another girl. He would look anxiously into a pretty face, engage in overly animated conversation, searching for he knew not what. He would try to ply the girl with extra drinks, attempt to hold her hand at the dinner table. He would be unusually assailable on the emotional level, would find himself extraordinarily touched by the pathos of a story or more appreciative than normal of a perfume or the beauty of a gown. He would be wittier than usual, would talk more, laugh more. He would find himself drinking more, moving around town more, visiting different clubs, spending more money than was wise. He would hope, sometimes, that he might be able to work up a genuine emotional involvement with one of these new women, but about this time the strain would usually become unbearable. He would wander about the apartment, feeling sour and unfulfilled, fingering scattered slips of paper, looking in the closets for some garment of Elaine's, searching through drawers for pictures of her.

He would think again of Helen and of the children, and would grow bitter as they seemed to be slipping away from him, as he felt drawn to the telephone.

His loins would begin to ache and he would curse himself for the powerful sensuality that would engulf him. And yet it was not simple release he required. It was not just appetite, or any woman would have sufficed. His thoughts would be filled with visions of Elaine, *her* mouth, *her* hair, *her* warm stomach, *her* hips.

He would jump up and walk around the apartment, go to the refrigerator and open a can of beer, look out the window, pick up a magazine, do anything to try to keep busy, to occupy himself, to keep his mind free of the tantalizing images that tortured him. He would try to read and for a few pages it would help, then suddenly he would realize that though his eyes had traveled down a particular page his mind would have no memory of its content, and he would throw the book down and pace the apartment again, animal-like. His loins would ache again and his stomach muscles would contract with remembered passion. He would rationalize with himself, go over the problem from the beginning, try to tell himself that passion was only passion, that he could even reawaken the old feeling for Helen.

Then, although he was never quite sure of what moment the decision had been made, he would hear himself saying into the phone:

"Hello, baby."

"Hello, darling," Elaine would say, tiredly, as if she were very sorry for him. They would talk eagerly and profess their love, and they would apologize and plan and explain and wonder and hope and dream and fear and then in a matter of minutes they would fly the one to the other and their bodies would come together and tremble, each holding onto the other for life itself.

Then it would be a reprieve, a rebirth, a homecoming, a triumph snatched from defeat, an opening of blinded eyes. There would be laughter and tears and a frenzy of passion and he would lie awake holding her in the night and wondering about life, wondering how it could generate such great love where love was not supposed to exist. When he was back with her he would begin to want to work again and they would awaken in the middle of the night and stagger together to the piano. She would make coffee and he would pick out melodies and try to write lyrics. Some of his best work was done in these exciting periods of delirious joy, and sitting beside him in a housecoat, blinking, pouring him hot coffee, she would berate the publishers who had not seen fit to accept any of Dan's recent songs. She would say, "Oh, I can just hear Bing doing that," or "Dinah would love to get her hands on something like this right now."

"I'll take it around to Miller," Dan would say, "or maybe I'd better show it to Dave Kapp." Dan would become enthusiastic about writing again, but somehow weeks passed and then months and he had not been able to place anything. They were writing trash these days, he would explain, or the vogue now was phony folk songs, or all that publishers seemed to want was something for Johnny Ray. It was terrible, Elaine would agree, and probably if Jerome Kern or George Gershwin were starting out today as unknowns they'd be thrown out of every publisher's office in town.

It had been easier in Hollywood a few years ago. Dan's contacts there were better, he told himself, refusing for even a minute to consider the possibility that his writing might not have its former verve.

Eddie Manning, another publisher he had approached, had

told him to lay off for a few months, not to even try to write. It was easy for Manning to offer advice. His success had come easily, and he was one of several in the business who seemed to have made the grade by accident rather than as a result of ability. Manning had been a small-time agent for years, had managed Betty Collins, married her and negotiated a deal with E. B. Marks Music to set up a small publishing firm for numbers that Betty recorded. The firm, oddly enough, had prospered. Manning had even written the lyric of one song that became big, a Calypso novelty that, though of no particular distinction, had sold over half a million records. There had been a lawsuit of some kind, Dan dimly recalled. He had read something in *Variety* about a Puerto Rican or a Cuban or somebody suing Manning, claiming plagiarism, but Manning had won the case and now, four years later, was a successful publisher, no longer affiliated with Marks, no longer affiliated with Betty Collins for that matter, for their divorce and his subsequent remarriage were distant water under the bridge.

It was easy for Manning to sit behind his desk, in the office on the third floor overlooking Times Square, and give advice. Dan had exposed himself to the lecture by dropping a hint about an advance on a song.

"Baby, if I could spare it I'd give it to you," Eddie had said. He was one of the first in the business to call other men *baby*.

The fact of Dan's professional insecurity now made him all the more dependent upon Elaine. He not only needed her physically, but his ego was propped against the solidity of her love and respect for him.

He hurried home this day and took her in his arms.

"Did I ever tell you," he said, still standing in the doorway, with his hat on, "just what it's like when you're gone?"

"Yes," she said, "but tell me again."

"When you're away from here," he said, "and I think you're not coming back, the apartment changes character. It's not a place to live in any more; it's a museum. The furniture seems no longer functional, the individual pieces seem to be on display. The living room in particular is a lonesome place, so I find myself hovering around the bedroom, picking up little things you've left on the dresser, looking at things hanging in the closet, idly searching like a dog in a vacant lot."

She clung to him silently.

"I'm thirsty," he said.

She laughed and began to mix the drinks.

After two or three drinks, he noticed, he would often develop a peculiar and acute sort of awareness, a poetic detachment which enabled him to see things from a fresh viewpoint. It wouldn't last long. He'd have two or three more and become unable to perceive anything clearly, become mired in meanness and dullness, sitting muddleheaded and mumbling a monotonous commentary on whatever subject staggered across the stage of his mind.

But, before that, for a while, an hour or so, he would feel better able to wrestle with all his problems. He would feel aloof and philosophical and actually able to speak some wisdom culled from the mysterious depths of his subconscious. He sat once on the floor of the living room watching carefully as she sewed a button on his shirt cuff.

"Thank you for doing this," he said with exaggerated precision. "Do you know something? It has just occurred to me that a woman loves to see a man wearing a safety pin where a button ought to be because it gives her an opportunity to be helpful."

"That's right," she said.

"And that's not all," he said. "A man, on the other hand, is appalled at the sight of a stray pin on a woman. He thinks, 'Here is a woman who can't take care of herself.' "

Another time, slightly drunk, he lay on the sofa eating a large Delicious apple. He filled his mouth with a cold bite, then held the apple close to his face.

"Did you ever look at the skin of a Delicious apple?" he asked her.

"No," she said.

"Well, you ought to. Everybody ought to do that. You know why?"

"Why, darling?" she said.

"Because if you looked at it real close you'd see that it's full of stars."

"Stars?"

"Yes, damn it. Stars. They're very little and yellow and they look just like stars in a bright, red Technicolor sky."

She took the apple from him and examined it carefully and found that he had spoken the truth.

One day they drove to Jones Beach to swim and soak up sunshine.

"I would like to to rent a small airplane with a loudspeaker," Dan said, as they stretched out on the sand on an old blanket.

"Why?" Elaine said.

"So I could get up in the air over this place and yell, 'Listen, down there, all you people. This is Jones speaking. This is my beach. Get to hell out, *everybody!*' "

Elaine smiled. She lay beside him in a tight woolen bathing suit with narrow horizontal red-and-white stripes, her left hand folded in his right, her right forearm over her eyes.

A small boy, wearing a chain with a Catholic medal hanging from it, walked slowly past them, eating a hot dog. To Dan he looked somewhat like Michael. On an impulse he rose and ran into the water. It worked. For a few minutes he was able to forget his problems, luxuriating in the salt water.

In a few minutes Elaine joined him and they frolicked and splashed in the surf, laughing and holding hands. Later, lying in the sun on the blanket again, Dan said, "I am familiar with the moral concept of invincible ignorance. I wonder if there is such a thing as invincible *weakness,* in a given situation. For example, the weakness that, a man having been threatened with having hot lead poured into his mouth, makes him divulge military information, or the weakness that makes a normally law-abiding and decent man commit violent crimes if he happens to become addicted to heroin and runs out of it, or the weakness that renders an alcoholic literally unable to resist taking a drink he sees on the table. Or the weakness that seems to make it impossible for me to give you up, no matter how hard I try."

"People always say that ignorance of the law is no excuse," Elaine said. "So I'm sure they would say that weakness is no excuse either. At least men, being hypocritical and short-sighted bastards, would say that. But God would not, I think."

"I agree," Dan said. "No one can be morally responsible for what he cannot help doing. The question is, of course, *can* I help myself in this situation? I know now that I am relatively helpless. If that is true, then I am relatively blameless. But am I also *absolutely* helpless?"

"Perhaps at some moments you are and at other moments you are not. Obviously you're not helpless at those times that you decide to give me up, those moments when you leave me."

"That raises an interesting point," Dan said. "I have tended to think of this as *one* sin—the sin of loving Elaine. But it actually comes down to a matter of an almost infinite number of individual sins. Every time I consider the problem and accept the alternative that involves running to you, or reaching out to touch you if you are already here, or just thinking with pleasure of the red curve of your smile and the soft warm spot in the crook of your elbow—every one of those times another sin is chalked up."

"Unless," Elaine said, "some of those times you literally do not have free will. Is that perhaps the solution to the age-old debate about free will? That we have it, but only *most* of the time."

"I don't know," Dan said. "In a mechanical sense, of course, it's perfectly obvious that at certain times, and in certain regards, man does *not* have free will. When we're asleep, for example, and I suddenly develop a desire for you, what do I mean by the word 'I'? When we are cut with knives we have no freedom of choice *not* to bleed. When we go a very long time without food we have no freedom of choice to remain alive. When we are slapped in the face something inside us responds with a lightning-quick flash of fury. A moment later we are free to throttle our anger, but the basic, the important thing, is that *the anger was there.* It appeared unbidden, from the deep, dark place where the body stores the secrets of human animal history, and never delivers them up to the individual. God," he said, sitting up, "I wish I had really gotten an education so I'd know what I'm talking about."

"Go on with that idea," Elaine said, turning toward him and kissing his chest. "Maybe you're working your way toward some sort of a solution."

"I was about to say," Dan continued, speaking slowly, "that very young children do not have free will, and the insane do not have free will, at least most of the time they don't. Now if we move in from the extreme boundary of outright insanity we find, I think, that there is no sharp line of demarcation between the sane and the insane but rather that there is a very gradual—well, you might represent it on a graph, with violent insanity being on the far left, jet black, and pure intellectual clarity and brilliance on the far right, absolutely white. Now what is in between is not various neat bars of very dark gray gradually changing to very light gray, but rather one single stretch of space that is black on its left, white on its right, and gray in between, but the chart is so wide and the change so gradual that there is absolutely no single spot you can put your finger on and say that right here is where there is a clear-cut change between a point and the spot right next to it, if you see what I mean."

"I do," she said.

"Now if we start again by saying that the insane do *not* have free will then we see that it is impossible to point to the exact spot on our chart where free will goes into effect. We are faced with the problem of the many different kinds of insanity, subtly merging into the many different kinds of almost-insanity, the neuroses, eccentricities. We're faced with hereditary and environmental factors, endocrine glands, nervous sensitivities, the size of this—" he pointed toward his penis, jokingly— "and, hell, I guess what I'm getting at is that there *have* to be degrees of blame."

"That seems inescapable," she said. "Even human judges take that into account, which is why jail sentences for the same offense will vary."

"Right," Dan said, sitting up suddenly with a feeling of intellectual excitement. "But now here's something I don't understand. The Church has two divisions of sin: mortal and venial. Now an individual priest in the confessional, or even a four-star theologian, would be able to distinguish between degrees of guilt for serious sin, but what meaning, what importance would it have if the sin involved were still classified *mortal?*"

"I don't follow you there," Elaine said.

"It's quite simple," Dan said. "At least it seems so to me at this moment. A mortal sin is one that will send you to hell if you die without having repented of it, without having confessed it. So you go to hell and you meet a fellow and you say, 'What did you do to get here?' and he says, 'Oh, I sent three million Jews to the gas chamber,' and he says, 'What did *you* do?' and you say, 'Oh, I was taking my girl friend home from a high school dance and we stopped to park on a dark street and started to kiss goodnight and the next thing I knew we had our clothes off and were fucking and the motor was still running and something went wrong with the exhaust pipe and the windows were up because it was a cold night and we suddenly were killed by the fumes.' "

"Well, the example may be off-beat but I think that—"

"No," he said. "It's not. I didn't make up either one of these cases. The killing of millions of Jews you've read about in the papers. The case of the high school kids found naked in their car, dead, is real too. It happened in Chicago, not far from where I used to live. Scared the hell out of all of us kids. Anyway, my question is: what practical results, in theological terms, follow from the concept of degree-of-blame for sin as long as a sin is still *mortal?*"

"Dan," Elaine said, after a long pause, "I'm perfectly able to use the word *neurotic* but I'm sure I couldn't define it scientifically. But do you think your attraction to me—not to mention mine to you—could be, at least in part, neurotic?"

"I don't know," Dan said. "It doesn't seem so to me. In other words if I were not a married man, if you and I had just met and fallen in love, the idea of our relationship being neurotic would never have occurred to us. People would simply have said, 'Isn't it marvelous? They're such a loving couple.' "

"But—I've been in love before, and so have you. This is different. This feeling I have for you, that we have for each other, is so *intense,* so—I can't think of any other word than *wild*. And it isn't just the need for sex. You've had that. I've had it. The need we have is definitely for each other."

"I think so too," he said, "and yet, what if we had never met, or if one or the other of us had never been born. Wouldn't the need have been expressed toward someone else?"

"I suppose so, but perhaps never in this way, never to this crazy pitch. From the first moment we met there was the feeling of being with a good friend, an old friend. There was the feeling of sharing a sense of humor, of looking at things in the same way, of the most complete relaxation and understanding. I've never known that before."

"Then how can anything so good be neurotic?"

"I don't know," she sighed.

"I have the feeling that there's an explanation for what happened to us," he said, "but I'm beginning to think that, unaided, we'll never figure it out."

They had been home about twenty minutes when the telephone rang. It was Hank, calling from the Coast.

"Dan," he said, "I just heard something that I think you ought to know about. Something about Helen."

"What is it?" Dan said, fearful that he was about to hear news of a tragedy.

"Oh, nothing serious," Hank said, sensing his reaction. "It's good news, actually. At least it seems to me you ought to take it as such."

"Fine," Dan said. "What is it?"

"Well," Hank said, "you've been gone a hell of a long time now and I'm sure you don't expect Helen to just sit out there by herself for the rest of her life, do you?"

"Certainly not."

"Well, all right then. Because she's not. I was out with some people last night and one of the fellows in the group happened to mention that he'd met a wonderful gal the night before. Turned out that he was talking about Helen. He didn't know that I knew you."

"Well," Dan said, "that's fine. I mean I don't mind. I certainly want whatever is best for Helen."

"Good," Hank said. "Look, get one thing straight. I'm not

202

telling you this just to be retailing gossip. The thing would have come to your attention anyway, I'm sure. I'm calling you because I thought this news might help—you know—relieve your guilt feelings. It seems to me that if you knew Helen didn't care what you did one way or the other you'd feel a hell of a lot better."

"Yeah," Dan said. "I guess I would at that."

"Well, that's about it, man," Hank said. "How's everything else? How's Elaine?"

"Fine," Dan said. "She's great. Everything's great."

"Give her my best," Hank said. "And take it easy."

"You too."

"Bye-bye," Hank said, and the line clicked.

"What did Hank have to say?" Elaine said.

"Oh, he just had a little bit of news for me," Dan said. "Helen has decided to stop moping around the house, I guess. Hank said he ran into somebody who had a date with her, or something of the sort."

"How do you feel about that?"

"Great."

"Are you sure?" She looked at him levelly.

"Yes," he said. "Well, to tell you the truth, I don't really feel *great* about it at all. Don't misunderstand me; I'm certainly not depressed. I guess I'm just a little blank, really. A little puzzled. In a way I have no reaction to the news at all. That's strange, isn't it?"

"I don't think so," Elaine said. "It's perfectly understandable. For months and months you've been torturing yourself because you were torturing Helen. Now that you think she might have gotten over it all, well—this will require some thinking. Let's suppose this man, whoever he is, turns out to be important to Helen. Let's even suppose she falls in love with him and wants to marry him. What then?"

"What do you mean?" he said, uneasily.

"Well, Helen's not a Catholic. If she loves this other man and comes to assume that you're a lost cause she may decide to get a divorce. Where does this leave you with your religious problems?"

"I don't know," he said, sitting down. "I just don't know."

"Of course," Elaine said, "we'd better not get ahead of ourselves. Hank may have been mistaken or the guy may never show up again. But it's something worth thinking about. If Helen got married, Dan, would you marry me then?"

"Sure, honey," Dan said. "Of course I would." But inwardly he was far from sure. He projected himself into the possible future situation. Helen married to someone else. Himself free. What would he do? At the moment he did not know. He was surprised to find that he still felt insecure and uncertain.

CHAPTER

NINETEEN

A FEW weeks later Hank came to town and telephoned.

"Where are you calling from?" Dan asked, when he recognized his voice.

"I'm at the Warwick," Hank said. "Just in town for two or three days."

"Business?"

"Yeah, have to see my attorneys about something, and I also want to get a couple of new suits and see some shows."

"Have you talked to Helen?"

"Yes," Hank said. "That's the reason I called you. She's still going with this fella I told you about."

"That's good. Is he a right guy?"

"Seems to be. I did a little prying when I called her and she told me all about him. She says the kids like him and that he's a good guy all around."

"What does he do?" Dan said.

"He's a lawyer, I think. And he also has something to do with a chain of ice cream stores. He's been divorced himself and has two kids of his own. They're quite a bit older than yours, though. I've checked the guy out and he seems to be A-number-one. Nobody has a bad word to say for him."

"Well, that's swell," Dan said. "Do you think they're serious?"

"Probably not yet," Hank said. "I think it's just a matter of two lonely people keeping each other company. She probably won't let herself fall in love with him until she's certain which way you're going to jump. And with the kids in the picture I guess she's going at it the right way."

"Yeah."

"But, look, that's not the only reason I called. This may sound weird, but I know a man who may be able to help you."

"What's so weird about that?" Dan said.

"I didn't finish," Hank said. "What I mean is, I'm not talking about an analyst or a doctor or a priest."

"Do I start guessing?" Dan said, purposely flippant. "What is he—a dentist, a plumber?"

"No," Hank said. "That's the weird part. No one is sure just what he is, at least I'm not. As far as I can tell he's just a wise man."

"Sounds Oriental."

"I know. We've all read about wise men. You find them in the Bible, in ancient literature of all kinds. And you do find them in the Orient. The one place you practically never find them, oddly enough, is in *our* civilization, where they're probably most needed."

"Who is the guy? Where does he live?"

"His name is Carter Marvell. He's English, I'm pretty sure, although he's lived in this country for many years. He has a cottage right now in Brewster, New York; it's upstate. I guess *weird* was too strong a word. I don't mean he walks around in a loincloth, living on roots and berries. He looks perfectly normal, writes books, lectures here and there. But there's something different about him for all that. Unlike the rest of us he seems supremely uninterested in money, fame, prestige. It may be only because he has a certain modest amount of all three, but I don't think so."

"How did you learn about him?"

"The same way you are right now. A friend told me about

him years ago. I was in a confused state. You may remember my telling you once that when I was a kid in college I was a Communist, or something close to it. I had cast off my religion. Eventually I saw that communism wasn't for me either and that, as far as I could tell, it wasn't for the world. I won't go into all that now, but the point is I was hung up. I had no philosophical base, nothing from which I could draw strength. And a girl I loved, or thought I loved, had just gotten married. Anyway, somebody told me about Marvell. I spent one evening with him and—I guess it sounds dramatic to say that it changed my life. That's probably an exaggeration. But it did me good. It helped me to keep my head at a bad time. So what do you say? You want to try him?"

"Yes," Dan said, "if you think he'll have the time to see *me*."

"I've already checked into that," Hank said. "He has."

It was a perfect day for the ride up to Brewster. Warm, clear, breezy. The Hudson River had a fresh, snappy look off to the left as they motored up out of the city, heading for open country. In the suburbs the trees were deeply green, wind-tossed, sparkling in the sunshine.

"By the way," Dan said, "how much?"

"What?"

"I mean, what do I pay this fellow?"

"Nothing," Hank said. "He doesn't need your money. I think he must have some family money somewhere, and then he's paid to lecture. But as for his personal time he just donates it to the world, although not indiscriminately."

"A wise man," Dan said, reflectively.

"Yes," Hank said. "Or so he seems to me."

"What is his religion?"

"Whatever it is, it's his own. He belongs to no church, although there are strange rumors about him. I've heard it said that he studied for the ministry. Somebody once told me it had been whispered about that he was an unfrocked Catholic priest but I'm sure there's nothing to that story."

"Can't you tell anything about him from his books?"

"Not much. They're not autobiographical. And then too,

he publishes them under a pen name. A. V. Fennel. His religion seems to me part humanist and part some kind of synthesis of the major faiths, especially their ethical content. And I think he's been deeply influenced by the Oriental philosophers."

They arrived in Brewster shortly after midday, driving leisurely through its tree-shaded roads. Hank stopped the car at a rural mailbox with the name Carter Marvell printed on it in small black letters.

"Here we are," he said, turning into a lane on the right. Dan could see nothing ahead but a narrow, rutted dirt path, barely wide enough to permit passage of the car, its edges merging into the tangled profusion of grass, weeds and trees. After a moment the lane curved and there was the sudden view of a rustic but well-constructed two-story cabin, an expanse of brilliantly green lawn, and off to the right foreground a small, irregularly shaped swimming pool in which a middle-aged, bearded man was splashing. At sight of the car he waved and clambered out of the pool.

"Hello," he called. "You're early."

"Yes," Hank said. "We made good time. Carter, this is Dan Scanlon."

The man approached the car, drying his hands on a large yellow towel.

"Delighted," he said, as Dan emerged. "Will you be able to spend the entire afternoon?"

"Yes," Hank said.

"Splendid." Marvell shook Dan's hand, gesturing to an arrangement of patio furniture beside the pool. "You might enjoy sitting out here for a while," he said. "I'll be with you shortly."

When he had gone into the house Dan said, "He looks a bit like pictures I've seen of George Bernard Shaw."

"A little," Hank said, stretching out full length on a green flowered chaise and lighting a cigarette. "You'll find him easy to talk to. I won't be around, naturally. I can busy myself in his library, or I might go for a drive. I know some people in the next town down the road."

"How long will he want to talk to me?" Dan said.

"That's partly up to you. If you want to cut it short I'm sure he'll sense it. But it's my guess you'll want to spend the entire afternoon with him. He spins off ideas like a Roman candle. And when five o'clock rolls around you'll wonder where the time went."

"We'll see," Dan said.

After minted iced tea and cakes had been served beside the pool by a Filipino in a white jacket, Hank excused himself. Marvell showed Dan to a large, airy second-story porch, enclosed by glass and screening. Full of bookcases and comfortable paintings it offered a striking view of the lawn, the pool, and the rustling forest and open sky beyond. For a few minutes Dan, embarrassed, stood looking out the window.

As he turned he saw Marvell pour himself what appeared to be a drink of water in a small paper cup, down it, and then make a notation on a pad of yellow paper, after looking at his watch. After a moment the older man seated himself in a large leather chair and smiled amiably.

"You feel slightly ill-at-ease, Mr. Scanlon, I'm sure."

"Somewhat," Dan admitted.

"No doubt of it," Marvell said. "And perfectly understandable. I once stood where you are standing now, and I don't mind admitting I was damned embarrassed. However, it may put you at ease if I tell you that it doesn't matter in the least where we start our conversation. Nor, for that matter, is there any obligation to start it at all."

"Well," Dan began, awkwardly, "Hank said he thought you could help me."

"How long have you known him?" Marvell said.

"Oh, let's see," Dan said. "It must be five or six years."

"So he said I could help you, did he?" Marvell said, laughing. "Well, he's wrong. I cannot help you, or anyone, directly, except in the material sense. I can give you my coat or food or money. But what I *may* be able to do for you is enable you to help yourself. It will have to come to that in the end, you see."

There was a long pause, broken only by the sound of the soft wind in the trees.

"You must have thought of suicide as a way out," Marvell said.

"Yes," Dan admitted, remembering his desperate walk at the edge of the gray Pacific.

"That's good," Marvell said. "It shows that you take all parts of your problem very seriously. To actually *commit* suicide, of course, would be absurd. But to consider it may be an indication of a willingness to explore all possibilities. Unless, that is, you have concentrated upon it to the relative or absolute exclusion of all other solutions."

"No," said Dan. "I haven't done that. Although I admit I haven't been able to think of very many other solutions."

"I doubt that," Marvell said. "If we listed them right now you would find that there are a number of alternatives. The thing is, none of them looks attractive to you."

"I guess that's it."

"While again emphasizing the absurdity of suicide I still want you to know that you ought not to think that you are losing your mind or anything of the sort merely because you have *considered* doing away with yourself. Camus, among others, asks: is suicide the logical response to the hopelessness of life?"

"Who?" Dan said.

"Forgive my presumption," Marvell said. "*Albert* Camus, a French author, and one who has more to teach our age than, I suspect, we are capable of learning."

"I don't read as much as I should," Dan said.

"Who does?" Marvell answered, uncrossing and recrossing his legs. "But, as I was saying, Camus asks: is suicide a rational way out? This, it seems to me, would be a fair question for the last man on earth, or a man resigned to a life alone on the proverbial deserted island. But if it be granted that there is one other human life on the island, or that the man is not the last of his species, then there is a reason to want to continue one's existence, whether or not there is a God. We evidently cannot be seized with absolute conviction that we have a purpose unto ourselves or unto the Universe, but we *can* be certain that we have a purpose and a function unto others. We see this in the fact that the race cannot be propagated by any one of us alone but that this must be effected by union with one other human being. And we see further that when the new individual is born he dies at once if left to his own resources but thrives if he can find adults to take an interest in his welfare."

"I see," Dan said.

"Good," Marvell said. "Now I would imagine that at the present moment you cannot possibly conceive of the time when you will not love the woman with whom you are involved."

"Yes, that's right," Dan said.

"Ah," Marvell said. "You feel alone, unique. But your case is, in the large sense, not unusual. Perhaps only more severe than most cases of a similar nature. But we have not even established that. Remember this: everything, however beautiful, dies. That will sound to you so obvious as to be hardly worth mentioning, which is to say that you can now grasp it intellectually (to employ the wordage of the psychologists) but not emotionally."

He paused for a moment and looked at the ceiling, then continued.

"The day man is born he begins to die, to travel a road that, into whatever sun-swept highlands it may wind, wends its way inevitably to the grave. But—the realization of this fact being unpleasant—man represses it, so successfully that, sometimes to the moment of his final breath, dying seems to be something that only *other* people do. This perhaps necessary psychological repression is what accounts, I suspect, for the common inability to entertain the possibility of, for example, nuclear cataclysm, all public and private discussions of which seem to take place in a comfortable and emotionless vacuum. But I digress somewhat.

"Men, if they force themselves, can—at least a few minutes at a time—contemplate the idea of death and try to relate it to themselves. But this contemplation really ought not to be as difficult as it is because we all are involved with many rehearsals for death. Not only does our one physical death fall into the slot of certainty, as it were, in the moment of our conception, but each of our individual activities, dreams, and plans throughout life begins to die at the moment it is born. Love affairs, for example, very rarely end with the death of one or both of the parties involved; more commonly they die gradually quite some time before the physical self dies, sometimes concluding suddenly and violently but more often passing away peacefully in sleep, as it were, so that one can never, looking back, put one's finger on the exact moment of their death.

"And every work of art, too, is eventually for the artist a piece of finished and dead business which may seem to have life of a sort for others but which for the artist is no longer a part of him in the present but merely a dead reflection of something he believed or felt in the rapidly receding past. And so it is with every commercial venture, social relationship or random plan. Each has its birth and its death. And all of these, if we but recognize the fact, could be interpreted as rehearsals for the last death."

"I am impressed by what you say," Dan said. "It's all reasonable, and even comforting. But my problem is an immediate pain, a present situation that I'm not sure will be relieved by philosophy, however right and agreeable."

"But of course," Marvell said. "I am not offering you a palliative. Understand this clearly. Your suffering will continue. Perhaps for a long time, although I believe it will not last as long as you at this moment fear that it will. But you will suffer, in part because of the trap into which you have stumbled—of which more later—and in part because suffering is natural to man. Because man feels alien to this world he sometimes imagines that if the earth had other dimensions, if the material means of his existence had other properties, life would somehow be different, better. But it seems to me that regardless of what conditions on the earth were, even if, for example, there was no disease but people simply vanished in a puff of smoke at seven o'clock in the morning on the first day of their sixty-fifth year, man would still consider his fate in general to be a tragic one. And he would be quite right in making such a judgment."

"I suppose that's true," Dan said.

"If all men were born with three legs," Marvell continued,

"there would be great weeping and wailing over the occasional genetic mutant who was brought into the world having only two. No, my friend, no physical improvements would greatly alter man's attitude toward the world, unless perhaps he saw them come into being and could compare them with an earlier time when they did not exist."

Dan stood up and strolled to the window.

"Hank tells me," Marvell said, "that you are a Catholic. This, of course, increases the pain you now feel. You are torn apart by guilt. Tell me . . . how firm is your faith?"

"I don't know," Dan said. "Before this all started I would have said that it was very firm. But in the last few months I've learned things about myself that I never knew. I don't think very much of myself. If I could give up a good wife perhaps I could give up a good religion."

"It is certainly to be considered among the possibilities," Marvell said. "Let me put you at ease about one matter. I will say nothing whatever to weaken your faith. In fact, I wish you knew your religion better than you evidently do."

"What do you mean?" Dan said, looking up.

"I have the impression that you think you are despised by God. That can never be. Though you were the greatest criminal the world had ever known you would not be despised by God. And every Catholic scholar knows this, but I have come to the conclusion that most Catholics do not. Statistics covering mental illness, alcoholism, narcotics addiction, and crime —alas—have led me to this view."

"Then you think religion has failed man?"

"Certainly. They have failed each other. But what is meant by the word religion? *Everything* has failed man. He can be destroyed by all natural forces, forces which in themselves have no consciousness, no will, and which consequently cannot possibly will his destruction. Because religion sometimes fails—or perhaps I should say because a specific religious solution to a given problem proves inadequate—it occurs to men that their salvation may lie in science."

"How can science help in a case like mine?" Dan said.

"Do not expect that it will provide a magic key." Marvell responded. "Those who believe in the Cult of Redemption

213

through Science are wide of the mark. Certainly, if man ever thought that science would turn this earth into paradise, he was mistaken. But this is not to justify either the denial of the myriad benefits that science has brought into our lives, or the refusal to improve both things and men by the application of rational principles. Man, some say, is a creature whose rational and vital processes are in organic unity, and there is no possible technique by which he can escape from the hopes, fears, and anxieties of his own individual existence or those of his nation or civilization. This, I submit, is simply not true. Admittedly man cannot become God; that is to say he cannot become perfect, by applying the methods of science to himself and his world. But it is a fact that he *can* escape from a great many if not all of the fears and anxieties of his own individual existence by approaching the question as to the *origin* of these hopes and fears, insofar as possible, with a spirit of scientific objectivity. To consider but one example of how this might be accomplished let us examine briefly the question of racial prejudice, which has brought man to so much misery and bloodshed. Religion and moral codes, which have had full and unencumbered opportunity to attack this particular problem for centuries, have not only proved to a considerable extent unequal to the task but have in all too many specific instances worsened the situation they might have been expected to improve.

"Now irrational prejudices or attitudes are developed within the individual either by simple indoctrination or else originate from his private insecurities and fears. Science, if given free rein, can dissolve this problem. The fact that it will not do so in all cases or that in some cases it will do so imperfectly cannot be put forth as an argument against the wisdom of the undertaking in the first place. Science, in this connection, is like Chesterton's Christianity. It has not been tried and found wanting but has rather been found difficult, and so, by the mass of men, never tried. He errs, to be sure, who puts his total reliance upon science. Man is, after all, not a machine. But those who persist in seeing this question in terms of the historic rivalry between religion and science ought by now to have observed that where formalized, narrow religion has locked horns with science she has been defeated.

"Religion, rather than continuing to harbor resentment against science, ought rather to realize that just as science can improve all other things, so it can improve religion. The forces of religion once absolutely insisted that the world was only a few thousand years old. They would possibly still persist in this absurd opinion were it not for the fact that science respectfully, tentatively, carefully, bowing and scraping, pointed out its error. It is most unfortunate that the word *science*, in the minds of some, has acquired a sort of mystic personification. It is seen in the mind's eye as capitalized and it calls to mind vague associations of cruelty, impersonality, eccentricity, or atheistic tendencies. Again, one must say: nonsense. Science is simply the business of man's knowing. Any true fact, whether it be discovered by a Newton or a village idiot, is a scientific fact. To put the matter in even more basic terms, there is very great doubt, since the field of religion has become a babble of argumentative voices, as to what extent formalized religion might be said to be the province of God. But, granted that God exists, there can be not the slightest doubt that science is of God. It is, let us say, at the very least questionable as to whether God does not want us to eat pork or to treat a particular breed of cow as holy, but there can be no question that the natural force of gravity is a force of and from God."

Dan sighed deeply, staring down at his interlocked fingers.

"So now," Marvell said, "let us take a closer look at your predicament, seeing whether we can apply both scientific and religious principles toward the discovery of a solution. I assume you were not ideally suited to your wife."

"I would have denied that once," Dan said, "but now I don't know."

"I think we may safely assume it," Marvell said. "Permit me to explain. If you were truly, deeply, satisfactorily in love with your wife, you could not have formed this obsessive attachment to the second woman—what is her name?"

"Elaine."

"Yes. Please understand me. You could easily, let's say accidentally, in a moment of weakness, become *sexually* involved. This, after all, is rather common to our society, a fact which our society persists in hiding from itself. But the cases where the outside-the-home attachment becomes literally overpowering are, fortunately, relatively rare. There *are* men with strange compulsions to indulge in extramarital affairs, men who go from one woman to another, men suffering from a Don Juan complex. But you are not one of these, for which you must be grateful. I am assuming you were not an habitual philanderer."

"That's right," Dan said.

"Very well," Marvell continued. "Then this reinforces my feeling that there is something of profound importance lacking in the relationship between your wife and yourself."

"I was never aware of it," Dan said.

"But you are now," Marvell said, "because you have accidentally stumbled over a vastly more fulfilling relationship. You are like the man who was born blind and so never really missed his eyesight in the way that a sighted man who is struck blind does. But now you have discovered what you were missing. Concentrate on that word *missing*. What *was* missing?"

"I'm not sure," Dan said. "I've always refused to look at my problems, until now. I always figured that Helen was my wife, till death do us part, no matter what, so why the hell rummage around under the surface and stir things up?"

"Ah, yes," Marvell said. "Why, indeed? Tell me, what happens when you try to give up the woman you love?"

"I go to pieces," Dan said, feeling embarrassed again. "I seem to have no will power. Oh, I can get by for a little while. Sometimes an hour, sometimes a day, sometimes three or four days. But every minute of that time something terrible and overpowering is building up inside of me, some terrible pressure. So far it's exploded every time."

"Do you blame the woman for this?"

"No."

"That's good. She is not entirely blameless but you must never make the mistake of thinking that she *did* this to you,

216

that you have no problems of your own, that she is the *cause* of your downfall. I take it she loves you very much."

"Oh, certainly," Dan said. "You know, I've never really been able to understand those cases of unrequited love. I mean I can understand some shock and disappointment at discovering that someone you love doesn't return the compliment, but I can't imagine mooning about it for more than a short time. No, what makes it so hard for me to give Elaine up is that I'm sure she *does* love me. So when I try to break away I have always on my mind the fact of her love. I know it's there, waiting for me."

"Well," the older man said, "it's good that you have not attempted to make her a scapegoat, as society may do. Remember: the day we are *born* we fall in with bad company. But also with good. And we have, all of us, the ability to distinguish. In time this ability causes us great concern, for it may teach us that those whom we had early regarded as good or wise are nothing of the kind."

Marvell paused at this point, selected a peach from a fruit bowl at his side—offered Dan one, which was declined—and began to peel it slowly with a sharp knife.

"And of course the fact of the children increases your sense of guilt, does it not?" he said at length.

"Yes," Dan said. "Is that supposed to be wrong? Is guilt out of style?"

"By no means," Marvell said, "although there are various kinds of guilt, appropriate for various kinds of offenses. One should, for example, feel more guilt for a crime committed with malice aforethought than for something done in a moment of weakness. But what must be clarified here is the point of *subjectivity*. Now *objectively*, in the eyes of a third party, let's say, the two crimes may look identical. So there's no question, it would seem, but that grave results of various sorts have flowed from your act. There is, however, a question as to how much you are to blame for all this."

"You're not suggesting I'm blameless?"

"No, I am not. But I'm not rejecting the possibility out of hand. I assume, however, that you *are* to blame, but probably to a smaller degree than you think. I do not, in other words, minimize the enormity of what has happened. The suffering your children feel, the suffering your wife and, for that matter, Elaine and yourself feel—that is all real. It exists. It must be reckoned with and dealt with. But you might be in better shape to deal with it if you could stop torturing yourself, wasting your energy *unnecessarily,* unproductively."

"I see," Dan said.

"It is further possible," Marvell went on, "that part of the violence of your attraction to Elaine is stimulated by your guilt."

"You mean the old expression: forbidden fruit, and all that?"

"That's part of my meaning," Marvell said. "But there's a mechanistic angle to the thing, too, I suspect. Guilt is a powerful emotion. It starts, in you, as an understandable and even, within bounds, *reasonable* reaction to the concrete facts of the situation. But it builds up. It makes you so miserable that you've got to take an antidote, got to find some sort of relief, some sort of outlet. Some people would take to sleeping pills, or alcohol, or narcotics. You just happen not to be driven to any of those things, but you *are* driven back into the arms of the woman you love. So that not only do you love her, in the normal, healthy animal sense, but you now *need* her, in a sort of desperate, or neurotic sense. It isn't merely sex. That's a rather common commodity and, though it's good with this young lady, you will, I am certain, admit that there must be other women in the world who are equally gifted at the art. No, there's something deeper here, something deeper even than a sexual need."

Dan coughed, to cover a small wave of embarrassment.

"I do not wish to embarrass you in any way," Marvell said, "nor can I do anything more than theorize about your case, since I am not really intimately familiar with its details, but it seems to me that you feel that the attraction which has you trapped is primarily sexual."

"Yes," Dan said. "I do."

"That *may* not be the case," Marvell said, "although the horizon of sex, for all our studious approaches to it, still eludes

218

us and—because each man is unique—always will. But
I suspect is really at the root of your attachment is an
tional need. It is this need which fans the sexual flames
were, and renders them so devastating. Is the young lady
beautiful?"

"Yes," Dan said.

"I see. But I have known of similarly compulsive or obsessive cases where the woman was *not* attractive, where indeed she was crippled or much too old or something of the
sort. Now where there is something clearly and identifiably
unusual about the woman it is often not too difficult to determine the reason for the obsession that develops. In every
case of which I have ever heard the explanation is found in
something that occurs in the early years, some circumstance of
childhood conditioning that renders a certain sort of woman or
a certain feminine quality *important,* terribly important. And,"
he sighed, looking out the window, "woe to the man who, already married, meets a woman with the quality or features
that, perhaps all unknown to him, he has always been searching for."

At Marvell's last words Dan felt an interior sense of understanding that yet baffled him because the precise face, the
particular clue, the final solution to the mystery, eluded him.
And yet the explanation that Marvell had offered seemed to
clarify the situation to some degree, as if a heavy mist had become less dense.

"The Old Testament," Marvell said, after a moment, "uses
the verb *to know* to describe the act of sexual union. Whether
the usage is merely euphemism or euphemism-plus-insight we
shall, of course, never establish, but I prefer to think it is the
latter. For love is the relationship in which we want, to the
very depths of our souls, to *know* another human being. It is
my own belief that the man who has never known the love of
a woman can never truly know himself. This is not to say that
he will remain in complete or even general ignorance of himself, but merely that there will always be a large area of himself
unexplored until he has explored it with the understanding
assistance of a mate."

After a long pause Dan smiled. "You seem to understand

me a great deal better than I understand myself," he said, laughing lightly.

"My dear fellow," Marvell answered, "you say that as if it were strange or paradoxical. It isn't. No man can clearly or easily understand himself. We can all learn much from studying others, and from studying certain classic human situations. I don't want you to suppose, by the way, that this pleasant afternoon's conversation is going to solve all your problems. When you drive away from here the problems will still exist. I am not an analyst, although I am a psychologist. A long-continued analysis, by the way, in the hands of a *good* man or woman, would bring you immeasurable insight. I agreed to talk to you only because Hank gave me an idea of the urgency of your case and because I thought I might be able to stimulate your own thinking. But remember this: don't force yourself. You've tried that. You've driven yourself mercilessly, and it hasn't worked. The reason is that you are just now quite literally not in control of yourself, in certain respects. No human being is completely in control of himself at all times, but in certain circumstances our degree of self-control falls below a danger point. You are going to have to work with the ingredient of *time* in this situation. I can only tell you what I am sure you already know. There is no easy way out. There is no quick way out."

They talked thus for another two hours, pausing from time to time to sip iced tea, munch thin cucumber sandwiches, or merely reflect. When it was time to leave Marvell stepped to a cabinet and removed two books.

"I want you to read these," he said. "The first thing that will strike you is that they have nothing whatever to do with your situation. But for all of that they can help you, I think. One is *Extraordinary Popular Delusions and the Madness of Crowds,* written long ago and recently republished. It will teach you something about the irrational element that lurks beneath the surface in all men, and sometimes not very far below. The other book is the *History of the Warfare Between Science and Theology,* written by an eminent Christian scholar named Andrew White. He was one of the founders of Cornell University. His book tells of the purification of religion.

220

It should not weaken your faith but strengthen it, although that will be entirely up to you."

"Thank you," Dan said. "How shall I return the books to you?"

"Simply package them and mail them to me here at Brewster. If you keep them longer than four months I may be in Japan for a time, so in that event simply keep them till you hear from me."

Standing in the cool, blue air of early evening, getting into the car, Dan said, "I can't find words to express my thanks."

"It was my pleasure," Marvell said. "I shall appreciate knowing what good, if any, will come from our chat."

Strolling through Central Park that evening, when Dan told Elaine about his visit with Marvell, she said, "Did he tell you that you had to give me up?"

"No," Dan said. "Come to think of it he gave me no specific instructions whatever. What he did was to put my problem in some sort of context, some perspective. And he gave me some clues. I hope I'm bright enough to follow them up."

"You are," she said.

"I'm not so sure of that," he said. "The philosophers get life figured out pretty well but the rest of us dumb bastards have to live it without the benefit of their knowledge. I suppose that about the time you do get a few things figured out the game is over and it's time to go home."

Dan looked up then at the stars and felt a deep yearning to *know*. To know *what*, specifically, was, at that moment, relatively immaterial. It was nothing less than the secret of the universe, the secret of time, that would have satisfied him. He was suddenly overcome with a powerful sense of the past, stimulated, he suspected, by the smell of the trees and the grass in the park. The past seemed to mean sadness, although he could not imagine why. He remembered weeping, some vague lost time long ago, and the tears remembered could have led to tears in the present had he not consciously controlled himself. But remembered laughter, he reflected, could also lead to tears simply because it was gone, irretrievable, swept back along the river of time. There was some imbalance involved in this, certainly. The future, perhaps, evened the scales, Dan thought, for even though humans wept for certain lost hours of joy they undoubtedly laughed before a host of unimagined tragedies that would come at unknown hours lying ahead.

Strolling past the lagoon he was reminded of the lagoon in Jackson Park in Chicago, remembered how he and his school-day friends used to go out in rowboats on almost forgotten summer nights, laughing at anything or nothing, put some-body's cheap pawn-shop trumpet to their lips and blow wild cracking off-key notes across the black lagoon, notes that echoed off the high imposing walls of the Museum of Science and Industry under the hot Chicago stars. They had deliber-ately rocked the boat, with the heedless impetuosity of youth, and laughed in rough animal cackles, disturbing lovers who floated dreamily past in their silent boats.

"It's a little muggy tonight," Elaine said. He nodded, lost in reverie. The damp air of the park seemed not a negative thing, as air usually did, but something positive, something that lay wetly in his nose and along his lungs' dark branches. At the park's edge a street lamp was framed by a spray of leaves, which it X-rayed greenly, hanging like an Oriental lantern on the night's lush calm. Something about that light, too, some-thing about those graceful branchlets on this warm and aching night was meant, he thought, for reminding. His mind flew, a searching moth, among the leaves, looking for itself, tran-scending time, fluttering among the fragments of the past: young hands intertwined, and cotton blouses, long walks alone or with a girl, water drunk from stone fountains, water that surprised you, splashing up your nose, youthful laughter, futile tears, hands tentatively, fearfully, guiltily placed upon firm young breasts in the cheap cotton blouses on warm spring and summer evenings long gone. This deadly tender night he walked in was certainly meant for reminding, he decided, and now forever after reminding of reminding.

He wondered if he would have thought such things while strolling alone. Was it the peaceful, fulfilling presence of the woman he loved, that—combined with the appeal of nature —was stimulating him to this mood? Love, in him, quickened all his senses, turned the volume up in his ear, made his fingers sensitive.

Ducks moved sedately in the shadows of the pond edged by 59th Street, their splashings reaching his ear distantly.

"I just thought," he said, "of a brand of soda-pop I used to drink when I was a boy. It was called Green River. I used to love it, not because it tasted especially good—it was just another cold drink—but because of the color and the name of it and because of the label on the bottle. It showed a river, bathed in green moonlight, as I recall, fading romantically into the distance, curving out of sight somewhere, somewhere I wanted very much to be. When I was seven or eight that label could transport me down the dark green timeless river to the land of anyplace-but-here."

"I remember that, too," Elaine said softly. "They sold it in Milwaukee."

"I used to sit in drugstores in the summertime," he said, "cooling my bony elbows on the cold marble soda fountains, drinking that stuff. I think I half believed that Green River was the water scooped from the river itself, sort of a magic liquid from—from, I don't know—some place.

"It's strange," he continued, "that when something is happening to you that later will be called a memory, with a capital M, you never seem to realize it. I mean when the thing is going *into* your mind you don't realize that twenty-five years later you'll be walking down the street and thinking about it. Just now, for example, I was thinking of something else from my childhood, of a boarding school I went to for three years—I think I told you about it before—and I remember lying one day in deep clover with a friend of mine, a boy whose name I forget, just lying there being brave about the honey-bees that floated around us, not interested in us at all although we thought they were. I remember how we lay on our backs, in our sweaty khaki shirts and corduroy knickers, looking up at the blue sky and trying to interpret the clouds as horses, monsters, old men, anything but clouds. I remember how, close to our faces, the pink clover-blossoms shook gently in the hot summer wind, and how we picked them, plucked each tiny prong of them, and sucked the sweetness out of it. The sweetness, the sugar, was so delicate you had to almost close your eyes to taste it. And we picked the stems of pregnant dandelions and blew the delicate fuzz-bombs apart and watched the breeze scatter the white specks over the grass. And then a bell rang, calling us back to a big gray building that we didn't want to be called back to. What was going on in that building was supposed to be the important thing, so why now do I remember only the other, the lolling in the grass?"

"I suppose," Elaine said, "that what happened to you both inside and outside that building left an impression."

"I just had the ridiculous notion," he said, "that it would be nice if at this moment I could somehow disconnect myself from the wheels and gears that make the universe go round, just hang myself by a thin black thread in the top of my head, dangle myself on this particular point of time till I had my fill of all that goes together to make up this moment—the quiet, warm city, you by my side, your hand in mine, your hand with its flesh and blood and delicate bone, your words in my ear, your words and the sweet, wet, red mouth they come out of, and the looking down sideways at your little racehorse ankles, the high heels of your red leather shoes, the smell of the park and your perfume and the ocean off somewhere not far away, and the speaking and *knowing,* before I ever say anything, that you will understand it. Yes, maybe that's the most important part of all. God, how few of us ever understand, really, what the others are saying. We're all like students of a foreign language, students who get by, get a passing grade, and can fake it through Italy or France or Sweden, always knowing the *gist,* but not more than the gist, of what is being said. But this is a moment I wish I could hold onto for a while."

"For how long a while?" she said.

"Oh, not long," he answered. "Perhaps a hundred years or so would do it."

CHAPTER

TWENTY

THE DAYS, and the weeks, dragged on. Dan could not later remember just when the point of decision was reached but eventually he and Elaine began to assume that, at some indefinite moment in the future, they would certainly get married. Oddly, he was able to discuss the idea of their getting married, but he was not able to discuss the idea of getting a divorce from Helen.

He began to lose some of his complacent good nature under the barrage of repeated exposure to people with whose opinions on a thousand and one matters he disagreed.

The good times now were costing more, emotionally speaking. There were brief ecstatic highs followed by longer, murky lows. His impatience with Elaine, with himself, was ever present. A slow, smouldering annoyance lay just beneath his emotional surface. One night it broke out at an unexpected moment.

They had gone to see an old film Elaine had read about in *Cue* magazine. It was a classic, one of the first of the episodic films, and even now, fifteen years after its introduction, they found it moving. But, sitting in the dingy neighborhood theatre in the eighties on the West Side, Dan gradually became conscious of feeling a full, vigorous hatred for the theatre-audience-in-general, the people who sat about him, whispering or talking openly to each other, laughing at the wrong times, crackling candy-bar wrappers.

He and Elaine were seated in the center of the theatre, in the first row of the balcony. Twenty rows behind them a gang of teen-agers guffawed and spoke aloud from time to time. The pathos and beauty on the screen came to be more and more in contrast with the ugly behavior of the audience. Dan's mouth straightened as revulsion for the motley assemblage mounted within him.

Now, here and there in the theatre, people began to shush each other. The air crackled with tension. Ushers patrolled the aisles. Dan sat grimly, watching Mae Robson in a touching scene laid in an old people's home. The morning mail had just been delivered and several old women were eagerly, fumblingly opening the envelopes they had received, hoping that each would contain a message from a loved one. One or two of the women were lucky and began to boast of their good fortune, to read aloud certain passages from sons and daughters and friends. One of the lucky ones suddenly turned to Mae Robson and asked if she had gotten a letter from her son. The camera moved into a close-up of her hands and revealed that the piece of paper she was at that moment taking out of an envelope was nothing but an advertisement. For a moment the audience was silent, gripped by the deep pathos of the scene. Dan felt a knotting of his larynx as Mae Robson said, "Why, yes, I have a lovely letter here from my boy," and started to read aloud to the other old ladies, making it up as she went along, keeping a brave smile on her face so that she would be spared the indignity of sympathy. At this moment one of the ancient women, one who had received no mail at all, rose from her bed and began shuffling painfully, handicapped by palsy and a partial paralysis of one leg, toward Mae Robson.

Dan could clearly hear sniffling from here and there, and he was blinking to keep back his own scalding tears. Suddenly there was a loud, animal laugh from the back of the balcony

226

and one of the teen-age boys yelled at the palsied figure hobbling across the screen, "Shake it, baby!"

There was a gasp and a giggle from the audience and then Dan heard a man shouting and was surprised to discover that the sound came from his own throat. He had leaped to his feet and was facing the rear of the theatre, fists clenched, and raw lust-to-kill bubbling in his throat.

"Will you please," he said, as loudly as he could, "shut your god-damned mouth!"

Ushers came running up the aisles and there was a sprinkling of applause. Surprisingly, the toughs in the last row were silenced.

When Dan sat down his heart was pounding and his anger gradually gave way to painful embarrassment. Elaine looked at him for a moment, stupefied, and then took his hand in hers and held it tightly in her lap, patting it from time to time.

When they left the theatre, Dan half expected to find that the neighborhood punks were waiting for him, but everyone seemed to have forgotten about the incident. They decided to walk all the way home.

"It must be nice to write fiction," he said, crossing 72nd Street, "because you can manipulate your characters and attribute to them whatever characteristics the situation dictates. Maybe in real life there's no such thing as a sad story with a really happy ending."

"You're moving too fast for me."

"I mean, well, take the movies." He yawned and rubbed his eyes. "You see a lot of sad stories, but most of them have happy endings. In real life I think there's rarely any such thing. In reality a sad story either comes to a sad ending or else it just comes to slow, pointless halt. The sadness stops finally but there's usually no *solution,* nothing that could really be called an *ending.*"

"What would you do with us, Dan," she said, "if we were just people in a book?"

"Oh," he laughed, "it would be wonderfully simple. First of all we'd make somebody the Heavy. Let's see. We might make Helen the Heavy. We'd make her a nagger and a spendthrift and an ugly, frigid bitch. The readers would hate her. Then you and I would be depicted as brave, noble, tragic lovers kept apart by her selfishness. Come to think of it," he laughed, "I saw a picture like that just the other night. Laurence Olivier and Jennifer Jones were in love but they were kept apart by the meanness of Miriam Hopkins and the hypocrisy of society."

Elaine laughed.

"Or we could make *me* the Heavy," Dan said. "To be a good one I'd have to be something of a cruel, unthinking, habitual philanderer. We'd write in a scene where my lovely wife and beautiful children plead with me to return, to give up The Other Woman. But would I? Not me. I'd laugh in my wife's face and say, 'I've Outgrown You, My Dear. You Don't Understand Me the Way She Does. I no longer care about you and if you don't give me a divorce I'll make your life A Living Hell!' "

Elaine smiled.

"Or we could make *you* the Heavy. We'd make you, let's see —a wealthy society playgirl, a conniving, unscrupulous bitch who wouldn't feel a moment's remorse at Breaking Up a Home. To give it the final touch we might even have you Throw Me Over after you'd Ruined My Life."

She did not speak.

"God, how I wish we were only people in a movie," Dan said. "In real life it's usually tough to find the Heavy. My mother's pretty good at that. In fact she spends half her time identifying the Heavies with whom she comes into contact. Only trouble is she's almost invariably wrong. For the most part people aren't really divided into villains and heroes."

"Are you sure?" she said.

"What?"

"Are you sure you sometimes don't perhaps think of me as an evil home-wrecker, a remorseless bitch?"

"Don't be silly," he said. "What have I been telling you? This whole thing is such a puzzle because there's been a crime committed but no one is ever going to know who committed it."

At twenty minutes to one in the morning, on another night, Dan sat on the studio couch beside Elaine, watching a late movie on television. After a while the picture concluded and a short film was presented as a public service. It was titled "Sermonette" and at its beginning a picture of Christ on the cross was superimposed over a background of rolling clouds.

Without thinking Dan started to rise to turn the set off. Then, succumbing momentarily to the appeal of organ music and the familiar figure of the crucified, he experienced a flicker of embarrassment at the thought that Elaine might think he had been about to turn the set off out of a feeling of uneasiness. He was deeply sick of the very word *guilt*.

Unhappily, she partly read his thoughts.

"Same old thing?"

"No, damn it," he snapped. "I'm just tired. We've been watching television since nine o'clock. Is there anything wrong with my turning off the set?"

"Don't bite my head off," she said, trying to be light, trying to dam up the emotional flash flood to which they had so unexpectedly become exposed.

The familiar lines of annoyance formed around the corners of his mouth. "Please don't," he said. "Don't hand me any more of that crap about—"

"What is it with you?" she interrupted. "Can't the subject of religion be discussed without your making an argument out of it?"

"Who was discussing religion?" he shouted.

"Oh, you know what I mean," she said.

"No, I don't. I don't have any idea what you mean. I simply got up off the couch and turned off the TV set."

"I know that. I'm not blind."

"Aw, hell," he said tiredly. "Let's not argue any more. These arguments keep breaking down into arguments about arguments. We can't even discuss things intelligently any more."

"You don't want to marry me, do you?" she said suddenly. "That's always it, isn't it? That's what's at the heart of all this bickering."

"I don't know. I don't know what I want. This is no time to throw a question like that at me. I'm angry right now. I'm annoyed at the turn this conversation has taken, so right now I don't want to marry you or eat or go to the toilet or go to sleep or do any of a million things that might be good for me."

She looked up then, and seemed so dejected and puzzled that he felt sympathy well up within him and he leaned down and patted her shoulder and kissed her on the forehead. He went into the kitchen and made two drinks of bourbon and ginger ale and brought them back.

They sat side by side and tried to smile. He put his head back and looked at the ceiling for a minute and then sighed and said aloud, "It's a bitch, isn't it?"

"What?"

"Oh, everything. You say we were talking religion? Okay, let's talk it. It's a bitch that the Catholic Church is so obviously right and the Catholic Church is so obviously wrong."

"I don't know what you're talking about."

"I don't either, but I can prove what I say. That's the trouble. It's so god-damned easy to prove anything these days. The Communists can prove their case like that," he snapped his fingers, "and the vegetarians can throw a library or Shaw at you, and the euthanasia people can make it add up one, two, three, and the Mormons can prove their arguments in five minutes to any man with an open mind. There are bookshelves filled with proofs for or against the truth of Catholic doctrine; take your pick."

"But it doesn't have to be so complicated, does it?" she said.

"Of course not," he said. "Not if you can take one story, believe it, and then refuse to listen to the opposition."

"I don't know much about it," she said, "but it has always seemed to me that the Catholic Church has been sort of re-luctant to allow humanity to take any steps—you know—along the path of progress."

"You're absolutely right," he said, "but I can prove you're wrong."

"You're joking now."

"Not exactly," he said. "I'm pointing out a joke, all right, but it's not a joke of my making."

"You said you could prove I was wrong."

"Sure."

"Go ahead."

"Well, if you were alive a thousand years ago it probably wouldn't have occurred to you that the Church was hamstringing progress."

"In those days maybe it wasn't."

"Then you're saying that something which was right a thousand years ago is wrong today."

"Does morality have to be absolute?"

"If it is to have any valid existence, yes. If it is to have any real authority behind it."

"What about relative morality?"

"Let's get down to brass tacks. What is morality? Just the ability to tell the difference between good and bad. Right?"

"So?"

"So man is the only animal who can do this particular trick. It must pertain to him and it must be important to him. It must also pertain to the motivations of his important actions; at least I think so. I mean it can't have anything to do with what suit of clothes he selects or how he plays baseball."

"It could."

"You know what I mean."

"Yes."

"All right. Man is so constructed that he has certain powers. Like the power of speech. Man can speak so that he may speak the truth. He was not given speech in order to lie. So telling the truth is in his nature. It must be part of the natural law of man to speak the truth."

"But you're taking an easy example. Nobody defends lying. There's no Society for the Preservation of the Lie."

"The hell there isn't," he said. "There are dozens of them. But do you agree with what I just said?"

"Well, so far, yes."

"Fine. Now I can prove how wrong I was."

"What?"

"A man knocks at the door. You know he's come to kill me. I hide in the next room. The man breaks in. He wants to know where I am. Would you be willing to tell him I was out of town? Or even shoot him?"

"Of course."

"Then you're a believer in relative morality."

"Then we all are."

"Right."

"I don't know what to think. But what about us? What about marriage?"

"The Church says the primary object of marriage is the birth and upbringing of children."

"But that can't be true any more in the old sense," she said. "What about the threat of world-wide famine? What about overpopulation? The starving villagers of India, China, Africa?"

"Fellow named Malthus did this bit," Dan said. "Long time ago. The Church still says you can't foresake principle for expediency. It says grow more food, tame the atom, create new fertilizers through chemistry, educate the villagers."

"But that only delays the solution of the problem another hundred years or so."

"Maybe," said Dan, walking to the kitchen for more ice, talking over his shoulder, "but that's the way she goes. It's a gamble, but the Church might win. In a hundred years we might import our grain from Mars or someplace."

"But mathematical progression will always keep the demand ahead of the supply. And there's the simple problem of standing room."

"Be right in," Dan called.

"I suppose, then, this particular argument is insoluble. They can always say that up to now the Lord has provided."

"Maybe," said Dan, coming back into the room, "but there's one loophole."

"What is it?"

"The Lord has always provided for the race, to be sure. But millions of times He has not provided for the individual, and is not at this very moment."

"That makes us sound like little more than animals. The preservation of the race at the expense of the individual."

"Well," said Dan, "as the comedians say on television, we all have to go sometime."

"To get back to marriage," she said. "If marriage exists just so parents can bring up their children then what happens if a man and his wife have done just that and the children have gone out happily into the world? If the husband and wife don't love each other any more is there any reason why they should stay together?"

"Yes," said Dan. "Procreation is not the *only* purpose of marriage."

"Agreed," said Elaine, sitting up straight, pressing her advantage, "but I'm talking about a marriage without love, or one where love has died. Why shouldn't the couple separate if they *both* want to?"

"Look what it would lead to, though, if every couple who were tired of each other just called it quits."

"That's just about the way it already is in this country right now," she said. "But what if the situation with this couple is even worse? What if the man is a bore and an alcoholic and a mess in general?"

"You've got me backed into something of a corner here," Dan said, half-smiling, "but I refuse to admit defeat. Here again is an example of the Church's teaching that the benefit of the race must come before the benefit of the individual."

"Like animals again."

"A little, yes, but that isn't necessarily evil. Maybe the woman owes the man a little loyalty. Maybe she has an obligation to stand beside him in all forms of sickness as well as in health."

"It sounds nice when you put it that way, but I say it's against human nature."

"Now we get on the real merry-go-round," said Dan, "because I think a lot of nice things are against human nature."

"What?"

"I mean two separate parts of a human's nature can be at war with each other. You walk down the street and see a beautiful girl. You want to grab her and make love to her. That's certainly a part of a human's nature, that kind of a desire. But there's another part of his human nature that's at war with this fundamental drive. Or you're swept off a boat into the open sea and a board floats by. It's strong enough to support only one man. You and one other survivor are in a position to struggle for it. It's certainly human nature, the most elementary sort of natural law, to grab that board and try to push the other man away from it, but what the hell happens to the issue of good and evil in a case like this?"

"Well, these extreme cases are—"

"They're not extreme. They're just simple and dramatic. Things like this happen to all of us every day. Take your average businessman. He's trying to keep his head above water, and woe to any competitor who tries to float on the same piece of driftwood, Christian or no. Or woe to his customers if he's not making a profit. Our consciences are formed when we're little kids. Aggression is wrong, humility is the thing. Be nice. Turn the other cheek. What the hell do you think rich men give so much money to charity for? It's because after they get their pile their methods begin to haunt them. It's conscience money they're giving away."

"You depress me when you talk like this."

"I'm sorry, sweetie," he said. "I can't help it."

"Isn't there anything we can be sure of?"

"Gosh, I don't know. Sometimes it seems like a waste of time even trying to convince *yourself* of anything, much less one other person or the whole world. Take the men who have done the big thinking with a capital T. The philosophers. Their books were hardly off the presses before other philosophers were leaping into print to expose their fallacies or say that they were wordy asses or whatever-the-hell. Take the great religious leaders. It's all well and good to sip tea and mutter warm little platitudes about all of us being on different roads to the same place and one religion being just as good as another and Buddha and Christ and Confucius and Mohammed and Joseph Smith and Mary Baker Eddy and Moses and Father Divine and you-name-him-we've-got-him being all great teachers presenting truth in different ways but by God it doesn't make sense to me!"

"But the world is full of intellectual confusion and other men don't seem as troubled as you by it."

"Maybe not."

"Then maybe the real problem is inside you. Do you think anybody could help you? Could you go to a priest or a psychiatrist or somebody?"

"No. All a priest could say to me is 'G'wan back to your wife and kids,' and I'm not sure what a psychiatrist could say but I'm not mentally sick."

"I didn't say you were."

"Besides, I've heard that psychiatrists don't really concern themselves with right and wrong."

"How do you know they don't?"

"I don't. I just think I read it someplace. And for God's sake, the psychiatrists or psychologists or psychoanalysts—I can never keep those words all straight—they argue amongst themselves just like everybody else. Freud doesn't dove-tail with Zh-ung or Yung or whatever his name was."

"Well, medical doctors argue amongst themselves, too, but they cure an awful lot of people. But I suppose you're right. I don't think you need to see a psychiatrist."

"My problem is really very simple," Dan said. "I did something wrong and I know it. It could be even simpler. Suppose I murdered somebody. Would I need a psychiatrist to tell me that I did something wrong? Would there even be any point in the guy's improving my mental state? Or even in explaining the reasons why I committed the crime? I'd still have to go to the chair. The victim would still be dead. In my case Helen is still hurt. Nothing will ever undo that. The kids are still wondering where the hell I am. No psychiatry for *me* can change *their* loneliness. And as long as they're lonely, I'll feel guilty."

Later that night, lying in bed, in the darkness, he thought back to the matter of psychiatry. It did not primarily concern itself with ethics perhaps but it might answer questions. It did deal in motives. Would there be any value, Dan wondered, in finding out why he had left Helen?

What was it Hank had once said? "Why waste time thinking about it? You left home because you couldn't give up a particular piece of—"

But other men became similarly involved and were able somehow to preserve their homes. Why had he not had the strength? Or did strength have anything to do with it? Was he unable to cope with the powerful physical desire he had for

Elaine only because it was the only other he had ever known in all the years of his marriage to Helen? Would it have been better to have played around when he was young, to have become more experienced, more sophisticated and relaxed about sex, like most of the other men he knew? He had known scores of men, his close friends, who had committed adultery, washed up, gone home, and forgotten about it. Why had he in particular not been able to give it up? Was it because of his early training, his virginal formative years? If so, then what of the value of premarital abstinence? If the inexperienced man or woman is more than easy prey for the experienced extramarital bed partner, then a good means had brought about a bad end and—again this line of reasoning enmeshed him in its hopeless windings and coilings and he fell asleep troubled and fearful as usual.

CHAPTER

TWENTY-ONE

O<small>NE DAY</small> there formed in Dan's mind the idea that he was going to bring Helen and the children East. This was his original rationalization for getting a larger apartment, and now the image occurred to him again and again during the following weeks. He could figure out no way to mention the idea to Elaine.

One night, lying in bed, he started to tell her, but got panicked and sidetracked the subject before he had opened his mouth.

"My God," he said, "I just had a frightening thought."

"What?" Elaine said.

"Wouldn't it be terrible if I got involved with you not only, or even chiefly, because of what *you* are, but because of what *I'm not?* One reason I now have such a low opinion of myself for not being able to keep my hands off you, not being able to stop wanting you, is that I am judging myself by the standards that I was taught as a child."

"They're still popular standards," Elaine said.

"Yes," he continued, speaking very slowly, frowning at the ceiling, "but what I'm getting at is they're very old standards. They're standards created when men lived in poverty and simplicity. But now I—most of the men in my society—we've *got* the things that earlier generations dreamed of and saw as Heaven-on-earth. We've got freedom from want and more physical comforts than we deserve, and yet our life today doesn't fill up all the holes, doesn't answer all the needs. There's no—I don't know—no adventure, no risk, no wrestling with hardship in the old-fashioned sense. I've always lived just for myself and, eventually, for my family. Now something inside me vaguely realizes that I want something bigger, some cause, something really less selfish. Maybe I was stunned by you and clutched at you so desperately because—because you were—oh, hell, *excitement* sounds like such an inadequate word."

"Listen," Elaine said, "why were you carrying that airline schedule in your pocket today? Are you planning another trip to the Coast?"

"No," he said, blurting it out, "I thought perhaps this time I'd bring the kids here for a change."

Elaine eventually had occasion, thus, to speak of the realities. At times she feared that Dan would never again force an issue of any kind.

"Sweetie," she said, and her tone made him apprehensive, for its tenderness and resignation informed him that she was about to discuss *the problem,* "what's going to happen? Helen and the boys are coming on. That means we're not going to get married, doesn't it?"

"Not necessarily," he said. "I can't understand why you're so aroused just because they're visiting me. I just get desperate to see the children, that's all. And the trip will be a nice change for Helen."

"I know, but when they come here you'll get used to having them around and you'll want me to go."

"No, I won't. Why do you say that you have to go? Obviously you can't stay here while they're in the city, but you don't have to run a million miles away. You could move back in with Polly or something for a few weeks."

"Honey," she said, "we're just delaying the execution. I'll go. I'll go when they come and that will be that. I don't know why I go on fighting month after month. I get just to the point of going because it seems like the best thing to do but then there's always one little doubt in my mind. I think maybe there's just one small chance that this love of ours is going to come out all right in the end, and that small flicker of hope makes me reluctant to walk away from the whole thing. It may be the best thing that's ever happened to me and so at the last minute I'm often afraid to give it up."

"I know," he said. "It's the same for both of us."

"Dan," she said, looking at the floor, "is it just religion? Is that the real reason you don't want to marry me?"

"I do want to marry you," he said.

"You know what I mean."

"No," he said. "At one time maybe it was religion, but I'm not sure any more. It's all so confused. Sometimes I think I no longer have a firm faith in the validity of the rules I think I've broken, if that makes any sense."

"God loves you."

"I'm not arguing that He doesn't."

"But don't you think He will go right on loving you regardless of what you've done?"

"Not necessarily. I mean—"

"Wouldn't you continue to love your children, no matter what mistakes they made?"

"Yes, of course. But it's not quite the same. I have no doubt that God is capable of loving all of us but there must still be some code we have to live up to; there must still be some way we have of showing that we deserve His love."

"Well, just what is your problem? Are you in an awkward position only as a Catholic rather than as a Christian in the broader sense, is that it?"

"That's something like the truth, but even knowing that much doesn't help."

"I don't understand."

"Well," he furrowed his brow and looked at the ceiling, "there seems to be little chance that I could ever rebuild my marriage, and if I get a divorce I can't very well just take up my religious obligations where I left off."

"Why not? A Lutheran could."

"I'm not so sure about that, but anyway I know I can't. Oh,

I suppose the technical possibility exists. I could give you up, never associate with another woman again as long as I lived, and lead as saintly and ascetic a life as possible. That would be all right. The Church says divorce is wrong but the actual sin occurs only when you marry again, only when you take unto yourself a new mate."

"I see. And that sort of arrangement would be difficult for you."

"For me, impossible. You're not supposed to think like that, I guess. You're not supposed to say that anything in the moral area is impossible, but I say nuts. I say that for me such a life is impossible. It was difficult enough to walk the straight and narrow when I was married. Now that I'm off alone how could I personally hope to practice sexual abstinence till the end of my life? Some men can do it. Or at least so we are led to believe. Good for them. Some men I know can play 'The Flight of the Bumblebee' blindfolded in double-time, but I can't. If a man can't attain to perfection in the arts and sciences why should he feel so damned certain he could live the perfect life as regards morals?"

"Dan, you talk as if you think you're evil. I know you, in some ways better than you know yourself, and I think you're good."

"Thank you, sweetheart. Sure, I'm good. You're good. We're all good. But we're also bad. That's what I'm trying to say." Suddenly he laughed.

"What's funny?"

"I was just thinking," he said, "here I am mouthing amateur philosophical commonplaces. I'm just an average citizen, just a lousy song-writer and I'm trying to settle problems on which the philosophers have never been able to agree."

"We're getting off the track," Elaine said. "What about your remaining a good Catholic?"

"Oh, yes," he said. "Well, as I was saying, it's impossible. I'm too much tied up with the world. I can't give up everything and run away to a monastery. I have to stay in the music business. It's all I know. I have to make money to support myself and those who depend on me. That means I've got to live in theatres and at cocktail parties and radio studios

240

and places where women walk by you with tight dresses and red mouths. I could give *you* up, theoretically speaking, but that wouldn't do any good. In five days I'd either be after you again or running after some other woman. We've learned that the hard way, you and I. We've learned how difficult it is to give up something that you want, something that brings you happiness or pleasure or both."

"Would you like it if I went away, Dan, and refused to come back to you?"

"No, honey," he said. "I wouldn't like it. But if you did go away, if you were hit by a truck tonight, that wouldn't really solve the problem at all. The problem isn't *you;* it's *me* and my desires and my drives and my requirements. If a man is going to fast and live on brown bread and milk in the mountains that's all well and good, but he will not be able to restrict himself to this diet if he happens to work in a fine restaurant. He can fight his inclinations just so long and then in his dreams, in his unguarded moments his animal self will assert its powers and he will have to start all over again."

"Maybe that's the key. Maybe it's all right to fail because you can always start all over again."

"That's good Catholic doctrine you're expressing," he said, with a smile, "and to a lot of people it makes good sense. It made sense to me for many years and would again, I suppose, if I were living in my own home in an orderly way. But don't you see what it means to me personally, in practice? It means right now, right this minute you've got to get up and put on your hat and coat and leave me forever, because there's no sense in saying you'll leave tomorrow. You can't say to yourself, 'I'll start living the good life pretty soon.' You've got to start right now if you're going to accomplish anything at all, if you're going to be honest."

"Then there's no hope for you in the Church?"

"I don't know. Because of the impressions left on my mind by my upbringing it seems a fearful thing to have to admit, but that may be just the size of it. There are people I know who *pretend* to be Catholics, who remain in the Church because it seems socially expedient, who remain in the Church for no other reason than that they're afraid to break away from it, but I'm not one of them. Or, hell, I don't know. Maybe I *am* one of them. It's just that the technicalities of my present situation prevent me from even putting on an act to keep my mother and friends happy. Otherwise I might remain in the Church as a hypocrite. If there's anything I've learned during the last year it's not to look down on others, not to judge them. We are all cowards and pawns of fate and any one of us might commit any sin in the world if placed in a certain position."

"Then what can you do, of a practical nature, to help yourself? What about becoming a Protestant of some sort? Perhaps an Episcopalian?"

"No," he said. "That would be no help. I think it was in James' *Portrait of the Artist as a Young Man* that somebody —yes, that was it—somebody asked Stephen Dedalus if, since he was giving up his Catholic faith, he would then become a Christian of another sort. I don't remember his exact words at all but he said something like this. He said, 'No, sir. That would be giving up an absurdity for an insanity.' Something like that. If the original Christian Church is wrong then organizations that have branched off from it seem to me to be worth a good deal less than their parent organization."

"I can't keep up with you," Elaine said. "Are you saying now that the Catholic Church is wrong? A minute ago I thought you were saying that you were simply unable to live up to your faith."

"I don't know," he said, tiredly. "Sometimes I think one thing; sometimes another. When I was about twelve years old and learned about men like Luther and Voltaire and the like, I said to myself, in all the mature wisdom of my years, that these men would never have rebelled against the authority of the Church if they had not found themselves unequal to the task of adhering to its principles. I thought to myself that *first* they sinned, *then* they rationalized. Now it seems that I am doing the same thing. As long as I was able to live within the moral boundaries laid down by the Church it did not occur to me, except fleetingly, to doubt the wisdom and omniscience and purity of the Church. Now that I am, if you will, a *sinner* my mind is full of doubts and questions."

242

"You must be terribly unhappy."

"I don't even know that," he said. "But I'll tell you something interesting. Sometimes I think that my real problem is not with God but with the people I know who are Catholics."

"What do you mean by that?"

"I mean that I feel a sense of guilt but somehow it doesn't seem to be directed from me to God in a straight line, if you know what I mean. It seems to go from me to other people, to my mother, for example. I'm sorry that I fell away from the Church more for the worry and sadness my fall will cause my mother and my people than for the worry it actually causes me. As far as I personally am concerned there is actually a sense of excitement, of discovery in the way that my mind is now being spaded up and turned over."

"That sounds hopeful."

"I suppose it does. It's perhaps a ghastly thing to say but I have the feeling that if my mother were to suddenly be assumed into heaven, if she were to die and give no further thought to my welfare I would actually be much freer and happier. Does that sound awful?"

"Not to me."

"What I mean is I can remember exactly what it is like to be a Catholic, to be girded with the armor of seemingly indestructible certainty. There is some comfort in being positive about the truth of your beliefs but there is also something bad about it all. Being that positive automatically makes you uncharitable toward those who do not believe as you do. And the attitude of the average Catholic toward a man who has left the Church is traditional and never varies. He feels first shocked and scandalized, then he may begin to pity a bit, although he still bitterly disapproves. He shakes his head and feels quite certain that the member who has strayed from the fold is doomed to perdition, unless he repents."

"Do you think that is the way your mother feels about you?"

"I do. That is the way every Catholic who ever lived felt about anyone who left the Church. There are degrees to the thing, of course. Some Catholics are more stone-headed than others, some have more natural charity in their emotional makeup than others, all of which has to do with the fact that they are human rather than that they are Catholic. But those still in the Church can, I think, only swing back and forth between presumption and despair in their attitude toward the wayward brother."

Elaine began winding her wrist watch.

"Why," she said, "does there have to be this eternal confusion about religion? Why don't we all just go back to the simple religion of the Bible?"

"Sweetheart," he said, "you're talking nonsense, although you've got a lot of company."

"Give me one reason it wouldn't be a good idea."

"All right," he said. "I'll give it to you in one word."

"What?"

"Interpretation."

"What do you mean?"

"Hell," he said. "Man can't even understand his income tax forms, much less the Bible. There has to be some authority to interpret the wordage in the Scriptures or else we're right back where we started from with every man his own authority."

"What's wrong with that?"

"What's *wrong* with it?" he said, rather loudly. "Why, don't you see? If ten men all state conflicting theories on a certain point they can't all be right. Either one of them is right or else they're all wrong."

"I don't know who these ten men are," Elaine said, not noticing the expression of exasperation that flickered across Dan's face, "but I repeat my statement. Let's get back to the simpler religion of the Bible."

"I don't seem to be getting through to you," Dan said curtly, "with what is up to now the very simplest point I've made. Look. Take just one sentence in the Bible. How about 'Thou Shalt Not Kill.' "

"Exactly," Elaine said. "That's just *my* point. Thou Shalt Not Kill. What could be simpler than that?"

"Good God," he said, wriggling out from under her, rising, pacing across the room. "Don't you see? It isn't simple at all. Nothing could be more complicated, as a matter of fact.

What does it mean to you? Tell me, right now. What do the words Thou Shalt Not Kill mean to you?"

"Please," she said, "don't insult my intelligence. They mean we're not supposed to kill. I don't know of any plainer way to put it."

"All right," he said, pointing at her. "Answer some other questions. Is it all right to kill a mouse?"

"Of course it is."

"Are you aware that there are some people on this earth who say that the words Thou Shalt Not Kill prohibit the killing of mice or bedbugs or any living thing?"

"These people are fools," she snapped. "Why bring them into the discussion?"

"Can't you see?" he shouted. "You can't keep them *out* of the discussion. What about the matter of capital punishment? Is it all right for the state of New York to put a man to death in the electric chair?"

"No," she said. "I don't think it is. The Bible clearly says Thou Shalt Not Kill."

She observed him triumphantly.

"Fine and dandy," he said. "But there are millions of fine, upstanding Christians all over this world who believe that it *is* permissible for the state to put a criminal to death."

"They're wrong."

"They may be, but that's not the point, honey. I'm just trying to make you see that there *can* be arguments, disagreements on the matter of interpretation."

"But you're not arguing fairly," she snapped angrily. "Any sensible person is opposed to capital punishment and any sensible person knows it's all right to kill a mouse. You're talking exceptions and nonsense."

He turned on her violently.

"What the hell is the matter with your mind?" he cried. "You argue like my mother, god-damn it! Won't you grant any points at all? Don't you know anything about the rules of debate? Would you ever kill a man?"

"Of course not," she said.

"Suppose," he said, crossing to her, pointing a rigid finger at her, "that a thug came in here right now and had a gun trained on my heart. Suppose you knew he was insane and a killer and that he announced that he was going to put a bullet through me. And suppose that you suddenly found a gun in your hands. Would you fire at him—to save me—to protect yourself?"

"I can't stand your tone," she said. "We've gone over this before. You don't have to talk down to me. You don't have to act as if you were talking to an idiot."

"All right," he said. "I'm sorry. I shouldn't shout at you and I admit it, but now that that's all taken care of can you see what I'm talking about? When I use the words Thou Shalt Not Kill as an example to prove a point don't get off the track and argue the merits of the admonition. My point, if you can remember it, is simply this: There is such a thing as a difference of interpretation."

"Well, any fool knows that."

He whipped his head around in a fury of exasperation.

"Do you mean to sit there," he said, "and deny that two minutes ago you were resisting what you just now admitted?"

"Stop it," she cried. "Don't talk to me like that! Who do you think you are anyway, with your superior attitudes?"

"Never mind," he said. "I don't think I'm anybody. I didn't mean for this to turn into an argument. I just can't seem to understand the way your mind works. It doesn't seem logical to me. Does it to you? I'm just asking."

She stood up again and walked out of the room angrily. He followed and caught her arm.

"Let me alone," she said, not raising her voice. "Your wife is coming East. I'm leaving."

"Where will you go?" he said, without knowing what answer he desired to receive.

"Oh, who the hell cares?" she said. "Maybe I'll call up some fellows I know and go out and have a little *fun* for a change. God knows I've put up with enough misery around here."

In a few minutes she was dressed and gone. Dan was left with his mind full of frightening pictures, feeling bitterly jealous in advance at the thought of her in another man's company. He feared the approaching night alone and stayed awake as long as possible.

His loneliness and longing were manifested in many strange ways; sometimes in an inability to concentrate, sometimes in a warping of his powers of optical expectancy. He would see strange women on the street, whose appearance was like Elaine's in only one respect, in that they might wear a large, black hat or a certain sort of red dress, or walk in a manner similar to hers, and for a few seconds his heart would leap and his eyes widen, for he would believe these strange women were Elaine.

At other times his love assumed the form of a passionate jealousy which recognized no bounds of reason. He would see good-looking young men on the street or in offices or riding in elevators, men who might presumably have appealed to her if she had met them, and at such times a furtive unreasoning hatred for these unknowing and unknown passersby would smoulder in his heart.

He awoke on the jagged edge of a dream, his mind still fuzzily grasping the impression of a skeletal bridge over water. Something was hammering on rusty girders, scraping against raw metal, chattering high and thin against wind-swept wires off to one corner of his mind, then gradually his eyes focused on the ceiling; the lightly chattering metallic sound became a telephone's ring.

He let it ring on.

After a while it stopped and for a long time he lay staring at the ceiling, listening to the whisper of rubber tires in the wet street. It was a familiar, soothing sound, a sound strangely pictorial. In his mind he could see quite clearly the squeegeed tracks the wheels were making in the film of water that glistened across the black asphalt, the lacy curve of moisture that spattered up behind the tires, the melting rainbows that writhed in the street where the rain washed over patches of oil-scum.

Now and then across the lazy, hypnotic swish from the outside the raucous shriek of a horn would cut sharply, making his heart pound unaccountably. Then he would lay with his eyes closed, listening to the blood pumping somewhere near his ear. A cool draft swept through the room and he shuddered slightly, turning over on his side, drawing his knees up to his chest, foetus-like, trying to drift back into sleep.

It was no good. After a time he rubbed his eyes and got up and went to the toilet. His tongue, as he looked at it in the mirror, was white and there was a smudge of blue under each eye. Sleep was supposed to refresh you, he mused, but somehow you always seemed to look your worst after sleeping.

While hot water was running in the tub he walked back into the room, shivering a little as the air from the opened window enveloped him. Warily he stood back from the window a few feet, so as not to be seen from the apartment across the street, and scratching his naked stomach idly, he looked down at the traffic. It was a typical rainy New York day.

By noontime the palliative of boredom with suffering had worn off and he was tense and anxious again. When he telephoned Polly's number there was no answer. Vainly, he called again and again over a period of two hours. He told himself that Helen was coming East and that Elaine had gone, once and for all, truly left him. He tried praying and was shocked to find that his fingers and toes were tapping a rhythmic beat of accompaniment to the prayers so that he was singsonging them as he had done as a small child. He ate neither breakfast nor lunch that day and tasted nothing but one can of beer.

Just at the onset of dusk he stood in the middle of the bedroom, sighing, and rocked back and forth on the balls of his feet. It was going to be all right, he thought. His mind was sodden, dulled, and the only sign of the flickering, guttering horror that he felt was the slow movement of his eyes, back and forth, the glance directed just above the lower lids, far to the left then far to the right. But it would be all right. After all, he was not pacing the floor of his room as he had seen animals pace the floors of their cages. He was standing in one spot, but the eyes paced. Back and forth, insanely, looking for escape. The lips were straight and there was a tenseness at the sides of his mouth. Now the eyes would flicker wildly to the ceiling, looking for escape, running like maddened mice up the wall, along the plaster ridge where the wall met the ceiling, to the window. Then, slowly, back to the floor. But it was going to be all right this time. Except for the eyes, the held breath, he could hang on, firmly push each picture out of his mind. It was eight o'clock now. Perhaps they would be having dinner. Elaine laughing. White teeth. Lips mockingly stretched across white teeth. A male hand placed suddenly, but casually, on hers, as it lay on the white tablecloth. She not withdrawing her slender hand. The male fingers tightening as the male mouth smiled.

"Waiter, two more."

Music, and the soft, distant sound of dishes and glassware being moved about. Where to now? I know a swell place over on 56th. She laughing. Joking softly in a taxicab. Doorman. A canopy over a street. Or perhaps, "A drink at my place." Thick rugs. "I'll fix us something. Hope this isn't too strong. Now tell me all about yourself." The male hand, manicured, moving familiarly through electric air. Settling on her hand. Casually, oh, so casually on her arm, or perhaps knee. Resistance? Acquiescence? Time, crawling like a worm, devouring. Red-tipped cigarette fragments. "I'll get some more ice." Perhaps the male lips brushed against the back of her neck from behind the couch. Casually. Laughter. And what would time do? Erase, perhaps, the casual? Replace it with the desperate, the not-caring, the necessary? The eyes moved faster now across the carpet, ran crazily up the walls. But it would still be all right. Straighten up the room. Move. Move. Keep moving. Release explosive energy.

He picked up the gray flannel slacks from the chair near the bed and shook them out, pinching the cuffs together. The pants-hanger gripped the soft cloth and then, as he draped the hook over the long bar in the closet, the heavy flannel pulled itself out of the felt grips and the trousers crumpled to the floor.

He had no warning. He had thought it was going to be all right. So much had gone wrong, but he had thought that just this once it would be all right. There would be nothing more than standing there in the middle of the room, aching dully, nothing worse than that. There would be control, and a shred of self-respect, even a semblance perhaps of devil-may-care resiliency. At that moment, as if the sound had been torn from a stranger's throat, he was shocked to hear a fierce strangled cry. It was the slacks falling on the floor so unexpectedly that had triggered the explosion. He had thought he was holding on, but now he fell back out of the closet, howling. The slacks he threw in a heap and then he was trying to follow the eyes, a tiger intent on breaking out of the cage. His chest went cold, then hot, and his eyes filled, blindingly. He ran across the room and slumped, without strength enough to hold himself erect, on the bed. Shaking violently, he pressed his hand against his mouth, to stop the shouting, the gasping sounds. His stomach contracted and he breathed loudly, like an enraged but exhausted animal brought to bay. The breaths became louder, merged into wheezing sobs, then the demoniacal howling started again and much moisture, tears and saliva (God! Not froth!), ran from his mouth, dropped onto the bed, ran through the animal fingers he pressed desperately to his mouth. The eyes rolling wildly now, running to the window. To the mirror over the mantel. He staggered to his feet and lurched across the room. His red-faced image almost shocked him into silence. His hair was disarranged, his mouth drawn down at the corners, drawn sickeningly down, the lower lip looking sub-human as it trembled and shone with spittle. The eyes burning, red, blinded. He shrank back from the mirror and threw his arms up around his chest, tightly, squeezing as hard as he could, trying to crush out of his chest the horror that burned there, pushed against his aching ribs, washed in stifling waves over his heart. His fingernails dug into his arms but he could not even feel the physical pain to the normal degree. The pictures came flooding back across his mind now. The male hand moving on her shoulder. The male lips crushed hard against hers. Oh, God, God, God, God, God, God, God, God, God, God, God, God, God, God, God, God, God, God, God, God, God, God, God, God, God! Her slender body moving slightly, with warmth, in response to the male arms. He fell to the floor now, his knees thumping hard against the firm boarding under the carpet. The pain boiled up out of his chest, cut off his breath. He retched drily, twisting his white-

250

knuckled fingers around the loose folds of his shirt-front. With the fleshy sides of his fists he pounded on the floor, suddenly overcome with murderous rage, growling instead of crying, growling gutturally, but the lower lip still drawn down at the corners, in true terror.

Her warm hands, her white hips, her slender neck, with the pearls left on, puckishly, after the dress had been taken off, the slip, the underwear. The pearls, and the mascaraed lashes, and the white teeth. Green water bubbling in a tub, rising and receding over her large breasts. Laughter and softly whispered love-jokes.

He drew himself to his feet, staggered, and fell back on the bed, and then at last, after many, many minutes, the storm faltered slightly in its fury, and the ache in the chest, in the blood, began to ease quietly. His eyes still burned, and lying on his back, he felt the warm salt water running down the sides of his face, tickling his ears, running out, down along his neck, running into the perspiration that bathed the back of his neck. The mouth growing dry, the eyelids feeling sandy now. The crying softer and human now, no longer fiendish. The breath coming more slowly, steadily, the ache dulling, still there, but dulling. Cold water on his face. A dry towel. Looking in the mirror. The eyes red, but the mouth firmer.

Shaving, putting on a fresh shirt, combing his hair, he wondered how soon the storm would rage again. And whether he could survive another such tornado. That night, while jotting down an idea for a lyric, he wrote the words *nervous breakdown* in the upper right hand corner of the page.

CHAPTER

TWENTY-TWO

ALTHOUGH he was back with Elaine two days later he could not seem to reverse the machinery that was grinding out his destiny. Helen was still coming, having accepted his falsely cheerful invitation.

Then there was Westport . . .

The whole Westport episode was quick and nightmarish. It was over and done with before Dan had even become accustomed to its reality. The day after he definitely decided to bring the family East he had gone to a cocktail party. He happened to say, "I'm looking for a place out of town," and somebody said, "Well, I know of a lovely house up in Westport that I don't *think* is rented yet, if you wouldn't mind being that far out."

"Why, no," Dan said. He took out a pencil and jotted down the telephone number of a real estate woman in Westport and the next day he called her and the day after that he drove up to look at the place and he liked it and decided to move right in.

It was all like that: quick and unreal. The whole thing reminded him of the sensation he always had for a day or two at the end of a long trip by air; he felt as if he were still back where he had been. It always took him about forty-eight hours to get used to his new surroundings.

He discovered that he was now a resident of an exclusive community, that people in New York said, "I live in Westport" with something like the pride exhibited by people in Hollywood who said, "I live in Bel Air."

He fought against the feeling of smugness that taking a house in Westport induced, but in the end he succumbed to the temptation, simply let himself go and allowed himself to feel just a slight bit superior when he mentioned his new address.

It was a pleasant little town in which to live.

Years before it had been a secluded community populated by old, wealthy families, prominent artists and well-to-do writers. Of recent years it has been somewhat overrun by television and radio executives, advertising men, industrialists and bankers but with little sacrifice of its sleepy, old-time charm.

The house he rented was on the edge of the Greens Farms section of the Westport community, where a great many large estates are to be found. His house, in fact, was on one of these estates. It had at one time been intended for service quarters but had evidently been rebuilt and added to several times, until now it was a sprawling, oddly shaped but comfortable one-story country house, shingled, shuttered and furnished with semi-antiques and vague, dark, old-fashioned, easily forgotten gold-framed paintings.

Two days before Helen and the children were due to arrive, he drove up from the city, went to a grocery store on the Post Road and bought two large cardboard boxes full of provisions, including cereals and Ovaltine for the children and special delicacies for Helen. It felt good to again be doing something homey, something fatherly. He literally felt a sharp pain in his chest whenever he accidentally allowed himself to think of Elaine, but most of the time, by keeping busy, by whistling and daydreaming and planning what he would do with the children he was able to get by without too much discomfort.

He walked about the chilly kitchen with his overcoat on,

putting things into cupboards, stocking the shelves, plugging in the refrigerator and filling it with meats and cheeses and eggs and milk and fruit juices. It would all be ready and nice for the family.

Driving back into the city he tried to keep his spirits up but the realization that he would see Elaine for only two more days depressed him and in the end he lost his cheerful outlook completely. By the time he reached her apartment he was morose.

They had an Italian dinner at a restaurant on 54th Street and then went back to his apartment. When they talked at all it was about the weather or about Westport. Elaine wanted to know if it was pleasant there and he told her, yes, it was.

They read the papers and talked about people they knew and then Elaine worked a crossword puzzle and, at last, sometime around midnight, they began talking about the fact that they were going to say good-bye again. They both believed it would be the final good-bye, the real one, the one that would stick.

"This will have to be it," he said. "Because now that I'm bringing the family back there'll be no retreat."

"That's right," she said.

They were sitting talking like that when the phone rang. It was long distance. Helen.

"Hello, hon," he said, embarrassed at Elaine's presence. She frowned when she realized who was on the line and got up and walked into the bathroom.

"How are you, honey?" Helen said.

"Oh, I'm fine," he said. "How are the children?"

"They're so excited," she said, "they can't wait to see you."

"That's good," he said. "I can't wait to see them."

There was an awkward pause.

"Are you alone?" Helen asked.

"What?"

"I said are you alone? Can you talk?"

"Oh, certainly," he lied. "When do you get in?"

"Seven fifty-five Friday morning. Is that too early for you?"

"Goodness, no. Don't worry about that. I'll be there to meet you." He looked at the bathroom and saw that the door was partly open. His hands became moist and sweat began beading on the black plastic of the telephone, running down over his wrists.

"I can't hear you very well," Helen said. "Can you talk a little louder?"

"Yes," he said, wincing. "What flight are you on?"

"Flight 95, TWA."

"All right. I'll be there to meet you."

"Dan."

"Yes, dear?"

"Is everything all right? You sound funny."

"Why, no. Everything's fine, hon. I'm just a little tired, I guess."

"Are you sure about all this? Are you sure you want us to come back there?"

"Of course I'm sure. I've got a swell little place for you. I guess I told you about that in the letter. I was up there today getting groceries and things."

"That's fine. How does it look for the kids?"

"Oh, great. There's a whole forest for them to play in, practically . . . and nice schools and everything. I think you'll like it."

"Whatever it is, it'll be all right."

"That's right."

There was another pause. He bit his lip.

"Are the kids in bed?"

"Yes."

"Oh. Well, I'm glad you called, Helen."

"Yes, I wanted to talk to you, to see how you felt about everything."

"I feel all right."

"That's good."

"It'll be good to see you, Dan. I've missed you."

He glanced at the bathroom door. God!

"I've missed you too."

"Have you really?"

"Of course."

"It's funny talking like this, with you so far away. I guess it'll be different when we see each other again."

"Yes, I'm sure it will," he said.

"Well, I guess that's about all for now, then. Goodnight, Dan."

"Goodnight, hon. Thanks for calling."

"We'll see you Friday morning."

"All right. Good-bye."

When he hung up he heard the sound of crying. He walked into the bathroom. Elaine was looking at herself in the mirror. Her mouth was turned down at the corners exactly like the mouth on the mask of tragedy. Her eyes were wet and her mascara was running.

"Don't cry," he said.

She turned away and wiped her face with a bath towel.

"I'm sorry," she said, sniffling and moaning softly. "I'm sorry."

He put his arms around her.

"I'm sorry, too," he said. "Please don't cry."

She clung to him and got lipstick on the front of his shirt and blubbered against his chest like a child and he became all at once filled with a nameless, maniacal, trapped fury and began to weep, angrily, bitterly.

They walked back into the bedroom.

"It doesn't seem real," he said. "I can't get it through my head that after tomorrow you'll be gone. Can you?"

"No."

"Oh, God," he said, sitting down on the bed, violently pounding his fist into the mattress again and again. "God, God, God! Why do things like this have to happen to people?"

"Don't act like that," she said. "Don't get yourself all worked up. It will be all right. I'll go and eventually you'll forget me and everything will be all right."

"But eventually isn't soon enough," he shouted. "Helen and the children will be here Friday morning. I should have forgotten you by *then* if there is to be any happiness between Helen and myself, don't you see that?"

"Yes, I do."

"The whole thing is just one wrong move after the other," he said, punching the mattress furiously again. "There's no such thing as the *right* thing to do in this god-damned affair.

I just have my choice now of several mistakes. I tell you, if it weren't for the children, I'd kill myself!"

"Don't say that."

"Why not?" he said, jumping up. "Oh, I *know* why not. I'm so damned tired of all this talk and this misery and this confusion and heartache and guilt and fear and the endless running around like an animal in a maze that I'd like to take a running jump against the wall right now and dash my brains out and have it over with!"

"Dan, don't," she said, putting her arms around him.

Suddenly the realization that he was smelling the perfume of her body, feeling the warmth of her arms for the last time in his life caught him between two fires, passion and despair, and raked him mercilessly. He crushed her to him and kissed her neck and mouth hungrily and the more his passion mounted the more intense was his fear of losing her and the more intense his fear became the more neurotic and unrestrained and desperate was his desire until at last he began running his hands over her breasts, her hips, clawing at her wildly, pleading, entreating her to grant him the nepenthe of physical love.

She, in her own way, reflected his emotions, ran her hands over his body, and in a few minutes they were in a veritable frenzy of love, desperation, fear and hot-handed, wild-eyed longing, clinging to each other like refugees in a hurricane, drinking the wine of forgetfulness that their bodies held out to them, drinking it greedily and deeply and with no regard for what was to come after.

They slept deeply that night, huddled close together, exhausted emotionally and physically. It was almost two o'clock in the afternoon when they awakened.

Dan got up and raised the blinds and stood rubbing the back of his neck, looking down at the sleepy face on the pillow, trying to just look at it and enjoy it because it was a pretty face, trying not to think that this was to be their last day together.

He showered and shaved and then waited for her while she used the bathroom and got dressed. They had breakfast in a drugstore, speaking hardly at all, scrambled eggs and coffee.

They bought the papers and then went back up to the apartment and Dan made a few phone calls and then they just sat quietly and looked at each other with immense curiosity, as if they had never seen each other before.

That night it was the same as the night before except that they never went to sleep at all.

They stayed up the whole night making love and laughing and weeping and then laughing again and wondering what they should do about writing to each other if either ever needed the other or was ill or desperate.

At dawn they filled the tub with hot water and climbed into it together and then later they dressed and went downstairs, walking stiffly and awkwardly, like robots, staring straight ahead, not seeing the elevator boy who moved like a whispering ghost in the early-morning loneliness of the lobby, not seeing the strangers who passed them on the street.

The lack of sleep, the emotional pitch at which they had been living had combined to offer their ravaged hearts something like an opiate. They felt cried-out, loved-out, depleted, resigned, almost content. There was no fight left in them.

Moving as if in a dream, he drove to a midtown garage, then walked her down Sixth Avenue, in the quiet arctic coldness of the early morning, to the apartment on Fifty-fifth Street. Outside her door he gave her a sort of fumbling high-schoolish good-bye kiss, mumbled something about always loving her and then turned and walked off with his eyes unblinking, his head held stiffly erect and his mouth sour and his legs weak and numb.

He got the car out of the garage and drove out to the airport.

The plane came in on time.

He felt a strange surge of something like happiness and hope as he watched the people filing off the airliner and when at last he saw two small familiar figures hopping down the steps his heart leaped up and he walked quickly forward.

"Daddy! Daddy!" Michael and Patrick screamed, running toward him at top speed. They leaped up into his arms and he caught them both and swung them around and laughed and then put them down and picked them up one at a time and kissed them and then he saw Helen approaching, carrying Barbara.

She looked pretty.

"Hi," she said, smiling tiredly.

"Hello, honey," he said, kissing her on the mouth clumsily. "How was the trip?"

"Oh, awful," she said, laughing. "This one is quite a problem child."

"Here," he said, "let me take her." He lifted Babs from her arms and kissed her on both cheeks and lifted her up in the air and said, "How is Daddy's big girl, huh? How is Daddy's big old girl?"

The child smiled shyly and took Dan's hat off and held it against her face.

Driving back through the city, picking up the parkway drive to Westport, it almost seemed like one of the Sunday afternoon drives of days gone by. They were all together, in the car, all talking rapidly, joking, making small talk, family talk. It felt good.

They were all very tired, however, and once or twice their tempers became a bit short and Dan had to reprimand the children, although he hated to have to do so after not having seen them in so long a time.

When they got to the house the boys were out of the car like jack-rabbits, running around the property, exploring, shouting, questioning. He showed them the house proudly, as if he had built it with his own hands, and then they all had a light lunch and got into casual clothes and the children stood by and watched while Dan made a fire in the fireplace in the living room.

That night they all went to bed early.

Dan had been relieved to see that there were twin beds in the master bedroom. It meant there would be some time before he would have to face the embarrassment of physical intimacy with Helen.

She sat on the edge of her bed, in the familiar blue chenille housecoat, smiling shyly at him.

"It's good to be here, Dan," she said.

"It's good to have you, hon," he said.

259

"How has your work been coming along? Have you been doing much writing?"

"Not a great deal," he said. "I don't see quite as much of Hank as I used to and there's been—uh—some delay on Halliburton's show."

"That's too bad. Well, good-night."

"Good-night, hon," he said, climbing into his bed.

"Aren't you going to kiss me good-night?"

He turned, caught off guard, and leaned over, kissing her on the cheek.

Before he had gotten back into bed he could tell, without looking at her, that she was angry.

"What's the matter?" he said.

"Nothing," she said in a flat voice, turning her face away.

"Don't say nothing is the matter when it's plain that something is," he said. "What's on your mind?"

"Are you sure you want us here?"

He felt cold and frightened and wanted to run.

"Of course I want you here. What do you think I took this big place for, for myself?"

"That isn't what I mean," she said. "I know when you took this place you thought you wanted us, but now are you sure you did the right thing?"

"Honey," he said, swinging his feet out of bed, "why are you starting like this? What's wrong?"

"I don't know," she said, her eyes filling with tears. "I don't want to cause any trouble. I'm just afraid, that's all."

He was seized with pity and fondness for her and quickly stepped over to her bed and put his arm around her and pulled her head down on his shoulder and patted her arm.

"Don't cry, honey," he said. He had said the same words the night before to Elaine.

"Oh, Dan," Helen said. "I'm afraid."

"Don't be," he said. "We're overtired and maybe things seem a little confused right now, but they'll work out all right. They've got to."

"Don't say it like that. They don't *have* to. That shouldn't be the way to look at it."

"Look," he said, "are you sorry you came?"

"I don't know," she said. "It's wonderful being here and I love you and I think this place is very nice, but it's just not the way I thought it would be. I guess you think of two people getting together after a long separation and you think of them running to each other and wanting to be together and kissing each other as if they wanted to kiss each other. You think of starting all over again and being happy, but somehow it doesn't feel the way I thought it would. Maybe I've seen too many movies."

"I don't know what to say."

"That's just it. All day we've been circling each other. You've acted like you were afraid you were going to have to be alone with me eventually. We've spent all day talking about the children and the furniture and the weather and we haven't talked about ourselves."

"What is it you want me to say?" he asked.

"I don't know," she said. "But don't you know what I'm talking about? Am I wrong altogether? Don't you feel a coldness, a strangeness?"

"I don't know. Maybe I do. Whatever I say I have the feeling it will be the wrong thing."

"Do you love me?"

"Yes."

"That doesn't sound like the kind of a yes I want."

"Oh, Helen, now stop this foolishness! We've been through a hell of an experience. I know it wasn't your fault but it hasn't been an entirely happy thing for me either, to put it mildly. I'm trying to do what I think is right, don't you see that? I want to do the right thing. Can't you at least give me credit for that?"

"Yes, but . . . Oh, I don't know. I don't know what it is I want. Maybe it's just love."

"I'm sorry. I'm sorry I don't feel like throwing my arms around you and kissing you that way right now, but I'm not feeling like I'm feeling just to be mean. I'm not *trying* to hurt you."

And so they talked in circles for over an hour and at last Helen went to sleep in tears and it never got any better between them during the days that followed. He tried to force himself to exhibit a physical warmth toward her but he could not bring himself to the point of getting into the same bed with her for fear that she would discover there was not the real right kind of love or desire in him.

They entered the children in school but the boys seemed to sense the bitterness that stood between them and Michael took sick and Patrick would not eat and then one day they awakened to find that heavy snow had fallen all during the night and Dan could not get the car out of the driveway and they were trapped in the house and finally they sat, the five of them, like wolves trapped in a cave, now and then snapping at each other, waiting for some sort of deliverance.

Dan was now half demented from frustration and remorse at the evil thing he had done. Again, in trying to do what was right he had done what was wrong. His self-contempt knew no bounds and he became more desperate and angry by the hour.

The house had fireplaces and central heating but it seemed impossible, in the wintertime, to ever completely banish the chill that crept in through cracks and crevices or filtered in some mysterious way even through solid surfaces, through glass and wood and stone, settled in sofas and rugs and drapes, found warm flesh and made it shudder, seemed to pass through it, too, as easily as it had through everything else, and to settle in the bone. They lighted bright fires and turned the furnace up high, but in certain corners of the room, at certain low levels near the floor, and waiting for them in their beds at night, lurking between the sheets, the chill lay in wait, ever in wait, drawing its own cruel strength from the snow piled outside, from the winds that congregated high in the bare skeletons of trees and rattled windowpanes not violently but gently and relentlessly.

If it had been a happy house for them, if it had been a house of love, the cold would not have brought such an air of loneliness and desolation with it, but while there was love in the house it could not flow freely then between any of them, could not unite in one spiritual blaze to warm their hearts and souls, but rather flickered weakly between them, seeking a ground, dissipated itself in the air, leaving them uncomforted, insecure, and cold. The children went out again and again, bundled up with leggings and scarfs, to play in the snow, the first they had ever seen, but even their play seemed subdued, their squeals of wonder and surprise muffled, like the cries of lost birds, free but starving birds trapped in the North.

Dan walked with them in the snow, looking at them the way a man who knows he is soon to die must look at his children, trying to crystallize certain moments and sights and sounds and preserve them in his memory. He saw their red cheeks and uplifted smiles, watched them struggle through snowdrifts on little legs, looking like lost explorers on a strange planet, and because he knew, or at least was afraid, that something might take them away from him again (for, yes, they had been taken away from him by *something,* even though he had performed the act of leaving, even though he had removed his body from the presence of theirs in the West) he stared at them hungrily as they rolled and fell and recovered with piping cries and wandered in the snow, stared at their faces the way men stare at the forms of loved ones through prison bars, the way the condemned stare at the sun and sky before the black bag is lowered over their heads, the way God must stare at the souls in hell (if there is a hell), and the way those souls must stare at God (if there is a God). He wanted to kneel before them and say—oh, say what? The only words that occurred to him, and dimly, vaguely at that, would have been incomprehensible to them as well as embarrassing. He wanted to say absurd things like: Oh, you little tiny human beings, you toy people whom I love so much, with your little toy noses and your ridiculous adorable voices and sweet trusting little hearts, how I wish it were possible for those of us who are members of the giant race that rules the planet to kneel on the floor and in the snow and in fields of flowers with you and get into your world, somehow, rather than dragging you into ours, to kneel with you and look very closely into your faces and say how is it in there and we are sorry, truly stricken, that we ever hurt you.

But of course it was all nonsense, the whole idea, and he knew it, so all he could do was look at them as the days passed, look at them as they climbed panting up the rolling white hills and slid down, as they built snowmen and wandered through the stand of trees that surrounded the house, look at them as they walked gnomelike under the cold winter sun and under the sharp, crisp glittering stars of early evening. All he could do was watch them and think: God, what a supreme joke! I, who would be tempted to kill anyone else that hurt you, am hurting you more than anyone ever has. And you will probably never understand, and how could I expect you to, when I myself do not understand. Ah, well, some day you will know, and perhaps you know it already in some very basic way, that my love for you *exists,* that it exists whether you are on my lap or thousands of miles away under other stars. Or is there any good in that? Is love, for a child, nonexistent if the one who loves is not present? Oh, enough! Enough and too much of this endless looking at you and loving you and wondering, trying to piece together a puzzle that now can never be put together because some of the pieces are missing, having been lost or burned or pushed over the edge of the universe, gone, ever gone. There is only the present, doled out to us second by second and at least you are here, now, at this moment, and that is something to be thankful for. I love you now, here in this cold forest, here in this quiet house, here in this lonely Connecticut lane, and you are here to know of my love so that is what I will have to settle for now. Tomorrow can take care of itself. It is idle to dream of freezing time in the *now,* sticking to one point of time, stopping all motion the way it is stopped by a photograph or a flash of lightning. I will pick you up now and kiss you and take you into the house and make you hot Ovaltine. Not to coin a phrase, my beloved children, we will eat, drink, and be merry, for tomorrow we die.

Helen had not had the time or the inclination to make any friends in Westport and after the first few days, after she tired of the scenery, tired of the trees and the snow and the clean, still country air, she had nothing to occupy her mind but her misery.

"Why in the name of God did you drag us back here?" she would shout. "We didn't need you. Why didn't you leave us alone? This was your idea. Not mine!"

He had no answer. She was right, and the very fact served only to increase his fury. Finally one night after the children were asleep she screamed at him.

"Are you still in love with Elaine, is that it?"

"Why do you ask me questions like that?" he said. "What are you trying to do?"

"So that's it," she cried. "You *are* in love with her! Oh, God, I could *kill* you." She tried to slap his face but he caught her arm and pushed her away.

"Shut up," he said. "Go to sleep. You don't know what you're talking about!"

"You love her, you god-damned son of a bitch, and yet you drag us out of our nice home and back to this God-forsaken shack!"

"All right," he shouted, wild-eyed. "So I love her. What do you want me to do? I gave her up, didn't I? What more can I do?"

She startled him then by screaming insanely in a full wild voice and cursing him foully and then she ran into the bathroom and locked the door and he heard her fumbling amongst the bottles in the medicine cabinet.

"What are you doing?" he shouted.

"Get away from me," she growled in a strange animal voice, crying. "Leave me alone. What do you care what happens to me?"

After a moment the door flew open and she ran out, red-eyed, her hair disarrayed.

"I just took sleeping pills," she said triumphantly.

"How many?" he said.

"All I had!"

"How many?"

"There were only four," she said, "but they're strong ones and I hope they kill me, you hear? I hope they kill me!"

"Lie down," he said, trying to think. "I'll call a doctor."

"Never mind the doctors, god-damn you," she said. "What difference does it make to you what happens to me?"

She threw herself down on her bed and sobbed till she almost made herself vomit.

He picked up the slim Westport telephone directory and thumbed through it with trembling fingers.

When he at last had a doctor on the line he felt embarrassed.

"Say," he said, trying to sound casual, "this is Mr. Scanlon in Greens Farms. I was just wondering . . . Mrs. Scanlon has taken some sleeping pills, by accident, that is. What—"

"How many?" the doctor said.

"Just three or four."

"She probably won't be in any *serious* danger then. Does she need sleep?"

"Yes."

"Fine. Just let her sleep it off. She'll sleep a very long time but eventually she'll be all right. Have her drink liquids later if you can."

"All right, doctor, I'll call you back if there's any change."

Helen was already getting drowsy. She moaned and buried her face in her pillow, torn by jealousy and fury. The children, in the bedrooms on the other side of the house, did not seem to have heard anything.

The next day Dan arranged to have a practical nurse spend the day at the house. He took the children out for a walk.

When he came back, late in the afternoon, Helen was up and about.

"I've made up my mind," she said. "We're going back."

"What?" His stomach tensed.

"It's what you've wanted all along. You don't want us here. So we're going back."

"Don't talk about it now," he said. "The children might hear you."

Stunned, he hurried into the room where the children were playing, half-watching a TV set. The children had always been able to make him laugh heartily and he loved to talk to them because it fascinated him to watch their minds function.

When Michael was only four years old he had gone through a period where he had trouble with his "r's" and "l's." "I wike Wichard," he would say, or "I've been wunning." They had thought it was cute but one day Dan decided to explain to

Michael that such pronunciations were faulty and might be improved upon.

"I want some waymuns," Michael said. He meant raisins.

"You want what?" Dan asked.

"Waymuns."

"You mean raisins."

"Yes."

"But that's not the way to say it. Say it slowly now. Rais-ins . . ."

"Waymuns."

"Here, now. Break the word up into two parts. First say *raise*."

"Raise," said Michael, carefully.

"That's fine," Dan said, lifting him to his lap. "Now say *ins*."

"Ins."

"Wonderful. You're a very smart boy. Now slowly say *raise—ins*."

"*Raise—ins,*" said Michael, concentrating.

"That's perfect. Now say it fast. *Raisins!*"

"Waymuns!"

Their three faces, turned now toward the television screen, made his heart leap. They were going to be taken away from him again, although he accepted all the blame for what was about to happen. After a moment Michael looked up with what Dan thought was a measure of apprehension.

"You kids getting hungry?" Dan said, in a casual tone.

"Not me," Patrick said.

"If anybody's hungry," Dan said, "I can bring you some waymuns."

They all laughed.

"Hey," he said. "Anybody want to go with me to get the mail?"

"It's too cold," Barbara said, and they laughed again. He left them there, put on a jacket, went outside and walked down the drive-lane to the mailbox on the road. There were three advertisements for the former tenants and an envelope from his mother. Standing there in the snowy cold he opened the envelope with stiff fingers and read her letter.

My Darling Son:

After all your kindness and thoughtfulness to me what must you think of me allowing so much time to pass without writing to you. It's constantly in my mind, but I don't do it. I wonder what is in a person that causes them to do things they don't want to do and leave things undone that they want to do.

Thanks, Dan, for sending me those magazines. I enjoyed reading them and I guess if it wasn't for the reading and the radio and the television I don't know what I would do sometimes. The set you bought me is still working just fine although I had to have the man replace a tube the other day. I am so grateful to God for the great gift of a good child. Our Lord said the good (meaning the ones that loved Him) would suffer much and carry a heavy cross. He said He came to bring them a cross and not a crown. God help the ones that don't believe in another life beyond the grave. How can they stand their troubles here? And everyone has them sometime, sooner or later in their life, whether they bring on their own troubles or not.

Dan, little Mike has a birthday sometime in March. I lost the dates of all their birthdays so I can't remember just what day it is but I wanted to remind you so you could get him something. He loves you so much.

I visited Nellie last Sunday and she and Ann were so pleased with the delicacies you sent them. You know Nell. She always has liked special foods. On my birthday Ann brought me over a whole dinner, dessert and everything.

Dan winced when he read the word *birthday*. He had forgotten again. Well, she would understand. He looked at the letter again.

Oh, Dan, by the way, thanks so much for the picture of the children and me. I wish sometimes that when you're moving around in important circles back there you could meet Fulton J. Sheen. I know you meet a lot of important people and I'm sure he could comfort you a great deal. I wouldn't miss his Sunday broadcasts for worlds. Such a speaker.

Honey, thanks for sending me the book *Show Folks*. It wasn't bad but it seems to be just an ad for *Variety* and Joe Bernie. It is far from being a really complete picture of what was going on in vaudeville, believe me. I really didn't expect them to

268

mention my name but, hell, in all fairness, I did originate a style of singing that a lot of the people he mentions stole, imitated, or profited by. While I was not, maybe, what he used to refer to as a "Standard act," meaning an act that just played big time or the "Two shows a day" theatres, I was still well known and certainly had more individual talent than Bernie and Boothby and their set. You could buy their type act for a dime a dozen and there were dozens of them all cut from the same pattern. But I didn't cater to or mingle with agents and the *Variety* gang like a lot of the rest of them. I bought ads in *Variety* when I could afford it and got good reviews but one time when they gave me a rave and then practically insisted that I buy an ad to quote the rave I turned them down. The following week I was playing Loew's and they gave me the worst panning in history. The stage door of the theater was right next door to *Variety's* office, so after the last show I walked into their office and barring no holds told them exactly what I thought of their rottenness for at that time it was vaudevillians that were really supporting *Variety*. Well, to make a long story short, from that time on I was in their black book and they never spared me. I boil when I hear people giving "the great Gus" all those glowing eulogies. Sure, he helped a lot of people: his friends and his bootlickers. Thank God I never was one. I'm so glad you have the knack of handling people and taking care of things cleverly. I was too hot-tempered I guess to use any finesse. My new landlady is good and generous. She brings me things to eat and how I am eating them. For the first time in years I am getting fat, but I'm having so much trouble with my feet. The weather here has been damp lately and it bothers me quite a bit. Very little sun and lots of storms. Maybe all those Las Vegas Atom Bombs and things they're doing over in New Mexico have something to do with it. Dan, take care of yourself and write and let me know how you're feeling. Thank God for your good mind and kind heart. Speaking of minds, last Sunday this friend of mine, Jane, and I attended mass where the mental patients of Sawtelle Hospital go. The priest hears confessions before mass in the back of the church and last Sunday as the men were filing back there one poor man who didn't know where he was followed them and the nurse ran after him and grabbed him. Poor dear, he was going to follow his buddies no matter where they went, confession or what. Be sure to wear your undershirts all the time. Love. Mother.

Dan slowly folded the letter and put it into the inner pocket of his coat as he walked back to the house. It was so typical of his mother. The rambling thoughts, the sharp, sensitive but teeming, undisciplined brain, alternately bitter and loving. It was difficult for him to sit alone at home for more than an hour and often at such times he would reflect that his mother spent most of her time sitting alone in her apartment. In his mind he could see her watching television, or making herself a cup of coffee in the small kitchen, or crocheting as she sat in the big chair by the window and he would wonder how she could possibly stand it. Perhaps it was the palliative of habit that enabled her to endure loneliness. He wondered if he would ever become like her, able to sit alone day after day, as he knew he one day must.

A long time later he found that he had only a strangely vague memory of the next few days. They were hardly more painful than countless other days and he was getting almost accustomed to misery but, for some reason he could not determine, his mind had attempted to blot out the period during which Helen made plans to leave Westport and return to California. It was, he at last concluded, something about the look on the faces of the children that drove special knives of torture into his heart. They had thought they had him back and now discovered that they had been misled. The truth was withheld from them, of course; it had been a lovely winter vacation, they were told, and now they were going back to their nice, familiar home in sunny Southern California, and just as soon as he could arrange it Daddy would come out and have a wonderful visit with them. They accepted it all externally but their eyes revealed and their hearts were sensitive to the realities of the situation.

He telephoned Elaine and told her the news the moment it was definite, but on the day the plane actually left he found that he did not want to run, just then, to her. It would be somehow like committing the original crime over again. He spent two days closing down the now tomb-like house, working himself deliberately to the point of exhaustion. When the job was done he moved back into the Park Avenue apartment, which itself seemed deserted and sepulchral.

That night he once more blindly walked the streets. It was about nine o'clock when he went into the Strand theatre. He had been standing on the corner of Forty-sixth and Broadway looking up at a large sign that said, "Eveready Batteries" and he had suddenly decided to see a movie, *If This Be Love,* starring Joan Bennett and Gregory Peck.

The usher gravely returned the other half of the ticket, pressing it firmly into his palm. He walked across the lobby vaguely aware of the soft carpeting underfoot. For a moment he wondered how much such carpet cost per yard and then he was groping his way toward a seat in the flickering darkness of the orchestra.

When he had found a seat to his liking, removed his over-coat and folded it across his lap, he perceived that the picture had been running for some time. On the screen, Joan Bennett was slapping Gregory Peck's face.

"You're rotten!" she was saying. "Rotten, clear through!"

Gregory slowly felt his cheek with the back of his left hand the way men always did in the movies when they were slapped, and smiled slightly.

"I hope you feel better," he said. "You should have done that a long time ago . . . gotten it out of your system."

This looked like a pretty good movie, he thought. Then, from somewhere close behind him, a woman's voice said, "He shoulda slapped her back."

"Yeah," said another voice.

Tears appeared in Joan Bennett's eyes.

"I'm sorry," she said. "That wasn't a very ladylike thing to do."

"That's all right," Gregory answered, still smiling. "I had it coming, I suppose, breaking in here like this. It's just that after your husband told me—"

"Please," Joan interrupted. "I'd rather you didn't mention . . . him. What's done is done."

"But don't you see," Gregory said, serious now, "he may have lied about you, and I had to find out."

The rasping voice from the next row back said, "My God, he's got a nose just like Harry's."

"Yeah," came the whispered response, "but Harry's got a smaller chin."

He uncrossed his legs and peered over his shoulder without actually turning around. On the screen Gregory Peck was putting some papers into a briefcase.

"I'll try not to bring it up again," he was saying.

"Where are you going?" Joan Bennett asked.

"Back to the hospital," Gregory Peck answered. "The prospect of performing surgery after only four hours' sleep isn't a pretty one, but it's too late to worry about that now."

"You'll let me know, won't you, as soon as there's news?"

"Of course. In the meantime *you'd* better get some sleep. Can I give you something?"

A man in the balcony emitted a loud and suggestive whistle and the two women in the next row cackled lustily. "Some doctor!" exclaimed one.

"Yeah," answered the other, "I read where he might get a divorce."

"Who?" said the first woman.

"Him," her companion answered. "One of them movie magazines said he might but they didn't think he would, something like that."

"Oh," said the first woman.

Dan turned almost all the way around this time and cleared his throat ominously. When he tried to concentrate on the screen again his heart was pounding slightly and his palms were a little moist. There was a shot now of Joan Bennett nervously tearing at a handkerchief and looking at a clock on a mantelpiece.

The clock grew larger on the screen and then suddenly it was another clock and was growing smaller and the scene was no longer Joan Bennett's living room but was now General Hospital, Surgery. Gregory Peck appeared clad all in white with a mask over his face and tiny beads of perspiration on his forehead.

"He's sweating," announced one of the interpreters.

"Yeah," said the other. "You'd sweat, too."

A nurse walked up to Gregory Peck and showed him a chart

attached to a clip-board, then they hurried together into a white-tiled room.

"He ought to let him die," one of the women suggested.

"He won't, though," the other responded.

"I would, a guy who'd beat up his wife like that."

"Nah, he won't let him die. Where's my shopping bag?"

"I got it over here."

This time Dan sat up straight and purposely made it obvious that he was looking over the adjacent seating area in the hope of finding a spot from where he could concentrate on the movie without distraction.

A snort of disdain was heard from behind him, but a brief period of silence rewarded his display of pique. Perhaps, though, they hadn't noticed him at all. Perhaps they had just run out of things to say. His heart was still pounding disturbingly, more from frustration than genuine anger. It wasn't only the annoyance, it was that he couldn't strike back.

Joan Bennett was back on the screen now, in a car, speeding along a twisted highway in the rain.

"Oh, no," said the familiar voice just behind his ear. He began to imagine he could detect the faint aroma of garlic. The woman was obviously a pig and a slattern.

"She must touch up her hair," said the second voice disapprovingly.

"They all do," explained her companion.

Again he cleared his throat, more loudly than he had intended, and turned halfway around in his seat. This caused his coat to slide from his knees and he clutched at with a great deal of venom, conscious now that perspiration was forming under his arms and trickling down over his ribs. To himself he said, "Son of a bitch!" and the epithet, unvoiced though it was, gave him a sudden desperate courage. He clenched his fists, waiting almost eagerly for a word from either of them behind him.

Joan Bennett, looking beautiful and blankly worried, was looming in close-up now, and he felt a hot flicker of sympathy for her as well as a broad, deep understanding of her plight. It was a fine story, this tale of two people kept apart by a sense of honor. Hatred for those dolts who could not appreciate its poignancy welled up in him and tightened in his throat.

"She's going too fast," a voice hissed in his ear. It seemed he could feel the sound waves against the angry hairs on the back of his neck.

He whirled, bared his teeth, and forced air through them, shushing violently. The two behind him evidenced both unconcern and a complete absorption in the images on the screen, but a girl nearby coughed and several people turned to look at him. From somewhere to the right a man's voice softly said, "Quiet."

He felt slightly relieved but guilty and decided to move to another seat. When he stood up his coat started to slip again and for a moment the man on his left refused to withdraw his legs and he was left standing there, trapped and uncomfortable.

"Some people," said one of the women behind him.

"Yeah," said the other.

The man on his left finally stood up to let him pass and then, as he was muttering an apology, he stepped on the man's foot.

The theatre was crowded now and he could see no empty seats till he had walked all the way to the back of the aisle. An usher opened a door and he walked out into the lobby and through it to the wind-swept street.

CHAPTER

TWENTY-THREE

Some time later, Helen informed him, in a strange, prim, brief letter, that she had resigned herself to getting a divorce. He turned the matter over to his attorneys. When he told Elaine the news very early one morning upon awakening, she looked at him sadly and then said, "Don't let her do it, Dan."

"Do what?" he said.

"Divorce you."

A tremor of fear shot through him. "Why not?" he said.

"Because you're not really convinced it's what you want. You're not controlling the situation. You're just letting the thing happen to you. It's all right, honey. I give up."

He threw back the covers, sat on the edge of the bed, and began putting on his socks.

"What are you doing?" Elaine said.

"I have to go out," he said. "I'm just going for a walk."

"Go back to sleep," she said. "You'll be tired all day if you don't."

"I know," he said. "But I have to go out. I can't sleep." His throat was knotted tightly and he was afraid he was going to cry. He hated to cry in front of her.

"Why don't you call Helen right now?" Elaine said.

"I don't know," he said. "I don't know."

"God, if I hear you say I don't know once more I think I'll scream!" She sat erect in her bed, took a cigarette from the pack on the night table and lighted it, inhaling deeply.

"I'm sorry," he said, staring at the floor, lacing his shoes.

"That's good," she said, bitterly. "I'm sorry, too. I'm sorry for everything. I'm sorry I didn't go home a year ago. I'm sorry I came back all those times you asked me to. I'm sorry I ever met you."

He stood for a moment, looking at a framed letter from Michael. *Dear Daddy.* He looked at the words, tears in his eyes.

"You're indulging yourself," she said. "Look, why don't you call Helen right now and get it over with?"

"It's five in the morning," he said.

"It's only one out there . . . or two." She could never quite get the matter of time-changes right. "And besides, it doesn't matter what time it is. It's *better* if you wake her up in the middle of the night to tell her you're coming back. I'm a woman; I know. It will mean more to her now, in the middle of the night, than it will if you call her tomorrow in the afternoon."

"I'm not going to call her now," he said, standing before the bureau, looking through the dresser drawers for a shirt.

"What will you say to her when you do call?" Elaine asked.

"I don't know," he answered.

"You can't go on saying that," she snapped. "What do you mean you don't know? I'm leaving. That's settled. All right. That's the way you want it and it's fine with me, but—"

"That's not the way I want it," he interrupted, but she seemed not to hear.

"—you've got to make up your mind just what it is you want. You've got to put it into words. Will you tell her you love her more than anything else in the world?"

"No," he said.

"Then, *what?*" Elaine said. "Will you tell her you've decided to come back because you realize it's your duty?"

"No," he said. "Why do you ask me this? What difference

does this make? I'm not going to come up with any surprises when I talk to her. I'll just say you've gone and perhaps she and I can get together again. It will be good for the children. That's all. You could have guessed that much."

"It just doesn't make sense," she said, relighting her cigarette. She sat naked in the bed, with the sheet pulled up to cover her. Tears came again into his eyes as he looked at her sitting there, so beautiful and so angry. He had known it many times, the feeling that a given moment might be the last. It always made his throat feel tight and gave his face a pinched, tense look. He bit his lower lip nervously. At such times he despised himself for his lack of emotional control, feeling weak and childlike in his inability either to mask his feelings or control them. Looking at her now he wanted to go to her, to sit on the edge of the bed and stroke her hair. He loathed himself for wanting to run to her. Her hair was mussed. She looked utterly exhausted.

"You're so beautiful," he said.

She gave him a look of exasperation.

"Why don't you take your clothes off and go to sleep? You'll be dead tomorrow."

He walked to the window and looked out, through the venetian blinds.

"Oh," he said. "It's raining."

"It usually is," she said disgustedly.

For several minutes he looked down at the wet street, shining dully in the gray light of dawn. He had wanted to walk in the park, in sunlight, seeing the sky and perhaps sitting on the grass, as he had done years before in Chicago when he was troubled.

"Where are you going?" she said.

"Nowhere," he said. "Just out."

"What will you do?" Elaine said.

"Oh, I can keep busy. I'll walk around for a while. Or maybe take a drive. Then when the restaurants open I can get breakfast. Then I can go get a shave and a haircut. I have a luncheon appointment with a publisher. I'll keep busy somehow."

"You'll get wet," Elaine said.

"Thanks," he said. "I'd go back to bed, but I can't sleep, honestly I can't. I was going crazy, just lying there. My mind goes back and forth like a tiger pacing in a cage. It—I don't know. I just have to get out. It makes me miserable . . . looking at you."

"Thanks," she said, and they both laughed a little.

The sound caught in his throat and for a second he feared he was going to lose control of himself again. He could not stop tears from filling his eyes. It made him angry.

"I'm like a god-damned woman," he said.

"Everybody cries," she said. "It's normal."

Suddenly he felt a desire to escape, to get away from the torture of seeing her, demure and warm, perched high up at the end of the bed, like a kitten. He tried to say good-bye, but he could not bring himself to speak. For a long time he stood staring at her, saying nothing. He felt at once numb and hysterical.

"I'll be back," he said, and hurried out of the bedroom.

The elevator boy looked rumpled and annoyed when Dan stepped into the elevator. He rubbed his eyes and clumsily buttoned his collar as he said, "Good morning, sir."

"Good morning," Dan said.

"Up early, aren't you?"

"Yep."

The street was dismal and cold. Occasional taxis hissed by, their tires flicking up a graceful spray. The city looked deserted. He got in the car and opened the windows. The rain was falling in a light mist and, blowing into the car, it felt good on his forehead. He felt feverish and stuck his head out of the window to cool his face.

Driving along Park Avenue he idled at twenty miles an hour, without destination. The avenue looked more beautiful than usual, deserted, uncluttered in the early dawn. Against the background of gray skies, gray, slick streets, and gray buildings the center-lane of grass and shrubbery looked especially green and fresh.

For a few minutes Dan believed he was calmer, thinking more clearly, then he found himself turning his head to the right, looking at the seat beside him, expecting in an insane way that someone would be sitting there. He pretended for a moment that Elaine was there, smiling, discussing people in her deft, analytical way. Then for a moment he pretended the children were in the car. He stopped unexpectedly for a red light and stretched his right arm across the seat the way he always had when the children had driven with him, sitting in the front. A taxi pulled up alongside him, waiting for the light, and he felt a flush of embarrassment, wondering if the driver had seen his lips moving, his arm outstretched.

He grimaced, trying to squeeze all expression from his face, trying to wring all thought from his mind by sheer physical effort. Passing St. Patrick's cathedral he stopped the car, on an impulse, and sat looking at the front door of the church. It had been almost two years since he had been in a church. The building seemed foreign and yet friendly now.

Parking at the corner of Fifty-first and Fifth he walked across the street in the drizzling rain and tried the side door of the cathedral. It swung open and he walked in.

The church was brightly lighted but deserted, except for two figures, sitting apart, far down the aisle. Slowly, listening to his footsteps, hearing a cough from somewhere in the far recesses of the cathedral echo throughout its length, Dan walked up the aisle toward the altar. He genuflected, succumbing to the reflex, and knelt in the third pew from the front.

His mind, so long accustomed to indecision, now betrayed him again. He felt simultaneously a desire to cry out, to prostrate himself, and a desire to sit calmly, condescendingly weighing the possibilities that suggested themselves to the sight-seeing agnostic.

Tentatively, he said the Lord's Prayer. Then, repeating it, he weighed each word, each sentence. He recalled the parrot-like rhythm in which he had recited all prayers as a small boy.

"Our *Fa*ther," he had said as a boy, over-accenting the first syllable, "Who art in heaven," hitting the word *art* with too much emphasis.

"Hail, Mary, full of grace," he said, after a while. "The Lord is with thee. Blessed art thou amongst women, and blessed is the fruit of thy womb, Jesus." The angel's words brought a mysterious but tantalizingly vague comfort, which he did not entirely trust, for their meaning contained nothing in the way of a reference to himself or his predicament. He recalled the speech emphases of boyhood again, particularly that which had destroyed the meaning of the last few words for children from time immemorial. "Blessed is the fruit . . . of *thywombjesus*."

But the Church had a knotty problem, after all, in teaching children to pray. How explain to a child of six what a womb is, without running the risk of losing control of the exposition? The meaning came with time, and the parents who said, "I will teach the children prayers when they are old enough to understand them completely," usually never got around to it. The children grew and didn't find time to learn the prayers.

He cursed himself. Here he was again arguing both sides of a problem. His mind, that seemed to see things from so many sides, that seemed able in an instant to discover all facets of a problem, angered him with its very technical omniscience and openness. He was continually at war with himself. His head was a raging, torn battleground on which were constantly being waged the historic philosophical battles, the ancient religious controversies, the metaphysical debates that had occupied men's minds throughout time.

He could take either side of a religious argument and defend it cleverly, but the ability to do so disturbed him, left him privately confused, weak, frightened, insecure. He could impart security to others, advise them wisely, but for himself he seemed able to do nothing. For every truth he thought he discovered, he was aghast to learn that he could think of countless exceptions to it. After all, there were men in the world arguing every conceivable viewpoint, all claiming to be right, all claiming to carry the banner of truth. Perhaps it was his casual studies of their conflicting theories that confused him. But no, he thought, it was something more personal, something connected with his particular mental equipment. His mind was in certain ways a machine, at war with itself, feeding upon itself, grinding itself down.

Someone coughed again in the cathedral, and the sound

waves echoed hollowly against the towering walls. No sound from the street penetrated the buttressed walls of the massive building and its inner silence was broken only, and always startlingly, by the clearing of a throat, or a footfall, or the muffled tinkle of something from the dimly lit area behind the main altar.

Sitting quietly, Dan almost dozed off. He looked at his watch. He had been there for over an hour. Unaccountably a joke he had heard came to his mind. Herkie Styles, a young comedian he had seen working at the Palladium in Hollywood with Benny Goodman's orchestra, had said, "I've only had this job for fourteen days. Gosh, it seems more like two weeks."

He sat trying to see into himself, trying to go back over his whole story, over all of it from the beginning and then, more important perhaps, over the part even before that. He tried to decide how it was that he had grown so far away from what he had been, how it had happened that he had gradually drifted away from the land in which he had lived as a youth with his family, drifted as inexorably as a raft in a tide, without having willed to do so.

How much, he asked himself, did he owe to his people, his mother, his aunts, uncles, cousins? He thought warmly of them all and wished them well and would have done anything material for them that he could but he was not able then to find it within himself to feel anything that could in honesty be described as love for them, with the exception, of course, of his mother. But what now was even his love for her? Certainly not what it had been when he was a child. It was now mixed with sympathy and sadness, with a gradually increasing understanding of her failings, and yet too it was diluted with disapproval, at times even with hatred.

Stephen Decatur had said, what was it, my country right or wrong? Was one also obliged to say, my mother right or wrong, my religion right or wrong? He tried to agree but he was not equal to the task. He could not agree with Decatur or with anyone who said you had to approve of the activities of a nation, or a parent, or a church if those activities did not seem consistent and logical and moral to you.

He tried to make out in his mind an imaginary balance

sheet. To exactly what extent was he indebted to the people from whom he had sprung, among whom he had grown up? He thought it over and said to himself, "I am indebted to my family for many things. They gave me food and clothing and money and as much love as they were able. They also taught me, however—by example—to despise Jews, and to sleep in my clothes, and to make jokes about Protestants, and to hang wet clothing on sagging ropes in the bathroom to dry, and to laugh at and tolerate Negroes but also to look down on them, and to wear my socks three or four days at a time and shirts until they were dirty to the point of embarrassment, and to refer to Italians as Dagos and Poles as Polacks, and to look upon sex as something evil, and to respect the political pronouncements of Father Coughlin over those of the Pope, and never to do anything the simple, logical way; never to open a box-top according to the instructions that suggested an opening be made along a dotted line, never to open things neatly and efficiently, but always to tear at them with animal fingers, impatiently and grossly. They taught me, by example, to bump into things and knock things down, to exhibit a complete lack of social grace in the presence of strangers. They taught me, by example, to run and hide when a knock came at the door and to refuse to answer a phone when one was ringing. They taught me to scurry about and feel trapped if strangers or, indeed, friends came to call and they taught me to regard everyone else in the world as an outsider, to be tolerated, perhaps even loved, but always to be considered an outsider. Some outsiders came to them and tried to take them individually away, to separate them with only love as a weapon, but more often than not they failed. There was once a man a long time ago for Aunt Mag, a long-lost, almost-forgotten creature known as 'Uncle' Fred, Freddy Johnson. He had come offering love to Margaret but the family, all the other members, had made crude jokes about him and called him 'stupid Freddy Johnson,' or 'that damned Freddy Johnson,' and finally he had gone away and Mag had not gone with him."

There had been much of that, much insulation against the outside world, and a certain amount of it, Dan knew, had stuck to him and he had had to fight against it, to cleanse himself of it, but he knew that he could never be entirely free of it, that some small trace would always cling to him.

"What else," he asked himself, sitting there in the silent cathedral, "have my people done for me? They have taught me, by example, how the warp and the woof of family tensions and fears are constructed. They have taught me the way women must hide in the bathroom to smoke a cigarette so that brutish brothers who do not think women should smoke might not be offended. But the brothers have taught me how to be hypocritical, for they knew the women smoked and would not admit it. Expert instruction in a great many other fields was made available to me, but I eventually refused to interest myself in it. I had excellent opportunities to observe first-hand how a man can come home drunk and knock women down and break windows and throw up in a toilet and get blood on rugs and furniture. I might have learned how, had I cared, to become a nervous wreck in the face of the absence of tobacco. Fortunately some of these things that my family showed me appalled me or disgusted me and so my inclination was, in these matters, to be as different from my people as I could. It has taken a long time to go over it all, point by point, and decide which of the things they taught me might deserve emulation and which could serve as warning signs. Because as a child I saw that drinking often caused vomiting and foul, angry talk and sickness and violence, I do not now feel irresistibly drawn to alcohol; I can easily stop drinking if I want to. Because as an infant I was made uncomfortable by the clouds of cigarette smoke that were blown into my face, I do not now smoke, although I feel in no way virtuous concerning these things. They are all largely matters of accident.

"I do not, as a matter of fact, either feel obliged to give any credit to my people for the good things they have done for me or to blame them for the bad things they have done to me. I cannot find it within myself to blame them at all. I can only feel sorry for them. If my childhood was confused and torn up and unstable and frightening, theirs was worse."

Now he began to think about his grandfather—a bearded

tyrant who tried to bring up his children with an iron hand and failed, a strange, aloof man who could not control his children and could not bend and become warm with them and roll with them on the floor and make them laugh as a father ought. He could not in the end do anything with them at all, and when the boys began drinking and getting into street fights, when the girls became flighty and independent he bade them all good-bye one day and walked off to the other side of the world and left them.

"Bridget," he had said to his wife, "I want to return to Ireland. I am not happy here. Will you come with me, bringing the smallest children, and leaving the rest to run like the wild creatures they are?"

Bridget, the simple, patient, saintly mother of sixteen (of whom half had died at birth or shortly after), could not bring herself to leave her new home. She could not understand what secret longings, what dark fears were driving her husband back to his homeland and so she refused to go with him. They never saw each other again. The old man went back to Killarney, back to his native soil, and sat and smoked his pipe, and looked bitterly into the western skies and finally died, none of them ever having seen him again.

So it was that the children were forced to shift for themselves, to support the home, to give up whatever feeble pretense they had been making at acquiring an education, to get out and go to work in shoe factories, in meat-packing plants, in railroad yards, to jungle-fight for existence in the gray, dismal back-of-the-yards section of old Chicago, to walk the streets of the Bridgeport section and try to find amid the saloons and back alleys and yawning empty lots some sign of love and approval and success. They found none of these. They knew instead only bitterness and poverty and frustration, and instead of helping one another to fight the world and force it to do their bidding they fell to arguing amongst themselves. The boys took to jealously guarding the virtue of the girls, frightening away strange young men, beating up prospective beaux, insulting visitors. And the girls took to fearing the boys and loving them from a distance, and all their lives they never

284

were to know a month's peace for worrying about the safety of their drunken, brawling, short-tempered brothers.

And it was all the fault of none of them.

The young bucks had not the money or background for respectable relaxation, and so all that was open to them was the saloon, the poolroom, the street corner. Lacking education they were unable to worship the mind, and so they worshipped the body and took to boasting about which of them was the strongest and which of them could defeat the others in hand-to-hand combat. They also took to drinking and carousing, and so in time destroyed the bodies which had been their only source of strength and confidence.

And yet they were not merely ignorant, pugnacious toughs. They were these things, indeed, but they were more. They were all witty, popular, and loyal. They were brave and devil-may-care and quick-thinking. They were not cringing, servile, or dishonest but were of good Irish peasant stock, of the blood that has produced many of America's priests, mayors, doctors, lawyers, teachers and even some artists. But some weakness of character handed down to them, some inability to overcome the burden of their environment, ordained that they would not be among the few fortunate enough to rise up out of the jungle.

So it was that one of the boys died at forty, in the prime of his life, weakened by drink and frustration and then carried off by disease, another, sweet and blue-eyed, died of tuberculosis at twenty-two, coughing piteously, weeping and joking, clutched in the loving arms of his sisters, saddening the family so greatly by his death that they could never after speak of him but in soft regretful tones, for perhaps he would have been the one of them all who might have amounted to something if he had lived. Another of the boys, Bill—the one with the best brain, the one who could add up a giant column of numbers with the speed of an adding machine, the one who had always held good jobs and then lost them because of drink or because of his inability to take criticism from his superiors, the one who had almost moved into the successful circle of Irish political life in Chicago, but who had somehow miscalculated just a bit and gotten in instead with gamblers and racketeers (perhaps because the one group merged into the other anyway)—had finally become involved in some sort of difficulty with the law (Dan had never learned the exact details) and as a result had spent almost ten years in the state prison at Joliet. By the time Dan was old enough to know Bill, his prison years were behind him. Dan could recall him only as a stern, brisk, balding man with a warm heart that was rarely allowed to manifest itself because of his short temper. He had fumbled around with various women and finally, when Dan was a boy of thirteen, he had watched the old man die, slowly, torn with the pain caused by a cancerous stomach, drinking to forget the pain, suffering then more from the drink, cursing his life and his wasted opportunities, sleeping on blankets on the floor, crawling about like a sick dog (with Dan looking in stunned horror at his exposed rump and testicles), throwing up and crying like a lost child.

This had been the way of the whole family, to know very little happiness but much misery, to be not masters of their fates or captains of their souls but rather to be poor, lost wanderers in a world that buffeted them about and frightened and embittered them.

So it was that Dan could not blame them for what they had done to him, for they had not known they were doing it. They had never sat down and reasoned the matter out on the question of, say, anti-Semitism. They had never said to themselves, "Well, let's see . . . it must be a wise thing to look down on the Jews because Jews are always taking jobs that the Irish should get, or because too many Jews are moving into our neighborhood and it's getting so an Irishman can't find a decent place to live in this city." They had never made any attempt whatsoever, even such an illogical one, to arrive at their decision to be bigoted and prejudiced. They had simply *been* prejudiced in as simple a way as they had been blue-eyed or strong-boned or quick to laugh. It was thus with all their faults. Most of them they did not recognize as faults, and the others they seemed powerless to correct. There was no point in hating such people and not wanting to have anything to do with them. Dan simply felt that he had grown away from them

286

and that he could no longer speak their language. It was not really anyone's fault.

Sitting there in the church, trying to figure out who he was, trying to identify himself and so predict his future, Dan became aware at that moment that Mass had started. The priest had now appeared on the altar. Acting on the conditioned reflex, Dan rose and stood listening to the soft mutter of the introductory prayers.

After a while, he knelt and experimentally tried to throw himself back into time many years, back to the time of his boyhood innocence when he had knelt wide-eyed in church, hands folded piously against his chest, looking eagerly at the plaster figures on the altar, hoping to see some sign of movement, daydreaming about miracles, wishing that the painted hand of Jesus might wave to him with some sign of encouragement or love.

He had heard stories that women were sometimes able to fall in love with Christ, almost in the way that they might fall in love with a man. He had heard stories of nuns who seemed to love Him in that way and he thought as a child that perhaps he could learn to feel something of that sort of love.

He had never known the love of a father, and he could remember looking up into the faces of many men through the early years, the faces of uncles and friends of the family, to see if he could discover love in them. As a child he had wanted an adult male to love, and in this desire, when he had been very young, there had been indications that he might be able to feel a son-to-father sort of love toward Jesus.

But he had never actually been able to do so. It had been difficult, or more correctly, impossible. There had always been the cold, unmoving statues; no signs, no proofs, nothing flowing back to him that he could feel.

There had been some emotionality involved in the performance of his religious obligations, of course. He could remember the childhood solemnity and sanctity that had permeated his soul when he had received Communion, the feeling of release and happiness he had known when he had gone to confession. But now, years later, he could not be at all sure that the feeling of joy one felt upon leaving the Communion rail was not merely a shy sort of pride, an exaggerated version of the "good-boy" feeling. He could not be sure that the joy at leaving the confessional might not be partly due to one's belief that one had been forgiven and partly due to one's relief that the embarrassing ordeal was finished. The feeling was, after all, remarkably similar to the sensation he felt after leaving a dentist's office. One was glad that the work had been done, one felt somehow improved, but a great deal of one's pleasure resulted from nothing more than the fact that the visit was over and done with and would not have to be repeated again for a while.

Standing up for the reading of the gospel, he cursed himself again for the ambivalence of his reasoning. He seemed to be completely unable to entertain an important idea without immediately thereafter welcoming exceptions to it, other ideas which were clearly in opposition. He sat down and closed his eyes in contemplation, and then fatigue hit him hard and he dozed off for a few minutes. The altar bell tinkled and awakened him and he shook his head and sank to his knees.

"This is My Body," the priest was saying, in Latin. It had been a long time since he had last taken the Host into his mouth. He could clearly recall its taste as it lay thin and brittle on his tongue, quickly dissolving and turning sweet as the ptyalin in his saliva turned the starch of the wafer to maltose.

Receiving the Host had been a pleasure to him as a child but later, when he was changing from a child into a man, he had been panicked and afraid to confess his new sins and afraid too to have his sinfulness revealed to the world by his absence from the Communion rail and so he had been driven by his abject fear to receive the Host unworthily. He had made what was called a "bad" Communion.

One of his teachers, a Sister Claudette, had told his class a frightening story about a man who made a bad Communion and who immediately thereafter began to cough and spit blood and had finally died horribly right in church with blood gushing from his mouth as punishment for his terrible sin. He was to learn later that he was not alone in this particular conflict, that many a trapped young sinner had been driven guiltily to

288

the Communion rail. Out of this experience he had first conceived the idea that it was possible that from a good thing could come bad consequences.

When Mass was over he walked across the street and had scrambled eggs and whole-wheat toast and coffee at Hamburger Heaven and then he got back in the car and drove around town, aimlessly.

In another hour the drizzling rain had stopped and the sun had begun to dry the streets. He parked the car in a garage and began walking, without direction, deliberately tiring himself, staring straight ahead, gliding like a ghost through the swarms of people who began to throng the streets. In time, the warm and oddly dry air evaporated the last trace of the early-morning sprinkle. Still Dan walked, once or twice despising himself for what was at least a *new* reason, that in his confused state he had momentarily visualized himself as a strange, lone figure in a motion picture, a forbidding avenger come to town to mete out justice with a gun or his fists.

By noon he had walked many miles, first one way and then another, allowing himself to be turned in that direction and this by a car that blocked his path, a traffic light that suddenly changed, an obstruction in the street. At last, almost as in a dream, he found himself in a strange land.

As far as he could see, far past the flat sweep of green in the foreground, beyond the clump of trees off to the left, the scene suggested one word: carnage. Bodies lay sprawled in poses at once grotesque and graceful and, as he passed among them, he observed with a shudder how some turned their glazed unfeeling eyes to the sky, though the eyes of most were respectably closed.

The most prominent figure, the one man on the horse, the cavalry officer, sat motionless, surveying the area without so much as the flicker of a muscle to indicate his reactions, right hand casually holding his drawn sword in such manner that it pointed down and slightly to the rear.

Following the line of the blade one's eye came at last to a pair of bodies lying face up, the arm of one lying across the chest of the other. Dan sniffed the air and winced as his nostrils detected odors in conflict: the clean green scent of the warm moist earth and the chill ugly smell of released gases.

Papers were blowing now across the fields as a vagrant breeze plowed up the still air. He shivered slightly and stepped away to the left, trying to keep his eyes straight ahead, trying not to gawk openly at the bodies flung all around, feeling at the same time an almost irresistible urge to bend low over them, to look into their faces and try to fathom their secrets, their pasts, feeling an urge to look into the vacantly staring eyes and try to detect with the bat-wing-fuzz of his subconscious whatever reflected images might still be giving off the subtle energy of only remembered light.

The bodies held a powerful fascination for him, but now it was weakened by the distraction posed by the mighty trucks that rumbled, motors grinding, along the nearby road. Overhead the sun stared down boldly, warming then reddening the exposed flesh.

The whole great city lay exposed before the golden eye and it was the hour of no-mystery, the time between the ageless pink surprise of morning and the equally timeless purple romance of dusk. Dan walked a hundred yards, crossed a street, stopped to wipe his brow with the back of his hand, and came at last to 59th Street. Behind him for miles stretched Central Park, crawling with nurses and baby carriages, with yellow and green taxicabs, with lovers strolling arm-in-arm, and with weary office workers and tourists who wandered off into the brush and across the vast lawns to fling themselves down upon the ground at last in the attitudes that had made the park look like a wide, peaceful battlefield on the morning after a bloody struggle.

He loved to spend small pieces of time in the park. It was the place where one could first find Spring in the city. Some dark night, when no one was looking, the shy season would slip into town and hide in the park. Though it could not be certainly discerned for weeks in the windy, dirty streets it could very early be identified in the park, rustling secretively amongst the trees, spreading a soft green carpet for itself over the tawny-colored fields.

He sat now on a bench looking along Central Park South and up Sixth Avenue, head tilted back to face the sun until at last a fat elderly man seated himself on the bench upwind and lighted a cheap cigar. Shortly the foul fumes obliterated the perfume of the surrounding greenery and Dan stood up frowning and walked away.

When eventually he returned to the apartment, he effected a simple, sad, animal reconciliation with Elaine, in the way that by now had become almost routine with them. But it was, as always, immensely pleasurable, warmly comforting.

Days passed again in a sort of truce state, a period during which the two of them simply did not discuss their problem. Dan sometimes thought, in idle moments, that it might be possible to go to his grave happy still in Elaine's company if only he could live hour by hour, day by day, refusing to face reality, trying to sneak by and enjoy what happiness he could while no one was looking, so to speak. But even these daydreamed fantasies could not sustain him for long. Always would come the fits of remorse, the periods of standing at the window looking down, wondering what the sensations might be if he jumped out. Would there be five or six seconds of panic and then one moment of unbearable pain and then oblivion?

Summer had come in full strength to the city. The tar was soft in the gutters and the city suffered.

CHAPTER
TWENTY-FOUR

AFTER one of their arguments he stayed away from her for five days, during which time he met a girl at a cocktail party, Shirley Harris, a secretary who worked for a music publisher. She was an overweight brunette with a bad complexion but he spent the night at her apartment. Shortly thereafter Elaine found, in one of his jackets, the girl's name and telephone number. He could not even remember having written it down.

After another argument he accepted an invitation from a publicity woman named Anne Kraft to spend a weekend on Fire Island. When Elaine found out about it she was furious.

"It was all just a matter of swimming and lying in the sun and walking around and visiting people," he said. "I don't happen to find Anne physically attractive."

"Well, isn't that good news," she shouted. "I suppose if you did find her physically attractive you would have spent the weekend in bed!"

She stomped out of the apartment. That evening, when she did not answer the phone at Polly's, he went to Fifty-fifth Street and waited for her on the corner for over two hours.

"Where were you?" he said when she at last appeared.

"At the newsreel theatre," she said. "Alone."

They walked the streets for a while, in silence.

"Well, honey," she said, as they window-shopped on Fifty-seventh, "what's new? How are you and God getting along these days?"

He laughed. "Just fine," he said. "He was asking for you."

"And how about you and the Pope?"

"Strangely enough," Dan said, "he doesn't seem to have heard about my case."

"Seriously, Dan," she said. "Do you feel any different about . . . well, about the Church?"

"To tell you the truth," he said, speaking slowly after a thoughtful pause, "it's difficult for me to tell how I feel about the subject of Catholicism for the reason that, although I was trained to love and respect the Church, most of the individual Catholics I ever knew, now that I think back, were dreadfully poor Christians."

"You're exaggerating."

"I don't think I am. At least I don't intend to be. I mean just what I say. Perhaps it's just that I grew up in an Irish-Catholic society, which I admit is not the same thing as an Italian-Catholic society, say, or a French-Catholic society. Then, too, I'm talking about the Irish Catholics in America, and the poor ones in Chicago, who may, for all I know, be quite different from the Catholics in Ireland. But the facts as I see them are simple. My grandmother, to the best of my recollection, was a rather saintly old lady, almost a stock dramatic type: the little, old white-haired Mother Machree, and I can remember a few priests and nuns who seemed touched with gentleness and sweetness and piety, but against this handful I can point to thousands of others whose only concept of sin seemed to be in the area of sex, who were absurdly scrupulous about sins of the flesh, but who were boorish, unfeeling, cruel, defensive, and thoroughly un-Christian in their attitudes toward their fellow man."

"It's tough to turn the other cheek."

"I know, but even that is secondary. It isn't the essential

thing about Christianity. The heart of the Christian message is love. You can turn the other cheek, if you can at all, only because first you love."

"Aren't Catholics taught to love?"

"I can't answer for the whole Church. All I can say is that I personally don't remember ever being really taught to love. Not at all. Oh, I was told to love God all right, but I don't remember hearing much about loving my fellow man. It's quite confusing, of course. I don't mean that man is more important than God and I'm not saying that the Church ignores the letter of the law of universal charity. It's just that I can remember a million nights and days of going to Mass and praying and kneeling and singing and contemplating but I don't know if I can remember hearing a single thing of a practical nature about experiencing the brotherhood of man."

"Not ever?"

"Oh, I *must* have heard it. It's there on paper, of course, and you find it in the better Catholic magazines, and goodness knows Christ was explicit enough about it. But in general the Church seems to deal too much with the idea as an eternal abstract truth and not enough in its concrete application. I know thousands of Catholics who are bitterly anti-Semitic and I'll bet not a *one* of them has ever confessed it. In fact if you stopped the average Irish Catholic on his way out of the confessional and said 'I heard you talk about the Jews in a sinful way the other night. Have you confessed the fact?' he'd probably think you were nutty. He wouldn't even know what you were talking about."

"Does that mean most Catholics, or let's just say Irish Catholics, are hypocritical?"

"No, I don't think it's so much a matter of hypocrisy as of moral stupidity. Or perhaps stupidity is too harsh a word. It's just that some of my people seem to have a moral blind-spot when it comes to the very vital center of the Christian message. Too many of them, at least of the older generation, think that being a good Catholic is just a matter of making novenas and lighting candles and hating Communists and sending money to missions. By God, the Church ought to rub their noses in the truth."

"Do you think the Church itself knows the truth?"

"Probably, but now we get down to the matter of defining the word Church. What is a church anyway? It's masonry and architecture and it's also a body of people and it's also a lot of beliefs written down on paper. I'm certain that there are some priests who know the truth, or who at least know what we can accept as the truth for purposes of this conversation, but there are, at least in this country, too many priests who seem to be as blind as the people . . . and I think in many cases they are Irish priests."

"But Sheen and the Jesuits who—"

"Oh, of course you can name *scores,* probably hundreds, of fine men among the clergy. That's the shame of it all, that there aren't more like them. But for every wise leader there are dozens of shortsighted parish priests who seem to be vain men with a narrow outlook. I knew a priest once in Los Angeles who said it was a shame there so many niggers moving into his parish. But we're digressing. I'm not interested in isolating instances. Every group has its bad apples. It's just that there are so many examples of cases where Catholics develop a callus on their souls."

"Don't we all in time?"

"Sure, but do we all continue to feel that we're better or holier than the rest of men? Now anything that wrong has to be somebody's fault!"

"Are you talking about this," she said, "just because it's on your mind or because it has some relevance to our problem?"

"I'm not sure," he said. "I don't think it has anything to do with what happened to me, but then again maybe it does. I guess I'm not bright enough to figure it out."

"Well," she said, "bright or not, you don't have forever. We've got to make a definite move sometime."

"I know," he said. To himself he added, "And the move has got to be away from you. I've got to give you up."

She was thinking the same thing. That day they made up their minds.

They were sitting at opposite ends of the long, wide, old-fashioned white tub, facing each other, soaking quietly in the hot water. The mirror over the sink was steamily opaque and a faint film of warm moisture was beginning to condense on the cold tiled walls.

Elaine picked a forest-green washcloth out of the water and applied it to her face, holding her breath under the hot terrycloth, exhaling noisily as she splashed herself again and again.

"Would you like me to brush your nails?" he said.

"Please," she said in a small voice.

He picked up a white plastic-handled nailbrush, touched it to the soap and began to scrub the tips of her toes, impersonally, absently, as a jeweler might polish a stone.

"It seems like such a waste," she said after a while. "Our parting, I mean. Such a waste of love, such a waste of passion. Is there really a reason for everything?"

"I don't know," he said. "There must be a cause, but there might not be a purpose. Give me your other foot." She lifted her left leg gracefully and he began to brush again.

"It's hard to avoid speaking lines," she said, "but it does seem like *such* a waste. There were so many things we could laugh at together and now it—that tickles."

"I'm sorry," he said. "It's done, anyway."

He dipped her foot into the water, washed the soap from it, lifted it, inspected it, kissed it and lowered it back into the water.

"Do you really have to go?" he said.

"Yes, baby," she said. "There's a time for everything. Timing is important. There was a right time for us to get married. It's past."

"I love you." He had not realized he was going to say it.

"I love *you*," she said, without feeling. "Oh, God, why do things like this have to happen to people?"

"As they used to say in the army, that's a good question," he said, thinking it out slowly, speaking slowly. "According to our standards everything we've done has been evil. We've hurt people, we've lied, cheated, and posed, and pretended. But the funny part of it is that the thing itself, the very heart of it all, the love that we feel for each other, there doesn't seem to be anything wrong with that. It's so perfect. That's why the whole thing is so damned ridiculous. They say no good can come of an evil thing, but they're wrong. This evil thing has been very good in many ways."

"It's crazy," she said. "It's too much for me. We've tried so many times to tear ourselves away from it, but it's never worked."

"I know," he said.

"But it will this time," she said, flaring suddenly into anger. "It will this time. And don't . . . don't you dare, not for even one minute, think that you can call me on the Coast if it doesn't work out between you and Helen. I'd never come back. You know that, don't you?"

"Yes," he said. They could never seem to sustain an emotion any more. They would swing sweepingly from one mood to the other, mixing hate with love, crying, then laughing, accepting numb resignation, then rejecting it in the hysteria of passion.

"You know I could never come back," she said. "And you know why."

"Why?"

"Because I would always feel that I'd been a second choice. If it doesn't work out for you and Helen, maybe you're thinking you can call me and I'll come running back. It's no good that way."

"I guess not," he said.

So this was the way you finally broke up. Really, finally. Speaking in subdued tones, almost off-handedly, as if you were discussing something of relative unimportance. Well, there certainly should be no more quarreling. There should be nothing, in fact, to upset this mood of dull, numbed disbelief. Perhaps you could hang on to this numbness for a long time and then one day say to yourself, "Well, I haven't seen her in almost four months, and it doesn't hurt so much any more." Perhaps you could do that. He would see.

"I hate to ask you," she said, "but I'll need money to pick up my train ticket tomorrow."

"That's all right," he said. "I'll make out a check."

She sneezed silently, stifling the sound in a way that had always made him smile.

"There's a draft from under the door."

"Yes," he said. "I'll fix it." He climbed out of the tub, took the undershirt he had thrown on the floor, placed it loosely along the crack under the door, and stepped back into the water, shivering slightly.

"You're beautiful," she said. "What will you do after I leave . . . and before Helen arrives?"

"I'll manage."

"The hell you will," she said, chin trembling. "You'll manage with some broad you'll pick up, that's how you'll manage."

"I haven't made love to you for over a week now," he said, "and I'm getting along fine. I've told you a million times that before I met you I wasn't particularly passionate. It's only with you that I'm that way."

"Then why did you have to sleep with that Harris girl the other night?"

"I don't know," he said. "That's different. I thought I wasn't going to see you again. I was angry with you and sad. I don't know why I do those things. I never did them before in my life."

"I don't do them," she said.

"I know, but women are different. You've told me that when you're away from me the thought of another man touching you is distasteful. Why it's not that way with me I don't know. Oh, I don't care anything about these other women. They're never really attractive to me, they're simply available. I drink, and I drink some more, and I feel something ugly and angry inside of me and the next thing I know . . ."

"You're in bed with them."

"But don't you understand?" he said. "They mean nothing to me. It's almost like going to a whorehouse, I suppose, though I've never done that either. But I guess it's very much like that, although it usually happens accidentally. I don't plan it, but when it finally happens it's impersonal, it's desperate and even sordid. It's very much like paying for it. Anyway, Shirley Harris means less than nothing to me. She's the last, believe me."

"Then you were telling the truth about Fire Island."

There was an unexpected jangling, a jerking short somewhere in his subconscious, a flow of body juices. He had unintentionally lied and he knew a moment of slight panic, the normal reaction of a trapped liar.

"What?" he said, as do all liars.

"Did you sleep with Anne Kraft on Fire Island that time?"

For a moment he planned to continue the lie. But they had had the talk about it all time and again. "The truth," she had said, "may hurt a little bit, but then it's over. You know what the facts are and you learn to live with them. But lying is no good at all. If I find out you've lied then the truth hurts more than ever. It's doubly bad. You've done something wrong and then you've lied to me, and I get so I can't tell when you're lying and when you're telling the truth. So please," she had said, "tell me the truth, no matter what."

"All right," he said. "Yes. Yes, I did." For perhaps five seconds her face was expressionless but Dan could see that underneath she was frightened and hurt.

He thought perhaps she would say, "I thought so all the time," or "You're disgusting," or "God, I hate you." But he was shocked and unnerved when she began to howl and gasp like an abandoned infant.

He knelt clumsily before her and put his arms around her, splashing water over the edge of the tub. "Baby," he said, "don't cry. It's all right. Everything will be all right." Later he could recall having thought that most of the time when people said to other people, "It's all right, don't worry, it's all right," that it never was.

She cried in a strange way, shouting uncontrollably, incoherently, like a witness to a great disaster. He put his hand on the back of her head and pressed her face into his shoulder to muffle the sound. "Darling," he said, "please don't. Don't cry, honey. Everything will be all right. I love you. Please don't cry like that. Ssshhh, baby. Ssshhh."

He could feel her mouth, hot and wet and blubbering against his chest. He looked at the top of her head and saw here and there gray hairs wisping up through the brown. He patted her head and loved her very much. She shrieked brokenly again and then injected a note of fierce anger into the sound, pushing him away, her hands on his chest.

"You . . ." she spluttered. "You son of a bitch!"

"What?" he said, startled.

"Take you hands off me," she said. "I ought to slap your dirty face!"

The mood was changing again. It was hatred now. Love, then numbness, then fear, then hatred. The simple primitive bitterness in her face frightened, then angered him. He stood suddenly, splashing more water out of the tub, and grabbed a towel.

"I could take all the others," she said. "But this was after you'd just come back to me. You came back to me and said you loved me. You said it, and then you . . . I *hate* you!"

He stepped out of the tub, feeling the white tiles cold against his warmed feet. He started to explain, to say that with Anne Kraft, too, it had been an accident, a thing not planned, but it was no explanation. He could not have explained to himself why he had done the thing. He felt trapped and resentful, and displeased with himself completely.

"All the others," she was saying, "I could have taken all the others. But you said—"

"Cut it!" he shouted. "That's enough."

He finished drying himself and stalked into the bedroom.

For a few moments she sat in the tub trying to regain mastery of her emotions. Gradually the hot, wild vexation subsided and was replaced by a calm, methodical antagonism, a cold-blooded desire to retaliate. Splashing up out of the water, she began drying herself, looking coldly, bitterly into the mirror. She could hear him in the bedroom, banging drawers, stomping around petulantly, getting dressed.

"I guess we might as well forget dinner, eh?" he said.

"Of course," she said. "You and Hank go somewhere by yourselves. I'll make other plans."

She stood naked before the medicine cabinet mirror, applying bright red lipstick, combing her hair. He looked at her once through the open door, felt the old familiar fluttering in his stomach, the desire to put his arms around her, and hated her in the instant for her power over him.

300

He selected a blue, button-down oxford shirt from a bureau drawer and stood in the middle of the room, putting it on. Drivers and their cars honked and swore and screeched and made grinding sounds down in the street. The city sweltered in the early summer heat and, partly from the warmth of the air, partly from the violence of his emotions, he began to perspire.

Not wanting to look at her, he walked to the window and stood looking down at Park Avenue, at the Catholic church on the corner of 84th Street, the Protestant church on the corner of 85th. Children were being let out of school and he could hear them plainly, laughing and shouting, the piping sounds floating up balloon-like on the stifling summer air.

She passed behind him, padding silently across the floor, and climbed back into her bed, pulling a sheet up to her neck. Only when she was angry with him was she conscious of her nakedness.

"I just can't understand it," she said, slowly. "The other times maybe you were blue, being away from me, although it hurt even then. But telling me you wanted me, telling me you loved me, and *then* lying to me and running off with Anne Kraft to Fire Island."

"I didn't run off with Anne Kraft," he said, wearily. "I had just planned to go out there because I'd heard so much about the place and it sounded as if it would be a pleasant way to spend a weekend."

"It certainly was," she said, teeth clenched.

"All right," he said. "Give it to me. Go ahead. Say anything you want. I'm a target."

"What do you want me to do, congratulate you?"

"No," he said. "But I'm just trying to tell you I didn't go to Fire Island for the purpose of sleeping with Anne Kraft. She had invited me to be part of a large party and then I simply didn't feel that being back with you was any excuse for calling her and telling her I couldn't make the trip."

"Oh, never mind, baby," she said, momentarily tender. "It doesn't make any difference now."

"I'm sorry."

"Oh, for God's sake, stop saying you're sorry. I'm sorry

301

myself! I'm sorry I ever believed you were capable of love and honesty and—"

"That's enough," he snapped.

"You bet it is!" she shouted, throwing back the covers. "You and Hank have fun tonight. Call up a couple of girls, because I won't be seeing you."

"I don't give a good god-damn!"

She began dressing. "That's fine," she said. "That's as it should be. And whatever woman you pick up you can bring her right here tonight, because I won't be here."

"Good!"

"It must be fun, weekending on Fire Island. I think I need that kind of a weekend myself."

He suddenly felt badly frightened. Adrenaline rushed through his circulatory system and his face turned white. He remembered the sensation that had struck him once after he had narrowly missed being involved in a serious automobile accident. His mouth hung open and he held onto his ribs, for the moment under the curious delusion that they had become loosened and were no longer capable of supporting his chest, protecting his heart. She was talking about going to Manhasset, going boating with the painter, whatever his name was, that she had met on a weekend with Polly, during one of their separations.

He walked into the other bedroom and picked up the color pictures she had taken that weekend, on a sailboat. There were three pictures of her posing in profile against the white sail, smiling into the sun. The other pictures she had taken of the man. Dan looked at him closely. Handsome, blond, innocent, out-doorsy, naked to the waist, he grinned directly at the viewer, his white slacks standing out sharply against the blue water that stretched off to the horizon. Dan felt weak and off-center.

When he walked back into the front bedroom he found that she had closed the bathroom door. Absently he finished dressing and left the apartment, dazed by jealousy and fear, not knowing his destination. Outside, taxis swooped for fares competitively, like sea-gulls after crusts of bread.

He climbed into a Yellow and went to the Brill Building on

Broadway. At Dave Robbins' office he made a few calls, made small talk with the office staff, and tried not to think of Elaine.

The afternoon yawned forbiddingly before him. For twenty minutes or so he stood on the sidewalk in front of the building, talking to other writers, joking with song-pluggers, sitting on the fender of a parked convertible. He heard all the late gossip, the trade talk, the new jokes. The jokes seemed to be all of a stripe. There was a fad in full swing as far as show-business jokes were concerned. People were not talking about Joe Frisco, or even dealing in the usual off-color material. They were telling stories about "the two boppers" in the same way Rotarians in Denver or Cleveland might tell stories about "the two Irishmen" or "the two Jews." Bop, the latest direction jazz had taken, was controversial as an art form, but it had opened up a new avenue for sidewalk humorists. The avenue was being traveled to its limits.

"Did you hear about the two boppers driving into the city?" asked Manny Gale, the publisher.

"No," Dan said, to be polite.

"Well, these two cats were driving into the city," Gale said, "and they start going through the Holland Tunnel. Well, they're driving along through the tunnel and this one character digs all this white tile, see? He looks at it for a while and then he turns to this other bopper and says, 'Man, dig this crazy men's room!' "

The small group on the sidewalk was shaken and scattered by laughter, the way a flock of pigeons is scattered by a handful of peanuts thrown on the ground. The men slapped their thighs and walked away a few feet and looked at each other and laughed some more then drew together to await the next story.

Artie Gale, Manny's partner, had an idea. "You guys must have heard the one," he said, "about these two cats in Philadelphia."

"I heard it," Dan said, "but go ahead. These guys probably haven't."

"Well," Artie said, "it seems these two cats are walking down the street in Philly and they're all tea-ed up, see? They're smoking up a storm and walking about three feet off the ground and all of a sudden, just as they're walking by Independence Hall, or whatever-the-hell the place is called, there's a big clap of thunder or something and the friggin' Liberty Bell breaks loose and crashes right down into the street in front of these two guys."

One of the men standing on the sidewalk laughed in anticipation.

"Well, the first bopper turns to the other guy and says, 'Man, what was that?' and the other guy says, 'E Flat!' "

Artie collapsed, enjoying the story himself, and the others laughed again and agreed it was a hell of a story.

Dan left them joking and talking business and walked into the open-air Turf café on the corner, where he ate a hot dog and drank a cup of coffee, standing at the counter and watching a baseball game being broadcast on the restaurant's television set.

From time to time he thought of Elaine and gradually built up an anger toward her that performed the function of anesthetic reasonably well. Anger was a good weapon against loneliness. The trouble was you couldn't sustain it long enough. You could bank the ugly fire and keep it burning fiercely for a few hours, but then when you were looking the other way the flames would sputter and go out and when you turned again to warm yourself there'd be nothing but cold and emptiness and fear.

He paid for the hot dog and coffee and went back to stand with the men in front of the Brill Building. They were identifying cars when he sidled up.

"It's a Merc," one of them was saying. "Has that new scoop thing in the front."

"You're right," said another. "From the way it was turned I thought it was the Olds."

"They're nothing alike," said the one who was better at identifying cars. "Nothing alike at all." It was remarkable, Dan thought, how the human heart could swell with pride over small accomplishments.

The ability to recognize, to identify, to classify was a source of great pride for the average person. Elaine would mutter "Toulouse-Lautrec" passing the window of an art shop, or Dan himself would say "Coleman Hawkins," hearing a fragment of a saxophone solo floating out of the night, or a small boy would say "DC-Six," as he squinted into the sky. It was a minor vice to which evidently everyone was addicted, the habit of casually parading one's knowledge before those possessed of less information.

After spending another thirty minutes with the men on the sidewalk Dan discovered he yet had time on his hands, not to say eternity, and that the afternoon still stretched discouragingly before him. He drifted away from the group, went to a haberdasher's and bought two ties, dawdling a long time in selecting them, then exhausted another hour in the Newsreel Theatre, had a quick shot at a rundown bar on Forty-sixth Street and finally, grateful that the finish line was in sight, concluded his race with boredom by meeting Hank for dinner at Howie's restaurant on Sixth Avenue.

They sat speaking sparingly, cushioned on dark green leather, now and then feeling the earthquakelike rumble of the subway that ran under the building, scuttling like a snake through the deep, hidden tunnel under the city's crust. Closing his eyes Dan could almost taste the moist, dusty air that drifted up out of the subway tunnels, but the air in the restaurant was filtered, fresh and cool. He realized that Hank had been speaking.

"I'm sorry," he said. "I was thinking of the subway. What did you say?"

"Just what I said before, that if Elaine really goes back this time you might be able to get her out of your system."

"I might," Dan said.

"Is it definite that she's going?"

"I guess so."

"I thought you had it all figured out a while ago here. I thought you were going to get married."

"So did I. And then I got frightened."

"What of?"

"I don't know exactly. Or maybe I do. I was frightened of closing the book once and for all on Helen and the children. I was afraid of what it would do to my mother, and my relatives."

"You have to live your life for yourself, Dan."

"I guess that makes a lot of sense, but when I think of my mother lighting candles and making novenas, and all my aunts and cousins praying and feeling sorry for me and thinking they know what's right for me, I don't know, I just hate to think of what my marrying Elaine will do to them. It will be saying that they've got to stop all that damned praying and resign themselves to defeat in whatever it is they're fighting for."

"Why don't you try going back to Helen then?"

"I'm afraid of that, too. I'm afraid that some night if I go back I may be just sitting around the den watching television or maybe standing out in the back yard burning papers in the incinerator and all of a sudden I'll start thinking of Elaine. I'll start thinking of her and wondering where she is and who she's with and what she's doing and I'm afraid of what that would do to Helen, and for that matter what it would do to me."

"Helen wouldn't *have* to know."

"Ah, if only that were true. But she would. You can't keep a thing like that from a woman. Maybe some men can. I read about men who get away with bigamy or keeping a mistress or who never talk to their wives about their past lives. I read about men who never make love to their wives or men who keep a big part of themselves aloof, but I'm not one of those men. If I have a feeling, the woman I'm with can see it. It's awful, it's really horrible to have a woman look at you and cry right in your face because she knows you don't love her the way she wants to be loved. She looks right into your brain and sees things that frighten her and you can't help at all because you can't take her in your arms and say, 'Baby, don't cry; I love you.' The only way you can pull down the blinds is to act distant, to keep away, to act preoccupied, and that's no good either. That's slow death. That's what I'm afraid of."

Hank sighed and looked into his soup.

"And another thing," Dan said, "I don't even know if Helen would take me back. She's going with this fellow out there now, you know. You've met him. He's a nice guy."

"Does Helen love him?"

306

"I don't know. I imagine she does in one way or another. It's been just a small shred of comfort for me to know that she's been able to find some happiness again, and as I said he's nice. He's good to her. Better than I was, I suppose."

"What about the kids?"

"He's good to them, too. They call him by his first name, though. None of this 'Daddy' or 'Uncle' stuff. I wouldn't like that, and I'm sure Helen wouldn't either. I still make it a point to fly out there pretty regularly to see the boys."

"Kind of makes you wonder what the hell it's all about," Hank said.

"Yes," Dan said. "The thing that has me in a squirrel-cage is that there doesn't seem to be any right answer to the whole thing."

"What do you mean?"

"I just have my choice of several mistakes to make, that's all. If I marry Elaine it'll be a great shock to my people, to the children. If I go back to Helen it will be a nightmare for her if I ever weaken."

"Would you have to weaken?"

"Not if you can tell me how you stop loving another woman," Dan said. "God, it's a hackneyed sort of line, but if there were only some button you could push, somewhere in your head, that would turn off love. If love were like an electric light that you could snap on and off at the right times, how simple life would be. But what can I do? How do you go about forgetting? It's hard enough to forget a woman even if you're forced to by being told to get lost. If Elaine told me she didn't want me any more I suppose I'd get over it eventually. Maybe a year or so and the pain would stop. Hell, maybe it would stop in twenty minutes if I knew she didn't love me. But that's just it. I know she *does* love me, and when you know that love is waiting somewhere for you it's impossible not to want it, not to want to go to it. It's like being half dead of thirst and trying not to take a drink when there's a bottle of ice water right in front of you."

Hank winced sympathetically.

"Nothing seems to do any good," Dan continued, talking half to himself, talking to pour out his feelings, to empty himself. "Sometimes I try to recapture a sort of simplicity I had as a child. I try to pray. But how in the name of Christ can you say, 'God, make me forget a woman,'? In the very act of making your plea you're defeating its purpose. What can you do when you close your eyes and try to look into your soul to see if maybe God is sitting in there waiting to talk to you and instead you see the woman's face? What can you do when you unexpectedly wake up in the middle of the night wanting her? How can you be blamed for a thing like that? I don't say to myself, 'I'm going to do an evil thing. I'm going to want Elaine.' I just want her; it's as if my will has nothing to do with it. Part of my mind seems to be holding a busted steering wheel, trying to make it work while the rest of me is rushing down a steep hill."

Hank stifled a small yawn.

"I'm sorry," Dan said. "I'm bending your ear."

"No, I'm just a bit sleepy," Hank said. "You meeting Elaine later?"

"No," Dan said. "What'll we do?"

"I was going to call this girl."

"Has she got a friend?" Dan said, and they both laughed.

"Could be. You in the mood?"

"I feel pretty down. Maybe I need a little companionship." He thought then of Elaine on Long Island, felt a pain in his chest as he pictured her with the artist, the man with the boat, the man who had sent her a book of poetry. She had been angry enough in the afternoon to do anything. She wanted to hurt him and she might—

"Why don't you call this girl and see if she has a friend," Dan said.

Hank called the girl. She had a friend. They picked up the girls and began touring drinking places. Here and there in their trip around town they encountered solitude; once Dan saw the spectre of loneliness huddled on a stool at the distant end of a bar, again he rubbed shoulders with panic as he entered a club, and another time he thought he recognized the will to die disappearing into a taxi.

He tried to impress the girl he was with by mentioning some of his songs, but she had only heard of three of them and

308

for a while she thought he was kidding her and that he wasn't a song-writer at all. They joked about it and he even wanted to go into a record store on Broadway to buy her an album of his songs that had recently been recorded by Tony Bennett but he didn't bother. The town swirled around them like warm water, faces bobbing on the surface, lights dancing on the turbulent stream. They drank more, and laughed a great deal for little or no reason. Some time before dawn Dan invited his girl to his apartment either for a drink or because she said she had to go to the bathroom; later he could not remember the reason. He fumblingly tried to make love to her when she sat on the couch next to him in the front room and she half-heartedly repulsed him. In the semidarkness her face suddenly frightened him, for first it looked like Helen's and then like Elaine's. The face seemed to reproach him and he turned out all the lights in the room. She insisted then on being taken home, and after a few minutes of rambling argument he agreed.

"Good night," he said a short time later, standing at her door. "You're a very nice girl, and I'm sorry if I've bothered you with my troubles."

"No bother," she said, blowing him a kiss.

She *was* a nice little girl, he thought, and fairly pretty; the sort of girl who looked as if she would enjoy doing the Charleston. He never saw her again.

Elaine did not return to the apartment that night, nor did she appear the next day. When Dan awakened it was twenty minutes after two and the sun was hot on the floor of the quiet bedroom. He lay scratching his stomach, more asleep than awake, then turned and looked at the other bed. The spread had not been touched. It was perhaps five seconds before he fully realized he was alone. She had stayed on Long Island!

The man with the sailboat. He felt a brief emotional paralysis and was intrigued by the fact that he was not being torn by the claws of jealousy as he had been the night before. Gratefully he climbed out of bed, smiling. Later, while he was in the kitchen eating corn flakes, the panic ripped into him and he stopped eating and held his head in his hands.

He remained in the apartment all afternoon and all evening, afraid to leave for fear he might miss seeing her. When the phone rang he leaped upon it like an animal but none of the calls was important. None of the people calling was Elaine.

He moped around during the evening, washed his hair, trimmed his nails, rearranged the books in the living room, cleaned up a little in the kitchen, drank a few beers. He went out once to get the papers but hurried back and sat up in bed, reading, listening to the radio, drinking more beer.

Once he tried to do a bit of work at the piano but gave up after a few minutes. He took out pencil and pad and did some worrying on paper about his finances, and then about four in the morning he fell asleep again.

When he awakened he looked first at her bed and went cold when he saw it had not been touched. Twenty minutes later she walked in while he was lying there looking blankly at the ceiling.

"Hi," she said with that detached, polite reticence that lovers affect after a quarrel.

"Hello," he answered coldly, furious that she could look so beautiful, so aloof, burning with curiosity to know where she had been, what she had done.

He got up and went into the bathroom and began shaving. For an hour they circled each other warily, pretending to be composed and blasé, speaking in brief sentences, making small talk. They ate breakfast and even smiled a little.

Then something dropped out from under them, something flickered between them and they were thrown into each other's arms and the world began spinning around again. They cried and quarreled and kissed violently and laughed and blew their noses and planned and wondered and then she found a glass with lipstick stain on it and they had a furious argument about the girl he had brought up to the apartment.

"What the hell difference could that make to you?" he shouted. "You were out boating overnight with your friend."

"I was not!" she blazed. "You idiot. I've been with Polly the past two days!"

He felt at once relieved and betrayed.

"But you said—"

"I only said that to hurt you, to worry you! Now I realize I *should* have gone out with Peter. You had a girl up here, another one!"

"But I didn't know you were at Polly's," he shouted.

"Oh, God," she said. "Never mind. It's just the same old thing, over and over again."

"Yes," he said.

"I'm going. I don't know why I kid myself. I came back this morning to say I was sorry, to say I was willing to stay, married or not, to say to hell with what your friends think, but what's the use?"

"All right," he rasped. "Then why all this talk? If you're going, go!" Then he wanted to take it back, to run to her and apologize, rub it all out and start fresh.

"The train leaves at five o'clock," she said. "Will you take me to the station?"

There was a pause.

"I don't want to," he said, feeling ill.

"But you've got to help me," she said. "I can't carry those bags by myself."

"It isn't that," he said, shivering. "I just don't think I can help you to leave me. I don't think I, personally, could put you on a train."

He moved all day like a robot, helping her pack, or sitting quietly, staring at the floor, shaking his head. Several times they cried and argued and wavered. Once they kissed and clung together for a few minutes but neither of them seemed able to forestall the thing that was about to happen. She was going to leave today. Really leave. Actually get on a train and go away. They had tried to reach this point a hundred times before. For many months this had been coming, and now that it was here it was so unbelievable that they were incapable of reacting to it properly. Any tragedy that does not cause actual physical pain may bring about a similar reaction. The center of the emotions is numbed by shock and finally tears cease to fall. Hysteria ends, the jawbone is tightened, the lips turn down and the body marches forward to its destiny.

As he carried the bags into Penn Station, he had the impression of walking in a nightmare. Faceless, silent bodies drifted past him; the luggage, though heavy, had no weight to his numb arms. Like an automaton he plodded through the crowd, hurrying now because the train was due to pull out in five minutes.

He wanted, in some distant part of himself, to stop the play, to run out on the stage and demand that the curtain be rung down. But the tiny characters in the enormous misty cavern of the station marched on, handed the red cap the suitcases, walked down the stairs to the train platform. The dialogue progressed as it seemed destined to.

"I can't speak," he said in a whisper as they walked along beside the train.

"I love you so much," she said, not looking at him. "I'll always love you."

"Yes," he said. "And I'll love you. I don't know what's happening." His head ached and his body was completely wet from the exertion of carrying the bags. "I'll send you some money," he said, "so you won't be short of pocket money when you get out there."

"Thank you," she said, "but I'll be all right."

He was afraid to lift his eyes from the ground because now they were scalded by tears and he did not want to appear an ass before the porters and conductors and well-wishers who were gathered on the platform.

"This is the car," she said.

"Yes," he said. "I guess this is it."

They stood completely still for several seconds, looking into each other's eyes, their faces very close.

"You're so beautiful," he said.

"Thank you, baby," she said. "I love you so much."

"I love you," he said. They could think of nothing else to say and they had said all that was important after all. He could not take his eyes from hers and he could not truly grasp at all that in a few minutes she would be gone. He simply felt a great sadness but, absurdly, could not bring himself to admit the reason for its existence.

"Booarrd!" said a bawling voice far down the platform.

"Better get on, lady," a red cap said. "She's about ready to go."

312

She handed the red cap some change and stepped onto the platform of the train. He could not bear now to look at her and, putting his head down, he shuffled forward and kissed her clumsily on the cheek.

"Good-bye, lover."

"Good-bye, Dan," she said. He turned and hurried away, walking fast. His throat ached and he wanted to cry out, to hide someplace and shout his lungs out. Halfway down the platform he whirled around and looked for her, hoping that she might have stepped off the train, thinking that she might be running to him. But the platform was empty now and the train had begun to move.

He walked back up the stairs and through the station, but later could not remember having done so. He found himself walking the streets, clenching his fists, doubly wretched because there was no place he could hide and cry.

After half an hour of aimless wandering he had forced his breathing back to its normal rate. He stopped at a Nedick's stand and ate a hot dog and drank some cold, watery orange juice.

He made the effort not to think of her, but every few minutes he looked at his watch and tried to estimate where the train might be at the moment and what she might be doing. He saw her sitting in her compartment, going to the ladies' room, adjusting her stockings, having dinner in the dining car, alone, a beautiful lady with a red mouth in a dining car, being seated opposite a strange man perhaps, at a table for two. He saw her in the club car and he saw her sleeping and he saw her reading magazines and all the afternoon he saw her and wanted very much to die.

There was one moment of complete panic, one moment when, his guard momentarily down, sheer terror overtook him, conquered him in the instant, and left him whimpering, crouching animal-like on the floor of the bedroom. It happened this way:

It is the habit of the deranged mind to find comfort in hallucinations and impossible images, and all day he had snatched intermittently at the absurd idea that after he had turned his back and walked away she might have slipped off the train and gone back to the apartment. He did not believe that this was actually the case, but throughout the day, walking the streets, talking to people, eating, he had given the idea sanctuary in his mind. He had not only allowed it to enter, he had welcomed it, entertained it lovingly, enlarged upon it, enjoyed it, been dizzied by it, and even once or twice chuckled over it. He had imagined what he might say to her when he walked in and found her sitting in the front room having a cold drink and listening to the radio. He had seen himself running to her and swearing that he would never again let her leave him. He had thought that, at that moment, he might have taken her by the hand and driven off to Connecticut to get married.

He had allowed his unsettled mind undisciplined reign, given it freedom to consider what the years might hold for them together. He had raced from the future to the past, drawn upon his store of memories and examined hundreds of them, mentally thumbed through pictures of the two of them dancing, swimming, driving, looking at wallpaper.

And yet at no time—such is the mystery of the mind of man —did he believe that she had really stepped from the train when he had turned his back. What stripped him of his last defense, although he did not recognize that he was being made vulnerable when the thing happened, was that he had left the light on in the front bedroom. He had left it on and forgotten that he had done so. So it was that when he parked the car in front of his building and glanced up automatically at the front windows his heart leaped. He had looked up from force of habit and when he saw, against the blackened face of the building, two squares of light his body stiffened and he fumbled with quivering fingers for his keys.

The elevator man opened the door and mumbled a sleepy greeting but Dan did not hear him. Putting the key in the lock he said to himself, out loud, "She's not here. She couldn't be here. But the light was on so—"

When he opened the door he saw that the vestibule, and beyond it the living room, lay in darkness. He knew then again what he had really known all day, that she was hundreds of miles away, on a train speeding now through Pennsylvania or

314

Ohio, or perhaps even Indiana, and the apartment was dark and deserted. He had known it all afternoon; he had known it while he went about his business and found himself forcing his face into a frozen, dazed smile. What he had not realized was that the desperate, impossible image he had clung to was the one thing that had enabled him to get through the day.

Now, as he stood in the living room, looking at lipsticked cigarette stubs in an ashtray on the coffee table, the image was jerked away from him by crashing reality without warning, and he was left utterly without strength.

He fought for the image, snatched it back from the iron fist of actuality that was pounding at him. Perhaps she had come back after all. Perhaps she was down in the bedroom where the light was on. Frightened, he ran along the hallway and burst into the room, to see, to find her if he could.

The image was slipping farther away from him as he leaped into the room, his eyes darting in every direction, and then it was gone irrevocably. That was the moment that panic overtook him. He began to talk to himself in the third person, complimenting himself on his good sense, his level-headedness. He began to comfort and to advise himself. He spoke to himself scornfully, bravely, wisely. And it did no good.

Tears filled his eyes and, catching a glimpse of himself in the mirror, he swore, despising himself for his weakness. He ran into the bathroom, quite unbalanced now, thinking that perhaps she might be hiding there. He opened the medicine cabinet and even looked under the sink, whimpering slightly. Later he could recall being frightened by his irrationality, he could recall the sensation that some small part of his mind was standing to one side, cool and detached, shaking its head sadly at what was happening to the rest of him. His brain seemed to be divided into compartments and what was in each of the compartments was warring upon what was in the others.

He called her name, and cursed himself, and called upon God without having any idea what it was he wanted God to do. He sobbed and ran from room to room, turning on all the lights, opening all doors, looking into closets, pulling out dresser drawers. He clutched at small things she had left behind—books, papers, handkerchiefs, gloves.

He suddenly felt uncomfortably warm and removed his shirt. Standing in the closet, putting the shirt into the clothes hamper, he found a pale pink silk pajama top she had left. His heart stumbled in his chest as if he had heard her footfall and he pressed the garment to his wet face, inhaling the faint perfume that clung to it, breathing in the agonizingly wispy smell of her powder, trying to suck it into his lungs.

He howled and paced about the apartment with the silk jacket pressed to his face, walked to the telephone once to send her a wire, to ask her to return. But he could not have talked to anyone in his unsettled condition and therefore he resisted the temptation.

He staggered out to the kitchen and inspected the dishes left from their breakfast. The maid had not come. Drinking again. For once, he was glad. There was still something of Elaine left in the apartment. Her breakfast plate, cigarettes in ashtrays, a lipstick-stained drinking glass. It was something tangible, something he could smell and feel. He thought for a moment that perhaps if he very nonchalantly walked back into the front room she might be sitting there. After all, her breakfast dishes were in the kitchen, her cigarettes were in the ashtray. It seemed very possible, really, that she still might be somewhere in the apartment, or that she might have just stepped out for a few minutes. When the realization of the truth came back again it hit him in great, violent waves, beating him down, literally, to his knees.

He fell back along the hall, holding his hand to his mouth to stifle the strange sounds he was making, loathing himself for his inability to stand bravely before the storm. The clock on the night-table clicked softly, taxis with grinding motors raced past the building, and his faltering, watery breathing rumbled in his ears.

He could remember this particular feeling of panic. As a small child he had awakened once from a fearful sleep and found himself alone in a strange hotel room. He had screamed for his mother and run out into the empty hall, afraid of the darkness, afraid of the unfamiliar long dim hallway outside the room. The memory went no further, faded off into a vague recollection of sitting on his mother's lap, smiling, and

316

snifflingly drinking a cold malted milk through a straw, out of a cardboard drugstore carton.

Thinking of his mother, he considered for a moment that if he were to call Elaine and ask her to come back to marry him it would be an unhappy thing. His mother was praying every night for him, and for what she thought was right for him, and if it turned out that he did not live the life she wanted for him she would be broken in spirit and disconsolate forever after. She would go on praying and looking at him in sadness, and when he thought of this he began to cry harder.

For a few minutes the sadness of all the world seemed to rest upon his shoulders, the sadness of children in orphanages, of the imprisoned, the condemned, the abandoned, the blind, the ill, the dying. He thought of the misery of nature, of the millions of beautiful, puzzled animals dying in the forests and jungles of the world, their flesh torn by disease or by the fangs of creatures more powerful, creatures themselves condemned to die in slow uncomprehending pain or sudden torture. He thought of the millions of humans condemned to die of starvation or from the cruelty of their fellowmen, of the millions whose blood and tears had lubricated the wheels of history. And then, in the next instant, his sense of universal tragedy was replaced by a more selfish turn of mind and the flames of his hysteria were fanned by powerful gusts of self-pity. He called Elaine's name again and called for the children. He thought of Helen, ached with sympathy and unsensuous affection for her, and literally tore at the flesh of his face in a rage of self-contempt over what he had done to her.

His nails dug deep into his cheeks and the pain sobered him for a moment.

He tried to pray. He said, "Our Father, Who art in Heaven, hallowed be Thy name." But his mind whirled and lost itself in meaningless analysis of the words of the prayer. He could not seem to pray satisfactorily any more. Either he was mumbling fearful questions, pleading superstitiously to be shown some light, or he was weighing his words, debating with himself about the interpretation of the phrases he parroted.

From physical exhaustion, hunger, and lack of sleep he

317

had now grown weak, and when the thought passed through his mind that he should not be lying like a beaten cur on the floor, when the idea came to him that he was contemptible, he seemed unable to respond to the stimulus. He willed to rise, but a stronger part of himself kept him huddled between the twin beds on the floor, shivering, although it was a warm night. He could remember then kneeling before, as a small boy, feeling cold and alone. At boarding school near Chicago. Kneeling in the face of a cold, October wind. It was very vivid, the memory.

The sky was churning, full of cold, gray, smoky clouds that boiled in slow motion toward the west, the wind that hurried them across the sky also swooping low, tousling the trees.

He buttoned his sheepskin-lined leather jacket tightly about his neck, sat down on the concrete walk, and put the palms of his bare hands flat against the cement. The sun had been out all morning and the heat that it had spread out along the ground was still trapped here and there, in walls, and small boulders, and here, where he was sitting. The heat seeping up out of the rock felt good to his palms, and reacting perhaps to some dimly felt vestigial instinct he twisted suddenly to a kneeling position and brought his nose down close to the sidewalk, where it could, like his hands, feel the warmth and comfort that still clung to the ground, under the cold wind.

Turning his head slightly he could see the jagged remnants of a ginger-ale bottle gleaming dully in the earth at the edge of the walk. He crawled to the spot and carefully picked up the three largest pieces, having decided to make powder of them. It was a game the children played, making gunpowder.

Sometimes, instead of calling it gunpowder they would call it medicine, or magic powder. The game was a lonely one. There was no element of competition in it, and it was usually played by but one child, when he had nothing else to do.

Now, he remembered, he had searched in the grass until his fingers wrapped around a small fistlike rock. It would serve as a crushing instrument. Placing a piece of jagged, bright-green glass on the concrete he slowly tapped at it with the stone,

318

breaking the large chunk into several small pieces, breaking these into still smaller fragments, and finally concentrating on a tiny pile of glass splinters, tapping them slowly, his mind now not even on what he was doing, tapping, crushing, grinding until before him on the walk there lay a little mound of beautiful pale green powder, which he sheltered lovingly with his hands against the wind. Once more he brought his face down close to the cement, feeling the warmth with his nose and chin. With his eyes close to the green treasure it loomed mountainlike and for a moment he slipped from one game to another; playing insect. Often, when the weather was warmer, he would lie with his stomach pressed flat against the grass, eyes only as high as the tallest blades. This, he thought, was what the world looked like to a bug.

Sometimes, if luck were with him, an ant or ladybug would come ambling into his view, looking hideously large. He would lie, thrilling, with his ribs against the earth, staring with fascination at the crawling creature until its proximity made his eyes cross and ache.

The wind was getting stronger now, and he realized that soon a bell would ring, and he would have to leave his green treasure unguarded. For a moment he wrestled with the problem of how to preserve the emerald dust and then, with the same impulse he felt when he suddenly decided to leap into water, or jump down from a high ledge, he straightened up, put his hands in his flannel-lined pockets, and watched grimly as the cold breath of the east wind swirled the glass dust into nothingness.

His knees ached slightly as he got to his feet. He could even now recall the exact sensation of numbness that had deadened his kneecaps. Sighing heavily, he walked into the bathroom and bathed his face with cold water. Well, that was that, he told himself, calling himself a weak-kneed son of a bitch.

That was that. You lost a good woman, you lost her sweet soul and her wonderful warm body and it broke you up. What the hell, what did you expect? Was it supposed to be easy? The thing to do was to go on living and trying to work, to go on eating and drinking and sleeping. He took off his clothes and sat on the edge of the bed. It was then that he realized he would be unable to sleep.

He took a copy of *Time* from the stack of books and magazines on the bottom shelf of the night table and also turned on the radio. Two distractions were better than one. Barry Gray was speaking from Chandler's restaurant, interviewing a man who said he was a lawyer and just wanted to say a few words, Barry, just a few words on a subject that is very near and dear to our hearts.

"Mr. Kaplan," Barry said, "the microphone is yours. But be sure to leave it here when you go because I have to read the news into it in about ten minutes."

The crowd at the restaurant laughed and Mr. Kaplan laughed and said, "All right, Barry. That was very good, but I'll only take a few minutes of your time, only a few minutes to say what I have to say, because I know these good people here would rather hear you talk to Denise Darcel and Yul Brynner and all these other wonderful celebrities, but there *is* something I'd like to say just a few words about because it's something that's very important to all of us."

Dan leaned over and turned the dial till he heard music, realizing at the moment what a godsend radio was to lonely people in the middle of the night. For a while he read *Time*, trying to concentrate on what he read. He saw a picture of the actor, Stewart Granger, and thought that his name sounded like a brand of tobacco. He turned to the section labeled "Religion," and read that a Methodist bishop had attacked the Catholic doctrine of papal infallibility and that an Episcopalain priest had joined the Catholic Church and that a Baptist mission in Uruguay had been assaulted by a band of Catholic natives and that two groups of Presbyterians had decided not to merge after all.

Then he began to think of Elaine again. His body began to ache for her and he felt great disturbing waves of sensuality sweep over him. He got up and went into the bathroom and poured cold water over his private parts to try to cool the fever that writhed in his loins.

It helped.

He lay for perhaps half an hour on the bed, dejected, spent, listening to the radio, looking at the ceiling, then arose, gathered several pairs of socks from the floor of the closet, took them into the bathroom and began washing them. It was something to do. When he had rinsed the socks and hung them on a towel-rack he walked into the living room, sat down at the piano, played a little, and jotted down a few random ideas for songs. Nothing pleased him and he threw his notes in the wastebasket, got himself a can of beer from the refrigerator and sat on the sofa inspecting the moles on his arm.

After a while, between the slats of the venetian blinds he could see straight, thin bars of pale blue. Morning came early during the summer. He had another beer, took two sleeping tablets, and lay back in bed, listening to the giant city waking up, wondering how long his heart would feel like a stone under water. He cried in his sleep.

CHAPTER

TWENTY-FIVE

It was a bad time, a rough time. For the first few days he ran to the telephone when it rang, but when he discovered that the only calls had to do with business or were wrong numbers or were from people he wasn't interested in talking to, he stopped answering the phone altogether. He played the piano frantically, till his back ached, and then paused only long enough to drink a beer or go to the toilet and returned to playing again. As the weeks passed he lost track of the days, the seasons.

One morning he left the apartment and hurried out into the street. The morning air was clear and cold; the city looked deserted. His watch said 7:09. He thought it was probably a Sunday. Manhattan had a longer, thinner look than usual because, standing on some of the lateral cross-streets, you could see from river to river, whereas on hazy days or at night you were only conscious of the Hudson and the East if you actually approached them. Looking lengthwise at the island—up or down Lexington or Madison or Third—the horizon, the end of vision, faded off into a hulking blur of buildings and rooftops and streets that narrowed to perspective's familiar point, but looking across Forty-ninth or Fifty-second Street he could see now as he drove about that in either direction the land ended and that there was clear space and trees and docks, and water beyond, so the island felt narrow under his feet. Also, except for the sensation of insularity, he thought that the city through which he plodded looked more like Prescott, Arizona or Denver, Colorado than New York, New York. It had to do with the openness, the clear, bracing air that felt strangely dry and cold, like the breath of sky over mountains, and the quiet, small-town sense of desertion.

He went into a small coffee shop on Madison Avenue for breakfast. At the top of the menu, punctuated by a cheerful exclamation point, were the words, *Good Morning!* His re-action was a minute flicker of gratitude, but then he considered that the counterman himself did not speak.

"Who is saying good morning to me?" Dan thought. It was actually no one in the restaurant that day at all; it was a face-less man in an advertising agency or a disinterested workman in a print shop. The phrase dangled in air, in time, its value being merely what the individual reader was led, by his own personal conditioning, that of his ancestors, and that of his civilization, to make of it. It meant no more in the way of true human communication than would a centuries-old note found in a bottle on a deserted beach, or a prayer worn to smooth meaninglessness by the abrasive passage of time and thoughtless repetition.

It was difficult for Dan, during the next few weeks, to get to sleep. He would sit in the kitchen and drink a cold can of beer, huddled in a chair with his legs crossed, looking through a magazine and rocking back and forth slightly the way old people do when they are alone for long periods of time. He would sit that way, wearing a flannel pajama top and a pair of shorts, and then after he had finished the first beer he would open another can and walk down the hall and get into bed and turn on the radio and read some more and listen with a part of his mind attuned to the radio. He would drink from the small, triangular holes in the top of the beer can and finally his eyes would get tired and he would put the book on the floor and then he would flick off the light and turn over on his right side and close his eyes. He would leave the radio turned on very softly so as to avoid having to concentrate on a silence, a void, a vacuum that he would feel obliged to fill with thinking or breathing or drumming his fingers on the pillow or getting up and going to the toilet.

Sometimes the beer and the soft music from the radio and the lateness of the hour and the graininess under his eyelids would combine to render him unconscious. But often he would lie awake listening to other sounds than those coming from the radio. He would listen to his heart beating and to cars driving by in the night and to the clock ticking on the dresser and to strange wooden clicks and crackings the source of which he was never able to identify. One night he was lying half asleep when he began to think he heard the sounds of love-making from the bedroom of the apartment above his. He could only dimly distinguish distant, muffled voices but the creaking and thumping of a bed were plain enough and, against the silence of the night, loud and disturbing and exciting. He sat up and turned on the light and looked at the ceiling, listening to the increasing tempo of the sounds that filtered down to him. He grew tense and angry and was filled with a great loneliness and a sensual longing. When the sounds stopped he was left anxious and unfulfilled and he lay back again and listened, hoping that he would be able to hear something more. He thought of Elaine and wanted her and somehow his twisted mind muddled its thoughts in the early morning stupor in which he lay so that for a while he tortured himself with the idea that the woman in the apartment upstairs was Elaine and that some other man was up there lying beside her. His fists clenched as he writhed in the grip of the image and his mouth twisted in a genuine and bitter rage.

Leaping out of bed he stood in the middle of the room trembling with anger and frustration. Then he walked about the apartment turning on lights and looking through drawers and searching closets, taking inventory of the few little things she had forgotten to take with her. He looked at one of her old letters, and picked up one black glove and walked into the bathroom and opened the medicine cabinet and looked at some curlers on one of the shelves. Burning with energy he knelt on the floor of the living room, took all of his recordings out of their storage cases, put jackets on all the records that were uncovered, tidied up the cabinet and put all the records back. Then he was hungry. He ate three slices of canned brown bread and drank a glass of cold milk and finally went back to bed and fell asleep with sunlight lying in yellow rectangles about the floor of the bedroom.

Sometimes he could not stop thinking at night at all and that was when it was the worst.

He would lie in the darkness at two or three in the morning and his thoughts would pour out in a great, random bubbling torrent, without organization or plan or constructive result or, sometimes, sanity.

Oh my, oh my, I'll sleep yes, I'll sleep. Sleep, eep, deep, reep, creep. Where are you, baby? Where is my Elaine? My little darling? Oh, crap. That's enough of that. Yessiree, bob! That's more than enough of that. (Lights on the ceiling.) Long time ago, watching lights, cars passing. How are my little darlings? Bless their little, fat old hearts. Yes. Little Mike. Ha-ha-ha! Have to fly out there. Yes. Fly away. Skeeters am a-hummin' on the honeysuckle vine. Fly away. Someone is a-something on the honeysuckle vine. Oh, God, where are you, baby? I wish you were here with me, with your red lips and your pearls. Where are you? Where is that hot stomach? Where is it? Oh, I want it. I want it. Gimme it! Gimme it! Ohhhhh. Where are you? Right now. Right this minute. Let's see. It's about three-thirty here. That means it's twelve-thirty out there. Just getting home maybe. Driving up to the house with some son of a bitch with a big Cadillac. Kissing him. Oh, no. Oh, God. No, no, no!

Please, baby! Please. Come on, baby. Come on. Oh, I love you. I'd like to swallow you up. What's the matter? What's wrong? What's wrong with everything? Everything? Nothing is right! Ohhhhh. Agghhhh! Hillbilly tune. What the hell was it? "I've Got Tears in My Ears from Lying on My Back in My Bed While I Cry over You." Funny, eh? Rubber crutch style. Oh, what the hell. Screw it all. Crying . . . ing . . . ing. Like a friggin' woman. Big shot. Big front. Crying in the dark like a friggin' baby. This is bad. This is very bad. Crazy. No,

*sir. (Legs twitching) What the hell. Goddam shakes. All right,
though. If you're worried you're okay. When they got it they
don't know it. I'm okay. Poor little Helen shook like this, I
remember. Poor baby. Cried and shook like this. Hands
twitched and everything. Oh, no, no, no. I screw everybody up.
I don't mean to. Mean any harm. Gaston B. Means. Means
B. Gaston. Gaston, Faston, Maston and Houston. Riding
through Texas or some place. Where are you, baby? We
played with that book driving in the car, driving, and no towels
in that motel, and the quiz games in the book and no heat
and your hot stomach. Your hot, little stomach. You with
your hands on me in the car, driving, and everything. Oh, you
doll! You big, red-mouthed doll. Gee-rusalem, you sure took
good care of me, you poor little thing, making shirts, and
knitting, and putting up those curtains in the kitchen and fixing
all those steaks. And now this damned brown bread in the
cans. Hey, Charlie, you got Prince Albert in the can? Go to
the store, Danny, like a good boy and get Uncle Bill some
Tip-Top. Corduroy knickers and the tobacco package was
orange and had a picture of horses dashing to a fire and the
old corn-cob pipe stunk and oh, God, poor old Uncle Bill
with the horse races and the cancer and the woman he wanted
and never could have or something. Poor old Uncle Bill.
Allentown, Pennsylvania. Some other woman and some meat
plant or something. Poor old bastard. What the hell am I
complaining about? Guys got arms and legs off. One side or a
leg off. Where are you, baby? And where are those legs?
Those warm legs. I love them. I love you, I guess. You don't
know anything. All you can do is guess. What's this third-
person jazz? I don't know anything. I guess. I guess. You
guess. He guesses. We guess. You guess. They guess. Amo,
amas, amat. Amamus, amatus, amant. Ska-dum. Ska-dum,
ska-dum and it's the Mexican hat dance and away we go.
Little broad at the station in Phoenix, Feenix, Feenalax, pink
stuff. Let's see. No name. Cute. Singing My Buddy, My Body.
My body misses you. Played that in the key of F. Old Cecil-boy.
Play some waltzes, guys. I'll be right back. The Mezona. All
the Mesa broads and everything. Crazy drummer. Blink your
lights, you bastard, or I'll kill ya. Dim your lights, you mother-*

grabber! Bastard was crazy enough to do it, too. Ha-ha-ha. Go to the store, Danny, like a good boy. Uncle Bill, or some- body. I forget. Can't keep anything straight. Prescott. Cold. Shell station. Used to call it Sheel. Kid named Frank Sheilds. His station. Got some ink. Bottle of ink in paper bag. Running across stone bridge over creek, hit bag, ink shot all over, afraid, paper soaked blue, scared as all hell, inky fingers. Funny cal- loused place on left side of the third finger on my right hand from writing. Hit him, Nell. Pretty good up to fractions then not so good at arithmetic. Mike is that age now. He's asleep. Good, sweet angel. God love him. Yes, God. There's no problem there. There is a God; that's not the problem. From there on in, how are ya? I'm afraid. Wonder why, bleeding before, when I went to the toilet, bleeding. Cancer. That's what they always say to watch out for. Silly. Say, doc, I think I got a cancer. Why, no, you're fine. Who knows? I wouldn't mind. Like to die. Like to die. But if it hurts, that's bad. Everything, all bad. Maybe that'll stop. Bleeding. Grandma Scanlon lying on that bed with two mattresses, up high, dying of cancer. How it smelled. She didn't know anything. How it smelled! Ugh. Little green radium things in little glass containers. Won- der what they were? In the trunk when everybody opened it after she died. Silverware. Old purses. Poor Grandma. Cancer. Tropic of Cancer. The crab. The old crab. Wouldn't mind it on the arm or the foot. Don't want nobody poking around inside me. Awful. Even that time with that doc. Funny. He thought. What's the matter, goosey? No, you're all right. It's no venereal infection. Oh, we don't know, these things are kind of funny. This won't hurt. A hundred thousand units. A hundred unit thousits. A usit hundred thouserds. Do it today. Don't delay. Radio things. Reck-nack. Spelled backwards. Awful to have cancer of the balls. What the hell is it all together for, down there? Why can't it hang off your elbow? Bleeding will stop. There are no atheists in the fox holes. There are no foxes in the atheist holes. Holes. Holes. Bleeding, bleeding, bleeding.

One night, in his sleep, he realized that he could no longer go on as he had been. He had to work, to travel, to kill himself, to do something. He visualized himself returning home, chastened and made mature by his experience. He saw himself traveling west in a plane. He saw the ocean from a great height, looking gray and finely wrinkled, like the skin of a wet elephant. There were clouds in his vision, packed low and thick and creamy-white, like a vast expanse of arctic snow, the illusion being here and there accentuated by high iceberg-like projections that loomed up from the generally level, rolling surface.

He saw himself at last on the ground in California, rolling his car through the soft orange mist of late afternoon, into the blue edges of the earth's shadow. Face washed in cool, swift swirls of atomized desert-valley air, he skeined the liquid breeze successfully for evidence of citrus-blossom, sea-salt, random along-the-way roses, and freshly mown grass. When he was finally fully awake and these visions had been forgotten he began making arrangements to return to the West Coast, although he could not bring himself to state clearly what he planned to do once he was out there.

One idea was rather clear to him, although for all its clarity it seemed essentially absurd. He had the idea that he had entered upon a new phase, or that a curtain had risen upon a new act of his drama. But when he found himself considering his case in such terms he at once dismissed the idea from his mind since it seemed inappropriate—why, he was not sure—to be regarding himself in a sort of third-person sense.

Dealing with reality he realized that he could not fly back to the West to stay at all, unless he sold his car in New York. But it would be cheaper, he realized, to keep the car and drive back. Although his income from ASCAP was dependable he was still spending just a bit more than he was making and consequently he felt constantly insecure financially.

A month later he recived a message from Helen that she had gotten a divorce, in Mexico. He had not answered the telephone for many days. Undoubtedly some of the calls must have been from his attorneys. He was now, in a sense, "free," but was surprised to discover that the knowledge seemed to have no emotional significance. He felt no more free than he had before. With the colored maid to help him he packed his

328

few belongings, shipped a small trunk to a Los Angeles storage company, and put four suitcases into the luggage compartment of his Buick.

As he drove away from the city Dan understood for the first time in his life that as far as hard, physical evidence was concerned no one else on earth could care quite as much about his suffering as he himself could, no matter how hard anyone tried. This, he realized, however dimly, was not because others were hard-hearted. It was just that when you were cut, *you* had to bleed; no one else could bleed for you. They could bleed *with* you, possibly, but not *for* you. Empathy was beautiful, but it was once-removed from personal reality. And, perhaps, if you had to suffer for yourself then you also had to cure yourself. You could get help, but the big effort was yours alone. This insight, when it came to him, seemed to bring with it a certain modest amount of strength. What puzzled him was that it also seemed to bring a low-simmering anger. He laughed aloud when he found himself thinking that there had to be a God because otherwise man, victimized by impersonal circumstance, would have no one to be angry with, to shout defiance at. Would God prefer to be ignored or to have fists shaken at him, Dan wondered. And there were events, daily events, that called for fist-shaking.

We are all shocked and made unhappy if we see a jackal devour a rabbit, yet at this moment white teeth are sinking into furtive fur and tearing panicked flesh in all the jungles of the world and we are unaffected by the knowledge.

We wince if we hear that in the saloon on the next block a man was cut with a knife, but across the world men are daily cut to pieces and we are unmoved. Distance lends unreality.

We teach that our mothers and fathers must be honored and we honor them not. We are accustomed to coveting our neighbors' goods and our neighbors' wives. We are not even certain which day *is* the Sabbath day, hence we have difficulty keeping it holy. We find it, ordinarily, impossible to fall in love with God. All of us make something of a habit of bearing false witness against our neighbor. One of the rare occasions on which we will not bear false witness against him is when we are able to broadcast some damaging truth about him.

Those of us who do not commit adultery are almost without exception those who have not the opportunity. The rest are merely those who have not the inclination.

We say it is wrong to kill, but we kill cockroaches and pigs and hamsters and daffodils and burglars and Jews and Negroes and intruders and time and initiative and joy or anything that is convenient for us to kill.

Two human beings pulled into a gas station outside of Indio, California, one day in late summer. It was two days after Dan Scanlon had left New York. The two were Mormons: Homer Snow and his wife Betsy. They had been visiting with Betsy's relatives in San Diego for three weeks and now they were driving back across the desert on their way to their home in Provo, Utah.

Homer was a bishop of his church but he was also a dentist. The title *bishop* does not mean quite the same thing to the Church of Jesus Christ of the Latter-day Saints that it means to the other churches of Christendom, so it was not unusual that Homer wore no ecclesiastical robes and that he pulled teeth and also sold a little insurance on the side.

The Mormons are a thrifty and respectable people and Homer had saved a considerable amount of money during the twenty-four years he had been married to Betsy. He owned the two-story building in Provo in which he had set up his professional offices, and since his time was largely his own he was able each year to take a month's vacation.

He was as rangily tall and easygoing as his wife was small and shrewish. And yet, for all his good nature and for all her calculating determination, Homer was the boss and Betsy meekly did his bidding.

They had raised four children, put them through high school and college, and seen them all happily married. One of the girls had taken a job in Dallas and married a semi-Baptist and fallen away from the church, but this was the only black mark on the Snows' religious record.

They were well liked in Provo, and though they had accumulated some riches and learned a fair amount about the rest of the world, they clung tenaciously to their faith and observed all its admonitions and restrictions. They did not drink coffee, tea, or Coca-Cola and Betsy had never tasted liquor of any kind, although once in a great while if Homer happened to be out of town alone and among strangers he would take a drink.

They had a large radio in their front room and they subscribed to *Time, Collier's,* and *Reader's Digest,* yet they still believed that Christ would return in bodily form to the earth during their lifetime.

During the war they had stored away vast quantities of canned peaches, pears, Spam, Florida orange juice, flour (in glass jars), blackberry jam, peas, baked beans, applesauce, soups, and pineapple, for the Church had passed along the word that a famine might soon fall upon the land and that the Saints would therefore do well to provide themselves with as many of the edible necessities as they thought would store well without spoiling. There was some embarrassment among the faithful when Washington let it be known that to hoard was unpatriotic; but by simply not thinking about the conflict of interests, most of the Saints were able to go about their business and do whatever *else* they could to help the war effort.

Homer got along quite well with the non-Mormon members of his community, although he could not abide the Catholics because of their conceit and their belief that they were the one, true fold.

Of all the non-Mormons he had met and discussed religion with, only the Catholics seemed to have a faith as strong as his own. He attributed their success and their alarming increase to the direct help of Satan, although he often thanked God that Utah was still largely a Mormon state. He was alarmed about the problem of communism but he was secretly pleased about the war between Moscow and Rome. He considered that it was the will of God that two such powerful forces for evil should expend so much of their energy battling against each other.

Stopped now outside of Indio, he hooked the scratched bronze nozzle of a water hose over the mouth of the open radiator of his 1951 Dodge. A faint wisp of steam issued from the open pipe, and as he leaned over to look down its length the smell of hot oil assailed his nostrils.

"Help you?" said the station attendant.

"Yes," Homer said. "Give me five regular."

The attendant moved around to the back of the car as Homer sprayed the honeycombed radiator front with water to wash away the bugs and cool off the motor.

"Want to get out and stretch your legs?" he called to Betsy.

"No," she said, "I'm all right." Scattered wisps of hair stuck wetly to the back of her neck and she fanned vaguely at her chest with a limp handkerchief, but Homer had known that she would not leave the car and go into the station to get cool. Betsy enjoyed being a martyr, and Homer was so used to her attitude by now that he would have been greatly surprised if she had suddenly changed. She had sacrificed much to raise her children, had learned to sew exceptionally well to save money on clothing, and had seen to it that the children had many of the "advantages" that she had been denied. It never occurred to her that, now that the children were out on their own and she and Homer had more than enough money, she no longer had any need to deny herself.

She wore no make-up, had never owned a fur coat, mended her own stockings, and had never taken a penny from any of the children.

She sat primly, looking out at the dry desert foliage and the hot empty sky. Homer had lowered the hood of the car and she could look straight ahead again. Heat waves wrinkled and waved the objects that she regarded, lizardlike, through the windshield, and after a few moments her eyelids became heavy and she dozed slightly sitting there in her mussed lavender cotton-print dress.

They had not slept well the night before in the motel in Pasadena. She had wanted to stay at a hotel, but Homer had preferred the convenience and the savings that a motor-court stop represented. All night long cars had whispered by on the highway outside. She had lain in the twin bed by the window, tossing and turning and muttering, "Goodness," and "Land." She finally had fallen asleep shortly after midnight and thereafter awakened fully only twice, but when she had gotten up in the morning she had groaned and said, "I didn't sleep a wink. Not one wink."

"You snored," Homer said.

332

"I did not," she said, walking into the too-small bathroom.

Lying in his underwear in the unfamiliar bed, listening to her washing her face and flushing the toilet, Homer had known a very faint flicker of desire and had felt himself briefly. Sitting on the side of the bed he thought for a moment of Sarah, his receptionist, for it had been at least ten years since he had actively desired his wife, and though Sarah was married he still could not keep himself from looking at her sometimes as she moved efficiently about the office.

Fortunately for his peace of mind, desire came upon him very rarely. He stood now, scratching his stomach and yawning and said, "It's only eight-thirty. I thought it was later."

"Time we were on our way," Betsy said.

"Remind me to pick up some postcards for Davey later, will you?"

"Yes. We can get them when we stop for breakfast."

Homer had little use for Betsy's people in San Diego but he loved his nephew, Davey Udall. Davey was five years old and blond and affectionate, and Homer made it a point to send him a little postcard message now and then. In San Diego or "Dago," as Homer rakishly learned to call it, he would take Davey for long rides or for walks along the waterfront. They would stop and talk to men fishing and Homer would buy Davey ice cream cones and tell him stories about Utah.

Pulling out of the gas station, he kept the car in second gear.

"Why are you driving so slowly?" Betsy said.

"Looking for a place to buy postcards," Homer said.

He saw another gas station joined to a grocery and novelty store and pulled the car off the highway and up into the shaded gravel near the building.

In a moment he was back in the car, smiling.

"Got some nice ones," he said. "One with a little Indian boy riding a jackass."

"That's nice," Betsy said.

They drove along the highway at slightly more than sixty miles an hour, not speaking. Occasionally a car would overtake and whip past them, edging Homer over to the right a bit, and he would shake his head and say, "Crazy fool," or "I hope he gets there on time."

That night they stopped in Phoenix at the home of Homer's brother, Joe. Joe was older than Homer by four years. He ran a used car lot.

"Why don't you folks stay over a few more days?" Joe said the next morning, standing on his front lawn, leaning against their car.

"Oh, you know," Homer said. "Betsy's anxious to get back and everything. We'd like to, but I'm afraid we'll have to wait till next time around."

They had an appointment anyway.

"Well, take care of yourselves," Joe said, backing off and waving, stooped-over, as Homer gunned the motor gently.

"You, too," Betsy said, waving a loose hand.

"Write," Joe said.

"You bet," Homer called back.

There were mirages before Homer on the highway now as he sped north out of Phoenix. Dips in the road ahead appeared to be full of water and the numbing heat of the desert pressed down upon the car, made the motor run hot, and dried the throats of Homer and Betsy.

They felt sleepy and Homer turned on the radio. He tried to find a newscast but there seemed to be nothing on but cowboy or jazz music and interminable, inane commercials. Betsy flicked a button and silence filled the car, broken only by the hum of the engine and the steady sigh of the tires on the hot pavement.

"Just a little love," sang Homer, "a little kiss. I would give you all my life for this . . ."

Shortly thereafter, about the time Homer ran over a rabbit, Dan was turning off Highway 66 and pushing his car steadily toward Phoenix. He had been on the road for three days and he was nervous and jumpy.

The first night out of New York he had driven on the Pennsylvania Turnpike and become lost for over an hour trying to get out of Pittsburgh. A stupid gas-station attendant had given him the wrong directions just before an important junction, and he had found himself getting deeper and deeper into the Allegheny hills above Pittsburgh, on a narrow road that became more desolate with each passing mile.

Below him in the valleys strange flames glowed in the night and layers of blue smoke hung thickly over the landscape. Irritably he screeched to a stop and shouted to a boy on a bicycle, "Is this the way to Wheeling?"

"No, *sir!*" the boy said, laughing.

"Goddammit," Dan shouted, whipping the car around. "Son of a bitch!" He had driven at least twenty-five miles out of Pittsburgh and now, on the way back to town, traffic unaccountably piled up in front of him and he could not make time. He drove all night to make up for the delay and did not sleep until almost noon the next day.

When he woke up in the dingy motel in the small West Virginia town, he felt dizzy and sick to his stomach. A shave and shower picked him up, but he was disgusted to see that it was after six o'clock and already beginning to get dark. He drove all night again, squinting at the lights of oncoming cars, stopping now and then to drink a Coke or have a hamburger and coffee while the car was being filled with gasoline.

At first he had eaten good steaks and heavy desserts and tipped lavishly, but now as he stood under the dim neon-blue light of a tiny gas station in Missouri, counting his money, he was startled to observe that he had only thirty-nine dollars in his wallet.

He thereafter ate less expensive meals, began taking peanuts and packaged cookies with him in the car and bought regular instead of Ethyl gasoline. He stayed at the cheapest motels he could find and counted his money again and again and finally figured out that he had lost a twenty-dollar bill somewhere along the way.

Now and then he would pass hitchhikers standing like patient statues along the road or under lamp posts at lonely intersections. Some fear made him refuse to pick them up. It was strange. Now that he was a motorist, now that he had money (somewhere, if not in his pocket), now that he had a big car with shiny exterior and a powerful motor, now that he rode like a baron unarmed in a strange forest, he was not inclined to stop or to think of how his speeding past affected the stolid, lonely people who stood with thumbs lifted by the side of the road.

He had possessions and he did not want to risk them. It was just one minor example, but it illustrated perfectly the difficulty of being truly Christian. It was the same old thing: the rule and the exception. The ideal and the expediency.

He listened on the car radio to a disc jockey playing Stan Kenton records and passed lonely figures in the night. He had been a hitchhiker and had stood angrily in gutters and beside ditches. He could still remember the feeling, still vividly recall muttering threats and orders at passing cars. Hitchhikers, he thought, with their veiled shoutings and demands, were like poets who are forever standing on verbal hilltops with their shirts open, shouting instructions to the elements:

"Roll on, thou deep and dark blue ocean, roll!"

"Blow, blow, thou wintry wind!"

"Stop, you mother-grabber, stop for me!"

He saw himself clearly, standing by the highway in Arkansas (or had it been Texas?), when he had run away from home years before. His mind picked up the thread of the memory.

Standing by the side of the road, he remembered he alternately prayed and swore as car after car passed him by. Sometimes after half a hundred cars had gone by, tires whining on the pavement, he would make little efforts toward improving his appearance. People were afraid of hitchhikers. Perhaps he looked too dirty, too threatening. He removed his hat, folded it flat, and shoved it up under his sweater, along one side. Then he took out his broken comb and combed his hair. His handkerchief was wrinkled and filthy, but he rubbed it on his face to remove some of the dirt. There was a chill in the air and his jacket was zipped up tight under his chin, but it would be better, he thought, if it were open at the neck and neatly folded back at the collar to show a little of his shirt. With the zipper lowered a few inches the air lay cold on his neck, but he knew that he looked a little more presentable, a little less threatening. Without the hat more of his face was visible and as cars approached he smiled, tried to look innocent, harmless, friendly, casual.

A car was approaching now and he slicked down his hair with one last pat, then edged out onto the road to make sure the driver could see him. He opened his eyes wide and smiled idiotically as he lifted his right hand. The car did not slow down.

The rush of air as the car hurtled past made his eyes water, and a sudden surge of anger forced the corners of his mouth down.

"Lousy son of a bitch!" he shouted, looking at the disappearing rectangle that grew smaller far down the highway. "Lousy son of a bitch!"

After a moment his anger subsided, but a feeling of sullen resentment remained. To hell with all the people with cars, the lousy, selfish bastards! It wouldn't cost any of them a cent to stop and give him a lift. No skin off their noses, the goddamn selfish bastards. He wished he had a gun. It would be great to give the next bastard that came along a good square chance to stop. Wave at him nice and friendly and show him the old thumb, and then if he didn't stop whip out the gun and blast the son of a bitch off the road.

His mouth turned down again as he fancied himself pumping bullets into the back of a car, into the back of the driver's head, seeing the vehicle careen and wobble off the road, seeing it turn over and burst into flame. The dirty, lousy bastards. It would serve them right. If *he* had a car he'd be glad to stop for *them*. Why wouldn't they show him the same courtesy? What the hell; they weren't any better than he was. Lousy hillbillies, they weren't as *good* as he was. Who the hell wanted to ride in their god-damned rattletraps anyway? All he wanted was to get the hell out of that neck of the woods for good!

He zipped his jacket up tight under his chin again. Why the hell should he catch cold to please a bunch of stupid hillbillies? He walked along for a while, disdaining even to turn and face the cars that continued to speed past him. For perhaps twenty minutes he stalked along, kicking at rusty beer cans and stones, cursing and growling.

The throaty, grinding rumble of a truck sounded behind him distantly and he turned, feeling hope again in the instant. Some truck drivers shrugged apologetically, pointing to the "No Riders" sign pasted on their windshields. They seemed like nice guys and it wasn't their fault if they weren't allowed by their companies to pick up hitchhikers. Others just didn't give you a tumble and they could go to hell. But a lot of them stopped. Truck drivers, mostly, were good guys. Maybe this one would stop.

He stepped out onto the road and lifted his hand, his head cocked eagerly, his ears alerted to pick up the slightest change in the roar of the motor that might indicate that the truck was slackening speed. It seemed to be a giant Mack, he thought, as it loomed larger.

He peered intently at the cab, wavered, then condescended to wear the simpering smile again, trying to see the driver, establish contact, read his expression. For a moment he could tell the man at the wheel had lifted his foot from the accelerator and then, miraculously, the juggernaut was slowing down. His heart leaped up and his smile was genuine as he trotted up to the side door. Two Negroes regarded him without expression through the open window.

"How far you goin'?" one of them said.

"As far as you are," he answered.

"Okay," said the driver. "You can ride in back." He trotted to the back of the truck and pulled himself up. The back was walled and deep like that of a coal truck, but when his eyes reached the level of the rim he saw it was piled high with what looked like dirty cotton.

As the driver gunned the motor tentatively, he flung himself over the tail of the truck and sank deep into the cloudy pile of fiber.

"Hey," he shouted at the men in the cab, clambering forward, "what is this stuff?"

"Cotton seed," shouted the man next to the driver. The rest of his words were drowned out by the grinding of the motor as the truck gathered speed again.

Riding in the back, Dan squirmed around till he was spread-eagled, his face to the sky, luxuriating in the resilient softness of the load of fiber-stuck cotton seeds. The drone of the motor, the yellow-streaked, late-afternoon clouds, and the pure sweet blue of the sky were all he could sense of the world as he stretched and lolled on his magic carpet. The air was still chilled but he did not care, snuggled in the cotton. He wished that he could ride thus forever and he felt guilty at the bitterness that had been in his heart. This was really beautiful country and from his royal vantage point he now surveyed the Southern sky and the tips and branches of trees with a warm and appreciative feeling. He drunkenly reveled in the comfort that had fallen his lot, turning over on his stomach, flexing his muscles, yawning loudly, rolling onto his back again to lose himself in the bare, limitless beauty of the sky. For perhaps a quarter of an hour he lay like a drunken Oriental potentate till, literally overcome by comfort, he relaxed completely and slept.

Recalling the feeling of warmth now, he smiled sleepily and reflected with slight sadness over the passing of youth's ability to appreciate pleasure in its own peculiar, delicious, rawly sensitive way. But still he did not pick up any hitch-hikers. Perhaps it was just as well.

Coming through Oklahoma he was eating more peanuts, drinking more Cokes and chocolate milk, and eating less real food. The money problem now was acute. He considered stopping and wiring ahead to Helen for money, but that would have meant waiting for twelve or eighteen hours in some out-of-the-way spot while she answered him, and so at last he decided to gamble on making the money last.

That night he did not go to a motel at all but slept in the car, twisted stiffly on the front seat. Actually it was almost dawn when he pulled off the road, stopped, curled up and went to sleep. When he awakened his mouth felt bone dry and bitter and his body ached.

He had had a dream about Elaine and as he began to clear the shrouds of sleep from his brain, he tried to remember what he had been dreaming about. It had seemed that he had been walking with her by a body of water, perhaps an ocean. They had walked along, hand in hand, on broken, furrowed earth that fell away and sloped down sharply, among rocks, to the water line.

He had stepped out onto the rocks and then been terrified to see that the water was washing the dirt away from among them. He was at last left high and dry on one tall, thin columnar rock that teetered in unstable sections beneath him. Elaine was somewhere near and he recalled having tried to hold her to him, to put his arms around her, and to put his hands on her body, but then she had receded and he had been alone and terror-stricken again at the precariousness of his position. When he was fully awake the memory of the dream left him, although he was left with a quivering, early-morning desire for a woman.

He pulled himself up to a sitting position and sat half dazed with his eyes closed, trying to pull himself together. Looking at his wrist watch he discovered that he had slept only a little over three hours. It was fully fifteen minutes before he could summon up enough energy to step out of the car and flex his muscles.

The morning air felt cool and refreshing on his face, and to stir up the blood in his head he rubbed his cheeks and chin vigorously with both hands, feeling the beard stubble sliding under his fingers.

His mouth was sour and he spat again and again and inhaled deeply to clear it out. With trembling fingers he took a package of gum out of his pants pocket and put two pieces in his mouth. The sugar was immediately sucked down into his system and helped a little to wake him up more completely. The flavoring in the gum made him less displeased with his mouth.

Cars slipped by at long intervals in the cool, silent morning air, and he waited for a few minutes till the horizon was clear on all sides, then stepped away from the car a short distance and urinated, shivering.

When he got back behind the wheel the car seemed hot and stuffy again, for the sun was well up in the sky and beginning to burn off the cold air that had accumulated on the desert during the night.

Half an hour later he stopped at a roadside market and

bought a pound of juicy purple grapes for breakfast. He also stopped for gas and washed his face with cold water, and when he got back in the car he was whistling a little, although he was still very tired.

For three days he had tried not to think of what he would have to do when he got to Los Angeles. At times he would think of the prospect of marrying Elaine and settling things once and for all and he would feel excited and happy, but then after a few minutes he would begin to worry and wonder about what Helen would say and what the children's reactions might be and he began to wonder how he would break the news to his mother. Then he would turn on the radio and try to become absorbed in a newscast or a soap opera.

Although he was hurrying to Elaine, things had not, it seemed, changed so much after all, and the knowledge saddened him. He had left New York in a mood of some defiance and conviction, but he had not been able to sustain the bravado, and now he could pull it back only by fits and starts. Sometimes the vague recollection of a simple physical longing for Helen would come to him and he found that he was able to convert the feeling into a mild sort of strength, a sort of armor for the battle that he feared lay ahead.

"Perhaps," he said to himself, "when I get there Elaine will tell me she loves someone else. I'll feel bad for a while, but then maybe that will make everything all right and I can go back to Helen."

Then the squirrel cage would begin turning again, and pros and cons would tumble back and forth in his mind so rapidly that he could not get them into any sort of order at all. But some of the time he had the idea in his mind that he was going out to Los Angeles to marry Elaine and he felt pretty good about the whole thing. After all, Helen was evidently happy with Randy. Maybe everything would be all right.

He began driving faster now on the road coming south toward Phoenix, although parts of the road were twisted and dangerous. His brain felt numb again and he began to get drowsy, but at each possible stop he would step down hard on the accelerator and say, "Just a little farther and then I'll pull up." For perhaps twenty-five miles he pushed himself past stop after stop, thinking each time that the next place would be more inviting. Once he found himself slowed to a crawl behind two giant trailer trucks that were held to a snail's pace by a slight incline in the highway.

He tried to pass them but the road ahead was either curved or blocked by oncoming cars, so at last he settled down to the speed of the trucks and crept along behind them, frustrated and furious, for several minutes. Finally an opportunity opened up and he swept past the two juggernauts and resumed his former speed.

The road wound its way into mountainous country now and he was glad, for the flat land made for monotonous driving. He blinked to clear his head and rest his eyes and began holding the steering wheel more firmly as fatigue assailed him again.

Shortly after noon he began talking to himself and said, "Go just fifteen more minutes and then stop at the very next place you come to. You have to stop and go to the toilet, rest, and have something else to eat."

He nodded, by way of agreeing with his decision, and began going just a bit faster so as to squeeze the last possible mile out of the time limit he had set for himself. The speedometer needle now showed that he was traveling between seventy and eighty miles an hour, although he did not realize he was going that fast. The car handled beautifully and hugged the road well on the long, gradual curves that unfolded before him through the mountains.

The scenery was striking, but because of his fatigue he appreciated it only dimly. The sky was desert-blue, cloudless, and hot, and the mountains were clearly etched in great, jagged, purplish masses against its background. Close by the road, stately saguaros loomed out of the desert floor, and a million heavy rocks lay baking at the foot of the mountains, the matrix from which they had been wrested by time and gravity.

The vistas were so far-reaching, the distances over which the eye could sweep so vast, that it seemed to Dan, when he looked away from the road, that he was crawling at a pall-bearer's pace and would never cover the long, wild, empty stretch to the next mountain range. In the mountains now there was much static on the radio and he finally could not bear to listen to it.

In Los Angeles at that moment Helen was bathing the baby, kneeling beside the tub in the front bathroom, saying, "That's it, sweetheart. Close your eyes while Mama gets the soap off your face and then we'll have a n-i-i-i-ce nap, won't we?"

Randy was at a Safeway store, shopping for the week's groceries, and Michael and Patrick were with him, helping push the wheeled basket down the aisles, asking him to buy Wheaties so they could send in the box top with a quarter and get a magic-code ring.

In Beverly Hills Elaine was having lunch with her mother, sitting in the kitchen, wearing a slightly soiled pink housecoat, saying, "Who called early this morning?"

"I think it was Jack what's-his-name," her mother said. "He said he was only going to be in town for two days. I told him you'd call back. He's at the Ambassador."

"Thanks," Elaine said, pouring herself a second cup of coffee.

Dan was holding the car steadily on the road now, his mind numbly calm, almost happy. He was wondering if the next stop would be a good place to eat. The fifteen-minute period was almost over.

He shook his head once to throw the dark specter of sleep out of his brain, and then began squinting carefully, trying to drive with his eyes half closed and his head tilted back so that he could see the road quite clearly under the lids. He felt warm and relaxed. As he was coming up out of a slight dip in the road his head nodded, forced down as the car climbed the incline out of the dip, and it was then that the other car bore down upon him. He did not know that he was driving in the center of the road, straddling the white line, and he was never to know it.

His speed did not slacken, but the driver of the other car jammed down violently on his brakes and grabbed the steering wheel hard when he saw Dan's Buick dead ahead.

The other car started to pull away to its right, but it was too late to help; the autos crashed together, not exactly head on, for the other car had angled itself a little to one side, but with tremendous force nevertheless.

The top of Dan's head hit the windshield squarely and his body was pushed against the seat, driven back by the steering wheel, which buckled in his hands and lifted his legs up off the floorboard, breaking them.

The man in the other car, Homer Snow, was thrown against his windshield at a slight angle and his steering wheel hit him a glancing blow, breaking his arm. His wife was dashed into the windshield as forcibly as if she had been shot out of a cannon. She died in the instant.

Lizards and rabbits and buzzards scuttled in terror among the hills as the deafening roar of the impact echoed across the desert floor and bounced back off the mountain walls.

The Buick stopped about thirty yards from where it had been hit, twisted halfway around so that it was facing off the side of the road; the other car rolled over three times and came to rest among the cactus and tumbleweed that edged the highway. It lay on its right side a full forty-five yards from the Buick, and when steam stopped pouring from its radiator an ominous silence fell over the scene, broken only by the soft whipping of the wind as it slipped among the desert brush.

Three minutes later a Pontiac with Michigan license plates stopped and a man got out and looked first at the Buick and then at the other car.

He walked fearfully over to the Buick and looked in.

"Holy God," he said and then broke into a run and got back in his car and raced off at high speed. Not far down the road he skidded to a stop at a gas station. Leaving the door of his car open, he ran into the station, knocking down a little girl who was playing by the door.

"I'm sorry, sweetheart," he said, picking her up. "Listen, is there a phone here?"

344

"Yes," said a tanned elderly man with short-cropped white hair. "What's the matter?"

"There's been an accident. An awful one. Right back up the road. You better get help, quick."

"Lord, God," said the elderly man, stepping out quickly from behind a counter, "that's the second one this month."

He took the phone off the hook and spoke loudly into the mouthpiece. "Get the highway police, quick," he said. "Another accident up the road here. Yeah, this is Charley. Tell 'em where, will you? Wait a minute." He turned to the man at the door. "Where was it? North or south of here? I didn't notice which way you drove up."

"Up that way," said the man, pointing. "Oooh, it was awful."

"How many people?" asked the old man, hanging up the phone.

"I don't know," said the other. "I only looked at one of the cars. That's all I had to do."

"It's awful," said the old man. "Just awful. Makes you kind of sick."

"Yes, it does," said the younger man, and suddenly he ran outside and went behind the building and vomited.

In a few minutes a highway patrol car whined past the station at great speed.

"There they go," said the old man.

"What happened?" asked the child.

"Nothing, honey," the old man said. "You go on and play. Your ma'll be back soon."

Another car stopped outside and a man and woman got out and walked briskly into the station.

"Has somebody called an ambulance?" the new man asked.

"Yes," said the proprietor. "It's all taken care of. The highway patrol just went out."

"We just saw them," said the woman, "but they'll need an ambulance, too."

"Must be one on the way," the old man said. "They got a radio in the police car."

"Oh, dear," said the woman. "What a sight."

"Yes," said the man from Michigan, "it was awful. I saw it a few minutes ago. Awful." He screwed up his face at the memory.

"Don't know what people mean, driving fast," said the old man.

"It's just awful," the man from Michigan repeated.

"You want to go back there, honey?" the new man said to the woman who stood behind him.

"No," she said, shuddering. "No, sir!"

"All right," he said. "Let's move on."

"Good-bye," the old man said. "Thanks for stopping in."

"All right," said the new man as he left, closing the door.

"Just last month," the old man said, "one of them big trucks. Burned right up. Now this. I don't know what's going on these days."

"Yes, it's awful," said the man from Michigan. "Makes you sick."

Back at the scene of the wreck more than a dozen cars had stopped and pulled off the road. The highway patrolmen had put out flares and a small red flag, though it was broad daylight. Some of the passing drivers were out in the road in their shirt sleeves, ready to wave off oncoming traffic, willing to help if they could. Women sat in several of the cars, fearful.

"Looks like a head-on," one of the patrolmen said to the other.

"Yep. I've called for the ambulance. May take a few minutes."

The taller of the two took out a pad and pencil and began making notes.

"The Buick has New York plates," he said. "What's on the other car?"

"Utah plates," his companion said.

"A mess for the families, handling it long distance."

"Yeah."

"They all dead?"

"Pretty sure. This guy is, that's for certain. And the woman looks done for. Might be a chance for the driver of the Buick, but I doubt it."

346

"Son of a bitch," said the tall patrolman softly, shaking his head from side to side. "What can you do?"

"Yep," said his companion. "All right, you people there, keep over to the side. Over! Over! We've got to keep traffic moving through here, Goddammit!"

"What happened, officer?" said a small man with a loud sport shirt and dark glasses.

"What do you think?" the patrolman said scornfully. "Keep out of the way there."

The small man stepped nimbly away and took a three-dimensional color camera out of a small leather case that hung by a strap over his shoulder. He walked carefully around the Buick and took three or four pictures, then walked down the road to the overturned Dodge and took two more. In a short time he had gathered a small group around himself and set up shop as an authority.

"Must have happened right over there," he said. "You can see the Buick was going south."

"Is that right?" said a woman, pushing her hair out of her eyes.

"Yes, that's the way I figure it," the man with the camera said.

CHAPTER
TWENTY-SIX

Dan Scanlon was never able to remember much of the next few weeks of his life and a large part of what he was eventually able to report about the period came to him as a result of asking questions. There were faint memories of the early days, of course, but they seemed remarkably like the memory of dreams. There were vague recollections of numbness, a buzzing sound, the soft voices of strangers, smells of ether and disinfectants, waves of pain, nightmares and sweats, frights and weepings and great periods of black-and-red nothingness. It was only later that he learned of the surprise of ambulance attendants when they had discovered that he was not quite dead, despite his great loss of blood and many broken bones. It was much later that he was told he had spent days in a small emergency hospital and that he had then been transferred to a hospital in Phoenix.

It had even been three days, he found, before they had known who he was since somehow his wallet and identification papers had been lost or stolen at the scene of the accident. By checking on his license plates they got his name and address but, since he had by now secured New York plates, it was the New York address. The official letters sent there were merely left in his vestibule by the elevator boy; there was no one there to read them and learn of the accident. This much he figured out when he was finally able to remain fully conscious for more than half an hour at a time and discovered that no one had called to inquire about him, no one had come to see him.

"Don't you want us to get in touch with someone . . . your family?" a boyish-looking young doctor had said.

"Not just now."

"Well, it's up to you, but I think you owe it to whomever you live with to let them know where you are."

"I live alone," Dan said.

"Well," the doctor said, "whoever your loved ones are they'll be wondering where you are eventually, won't they?"

"Look, doc," Dan said, "if it's money you're worried about, forget it. I'll be able to pay."

The doctor stiffened and then forced a smile. "Okay," he said. "I'm here to help you, not argue with you. Don't worry about a thing. Get yourself some more sleep."

It seemed easy to Dan to pass out or fall into a peculiar doped sort of sleep, but sleep of the sort to which he was accustomed began to come only with difficulty. There were casts on both his legs and both his arms and no matter how he moved himself he could not get into a comfortable position. The sessions with the bedpan and the nurse embarrassed him painfully and he grew angry because there was no way out of the embarrassment. If he tried to delay relieving himself the absurdity of the effort became immediately apparent to him and yet each time the prospect of the nurse lifting him up, sliding the hard white pan under him, emptying it, smiling primly, saying "Upsidaisy" in an inane but well-meant way made him feel so deeply ill-at-ease that, absurd or no, he usually put off as long as possible emptying the waste from his body. He even felt a retroactive sort of embarrassment at the thought of the care he must have been given during the days before he had fully regained consciousness. How miserable was man, helpless on his back in all the hospitals of the world. Hospitals were like prisons, orphanages, concentration camps, insane asylums. They were all warehouses where society stored its troublesome members, largely—Dan felt during those days—to avoid having to look at them, to avoid having to *feel* for them.

In four weeks, when he finally felt prepared for it, he telephoned Helen.

"Where have you been?" she said.

"Well, that's a long story," he said, chuckling. "I started to drive out to L.A. and had a little accident. No, what the hell do I mean 'little'? I had a pretty *bad* accident."

"Oh, that's terrible. Are you all right now?"

"Yes, I'm fine. That is, I'll be fine in a few days. Don't worry about a thing. I didn't want to call you before now because I—"

There was a pause. His mind felt blank.

"Because why?"

"I guess I'm still a little dopey," he said. "Anyway I didn't want to worry you or the kids. How are they?"

"Oh, just fine," she said. "They're down at a goofy-golf course right now, with Randy."

"That's nice. Kiss them for me," he said. The conversation was already dragging.

"Well," she said. "When will you be up and around?"

"Oh, I don't exactly know. In a couple of weeks maybe. But don't worry. I'm coming along fine."

"That's good." Then, "Where did the accident happen? Where are you *calling* from, by the way?"

"I'm in Phoenix," he said. "But nobody in town knows I'm here. I'm lying low." Then he laughed. "In fact I'm lying lower than I ever did in my life. I'm at St. Joseph's."

"Is there anything I can do for you? Do you need anything?"

"No, thanks," he said. "I put through a call to my attorney in New York and told him to take care of the bookkeeping for me. Other than that all I have to do is lie here and wait to mend."

After a long moment Helen said, "Dan, I don't want to bring up anything that will disturb you if you aren't well enough to talk about—what I mean is, have you come to any decision? About us? Does our divorce stand?"

"Why, yes," he said. "But I'd rather not discuss it over the

350

phone. Tell you what, I'll get off a letter to you in a few days. In fact I've been running it over in my mind. I've got things pretty well straightened out, I think, but I'd rather not talk about it right now."

"All right," she said.

After his casts and bandages were removed and he was finally able to get about the business of learning to walk again, fighting the dizziness and the strange weakness in his arms and legs, he remembered the letter he had promised to write. For three days he thought about it and then one morning, after he had shaved and put on fresh pajamas, he asked for pen and paper and, seating hmself in a comfortable chair near an open window, through which wafted the warm familiar air of Arizona, he began writing.

Dear Helen:

If Randy is near when you receive this letter perhaps it would be wise if you called him and asked him to sit beside you while you read it, for it will have consequences upon both your lives. It is a letter that has been written only after much soul-searching, much remorse and despair, and I undertake its composition in the spirit of honesty.

For almost two years I have been fighting a battle that it now seems I was never destined to win: the battle to restore my life to its former state, to bring it back to the circumstances and conditions under which it existed prior to the time I met Elaine Sterling.

You have stood by during this time, unable to help me in my struggle, although your aid was willingly offered. I have learned that no one could have helped me and that there are some things that we must face by ourselves. Literally hundreds of times, unknown to you or anyone, I have reached decisions of one nature or another only to see them crumble in the face of reality.

I have known the hopelessness of a struggle where every move seemed to be a mistake and no solution seemed right. I have felt both the blameful perpetrator of a harmful plot and the innocent victim of cruel circumstance. The time of struggle has not been without its respites, even its joys, but always there has been present the torment that is the lot of the man who brings suffering to those who love him.

The battle now may be over, or it may be that its ending is only an illusion and it will continue all the days of my life, but I have finally come to the belief that I can bring less pain to all concerned by adopting a firm stand upon that corner of the field to which life has forced me. You and I have now been divorced for some time and since there seems no possibility that I could remain unmarried for the rest of my life I have come to the decision to marry the woman whose lot fate has thrown in with my own.

I know that in the past one of the chief factors contributing to the unhappiness of all of us involved in this matter has been my indecision. I realize now that only a definite, irrevocable move in one direction or the other can enable us to build a future with any concrete form and dimension.

This has not been an easy-to-make decision. You have said once or twice that it was your belief that I had no real conception of the torment I had caused you. Such, unhappily, is not the case. Not only have I seen, with my own eyes, evidences of the misery which the early stages of our breakup brought to you, but during this unhappy period I have suffered a great deal myself. My former way of life has been changed, and I have labored under an intense feeling of guilt because of the unhappiness I have caused you, the children and my mother. I have fallen into intellectual confusion; all my old emotional roots have been torn up.

I have learned that we are not, after all, the complete masters of our fates and the captains of our souls. I would not have ever made a decision to fall in love with another woman any more than I could have made a decision to become wet from standing in the rain, or to be hit by a random bullet on a battlefield. But the thing happened and although, in itself (if my relationship with Elaine can be considered objectively as a detached and impersonal thing), it may be said to be good, I was nevertheless appalled by its consequences. I suppose man never deliberately courts unhappiness, but unhappiness seems to shadow him all the days of his life, lurking around every corner to pounce upon him when it is least expected.

Even my relationship with Elaine is not the simple thing it might have been had we met in another age under other circumstances. While that relationship is very broad and deep, and while there are many fine and comforting things about it, we can not forget that the world will not look upon our union with favor.

We do not consider ourselves evil people and yet we have done an evil thing. We were blinded and moving in darkness and in so doing we stumbled over others and hurt them. We may say that we intended no hurt, and such is indeed the case, but the harm has been done and the pain of those who have suffered is as great as if the injury were vindictively afflicted.

Guilt feelings, of course, are normal to one in my position, but they have been multiplied greatly by the complete lack of selfish justification for my actions insofar as your part of our relationship is concerned. In other words, had you been in any way remiss in your wifely duties, had you been unsatisfactory to me, cruel, nagging, or cold, I might have found some comfort in at least a shred of justification, if only in the selfish, animal part of my nature. The fact that you were, as far as I am concerned, without fault in our relationship gives me complete exclusivity to the role of villain in our drama and this, as I say, has contributed greatly to a realization, perhaps even an exaggeration, of my guilt.

It was heartening to me to have you say, in one of your recent letters, that you still regard me as a friend, for that is certainly the way it should be. Though I have done much to hurt you, I still have a very real fondness for you. In a broad sense I have, I believe, a love for you, and I hope that we shall always be on good terms, for our own sakes, as well as for the children's. I will always consider myself under the obligation to see that you and the children are supported in the style to which, as the saying goes, you have been accustomed and you need have no fear that my marriage to Elaine, or yours to Randy, will work any financial hardship on you or the kids.

I refer to your marriage to Randy as foregone, for I know that he loves you and is an excellent man, and, as we have discussed, his character is evidently better suited to your emotional make-up than was mine. Even in our untroubled days I remember I frequently caused you unhappiness of various sorts. There is nothing to be gained now in going over my inadequacies as a husband; suffice to say that they existed.

There is still to be faced, I am aware, the religious objection to the move I am making and of that I can say little except that I would have preferred that life had not taken the course it has. The observation that much of what looks like virtue is simply due to lack of temptation is, I now think, a very sound one, for history itself is a record of man's inability to live up to his ambitions. I have no relish for moral weakness, nor am I anxious to be looked down upon for what I have done. We all hunger for approval, first from our mothers as infants, later from our families and friends and then from the world. I have no appetite for the hurts that I will suffer at the hands of morally righteous people but if these people have discovered a means whereby man may completely control the wild, undisciplined giant that is his secret mind I will be happy to credit them with the most monumental discovery in the history of human progress.

To a not inconsiderable extent man is, after all, powerless to control his thinking. He cannot will, for example, not to *think* of something since such willing automatically accomplishes the opposite of its desired end. His mind normally reacts to stimuli which are beyond his personal control, and though a man may pray to discipline his thinking he cannot pray twenty-four hours a day. Perhaps the only really holy people are those who do pray practically twenty-four hours a day, in the monasteries and convents, or in the mountains and villages of the Orient, but I am not one of these and though I have done my best it is painfully evident that my best was not good enough.

I suppose that about covers what I wanted to say, Helen. I do not know if you will feel a certain amount of hatred for me through the years or if you will be able to accept me as a friend, but I know that your reaction will be automatic and one which you are largely unable to control, so all I can do is hope that it will be sympathetic. Give the children a kiss for me. I will try to see them soon.

Happiness to you,
Dan

He did not receive an answering letter.

During all this time, strangely enough, he did not communicate with Elaine. He thought of her frequently during the long days and nights but he could not bring himself to call her, although several times he got so far as reaching for the phone or writing a few lines of a letter.

When he finally left the hospital, he weighed sixteen pounds less, had a long scar over his right eye, was very pale, and carried a cane, which he had been told he might need for a while but would eventually be able to discard. His left knee ached if he walked much or remained standing for longer than ten minutes.

After buying some new clothes at a Phoenix shop he took a plane to Los Angeles, registered at the Beverly Hills Hotel and stayed there for a week, letting no one know that he was in town. Every day he swam in the hotel pool and soaked up the sun. When he had finally gotten himself into the right state of mind he called Helen and said he would like to come out and visit the children. That morning he stopped and bought a second-hand but late model Chevrolet.

When he arrived at the house he had a strange feeling of having come back from another planet to discover that earth was a smaller, paler, and yet somehow dearer place than he had remembered. The children, as it happened, were playing on the front lawn. They surrounded him like squealing gulls and covered him with kisses and embraces. Looking up he saw Helen standing on the front porch.

"Hi," he said, shyly.

"Hi," she said. "How are you feeling?"

"Oh, fine," he said. "Not quite ready to play football but I'll live. Randy around?"

"No," she said. "He thought it would be a good idea if you had the day with the children to yourself."

They spent the afternoon playing games with the children and making small talk. He inspected the property, commented that the shrubs and trees were looking fairly well, that the lawn was brown and faded in spots, and that the house seemed much improved by the new colors added to the walls of the den and kitchen.

After dinner they put the children to bed, working together as they had so many times in the past, kissing the children's necks, joking with them, turning out the lights, whispering softly.

Helen led the way back into the living room. She opened the window near the sofa and sat sniffing the night air.

Dan lowered himself into a chair and looked at her.

"They're such angels," she said.

"Yes," he answered. With hands clasped he inspected his knuckles as if they were new. It was the first moment the two of them had been alone and unhurried and he knew they were going to talk. He felt ill at ease and withdrawn.

"The place looks nice," he said.

"How is Elaine?"

"What?" he said, inanely.

"It's all right," Helen said. "You can talk about her. I don't care."

"Well," he said, "there isn't much to tell. She's fine."

"Is she in town?"

"Yes. As a matter of fact she came West quite a while before I did. She hadn't seen her mother in quite some time and thought she ought to come out for a while."

Helen kicked her shoes off and lighted a cigarette.

"Dan," she said, "I'm sorry you don't feel free to talk to me . . . about Elaine . . . about everything. Believe me, I can talk about it now. There was a time when I couldn't, but it's past. I'm all right now."

"That's nice of you," he said. "I don't really know why I should feel this way, but I do. Even though we should be able to discuss it now . . . I don't know, I can't seem to feel free about it. There's been so much misery connected with it that it's just difficult for me to discuss it impersonally now."

"But you shouldn't let that feeling prevent you from having an adult conversation about the problem. I've talked it all over with Randy and I think we all owe it to each other to be honest. Maybe I can help you."

"That's wonderful of you," he said. "It's nice of you to feel that you want to help me. I—"

"I mean it," she said. "I care a great deal about you. It's not the same feeling I once had for you, but still you're something close to me. You're still the father of my children. I worry about you."

"Thanks."

"Do you love Elaine?"

"Yes, I believe I do."

"You *believe* you do?" she said. "Remember, you can say

what you're thinking. You don't have to soften any blows for me, because they can't hurt any more."

"All right. I love her."

"I wasn't sure that you did."

"Why not?"

"Because it seems to me that if you really loved her, nothing in the world could have stopped you from marrying her before now."

"I've come close to it."

"I know. When I got that letter I thought it was all settled."

"But then I get afraid. It's all so final, and it means so much unhappiness to my mother, and——"

"I know exactly what you mean. Randy and I have discussed it all, too. I want to marry him, but it seems like such a tremendously big step, and there's no retracing it. Sometimes I look at the children and tears come into my eyes. I'm not crying for *you,* you understand; it's just such a damned rotten break for them, that they don't have you around all the time, the way they feel about you."

Dan winced and shook his head slowly from side to side.

"I'm sorry," she said. "I didn't say that to hurt you."

"I know."

"They miss you a great deal. That should make you happy, in a way, knowing how much they love you. Randy is wonderful to them, and they're very fond of him. But it's not the same. He's not their father. It could never be the same for them."

"God, what a lousy trick we all had played on us," he said, angry.

"Yes," she said. "Although I don't hold it against you any longer. For a long time I was bitter and full of hate, but that's a road that leads nowhere. Pick up a paper. It happens every day."

"But, dammit," he said, "it shouldn't happen! What the hell's the matter with the whole scheme of things when life holds out to you what you think is your rosy future and then snatches it away?"

"Maybe it was building up for a long time and we never knew it. Would you like a drink?" she said.

"Yes," he said. "I'll fix it. You want one?"

"Yes," she said. After they each had finished a bourbon and soda it became easier to talk.

"I know our marriage wasn't perfect," he said, "but I never thought I was hoarding the imperfections in a box and looking them over in my secret mind."

"That must have been what you were doing," she said. "Brooding over our physical relationship, looking for things to bicker about, waiting for an excuse to break out."

"It's inconceivable," he said, then laughing softly, "but it's possible. I know I was always a little sorry because I didn't, you know, *satisfy* you. My religious upbringing was super-imposed on our sexual relationship, and your acceptance of the set-up must have prevented you from obtaining the satis-faction you were entitled to."

"It's strange how we can talk this way now," she said. "Perhaps if we'd been able to a long time ago——"

"Perhaps," he said. "I'm convinced sex had more to do with our unhappiness than we realized. If you'd been a Catholic, or if I hadn't, we would have looked at things in the same way, but with us every love-making was overshadowed by the fear that you'd become pregnant."

"That's right," she said. "That's why I could almost never——" she fumbled "——achieve climax. Do you disapprove of my saying that?"

"Certainly not," he said. "It's too bad we couldn't have been this frank when it might have done some good."

He sat looking at her and thinking of the barriers that each had had to overcome all the times he had made love to her. They had never used certain words, normal words. Nouns had been replaced by pronouns. The long periods of self-imposed abstinence between the acts had rendered him unstable and erratic in her arms. He could never wait for her, never com-pletely satisfy her, and so she could never completely satisfy him. The near-frenzy that would preface their embraces would give way to a feeling of unfulfillment and despond-ency. It was strange. With Elaine it had been imperative that she not become pregnant and therefore she had simply worn a diaphragm and Dan had accepted it as absolutely

358

necessary. Consequently with Elaine he had been free and open. He would subconsciously (and sometimes even consciously) wish either that he had married a girl of his own religion or that he had become mated to a wild, uninhibited pagan. He was always walking a tightrope, balancing on one hand his morals, arrived-at and automatically acquired, and on the other his impulses and desires.

"That must have been what we were always fighting about, although we never knew it," he said.

"I think so," she responded. "I always had the feeling that you didn't love me as much as I loved you, that you had reservations about my body, that you were holding back part of yourself. And that was no good. Love has to be free. Do you think," she said suddenly, "that if you had never *told* me about Elaine, the deceit and back-street skulking eventually would have . . . you know, made the thing wither away of itself?"

"I don't think so," he said. "That's what was so sad about it all. Perhaps every man has one stupid fling in him. Some men make it a habit. But even men who believe in being honest can fall. If they're lucky they make their mistake with some cheap broad who makes them sick when they look at her in the daylight. I wish that had happened to me, if the thing had to happen at all. I wish I had met some pushover with the morals of a man, some girl with lacquered fingernails and halitosis, and a little black book full of men's phone numbers. Instead it was my misfortune to meet someone whose qualities I admired."

"I see," Helen said, somewhat primly.

"Oh, Lord," he said. "I don't want to make you unhappy again. I'm only discussing all this because you said you wanted to."

"I'm all right," she said, wide-eyed. "Really. I like your being honest with me. You can't hurt me any more. You keep forgetting that."

"I'm glad," he said. "I mean I hope that's the truth."

"You're good to me in all the ways you can be," she said. "You give me as much money as you can, you love the children, you seem more thoughtful now."

359

"I can't even respect myself for that," he said. "It's probably due to my feeling of guilt. I don't suppose it's possible for me to perform a completely unselfish act."

"Maybe it's not possible for anyone."

"Maybe," he said. "I guess the only person in the world who could do an entirely unselfish thing would be an anonymous atheist. If a Christian does something kind he's doing it because it makes him feel good or because even though it's a strain on him he's currying favor with God."

She pondered the point for a moment and then said, "I think there's a little part of love that isn't selfish."

"Maybe," he said, musing. "Faith, hope, and charity. And the greatest of these is charity. I guess that means it's even more important to love your fellow man than it is to love your God. It may be difficult to love God, because it's hard to see Him, so you have an excuse for losing your *faith*. You can open any paper or turn on any television set and find an excuse for losing your *hope,* but there's a great big, crying vacuum that wants to be filled with *love*. There are people standing around weak, or sick, or in pain. There are infants waiting to be picked up, the hungry waiting to be fed, there is beauty to be admired. If you can't love you're really worse off than if you can't believe or hope. Perhaps love is a condition without which faith and hope cannot even exist."

They talked thus for many hours, unmindful of the time. Twice he went to the kitchen and got cans of cold beer out of the ice box, and shared them with her.

She spoke of Randy and he spoke of Elaine and they found that in a mysterious and subtle way they could be close and good friends and feel a warm bond, one unto the other. Physical attraction seemed to have disappeared entirely, and although he could plainly perceive that she was prettier now, and thinner, and smoothly tanned by the sun, his sexual self felt no inclination to move to her. His loving self, however, on several occasions brought him to her side, and he patted her shoulder and once even kissed her cheek.

Twice later that week he drove out to the house to visit with the children for an hour or so. At the end of the week he

360

checked out of the hotel and into a one-room-and-kitchenette place on Franklin Avenue in Hollywood. He still had not gotten in touch with Elaine.

One afternoon, however, he drove out to her house and parked across the street. For a long time he sat there, staring up at the window of the apartment he presumed she still shared with her mother. He could not understand why he would not permit himself to call her.

The next day he did the same thing, parking across the street from her apartment and sitting there in his car, for over an hour.

As he was sitting there on the third day a new Packard convertible pulled up in front of her door and a good-looking man with sandy hair and glasses honked his horn in a shave-and-a-haircut rhythm. His arrival did not strongly impress itself on Dan. Then suddenly the front door of Elaine's building opened and she walked out, radiant and smiling.

The man in the Packard leaped out and ran around to let her in the other side. She came toward him, talking brightly, wearing a wine-red wool suit, and did not see Dan who, momentarily stunned, recovered himself, turned his ignition key and sped off, his heart pounding. He drove about the city, aimlessly, for the rest of the afternoon. At last, his heart bursting with love, he parked the car, went into a drugstore, and dialed her number. There was no answer.

On the spur of the moment he went back to his room, packed, and checked out, not bothering to try to recover any of the full month's rent he had paid. With no destination in mind he drove out along the ocean highway, moving at a leisurely rate of speed. South of Malibu he passed the beach motel where he had first made love to Elaine, recognizing the neon sign with a quick sinking sense of loss. A few minutes later he stopped, parked the car, and walked along the beach thinking back over the whole story, toying with the idea of suicide, laughing when the sudden attack of a wave made him leap back to avoid getting his feet wet. Passing the old motel had been a shock, although he had been able to take it in stride. But God, were there to be these constant reminders? Had heart no reason, love no logic? Was he condemned for the rest of his life to be the sport of skies, of charging clouds, of flowers? How had she hurled sweet hooks into his flesh, not taking aim? He was not sovereign. He had been overtaken. Gone were all his boundaries, or merged with hers. His heart was the kingdom of the incomplete. Drunk now with the beauty of the seacoast and the remembered beauty of Elaine, he walked along, through a mist of light, shadow, color, the sound of breathing, eyes, oh, eyes, remembering now the taste of tears, the desperate part of love, the abject bargaining for moments, grateful for a glance, but never, never satisfied by even the most gluttonous hours, for he could take sufficient food or drink but never quite enough of her, however much she gave.

The sweet fruits of summer that had lain upon her tongue he envied now. Rich symphonies that she had heard but he would never hear disturbed his peace, for what was past was gone and what to come unsure, and he wanted to share all the world with her, past, present and future.

In a confused and sensitive state he got back in the car and drove north for many hours until at last, in rugged, mountainous country, he pulled up at a small inn. Since it had gotten dark, he could not clearly tell what sort of building he now proposed to enter but it looked to him old-fashioned, rustic, and somehow foreign, perhaps German or Scandinavian or Swiss. As he entered through a side door off the gravel parking lot a large, elderly woman approached, fanning herself.

"Are you serving dinner?" he said.

"Yes, indeed," she said. "For one?"

"Yes."

"Right this way. The girl will be with you in a minute."

He seated himself at a small oilcloth-covered table, decorated with a small blue glass vase full of mixed pink and red flowers. In a moment a teen-age girl with a pony-tail hairdo approached and solemnly handed him a menu.

The food, pot roast and fresh vegetables, turned out to be so good and the atmosphere so homelike that as he was paying his check he impulsively said to the elderly woman behind the counter, "By the way, do you have any rooms open?"

"They're almost all open right now," she said with a smile.

362

He paid a week's rent and moved right in. As he was bringing his bags in from the car he said to the teen-age waitress, "Say, where am I? What's the name of this town?"

"Well," the girl said, "it's not exactly a town. It's called Big Sur."

During the days that followed, Dan, for the first time in his life, developed a feeling of true intimacy with nature. Big Sur, he discovered, was a pure and undefiled place that, except for the thin ribbon of highway that wound through its mountains and the scattered homes and inns, must look today as it had a thousand years earlier. He spent long, happy days exploring its canyons and beaches, impressed to his soul by the area's high brown mountains that stand with serene dignity shoulder-to-shoulder like a herd of enormous blind buffalo, sensing the sea, fierce heads lowered, locked feet awash in the surf.

One of the beaches was bordered, on its southern side, by a scattered profusion of small, medium, and large rocks, upon which, after the strength in his arms and legs had almost fully returned, he loved to clamber, stretching out on one of the larger and flatter rocks from time to time to rest and breathe deeply of the healing salt air. During all his years he had never before been really *aware* of the earth's oceans, even though he had lived in California, and now he became infatuated by the Pacific.

Below him, endlessly and still and again and ever, the water came on, now liquid pearls, crystals, alabaster, diamonds, flashing magnificently in the cold, haze-filled light of the afternoon sun, splashing in wild profusion as the sea scattered its treasures upon the shore.

The sea, bunching its muscles, hurled itself endlessly upon and over and through the rocks off to the left. Where there were narrow clefts in the gnarled fists of stone the water altered its personality utterly, being no more the placid, pacific, timeless sea but rather a boiling, seething mass of currents, millions of separate veins of water that jostled each other for position, twisting, turning in a roaring, sudsy, chaotic stream.

Through the thin passageways the water sprayed thunderously, rolling, hissing, rumbling, the sight of it washing Dan's eyes, seeming to shoot the essential idea of itself through them into his spirit, cleansing it in the same way the wild flow washed the ageless, indomitable rocks.

Lying thus on the high flat rock he became thirsty. Leaning on an elbow he looked down at the cold, thrashing water and drank it with his eyes. It would be exquisite torture, he thought, to die of thirst in sight of that water, or die of hunger in sight of food, or die of unsatisfied lust in sight of one's beloved.

At that moment Dan Scanlon finally admitted to himself what he had for so long refused to accept, that in his arms Elaine had not just been Elaine but *Woman* and that he had learned to desire Woman, to need Woman, from the young blue-eyed mother who had held him to her breast as an infant and then, unable to help herself, had been forced to abandon him, time and again. He laughed bitterly like a savage, opening his throat freely to the wind, knowing that his animal shout of understanding would be drowned out by the sea.

Off to the right one huge, craggy hump of brown rock, as high as a five-story building, stood bedded, seemingly, to the earth's core, awash in the surf several yards from the glistening sandy shore, an immovable object assailed at every moment of its existence by the irresistible force of the endless ocean. An open corridor in its middle permitted wild waves to roar through drunkenly, splashing spray high against the rock walls, fighting, forcing their way through the narrow shadowy passage only at last to fan out, relax, and either sink with a whisper into the sand or stand about in sudsy, shallow pools along the beach-rim.

When his soul had drunk its fill of the sea Dan would repair to the canyons and ravines nestled back in the mountains. One day he discovered a canyon, new to him, that was particularly beautiful. The deep bottom of the angle formed by the juncture of its two steep mountain-sides was a quiet, green, enchanted place. Along its broken, twisting surface a creek descended, as it had for a million years, here splashing riotously through narrows and over embedded rocks, there pausing momentarily in silent crystal pools, as if to gather its strength before continuing the downward plunge to the sea.

High overhead, Dan could see, the sun was shining powerfully but so thick was the vegetation in the canyon, so ponderous were the trunks and branches of the mighty redwood and fir, so lush the leaves and fronds of the smaller trees and bushes, that at ground level all was hushed mystery and shadow, pierced here and there by dazzling golden shafts of sunlight that rocketed down from broken patches of open blue sky. The sun, where it could force its way down into the cool cathedral-like air, crashed through certain broad flat green leaves, turning them into such glowing patches of color that they seemed to burn with an apple-green fire. In one shaft of sunbeams pale gnats whirled sedately, atoms in a giant cell of light, planets circling through clear and infinite space.

In the creek bed a glorious frozen disorder prevailed, the result of ancient storms and floods. Enormous boles and limbs of trees—torn out of place by lightning bolts, by winds, by avalanches, by swollen angry cascades, by time—lay strewn about, the wreckage of centuries, contrasting strangely now in their sleepy peace with the brutal violence that must have occasioned their fall. Boulders of all sizes, too, lay awash in the gurgling water, some submerged, some providing Dan footing as, moving uphill, he crossed and recrossed the stream.

Seating himself on the smooth, stripped trunk of a fallen redwood that bridged the flow, he stared dreamily down into one of the tranquil pools where the water paused. After a few minutes he removed his shoes and socks and, sliding forward, lowered his feet into the ice-cold water. For a long time he sat thus, luxuriating in the tingling chill that gradually numbed his feet and ankles and reminded him of the old ache in his broken legs.

When at last he put socks and shoes back on he felt greatly refreshed. Such hikes were good not only for his body but for his soul. The accident seemed to him now to have been a punishment, a penance, a fire through which he had come successfully, bloody perhaps, but unbowed. He had almost been killed (or killed himself) in body and in spirit but now he lived and reveled in the pure simple fact of his existence. He felt prepared for some heroic act but conjectured drily that life would very probably present him with no dramatic opportunities to manifest his new-found strength. And, after all, all heroes in reality (as distinguished from the heroes of literature and motion pictures) were condemned to go on living. They could not exist forever in heroic form but had to stand about shifting from one foot to another while time cut them back down to human size. So he would be heroic only in his secret heart, content to keep his spiritual muscles sinewy only by wrestling with himself, the only adversary after all, perhaps, capable of defeating him.

CHAPTER

TWENTY-SEVEN

Within a couple of weeks Dan had begun to make friends at Big Sur, although he chose, most of the time, to keep to himself. Now and then he would visit a writer, a painter, a sculptor, a retired newspaperman, a young Bohemian couple, in one or another of the houses that perched high above the sea on a small terrace dug out of the enormous mountains. He looked longingly at the children he met—laughing, wind-blown creatures seemingly more free than the city-bound little ones he knew, infinitely more free than his own self of childhood days.

For the first few days the silence got on his nerves but soon he became accustomed to it. The geographical Big Sur, it seemed, purposely rejected the rest of the continent, ignored it, and kept its gaze resolutely fixed upon the Pacific. In time, Dan found himself doing the same. He thought of those he had left behind and upon occasion ached to see them, but he knew that to do so he had only to get in his car and drive south and yet he did not do it. Borrowing books from his neighbors he became engrossed in poetry and philosophy, two subjects in which he had up to now had little or no interest. On an impulse he drove up to Monterey one morning and had his hair cut short and monk-like. His usual garb now was levis and a zippered leather jacket or, when it was warm, open-necked short sleeved shirts. Within a month he was back to his former weight, tanned, and hardened by hiking through the canyons and swimming in the surf.

After a while Dan became aware that there were other residents of the Big Sur country besides the artists and intellectuals. High in the wild Santa Lucia hills the descendants of the pioneer settlers, who still raised sheep and cattle on vast ranches, hunted in the upper wilderness and fished the icy mountain streams. There were the old retired people, too. Dan met some of them in the inns and restaurants or at the homes of the few people he knew.

Even after the silence of the place ceased to disturb him he was frequently conscious of it, nevertheless, particularly at night. It seemed almost tangible, to have a positive rather than merely negative quality. It was as if it *came* from some place, out of the depths of the sea or the frozen bowels of the rugged earth or from the timeless stars that were splashed nightly across the black California sky.

Dan came, in time, to know every hour of the Big Sur day and night. He watched the sun go down, retired, and was up in time to see it rise. He became intimately familiar with the mountain flowers and the grasses and winds and the always close blue daytime sky. He knew well the morning fogs that sometimes conquered the willful sun but almost always lost their battle with it by early afternoon. He discovered a small motel-inn that featured natural hot spring water baths and got into the habit of bathing there once a week, luxuriating in the rich, sulphurous water in the large rough concrete tubs that were open to the sea and sky. One day as he lay soaking in the hot water a wild storm broke in the sky and he watched, enthralled, as the fierce drama of black angry clouds, lightning and thunder was enacted before him.

Another time, learning that a Catholic mission existed not far away, he drove to its walls and sat in his parked car looking at it but somehow unwilling to get out, as he had not long before sat before Elaine's apartment in Beverly Hills, just waiting and staring. Instead of entering the hermitage Dan drove away and spent the morning in the company of wild lilac, poppy, sagebrush, sun and sky.

One afternoon, while attending an open-air cocktail party on the eagle-nest terrace of a bearded novelist, Dan looked up from a tray of iced carrot strips and cream cheese and saw standing before him Carter Marvell. When Marvell had finished speaking to a full-blown blonde woman Dan approached him.

"Hello," he said. "You may not remember me. Dan Scanlon's the name."

"I remember you perfectly well," Marvell said. "How are you?"

"Fine, thank you. Since I saw you last I've read the books you gave me."

"And?"

"They had a definite effect on my thinking, although I'm not able to say for certain just what that effect was."

"How refreshing," Marvell said. "Come, I'm curious to hear more. Sit down and tell me what has happened."

They seated themselves on a rough redwood bench.

"What have you learned?" Marvell asked.

"That my problem was essentially one of communication. All the theorizing about incompatibility and love was just a way of coming to grips with that fact. I never learned how to communicate with some people. Unfortunately I happened to marry one of them. I've somehow got to get myself opened up."

Marvell nodded. "What else have you learned?" he said.

"To stop arguing with myself," Dan said, "because myself always wins."

Marvell threw back his head and laughed.

"Then," he said, "you would seem to have come to an understanding of the essentially obsessive nature of the predicament you were in. Ah, me," he continued, looking off dreamily, "deliver us from the cruelty of the virtuous. The cruelty of the man who *knows* he is cruel, or who at least has a reputation for being so, is one thing. It is more or less to be expected, although certainly not condoned. But the cruelty of the pillars of society, the good, law-abiding majority, is what has worked most of the world's mischief after all. For if the supposedly virtuous were really virtuous they would not eternally be so available to do the dirty work of the admittedly evil. What I am getting at, perhaps in rather a roundabout way, is that your—well, what society calls your *better* self was being very cruel with your inner controlling spirit, which is not, by the way, the same thing as the Christian *soul*. You were arguing with yourself fruitlessly, as you have now come to appreciate. When I stop to think of the millions of people in the world *arguing*—*arguing* with homosexuals, *arguing* with alcoholics, *arguing* with narcotics addicts, with arsonists, with klepto-maniacs, with neurotics, with psychotics, I am greatly sad-dened. It is all wasted breath, every last word of it. *Advice* such misguided creatures surely need, and help and love. But argu-ment is not only absurd, it is frequently harmful in that it weakens an already shaken ego. People who do not have a particular problem themselves find it almost impossible to understand the problem in others. They tend to see it in terms of their own usually quite irrelevant experience. They say to themselves, '*I* don't have to have a drink, so why on earth does my father need one?' Or, 'Bill has himself a fine young girl for a fiancée; why is it that his brother Tom keeps com-pany with homosexuals?' A strange part of it is that their minds are actually giving them a clue, but they are overlooking it. Their reasoning mechanisms are putting out the word *why,* the importance of which is crucial. But they ignore the clue and do not really mean *why.* They really mean the question only in a rhetorical sense, as a more genteel way of saying, 'Isn't so-and-so really a stupid and sinful ass for doing or want-ing what he does?'

"You probably feel," Marvell continued, "that there is something wrong or peculiar about you because of the way you have reacted to the situation. On the contrary your re-actions establish that you are normal. I am reminded of the classic experiments conducted by Pavlov. In one of them a dog was trained to react to the appearance of a circle on a wall, which was invariably followed by food. Eventually the dog's mouth would water when the circle appeared, with no food whatever in evidence. Then the dog was presented with

370

an oval shape but this was *not* followed by food. In due time the dog was able to tell the difference between the two. This was evident because, when the circle was shown, the dog would salivate, whereas when the oval appeared the dog would not salivate. Then the experiment took an ingenious turn. The oval shape was altered slightly so that it became closer and closer to the circle. When the oval was very nearly circular, the unfortunate dog became hysterical as a result of its inability to arrive at a decision. It barked, howled, and turned on its keepers. In other words it had what we call a nervous breakdown."

"What you are telling me is very enlightening," Dan said. "But it makes me feel like an animal."

"We endanger ourselves," Marvell said, "when we forget that we *are* animals. But in any event I am trying to draw your attention to the fact that it is not only the situation in which you find yourself that leads to your present state. It is the element of *indecision* which is crucial. If the young lady with whom you are in love were, let us say, suddenly killed by a bolt of lightning you would suffer greatly at losing her but, because the problem would have been automatically solved for you, you would almost certainly find that in a short time your mental state would considerably improve."

"I have already come to suspect as much myself," Dan said. "Tell me, where have you been since we last met?"

"In Japan, mostly," Marvell said, "but don't you want to go on talking about yourself?"

Dan laughed, noticing the twinkle in the old blue eyes. "You must become bored by the problems of others," he said. "Have you none of your own?"

"Of course," Marvell said. "But they seem much less important when I see them in relation to the problems of others. In any event I do what I can about myself and then concentrate on others. It is, after all, in forgetting *self* that we find much of our happiness. The happiness of love, you see, is so great partly because it makes us forget ourselves. We think of nothing but the loved one. We glimpse, or think we glimpse, perfection in her. It is as near as most of us ever get to it."

"Is simply being in love, then, the solution to the mystery of the pursuit of happiness?"

"Not really," Marvell said, looking off to the sea. "For remember, when you say *I love you* you are talking about yourself. But if you have known true love, even if you have lost it, or even if the glorious plant flourished in soil that could not long sustain it, be thankful. As Kahlil Gibran says, 'If in your fear you would seek only love's peace and love's pleasure, then it is better for you that you cover your nakedness and pass out of love's threshing-floor, into the seasonless world where you shall laugh, but not all of your laughter, and weep, but not all of your tears.' "

Dan was about to respond when a Japanese sculptor approached and prepared to spirit Marvell away. Dan thanked him, shook hands gravely and watched as the elderly man moved off, his white hair blown by the breeze, his fatherly smile lighting up the faces of those he approached.

Suddenly Dan turned away from those about him, stared fiercely at the mountainside and its flowers and felt his eyes brimming with tears at thought of the staggering beauty of the universe. The moment was noteworthy in that it was the first time in his adult life that he had wept without despising himself for his weakness in doing so.

That night he wrote a warm letter to his mother and sent postcards to the children. Then, since the moon was full and the breeze warm, he spent a long time walking on the beach. As a child, and even to some extent in later years, he had been uneasy in the dark. Now—also for the first time—he felt strong in the dark.

When Helen had been married to Randy for about four months they were in a restaurant on Ventura Boulevard one evening when she suddenly gripped Randy's arm.

"What's the matter?" he said.

"My God, you'll never guess who's sitting right over there."

"Who?" He turned to look.

"Don't turn around," she said. "It's Elaine Sterling."

"Are you sure?"

"Yes. I've never told you this but once, about a year or so ago, I drove over to her place to have it out with her about Dan. I couldn't make myself ring her doorbell though. Then, while I was standing there on the sidewalk, she came out and got into a car."

"Did you speak to her?"

"No. She never knew who I was. Never noticed me."

"Well, forget about her. Enjoy your dinner. What do you care about her now?"

"I guess you're right. It's all over and done with. But somehow, seeing her like this— I don't know."

"Is Dan going to marry her?"

"I don't know. He's written a couple of letters from Big Sur and I'm pretty sure he's living alone up there."

"She's with a man."

"Yes. I guess that means she and Dan have split up. I wonder why they did?"

"God knows. Don't worry yourself about it."

"You're not jealous, are you?"

"No, honey. I'm not. It's all right with me if you worry about Dan or talk about him. No matter *why* people break up, even if they hate each other, they always leave a piece of themselves with the other person. There's always a sort of echo of love, a memory of love that remains. Wait a minute," he said. "I've got an idea. You say she doesn't know you by sight?"

"I don't think she does."

"All right. I'll be right back." He rose and walked over to Elaine's table. She looked up as he approached.

"Excuse me," he said pleasantly, "but is your name Sterling?"

"Yes," she said.

"Well, I believe we have a friend in common and I've been wondering how I might get in touch with him. I thought perhaps you could tell me. His name is Dan Scanlon."

Her face expressed pain and she looked nervously at her companion.

"I'm sorry," she said. "I haven't seen him in quite some time. As far as I know he's back in New York."

"Oh," Randy said. "Well, all right. Hope I haven't bothered you."

"Not at all."

Dan did not see Elaine again but he did keep in touch with Helen. From time to time he would drive to Los Angeles to visit the children. For a while, on a whim and not really because he needed the additional few dollars, he signed on to work at a gas station on the coast highway, and then later he moved to San Francisco and lived there for a few months. He bought a typewriter and began writing short stories, but they were all returned by the magazines to which he submitted them. The tenth one he produced, however, was a remarkable improvement over the first. During the same time he wrote poems and was greatly pleased when a small *avant-garde* San Francisco publication accepted one of them. Later, Helen heard that he had taken a trip to some part of the Orient on a tramp steamer but whether as a passenger or a worker she did not know.

A friend reported having seen him the following spring in San Francisco, in the company of a pretty girl who seemed much younger than himself.

After a while Michael, Patrick and Barbara, having grown to think of Randy as man of the house and father, ceased to miss Dan acutely. On one of his visits Dan sensed the change in their attitude and was, or so he told Helen, actually glad of it, for the sake of the children.

"I do not want to cause them any pain," he said, in a very matter-of-fact, unsentimental way.

Helen stood on the front lawn as he drove away. It was a cold, foggy afternoon and she folded her arms about her breasts, trying to keep warm. The car receded slowly in the distance and then was at last swallowed in the mist that drifted in across the sprawling city from the sea.

ABOUT THE AUTHOR

The majority of the world's talented people are content to enter the Hall of Fame with a single ticket. Not so Steve Allen—he's got a fistful, any one of which would guarantee certain admission.

Allen is not only a top TV and motion picture star, but has also achieved prominence as a comedian, lyricist, composer, public speaker, pianist, and serious author, well-thought-of by the critics for the eight books and numerous magazine articles he has written. Currently the industrious Mr. Allen is working on no less than three additional books.

Along with his literary pursuits, he has found time to make a mark for himself as a serious actor. After starring on Broadway in *The Pink Elephant,* he played the title role in *The Benny Goodman Story* for Universal-International. Also at Universal he co-starred in *College Confidential* with his wife, actress Jayne Meadows. As a pianist, orchestra leader and composer, Allen has some thirty albums to his credit.

Oh, yes. He has written more than 2,000 songs, too, including such popular standards as "This Could Be the Start of Something," "Pretend You Don't See Her," "South Rampart Street Parade," "Picnic," and "Impossible." His words and music for the NBC-TV spectacular "The Bachelor" won him a Sylvania Award, and Broadway recently called him to write words and music for the musical *Sophie.*

How does a man feel who has been blessed with the apparent ability to accomplish almost anything he attempts? Steve Allen presented his personal views on talent when he delivered a lay sermon at a New York church. His subject was "Pride." He said: "Whatever a man can do, if he possesses unique talents, is as surely given to him as his ten toes and ten fingers. He is powerless to resist the temptation to do what he can."

M